The New Friend

The New Friend

Alex Kane

hera

First published in the United Kingdom in 2021 by

Hera Books
Unit 9 (Canelo), 5th Floor
Cargo Works, 1–2 Hatfields
London, SE1 9PG
United Kingdom

A CIP catalogue record for this book is available from the British Library.

Print ISBN 978 1 80032 612 5
Ebook ISBN 978 1 91297 380 4

Look for more great books at www.herabooks.com

Printed and bound in Great Britain by Clays Ltd, Elcograf S.p.A.

1

This book is for my Dad. It's been a tough couple of years, but we've got you. X

Prologue

Being buried alive wasn't something he'd thought would ever happen to him. He was the one who did the killing; he was the one who committed the crimes. But as he lay in his coffin, wrists and ankles bound by tight tape, his throat dry and scratched from screaming and crying out for mercy, he knew that this was the end of his life.

Maybe this was the way he was supposed to go; justice for all the awful crimes he'd committed. He had been responsible for many deaths. Even though he was on his back looking up at his own coffin, he didn't regret his killings or his callous character that went hand-in-hand with being able to put a bullet in someone's head, or a knife through their skin.

Grit and soil fell through the gaps in the wood and peppered his face. He closed his eyes to protect them. It would be the last time he ever did.

2001

Chapter One

The school playground was busy and as Arabella MacQueen looked down at her school shoes to see the tiny hole at the toe, her white sock poking through, so did her friends. She called them friends, but they weren't really. They were the girls that the teacher had asked to include Arabella because she didn't *have* any friends. She felt quite pathetic about that.

'Oh my god, look at your shoes. Ew, tramp,' one of the girls mocked.

Arabella bit her lip, trying to stop the tears as they threatened to well in her eyes. They burned as she tried to hold them in.

'*Trampabella MacQueen*,' another girl laughed. Erin, the school bully. She was forever picking on other kids. This time, it was Arabella's turn.

Why were they being so cruel? It wasn't her fault that her mum couldn't afford to buy new shoes for her. Arabella had never owned anything brand new in her life. It was all second hand, hand-me-downs and charity shop finds.

But her mum needed the little money they had to buy food. At least that's what she told her. Arabella might only be eight years old, but she wasn't stupid. She'd been around alcohol her whole life, had seen what it was doing to her mum and to her. Unless Arabella made herself something to eat, then she went hungry. There was only so much she could make without having to use the cooker. Sandwiches, toast, cereal – and that was only if her mum had bought bread and milk. The only thing that was ever in the fridge at home was wine, vodka and a few bottles of Coke which Arabella wasn't allowed to drink because it was for the vodka. The most humiliating thing for her was how she was always starving at school, and as well as finishing her own school lunch in a matter of minutes, she would often steal the leftovers from her peers too.

'Shut up,' Arabella spat.

'Make me,' Erin shouted, raising her hands and pushing Arabella so hard, causing her to stumble backwards. Arabella fell into the bin in the playground and already the other kids around her were beginning to chant.

'Fight, fight, fight...'

Suddenly, a crowd had gathered around them and Erin was standing with her hands on her hips, a wry smile on her face.

'Come on then, *Trampabella*.'

Arabella got to her feet and stood for a moment, staring at her. She wanted to punch her in the face but didn't know if she had the guts to do it. She'd get into trouble. Although that didn't really matter because even if the school did phone her mum, she wouldn't care. So long as Arabella was able to pick up the juice on the way home from school so her mum had something to mix her vodka with then everything would be fine.

'Oi, you deaf as well as a tramp?' the girl shouted. Before Arabella had the chance to answer, she had to raise her hands to defend herself as the girl began to attack her. Her balled-up fists were small, but they hurt. Arabella didn't want to fight; things were bad enough without getting into trouble from the teachers and bringing more unwanted attention her way.

The girl was relentless and continued to beat Arabella, who stumbled back and fell to the ground, tears streaming down her face. The girl stopped and began to laugh in her victory. She turned her back on a beaten and bruised Arabella, who noticed a stone lying next to her foot, the one encased in the holey shoe. It was the perfect size to clobber the bitch around the head with.

Reaching for it, Arabella picked it up and got to her feet. The girl turned back, saw the stone in Arabella's hand and glared into her eyes.

'No weapons allowed,' the girl said over the shrieking chants.

'Said who?' Arabella said, before rushing forward and throwing the stone at the girl's head. She fell to the ground and clutched the side of her head and Arabella dropped the stone before she began kicking the side of the girl's torso.

The chanting grew louder and Arabella knew she should stop hurting her bully. What she was doing was wrong.

'Don't you *ever* call me Trampabella again, you hear me? I'll fucking kill you if you say it again.'

The crowd didn't hear her, they were too loud. But she could tell the girl heard every word as she tried to defend herself.

Arabella had heard her mum say something similar to one of the men who'd been hanging around the house recently. He'd slapped her but her mum didn't lie down and take it. She'd taken off her high-heeled shoe and skelped him over the face with it, shouting that if he touched her again, she'd fucking kill him. Her mum hadn't known that Arabella had seen the whole thing. It was night time and she was meant to be in bed but Arabella had heard them arguing, had peered into the hallway of their flat and watched it all happen. She'd been scared but also proud of her mum for standing up for herself. That was all Arabella was doing now, wasn't it? Standing up for herself?

A coldness washed over Arabella then. A silence that hadn't been there before now. The chanting had stopped and Arabella relented. Stepping back in horror, she began to sob.

This was the kind of violence she'd been subjected to in her home life. Her mother's endless stream of violent men, drunk men, men who made her feel unsafe or unwanted. All the years of abuse she'd witnessed, all the neglect, it came out in the attack.

Erin lay motionless on the ground. Arabella looked down at the beaten body of her tormenter, blood pouring from her face and head, and realised she was the bully now; she was the predator. She had never felt more ashamed of herself. She was just a child, trying to get through each day while fighting off hunger and bullies, and now things were worse than ever before.

That was when Arabella felt hands on her shoulders. A teacher, pulling her away, dragging her towards the school office as two others picked up the girl from the playground and rushed her away from the crowd of now crying children.

—

If Arabella had known that social services would turn up and remove her from her mum's care, she'd never have smacked that stupid girl over the head with that stone. She'd never have retaliated.

'I'm sorry. I didn't mean to hurt her. Please, just take me back to my mum. She needs me. If I'm not there, she won't eat anything. She'll just drink the wine and make herself sick again.'

The woman, who Arabella understood to be a social worker, looked at her with a sadness in her eyes that made Arabella want to be sick. There was nothing in her expression to suggest that she would even consider letting Arabella go home.

'Sweetheart, that's why you're here. Your mummy hasn't been looking after you properly for a while. Your house was very unsafe. But I promise, someone is looking after your mummy.'

The woman's voice was soft and Arabella wanted to believe her.

'So I'll get to go home when Mum is better?'

The woman smiled, but instead of answering her question, she asked, 'Would you like something to eat?'

Arabella wasn't stupid. She knew that if social services got their way, she would be looked after by someone else for a long time.

As the thought entered her mind, she immediately began to miss her mum. She drank too much and brought back various men on a regular basis, yes. But she was still her mum. Arabella thought back to a time before things had got really bad. Arabella had found a doll in a suitcase under her mum's bed. It was old and a little frayed, but Arabella had thought it was beautiful. Her mum had come into the bedroom and smiled when she saw Arabella holding it.

'It was your gran's doll. She gave it to me when I was a little girl,' she'd said.

Arabella gazed at it, amazed that it was once owned by the gran she'd never met. She'd died before Arabella was born – a long time before, according to her mum.

'What's her name?' Arabella asked.

'Oh, I named you after the doll. I'd always liked the name and when I found out you were in my tummy, I knew right away that you were going to be an Arabella.'

Arabella smiled at the memory, even though, at that precious moment between them, her mother had still had a glass of wine in her hand.

'Can I have some water please?' Arabella asked the social worker.

She nodded and got up to retrieve a bottle of water from the fridge in the corner of the room.

'Thank you.' She opened it and took a tiny sip.

'What were you smiling at just now?' the woman asked, her voice soft.

'I was thinking about my name. My mummy told me that she named me after a doll my gran gave to her. It's my favourite doll.'

The woman smiled. 'It is a lovely name. Do you get to see your gran often?'

Arabella shook her head. 'No. She died before I was born. I think Mummy still misses her.'

The woman nodded sadly.

Arabella knew that her gran had died in an accident at home, she'd fallen on the wet kitchen floor and banged her head. She hadn't chosen to leave her daughter. Even though Arabella was only eight years old, she understood that her own mum on some level had chosen alcohol over her. She loved her mum, but already she was beginning to wonder if she'd ever be able to forgive that choice. Because now Arabella was alone except for this stranger and she had no idea where her mum was or if she would ever see her again.

Chapter Two

'If you walk out that door, don't expect it to be unlocked when you come back crying that you got it wrong and that you should have listened to me.'

Roxanne finished packing her bag and zipped it up. She had her passport, cash and a one-way ticket. It didn't matter what that cow said, there was *no way* Roxanne was staying in the shit hole she'd lived in her whole life, even if it was the only thing she'd ever been able to call home.

'Oh don't worry, I'm not even taking my keys,' Roxanne said, throwing the bag over her shoulder and gripping the handle of her suitcase. 'Do you think I'd really stay here and clean toilets in the local pub for the rest of my fucking life because you need dig money to survive? You can go and clean the bogs down the Hilly Bar yourself. And while you're at it, I hear blowjobs are a fiver a go. But you'd know all about that, wouldn't you?'

Roxanne's mother looked at her in shock. But she didn't get the chance to retaliate.

'Aye, that's right. I've heard the rumours. Sucked off nearly every guy in there for a free bevy. You make me sick and I'm not hanging around here to get tarred with the same brush. I'm out. There's a world out there where I won't have to lower myself to your fucking standards just to bring in a few quid.'

Roxanne took a breath. She couldn't believe that she'd actually said it. She'd been building up the courage to stand up to her mother for years. They were all the same around the scheme – single mothers, alcoholics, drug addicts. Roxanne didn't want to turn out like that. So she'd jumped at the chance to go away with her mate and forget about life in Glasgow, the shit hole that it was.

'You can't fucking speak to me like that,' her mother began. 'I'm your mother.' Roxanne had to laugh at that one. The way her mother said it made it sound as though their relationship had been perfect up until now, when in fact it had been quite the opposite. The woman wouldn't know the meaning of a good role model if it jumped up and slapped her across the face.

Without responding, Roxanne was already out the door, slamming it behind her. She could still hear her mother's voice echoing in the close as she called after her. But Roxanne wasn't listening. Finally, she was free from her alcoholic slapper of a mother. Now, she could start her own life. Now, she could finally live the way she wanted to, far enough away that she wouldn't hear the rumours, the disgusting stories of old Mandy McPhail, the local bike.

Climbing into the taxi, she told the driver to go to the airport. He asked her if she was going anywhere nice.

'Anywhere away from this shit hole is nice,' she replied.

'Fair point,' the man laughed.

A short while later, Roxanne had checked her case, had a drink for Dutch courage ahead of the flight and was now sitting in her seat, awaiting take off. This was her first time on a plane, her first time ever leaving the country and she'd had to get herself her first ever passport just for the occasion. She'd never stepped foot out of Scotland before. If Roxanne was being fully honest with herself, the drink at Departures hadn't done its job. She was shitting herself; the whole situation was completely overwhelming. The idea of leaving all that she'd ever known behind to start a new life abroad was scary enough, let alone her first flight.

'Ladies and gentlemen, our cabin crew will now give our safety demonstration. Please direct your attention to the crew for the next few minutes.'

The voice made Roxanne's stomach flip. Safety demonstration? She hadn't thought about safety when booking the flight. Turning her eyes to the woman dressed in a blue skirt and jacket, white blouse and hair tied so tightly at the top of her head she wondered if it hurt, Roxanne watched and listened as she demonstrated where the oxygen masks were, where the exits were and how to put on the life jacket.

'First flight?' An older man beside her asked. 'I can tell by the look on your face. My wife was the same. Just take a few deep breaths and ask for the bottle of vodka when the drinks trolley arrives.'

He smiled, but Roxanne couldn't even fake a smile in return. She felt utterly terrified that she would die in a plane crash before she even got to start her life. The man clearly saw the look of fear in Roxanne's eyes, because his wide smile softened, as did his eyes.

'Oh, don't worry. They say you're more likely to die in a car crash than a plane coming down.'

Roxanne closed her eyes and rested her head on the seat. If that was supposed to help, it really hadn't.

Pushing the man's voice out of her head, Roxanne imagined herself lying on the beach with a drink in her hand and her best friend by her side. As apprehensive as she was of flying, she knew it was a necessary evil. She had to put herself through it to get to her paradise.

The pilot introduced himself over the speaker, informing the passengers of the time it would take to reach their destination and that he would speak to them again soon. Roxanne hadn't been listening properly; she was too busy looking out across the tarmac at the plane beside her as the one she was sat on began to taxi out to the runway.

There was no going back now, she thought. The sooner the flight was over, the better.

—

'Oh my god!'

Roxanne glanced up as she tucked her passport into her bag and had to brace herself as her best friend almost flattened her.

'I can't believe you're actually here.'

Roxanne laughed. 'Well, I won't get to see much of the place if you suffocate me before I've even left the airport.'

Charlene laughed and let go. 'Sorry. I'm just so fucking excited that you're here. Honestly Rox, you're going to love it here. It's sunny all day, every day. The place doesn't sleep and it's so easy to get a job. In fact, I have one lined up for you already. You'll be working in the same place as me.'

Roxanne smiled and felt like she wanted to cry with relief.

'How was the flight?' Charlene asked.

'Fucking awful. Felt sick the entire time. And what the fuck is turbulence? I mean seriously, that shit is enough to give you a heart attack,' Roxanne replied, still feeling jittery.

Charlene laughed loudly. 'You're here, on the ground in one piece. Let's get out of here.'

They got into a taxi and Charlene told the driver in Spanish where they were going. Impressed by how quickly her friend had learned the language, Roxanne gave Charlene a playful slap on the arm.

'Get you,' she said.

'I know. But if we want to stay here, we need to make an effort and learn the lingo, don't we?'

Roxanne nodded and looked out of the front window as the taxi pulled away. The sun was already hot and the place had a different smell to it than she was used to. It was hot and sweet, unlike the damp and miserable Glasgow which smelt like rain and car fumes, along with that particularly familiar stench of salt and vinegar from the chippy, laced with strong notes of weed.

It didn't take long before the taxi turned off the road away from the tourist hot spots and began to drive them into a more residential area. Roxanne hadn't known what to expect of the place, but she was intrigued by how white the buildings were, how dry and scorched the grass looked.

Charlene said something to the driver in Spanish and the taxi stopped. Charlene paid him and they got out, the driver helping Roxanne with her luggage – not that she noticed; she was too busy looking up at the building complex.

'This is it, our home. It's only a small apartment. The advert said it's a two-bed, but the second room is so small you can only really fit a bed and a wardrobe in. I hope that's going to be okay?' Charlene said.

Roxanne nodded as she gazed up at the place that she would now call home. Charlene had been living out in Spain for the last six months and had been trying to convince Roxanne to join her. Now that she was standing there, she was glad she'd agreed to it. The only reason it had taken her so long to get out there was because she'd been waiting on her passport to arrive.

'Charlene, I'd happily live anywhere if it meant I wasn't sharing the same country as my cow of a mother.'

'The bold Mandy still frying your head then?' Charlene laughed as the taxi pulled away.

'You don't even want to know, trust me.'

They walked through the main entrance and got into the lift. The apartment complex stood six stories tall, each with a small balcony or terrace. When they got to the fourth floor, Charlene stepped out of the lift and Roxanne followed. The place seemed immaculate, unlike the building she'd lived in with her mother. For a start, there wasn't dog shit every few steps. The terracotta tiles were clean, and there was a smell in the air as though they'd just been mopped.

Charlene stopped outside one of the doors and inserted a key into the lock. She stepped to the side and allowed Roxanne to go inside first. She couldn't believe that this was where she was going to be living. In an apartment in Majorca with her best friend. It was something she hadn't dared dream of.

'What do you think?' Charlene asked.

'I think I died on that plane and went to heaven. Is this really yours?'

'Well, it belongs to the landlord. I just rent it. But it's home. And it'll be easier to afford now that you're here. You don't have to pay me any rent until you get your first wage, by the way. And the landlord knows you're staying here so you don't have to worry about that.'

Roxanne nodded as she dropped her bag to the floor. She stood in the middle of what she assumed was the living room. It was very different to the one back in Glasgow. No smelly old worn carpet. The same tiles as out in the hallway. Small frames with hand-painted pictures hung on white-washed walls and at the far end of the room the sliding doors led on to a balcony.

Through to the left of the living room was a small kitchen, and just off that was a bathroom with a shower. On the opposite side of the living room were the two bedrooms, the smallest of which was Roxanne's.

'You like it, then?' Charlene asked.

'Already feel at home,' Roxanne replied, pulling off her denim jacket and allowing it to fall onto the couch. 'What's it like, living here? Is it quiet?'

'It is, thankfully. I get enough noise at work every night, the last thing I want is to be surrounded by noise and parties after a shift.'

Roxanne smiled. She was hoping that Charlene would say that. That was another thing she hated about living with her mother. She was always inviting people back to the flat after the pub, mostly men. There were always noisy, drunken idiots banging around while Roxanne was trying to sleep. Her mother never gave a shit about Roxanne or what she wanted. All she cared about was getting dig money off her so she could piss it against a wall.

Roxanne took her case into the small bedroom that she would now call her own and began to unpack. She could just about fit her things in the wardrobe and was able to slide the case under the double bed. Looking at it, she wondered if she could class it as a double but she didn't care if she slept on a mattress on the floor; it was hers and that was all that mattered.

'Right, lady, you ready for your first night out in Magaluf before you need to start work?' Charlene asked, dangling a bottle of vodka in front of Roxanne's face.

'I thought you'd never ask.'

Roxanne and Charlene sat down on the sofa and poured themselves a generous measure of vodka, topping it up with Coke.

'Not only is this the best place to be living right now, but I've met a guy out here too,' Charlene said.

'Oh?' Roxanne teased. 'And from the look on your face, can I assume you're smitten?'

'It's early days, but yeah, I really, *really* like him.' Charlene's smile widened and Roxanne couldn't help but mirror it.

'So, here's to us, living it up in Magaluf,' Charlene said. 'Here's to fun, making new friends and having a fucking shit-hot time.'

Roxanne clinked her glass against her friend's and smiled. 'I'll drink to that.'

Chapter Three

He stood by the door and watched his big brother struggle downstairs with his suitcase. Brian was getting to disappear from the shit hole where they lived and he was leaving Cole behind.

Staring up at Brian through narrowed eyes, he wished he could climb into that case and go with him. But Brian only had enough money for one ticket. Not only that. Cole was sure that his twenty-three-year-old brother wouldn't want his younger sibling following him to a job.

'Don't look at me like that, Cole. If I could take you with me, I would. You know I would, mate. But you're only fifteen.'

'Why can't you take me? I don't get it,' Cole whined. 'You could be my responsible adult.'

'You know what Mum's like. There's no way she's gonna let you out her sight after you smashed that shop window last week. You ain't even allowed out the door, never mind out the country.'

Cole smiled at the memory of putting the brick through the old cow's shop window. That's what she got for accusing him of stealing from her stupid shop.

'You're lucky the police haven't come and taken you away,' Brian said as he reached the bottom of the stairs.

'The old bill ain't gonna touch me. I'm just a kid,' Cole laughed.

'Yeah, well if you go through life with that attitude, you ain't gonna get very far.'

Brian ruffled Cole's hair and Cole tried to pretend that it wasn't killing him that his brother was leaving. He wanted to be just like him. He was handsome, always had a girl on the go and always said that one day, he'd own his own building company. He'd promised that when Cole was old enough, he'd train him up and get him off the streets of London. Being part of a gang wasn't what Cole should strive for in life.

'How long you gonna be gone?' Cole asked, pulling away from Brian's hand and fixing his hair.

'Dunno, mate. But I'll phone you every night, make sure you're behaving yourself. And as soon as you're old enough, I'll take you with me on every job. I promise.'

Cole nodded, but was sulking. He was annoyed there was such an age gap between him and Brian but there was nothing he could do about it.

'Now,' Brian said as he opened the front door. 'Say bye to Mum for me. And don't go trying to steal my girl when I'm gone.'

Cole laughed. 'She probably fancies me more than you anyway.'

Brian playfully punched Cole before dragging the case out to the street and climbing into the taxi. He waved his hand out of the window and Cole waved back until he couldn't see him anymore.

Chapter Four

'I have to say, Jez, I have never known anyone to pick up the job as quickly as you. Tell me, did you come out here with the idea of never returning home?'

Jez smiled and shook his boss's hand. Three weeks, and from the first night he'd been working in Rafa's Bar. What had been planned as a boy's holiday had turned into a career opportunity almost as soon as he found the bar in the resort they'd booked to stay in.

Jez thought about his life back in Glasgow and shook his head. 'No, I just love it here and I'm young enough that I can give it a go.'

Rafa looked at Jez and it was obvious he knew that Jez wasn't being fully honest. But Jez wasn't about to tell his boss about the crap back in Glasgow. How he had left trouble back home and had no intention of going back to face it. He had no family there anymore, so there was less chance he would ever have to.

'Well, keep up the good work, Jez. If you do, you might go far in this business.'

Jez wanted that to be true. He could imagine himself living his life out in Spain. It would be like one big holiday, but he would be working to earn his living.

Jez headed back out to the bar and stood back, happy to have a permanent job there. He'd told the boys that he was planning on staying, but they hadn't believed him except for Billy. Marty and Stevo just laughed it off and stuck more coke up their noses.

'So, it's official,' Jez said as Billy approached the bar. 'I'm staying.'

'He offered you permanent work?' Billy asked.

'Aye. Looks like Scotland is a distant memory now.'

'Well, I'll drink to that. Congratulations mate, fucking brilliant.'

Jez poured them both a holiday measure of Jack Daniel's and Coke and they drank quickly. Jez wouldn't miss Scotland one bit. It had only ever brought him problems.

'Where's Marty and Stevo?' Jez asked.

'Where do you think they are?'

'They're at the strippers again? Filthy fuckers,' Jez laughed.

'Aye, they said that they wanted to see as much tits and arse as they could before heading back to Glasgow. Now, this is a direct quote, "the burds in Glesga are bogging compared to the wee Spanish hotties out here."'

Jez laughed harder this time. 'Do you think they realise that the girls in the strippers here are mainly British?'

'Are you kidding? With the amount of booze and drugs they've had since we got here three weeks ago, I'm surprised they can even see. I'm telling you, they'll end up like the rest of the jakeys in the scheme if they don't watch what they're doing. The end of Marty's nose is already glowing red and he's only fucking twenty. And Stevo's permanently sniffing as though his nose is on the hunt for a line every second of the day.'

Billy sat down on a bar stool and leaned on the surface of the bar. Jez could see that he was mulling over what he was going to do when he got back to Scotland. He had a decision to make about his life and he still hadn't spoken about it even though Jez knew about it all. Jez knew Billy better than he knew himself most of the time and even though Jez didn't agree with the choices that Billy was making about his career, he still respected him. Billy had a life-changing opportunity and if he decided to go for it, it would mean that their lives would take very different paths. Jez would be living it up in Spain and Billy would be up to his neck in his work back in Glasgow, so their friendship was likely to take a back seat, diminish over time. It was something they'd both silently accepted. Billy would likely distance himself from Marty and Stevo. He'd have to if he was going to make a go of a decent future.

'You cool over there?' Jez asked as he watched Billy stare into space.

'Aye, just thinking.'

The bar was quiet tonight, only a few people in and out. It was the start of the season, so things would pick up soon, according to Rafa.

As soon as the boys had arrived in Majorca, Jez had seen the advertisement taped to the door of the bar. *Barman wanted.* There was no thinking involved; Jez had simply gone inside, asked to see the owner and within thirty minutes he had the offer of a trial shift. At the end of that first night, Rafa offered him a permanent job. And that was when Jez had decided that he was definitely not using his return ticket to Glasgow. Getting a job while on holiday was the perfect solution to starting his life over, although it meant he hadn't really been able to spend any time with the boys. But if he wanted to get a head start on his plan then that meant making the sacrifice. The strange thing was, he didn't feel like he'd missed out on the carnage of a boys' holiday. It was all part of the bigger picture.

'Thinking about what? Whether or not to go to that college? You got in, didn't you?' Jez asked, pretending not to know much more than that, while keeping his eye on the door for more punters to arrive.

'Aye, I got in. Got through the interview stages and everything. I didn't think I'd manage it. But somehow I did.'

'So what's the problem?' Jez poured Billy a pint and passed it across the bar before sliding some of his own money into the till.

'Och, I don't know. I mean, is it really me? Will that life suit me?'

'You're only asking that because it's real now. You've got a start date. This will probably be the last boys' holiday you'll have. And if I'm staying out here to do my thing, then we'll not be seeing each other as much. It's the end of an era, mate. We've been mates since the beginning of primary school, Billy, it'll be hard to adjust without my brother by my side. But that doesn't mean you can't come out here when you've got time off. Just don't bring those two twats with you, eh? They'll try to shag every stripper on the fucking island.'

Billy laughed and Jez smiled. That had been his intention. As much as he agreed with Billy that the life he'd chosen for his future didn't suit him, he wasn't about to voice his opinion and alter his mate's choice. It wasn't his future to change.

A few hours had gone by; Jez had been serving a few punters as they came and went. But there was one guy at the end of the bar. He'd been there all night by himself, drowning his sorrows by the looks of it, Jez thought. He'd noticed Billy talking to him a few times. Two guys at a bar by themselves, why not? But Jez saw that something wasn't right. A look on the guy's face, a glint in his eye. He looked like the typical trouble-maker, always wanting to stir shit up after a few drinks.

As Jez was about to take his break, he saw Billy heading outside for a cigarette. After a few moments, the other guy went outside too. Jez decided to keep an eye on things as soon as he'd finished cleaning the tables ready for the next group of drinkers to come in. Quickly clearing away the glasses, he stacked them inside the dishwasher under the counter and grabbed his cigarettes from his pocket before heading out to the back to join Billy.

Opening the door, he heard the unmistakable crunching sound of fist meeting face.

He flung the door wide, rushed out to the concrete at the back of the bar and found Billy acting in a way he'd never seen before. Jez had always been the more aggressive and violent of the two, but here Billy was, stamping on this guy's head. The sound of bones cracking under the force made even Jez wince.

'Jesus, what the hell are you doing?' Jez said, launching himself at Billy and dragging him off the guy. 'You'll kill him.'

But Billy wasn't aware of Jez's presence. He was in a daze, far away in another place like he was having an out of body experience. Jez shook him, gripping his shoulders as hard as he could. Billy glared down at the body which lay perfectly still on the ground and then back up at Jez. His eyes slowly filled with terror.

'Is he...? Is he dead?'

Struck with horror, Billy stood as though paralysed, before Jez gave him a sharp shove.

'Go. Now.'

Turning, Billy left, running up the hill and along the back streets of the main drag. Jez hoped that Billy would be covered by the darkness of the night – that they both would.

Jez looked down at the body, the face a mash of blood and more blood. Unrecognisable. He shook his head, wondering what in the fuck had possessed Billy to do this. Right now, Jez couldn't think about that though; he had to get rid of the body before Rafa saw it. Before anyone saw it.

Glaring at the large bins lined against the wall, Jez had an idea. Rafa had recently had new carpet laid in the office. The old one was sitting up against the wall. Glancing back at the lad on the ground, Jez bent down and listened for breath. Of course he was dead; Billy had stamped all over his brain. Jesus, what a mess, Jez thought, although to be fair, this wasn't the first body Jez had had to deal with and he was now a little desensitized to it.

Getting back up, Jez glanced around the grounds. There was no one around, not a single soul. Without finishing his thoughts, Jez gripped the guy by the ankles and pulled him towards the wall. Then he stopped, held his breath. There was someone coming. Footsteps, stumbling. Looking at the doorway, he saw Marty and Stevo standing there. Swaying a little, they glanced down at the body at Jez's feet and then at each other. Jez could tell they were off their faces.

'What the fuck did you do?' Stevo asked, his eyes wide and his jaw tense.

'Bastard tried to jump me and I sorted him out,' Jez lied. It came out of his mouth so fluently because he knew he had to protect his friend and his future. 'So, you two going to help me with this or what?'

Marty hesitated, but Stevo was by Jez's side in a second, the coke in his system clearly making him feel more macho than he was. Looking up at Marty, it was obvious to Jez that he hadn't taken as much, or the drugs weren't having the same effect as they were on Stevo.

'Marty, if you're not going to muck in then fuck off.'

Marty didn't respond; instead, he moved closer and eyed the body at their feet.

'Not a fucking word to anyone. Just get him wrapped up in that old carpet and into that bin. Let me worry about the rest.'

The three of them did the job as quickly as they could before Jez told them to go back to their apartment, get cleaned up and ready for their flight home the next day. He'd expected an argument from them, but they said nothing and followed his instructions. Marty and Stevo weren't people Jez classed as true friends. With Billy it was different. They'd been friends since they were five years old, so of course Jez was going to sort this out for him.

That's what friends did for each other.

Chapter Five

'Mate, are you fucking mental? You near enough mutilated that guy back there.'

Jez paced the floor, back and forth, his hands on his head as he looked at his best friend. The best friend who had never in his entire life put a foot wrong with the law until now.

'He was fucking winding me up, Jez. He'd been at it all night, knocking into me, spilling his pint all over me. And you didn't see the way he was looking at me from the other side of the bar. It was like he wanted to start something with me, wanted to get me fucking angry.' Billy sat with his head in his hands. He hadn't looked at Jez since they'd got back to the apartment.

'Well you gave him what he wanted then, didn't you? Jesus Christ, Billy, do you know what you've done?'

'What am I going to do, Jez? I can't go to prison. Not here. They'll throw away the key.'

Jez stopped pacing and let his hands fall to his side. Billy was his brother in every way bar blood, had been there his whole life. Billy's mum had taken Jez in when his own mum died, leaving him without family at the age of fourteen. Even before those days, when they were younger, they'd stuck by each other through everything. Popular at school, with their mates and the girls, Jez and Billy never let anything or anyone come between them. If Jez got into a fight at school, Billy backed him up. If Billy was caught with a bottle of booze, Jez said it was his. And those were just the early days.

Jez couldn't leave Billy to deal with this on his own. Not when his family had done so much for him, not when they had a bond stronger than any other.

'Leave it with me, Billy. I'll sort it.'

'How? How can you sort it? We don't even know if the guy's dead.'

Jez could see tears in Billy's eyes. He was terrified. Jez wanted to tell Billy that in actual fact, he did know that the guy was dead and that he'd already put into play the first part of getting rid of as much evidence of what happened as he could. However, Billy didn't need to know that Marty and Stevo were involved, just as they didn't need to know that it was Billy who'd killed the guy and not Jez. This was Jez's thing; this was what he did best. Sorting things out. He'd certainly sorted things out back in Glasgow before they'd flown out to Spain. There was one less person back at the scheme who would be looking for them all when the holiday was over and Jez wasn't there to fight their battles. Just by keeping that to himself, he was already protecting Billy.

'I said I'll sort it. Just trust me on this one, alright?'

-

The place was quiet and the bar had been shut up for the night. The season was only just starting, so the resort wasn't as busy as it would be come mid-summer. The boss had gone home, as had the rest of the staff. The cleaners weren't due in until nine in the morning. This would be the only chance Jez would get to fix Billy's mess, or at least try.

He went to the back entrance of the bar and stared at the ground. No blood stains, no signs of a struggle. Jez had cleaned up well.

He went through to his boss's office. He had been in there a few times, but wasn't usually allowed inside unless the boss was present. Jez had really shown Rafa what he was capable of in the short space of time he'd worked there. Rafa had told Jez that he liked his work ethic and could see that he would go far in the business. Jez had really felt Rafa's trust, hence why he'd been shown around the office. It was almost as though he was second in command to Rafa and Jez was happy with that.

Jez knew where everything was; spare keys to the storage cupboard for the cleaners, keys to the stock room. But those weren't the things he needed. He needed access to the CCTV from earlier that night. Luckily for Billy, and unluckily for the guy who'd been winding him up, the attack had taken place outside the back entrance. From what Jez could tell, no one else had witnessed what had happened. But that didn't mean that Billy was in the clear.

Jez sat down at his boss's desk and switched on the computer. The tower beneath the desk came to life, the sound unnaturally loud in the silence. The screen lit up and he clicked on the CCTV link from the file on the desktop, opened up the recordings from the last twenty-four hours and hit the forward button. Stopping around the time at which Billy had arrived, he sat back on the seat and watched as Billy took his seat at the bar. He'd been there for hours, taking in the last night of the holiday and spending time with Jez.

Jez sat forward, his face close to the screen as he studied for evidence of an altercation. Billy had been talking to someone at the other end of the bar, but the camera hadn't picked it up. Jez opened up the file for the other camera at the opposite side of the bar, and to his surprise and insanely good luck, he found the lens was cracked on that particular camera. It hadn't even been switched on that night.

'Thank fuck for that,' Jez whispered.

He continued to study the footage from the working camera and hit the forward button. There was a lot of Billy drinking, chatting to Jez as he stood behind the bar, serving Billy and a few other punters. Then Billy turned, got to his feet and moved in the direction in which the other guy was sitting. But what had happened there wasn't in view of the camera. Then he watched as Billy left the bar and the other guy followed him.

He sighed loudly. It was only a matter of time before something like this happened. Jez knew Billy better than he knew himself. Billy and drink weren't a good mix. He was an angry drunk when he went over the score. When Jez was there, he was always able to bring Billy back round. But Jez hadn't been there to stop things before they went too far. He was usually the good, quiet one of the pair. Not this time.

Jez flipped to the CCTV which captured the exterior surroundings of the bar. His stomach flipped. The entire attack was caught on the camera outside. Jez watched as Billy and this guy got into an argument, a scuffle. The guy was goading him, but of course there was no audio to go with the footage, so Jez had no idea what was being said. At one stage it looked like Billy was going to walk away, leave the guy to argue with himself. But then the guy suddenly threw a punch in Billy's direction, his knuckles skimming Billy's jawline. Then there was a switch and even from the screen, Jez saw the change in Billy's expression. It was almost as though Billy was thrilled that the guy had taken a swipe at him, like he was waiting for a fight.

Suddenly, Billy was on top of the guy, fists hammering down on his face, his chest. The guy rolled up into a ball and Billy got to his feet. Jez shook his head as he watched.

He watched as Billy kicked, feet pounding into the guy's back, his ribs and his head. It was then that Jez saw himself appear on camera, pulling Billy away and shaking him.

The situation wasn't a worry for Jez. He was used to a certain level of violence because it was how he'd got by all these years. More shocking than the stranger's death was the fact that it was Billy who'd done the job.

Jez pulled the USB stick out of his pocket, inserted it into the USB port and transferred the files over, before permanently deleting them from the system. There was no way he was going to allow Billy's life to end up down the shitter because of what he'd done. He was a good guy at heart, with a good future ahead of him. Equally, Jez wasn't going to let his opportunities in Spain be ruined because his mate couldn't just walk away from a bad situation. All four of them would never have to worry about this.

He safely removed the USB and tucked it into the back pocket of his jeans, before locking the bar back up and heading outside. He would keep the footage on that stick in a safe place. It would do Billy good to be reminded of his behaviour if he ever tried anything like this again. It would be for his own benefit if Jez had to sit him down and show him what he was capable of under the influence. There wasn't much Jez could do to stop Billy hitting the self-destruct button again, but perhaps keeping the memory stick with the whole nightmare recorded might help.

The sun wasn't due up for another hour, but the bin lorry would be due on its rounds in the next few minutes. Jez lit a cigarette and made his way across the road towards the beach, before sitting on one of the sun loungers. He smoked in silence, listening to the waves as they washed up on the sand. Then in the distance, he saw the orange flashing light from the lorry as it approached, stopping every few meters to collect the bins from the kerbside. It didn't take long before the lorry stopped outside his bar.

Jez watched as the bin was attached to the machine at the back. The lads operating it weren't even watching, they were too busy chatting.

The carpet, along with the body and the rest of the rubbish from that night and the previous were inside being crushed as Jez took the last draw of his cigarette.

The orange flashing lights made off in the distance and Jez watched them go. He got to his feet, extinguished his cigarette on the edge of the lounger, tucked it into his back pocket and took a deep breath.

What a way to start his new life in Spain, he thought. Three weeks in and one murder down.

Chapter Six

Roxanne McPhail lay on the sun lounger next to her best friend Charlene. The sun beat down on their sun-kissed skin. Roxanne sighed as she sipped on her Sex on the Beach cocktail and listened to the club music as it pumped from the speaker at the opposite side of the pool. It had been two months since she'd landed in Spain. Two months of feeling free from the shitty life she'd had back in Glasgow. She and Charlene had fled the scheme in which they'd been brought up – or should she say *dragged up*? – and promised that they'd never return.

At just nineteen, she was living the dream. They had jobs in a strip bar on the main drag of the resort and so far they were making good money. That meant they could party as much as they wanted when they weren't working and not have to worry about running out of money. This was what Roxanne was born for, living free.

'My cocktail is too strong,' Charlene said, screwing up her face and placing the glass on the table between them.

Roxanne raised a brow. 'You're such a lightweight. You're from the hardest scheme in Glasgow and you think that's too strong? I vividly remember you drinking a quarter bottle straight down the woods one night when we were fourteen just to impress that idiot from Edinburgh who was visiting his cousin. What was his name again?'

Charlene laughed loudly, adjusting the strap of her bikini. 'Oh god, remember that? I fancied him so much. What was his name again? Chud or something like that?' Charlene paused for a moment. 'I don't think I ever found out what his real name was actually. My dad went ape-shit on me for rolling through the door blind drunk that night. He asked me to open a can for him and I opened it with a fucking tin opener. That's how he knew I'd been drinking. I spewed all over the sofa and he slapped me sober.'

Roxanne was belly-laughing now. 'He was probably annoyed that his daughter was more hammered than him.'

'Aye, scheme life was fun when you didn't understand it but as we got older it was just shit. So glad we got away from that place. Now look at us, sipping cocktails in the sunshine before we have to take our clothes off in a sweaty club.'

'Don't pretend you don't enjoy it, Charlene. It's brilliant, the money's amazing and it's better than what we had back home.'

Charlene nodded and got to her feet. 'I'm off for a swim. You fancy one before work?'

Roxanne shook her head. 'No, I've got some stuff to do before we start tonight. I'll catch up with you at the flat later. Unless you're spending the night with your man?'

Charlene smiled and Roxanne noticed how she blushed. 'No, he's working tonight. Although I might be able to catch up with him afterwards.'

'Look at you, you're like a soppy teenager,' Roxanne teased.

'I am a soppy teenager,' Charlene laughed. 'Why wouldn't I be? I'm living in the sun with my best friend and I've found the man of my dreams. You know, I really think he's going to pop the question. He's been talking about us in the future tense, where we'd live, how many kids we'd have...'

Roxanne smiled. 'Is that right? Well, you don't hang about, do you?'

'When you're in love, why bother waiting?' Charlene smiled widely.

'So, am I ever going to get to meet this guy?'

Charlene nodded. 'Eventually. He's just so busy that your paths haven't crossed yet. But I promise I'll arrange it soon.'

Roxanne felt guilty about asking when she was going to meet Charlene's boyfriend when she hadn't even told her that she was seeing someone herself. But it was early days, even though she'd never felt like this about anyone in her life. Not that there was a lot of choice where they were from.

Roxanne watched her friend walk towards the pool before diving in. They'd always talked about coming to Spain together and making a life for themselves. She couldn't believe that they were living that reality. It had been an idea for longer than she cared to remember. Now they were both seeing people, Charlene talking about marriage and the future. It was the best feeling.

Feeling emotional, Roxanne swallowed the lump that had formed in her throat, gathered up her things and headed out of the complex. Taking her mobile out of her bag, she saw a text from him and her stomach flipped. He had such a strong, physical effect on her.

As she headed for the café where she was meeting him, Roxanne could see him standing outside, his back to the place, facing out to the beach. He was on his phone, but as soon as he caught her eye, he ended the call. His smile was infectious and she couldn't stop the corners of her mouth rising in response.

'Hey gorgeous,' he said, leaning down and kissing her on the cheek.

'Hi.' Roxanne replied.

A young entrepreneur who owned one small bar just off the strip, Jez was forever talking about how he was going to be the island's biggest businessman. He was a little taller than she was. His dark hair and chiselled chin gave him an Italian look. But he was all Scot and had been living on the island a while longer than she had, and she had been seeing him almost since she'd arrived.

'So, how's things?' Jez asked as he sat down next to Roxanne.

'Yeah, good. How's things going with the bar? All okay?'

Jez smiled. 'Yeah, business is booming so can't complain considering I've not been here long and already own one of the bars on the main strip.'

Roxanne hadn't asked how that had happened, how he'd come to be a business owner in the party scene having only lived on the island a short time. She wasn't stupid, she knew where Jez came from just by the sound of his Glasgow accent – a scheme much like her own where sources of income for people like them weren't always legal. It didn't matter how far you went, sometimes those habits followed you.

'So, you missing Glasgow yet?' he asked.

Roxanne shook her head. He hadn't told her much about his past, or where he'd come from. And she hadn't asked because she didn't exactly have a great story to tell herself.

'Shite, isn't it?' He laughed. 'I hated the place, but your voice makes me hate it less. You remind me of the good times I had there.'

Roxanne smiled, still unwilling to tell him about her shitty excuse for a life back there. She chose to change the subject.

'So, I wanted to introduce you to my friend. The one I moved here with. She's seeing someone too so maybe we could all get together. Make a night of it?'

Jez wrapped an arm around her and kissed her gently. 'Babe, it's not that I don't want to, I'm just busy, that's all.'

'So that's a straight out no then?'

'Not a no, just not right now. Look, I've only just taken over the bar I was working for. I can't exactly just drop that to meet a mate of yours, can I?'

Roxanne shook her head. He had a point. Maybe she and Charlene could go to the bar and they could all meet together while he was working? It was a thought that she chose not to share with him. He'd only say no. Instead, she'd plan it as a surprise. Tell Charlene to bring her man along.

Best friend, boyfriend, new life in Spain. That beat scheme life any day.

Roxanne applied red lipstick and smiled at her reflection in the mirror. She was going to surprise Jez at work before she started her shift, and she would look incredible doing it.

Taking out her mobile, she was about to text Charlene and tell her that she was going to take her to meet her new man, when the front door of their shared apartment opened and Charlene stood there, eyes brimming with tears and looking as though she was about to collapse.

'Jesus,' Roxanne said. 'What's wrong?'

She went to her friend, wrapped an arm around her and led her to the sofa. Charlene's whole body shuddered as she sobbed loudly.

'I'm pregnant.'

Roxanne felt her eyes widen in shock. She tried to hide the expression, but couldn't hide the shock in her tone.

'Oh fuck. *Charlene*. What contraception were you using?'

Charlene buried her face in her hands. 'None.'

Roxanne exhaled loudly. 'Oh, for fuck's sake, Charlene.'

'I know. I know it's stupid. I can't believe this. I've only been seeing him a few months. And I know that we've been talking about our future together but what if he freaks out?'

Roxanne shook her head. 'If he freaks out then he's not worth being with. But from what you've told me I doubt he'll be anything other than supportive. There're worse things in life than having a baby.'

'You think?' Charlene sniffed.

'Definitely.'

'But he's really career driven, Rox. I doubt he'll want to get lumbered with a girlfriend and a baby right now. Will you stay here? I've asked him to come over so I can tell him. You don't have to sit in with us during the conversation, just kind of be here in case he does a bunk.'

Charlene laughed but the humour didn't reach her eyes. The poor girl looked terrified but Roxanne would be there to knock the guy's teeth out if he even thought about leaving Charlene on her own to deal with a baby.

'Of course I will.'

Chapter Seven

Sitting on the sofa, she waited for the knock at the door. How could she have been so bloody stupid? At least if things didn't work the way she wanted them to, she'd have Roxanne to help her figure out what to do.

Roxanne stood at the balcony door, looking out as the sun began to set over the horizon. Even in paradise, Charlene felt like she was in hell.

A rapid knock at the door jolted Charlene, and Roxanne turned to face her. 'You ready?'

Nodding, Charlene got to her feet and went to the door. This was it, the moment she would tell the father of her baby that his life was about to change forever.

Gripping the handle, Charlene pulled the door open and there he was, standing outside, dressed as handsomely as always, his scent wafting through the apartment and almost knocking her off her feet. She smiled and opened the door wide to welcome him in. But he wasn't looking at her. His eyes settled on Roxanne and his face paled.

'Oh my god, what are you doing here?' Roxanne said and Charlene turned to see her friend smiling at Jez.

'I... erm... shit,' he said, pulling his gaze away from Roxanne and back to Charlene.

Frowning, Charlene slowly grasped the situation. Was this real?

'Look, babe,' Roxanne said, stepping forward and kissing him on the cheek.

Charlene froze as she watched them both. Her man and her best friend embracing in a way that should only take place in her worst nightmares.

'This isn't really a good time. This is my best friend, Charlene. She's pregnant and the dad is about to turn up any minute so she can tell him.'

Charlene let go of the door handle and moved back, the shock almost knocking her to the floor.

'What the *actual* fuck?' Charlene said. But she wasn't looking at Jez. She was staring at Roxanne.

Turning, Roxanne frowned. 'What is it?'

'Well,' Charlene said, casting her eyes on Jez. 'Go on then. I'm pregnant, what you going to do about it?'

Jez, stunned and unable to speak, turned and headed along the corridor towards the exit.

'Wait,' Roxanne said, her tone telling Charlene that the penny had dropped. 'You're the guy Charlene's been seeing?'

He stopped and Charlene shoved Roxanne. 'You've been shagging my boyfriend? Are you fucking kidding me, Rox? You've only been here five minutes and you're dropping your pants for my man already? Like mother like fucking daughter, right enough.'

Roxanne retaliated and shoved her back. 'Oi, I didn't know he was your man. You've been so bloody secretive about him, how was I meant to know? And don't fucking dare speak to me like that. Just because you were stupid enough to get up the duff. It's not my fault.'

An angry fog descended and Charlene grabbed for Roxanne, pulling at her hair and rattling her head off the frame of the door. A flurry of fists and hair, Charlene laid into Roxanne as a frenzy took over. The same thing had happened when they were sixteen. Roxanne had slept with her on-off boyfriend, Colin, and pretended that she hadn't known they were together, got her slag of a mother to lie about it. Roxanne had professed innocence, apologised and begged Charlene to forget about it. But not this time; Charlene wasn't buttoned up the back.

'You're a fucking bitch, I bring you out here to get away from that shit hole and this is how you repay me?'

Roxanne struggled to loosen Charlene's grip, but she didn't have to. Jez reappeared in the apartment and pulled Charlene away, his arms wrapped around her as he dragged her along the hallway.

'Calm down, Charlene.'

With one last pull, Charlene tugged as hard as she could and a large clump of auburn hair came away in her hand. She let out a laugh and spat at Roxanne.

'Enough!' Jez shouted, pulling Charlene harder.

'I'll fucking kill her,' Charlene screamed. 'You hear me? I'll fucking kill you, bitch. Don't think I'll forget this because I won't. You better pack your bags and head back to that mother of yours, Saint Mandy, *love*, because you're not fucking welcome here anymore.'

Charlene felt tears burn her eyes as she shrugged Jez off, but he gripped her hand. After pulling her into the lift, they reached the ground floor. They were outside now and he was pulling her towards his car.

'Get in,' he said, moving towards the passenger door and opening it.

'Fuck off, I'm not going anywhere with you.'

'Don't argue with me, Charlene. Just get in the fucking car. We've got things to talk about.'

Charlene hesitated, glancing up at the apartment. He was right, they did have a lot to discuss. But what would he have to say for himself? He was the one shagging someone behind her back while she was busy growing his bloody child.

She climbed into the car and put on her seat belt as he sped off down the narrow street and along the back streets towards his apartment. They said nothing as Jez drove and Charlene had to bite her lip to stop from crying.

Charlene felt sick. This was all such a mess and so raw. Just an hour earlier she'd poured her heart out to her best friend and now she'd found out that the guy who'd made her pregnant was cheating on her with said friend.

Turning, she faced Jez and raised a brow. 'Explain yourself, then.'

As he cleared his throat, Charlene noted the beads of sweat on his brow. Good, she thought. He should be bricking it.

'Right, first of all I didn't know she was your best friend. I had no idea and I can promise you that she didn't know I was seeing you either.'

'*Bullshit*. Next lie please,' Charlene said with a venom to her tone she didn't know she could muster. She watched as he rolled his eyes.

'I'm not bullshitting you. I swear I didn't know you two were friends.'

'So that just cancels out the fact that you were cheating on me, does it?'

Jez shook his head. 'No, of course it doesn't. Look, I'm not into this whole monogamy thing. We're living in fucking Magaluf for fuck's sake and—'

'Oh,' Charlene interrupted. 'So basically, you're telling me that you give zero fucks that I'm carrying your child. You just want to live out here with no attachments? And where does that leave me, eh Jez? You were talking about moving in together, and all of a sudden you're "not into this whole monogamy thing". That's all I have to hear, Jez. I'm not interested in anything you've got to say for yourself.'

'Charlene—'

'I said I'm not interested.'

The car began to slow and Charlene opened the door. 'Let me out. I can't stand to be anywhere near you right now.'

Waiting for him to protest, Charlene felt the lump in her throat grow when he didn't. What was she supposed to do now? She'd lost her best friend, her man and her future all in one night. Now that she was pregnant with his baby, she'd never be able to forget him.

Jez stopped the car and Charlene got out. She'd half expected him to tell her to stay, so they could try to work things through. She wouldn't have, anyway. She needed to be alone with her thoughts. Stress and pregnancy were not a good mix and being in Jez's company wasn't good for her at that moment.

'Are you really doing this?' Jez said, but before she allowed the poison to trail from her tongue, she slammed the car door and walked away. She had no idea where she was going. Not back to her own apartment. She couldn't be in the same room as Roxanne. She'd walk. Think. Try to push the images of Roxanne and Jez out of her head.

There was one thing she'd never forget though. Roxanne's betrayal.

Charlene would take her revenge on her one day. She'd take them both down.

Chapter Eight

Roxanne opened the front door and turned to grab her suitcase. As she did, she heard footsteps and upon turning back to the door to leave, she found Jez standing there. He'd come back to Charlene's apartment by himself. His expression was flat, and Roxanne tried to work out what he was thinking. Roxanne's head still throbbed from where Charlene had pulled out a clump of hair.

'You're leaving Magaluf?' Jez asked, stepping into the apartment.

'That's none of your business. Now, if you'd move so I can get past,' Roxanne said, trying desperately not to make eye contact.

'I'm sorry,' was all he could manage. Then he said, 'If she wasn't pregnant…'

'You're a fucking idiot,' Roxanne said as she pushed past Jez on the way out the door. 'So what? You're just going to stay with her out of guilt? Does that make you feel like a man?'

Jez shook his head. 'If she wasn't pregnant…' he attempted again, 'then you know I'd stay with you in a second.'

Roxanne laughed venomously. 'Are you fucking serious? You think I'd *stay* with you after this? Has it not occurred to you that what you did was the single most shitty thing a man can do to a woman? Even if you didn't know we were mates, Jez, you still cheated on us both. And she's so head over heels for you that she thinks I've fucked her over.'

Jez moved towards her and put his hand between her and the door. 'How is that my fault? Before you even got here, she said you shacked up with her man back in Glasgow, so don't go blaming me for your choices before we even met.'

Roxanne felt the anger bubble to the surface and shoved his arm out of her path before heading out the door. She only just had enough money to buy a ticket back to Glasgow. She didn't even know where she was going to stay when she got back. She certainly wasn't going back to her mother's flat. The last thing she needed was the inevitable 'I told you so' lecture.

'Drop dead, Jez,' Roxanne said, hearing her voice crack. The tears fell then. She'd not been seeing him long in comparison to other relationships she'd had in the past, but she'd truly begun to feel things for him she hadn't felt with anyone in the past and now he'd gone and ruined it.

'Rox, I'm sorry. I didn't mean to hurt you.'

'You haven't,' she lied, pressing the button for the lift multiple times. 'I'm just glad I got out now. But she's stuck with you for the rest of her life. Shame, really. I mean, she hates me and I'm sure in time I'll get over that. But we could have fallen out over someone much better than you. You're a prick, Jez. Take away the flash car and the club and you're nothing but a boy from the scheme, pretending to be something he's not. A plastic gangster.'

Roxanne stepped into the lift and made sure to keep her eyes off him as the doors slid closed. And that was when she burst into tears.

She hated Jez for what he'd done. And she hated Charlene for the fact that she didn't believe her.

Now, it was back to Glasgow. Dreich and gloomy, as was her life.

2020

Chapter Nine

Arabella drew no comfort from the old-school music around her or the sounds of her friends laughing, joking and taking the piss out of each other. It didn't stop the impending doom of loneliness and past traumas that often crept up on her. It just accelerated it.

'Here.' A voice came from across the table. 'You want some?'

Arabella looked at the girl sitting beside her high school friend Shona, but said nothing. High school had been some of the toughest years of her life, and Shona's. Although Shona was one of those people who had a different best friend every other week – Arabella had been one of them on and off – she'd had her own problems with drink and drugs, and two young kids who'd been taken off her by social services when she was just seventeen. Apparently, she was allowed supervised visits now.

Arabella sighed. What was she even doing here? Her earlier argument with Eddie had caused her to put her guard up. All he'd said was that he didn't think it was a good idea for her to go mixing with old friends and he was right. But Arabella already had a drink in her by that point and snapped at him, telling him that she'd had no control over her life up until now, and she wasn't going to let him take that away from her by telling her who she could and couldn't be friends with. It hadn't been long before she found herself in the company of her old school friends at this house party, feeling sorry for herself and feeling like she was falling back into that old black hole of depression that often waited for her in the shadows.

'Oi, are you deaf or something?' the girl next to Shona said. Her name was Amy, another girl from high school, although she was more of an acquaintance. A friend of a friend. Arabella had met up with her again during community service for her last offence of breaking and entering. A property in the east end. Arabella hated getting into trouble with the police but it was something she couldn't quite seem to avoid these days.

'No, I'm not deaf. And no, I don't want a line,' Arabella replied, picking up a can of cheap cider and taking a large glug.

Why hadn't she listened to Eddie earlier? He was right about these people. They were a mess. *She* was a mess – 'a riot' some used to say. Just like the rest of the girls who'd grown up in care. It didn't matter what she did, how many times she brought trouble to his door though, Eddie just loved her and that was that. But for some reason she just couldn't accept it. Arabella knew he loved her, but anyone who said that would often disappear at some point in her life. Keeping him at arm's length was the safest way to protect herself if he ever got bored of her and left. That's what happened when you became a statistic, because that's what she was: a statistic. Once in the system, never out of the system. Once damaged, always damaged. Storming out on Eddie and into the company of these idiots proved that.

'What the fuck's her problem?' Amy muttered. Arabella was sick of the way people spoke about her as though she couldn't hear them.

'I don't have a problem just because I don't want to shove that shite up my nose,' Arabella replied before taking another gulp of cider. It had been a long time since she'd had a line, or even thought about taking one. Eddie would definitely leave her if he thought she was out doing drugs.

'Arabella, just leave it, eh? You're always so fucking tense, been like this since we were kids,' Shona said.

She didn't answer. Instead, Arabella got up, slammed the can down on the table, got to her knees and sniffed the powder up her nose without considering the consequences. That was how she grew up – do now, think later. 'There, you *fucking* happy now?'

Everything seemed to buzz then. The music, the chatter of voices around her. She sprung to life and got to her feet. She glared down at Shona, at Amy. They were scum from her past, but now that she had coke in her system, she didn't care. Picking up the can of cider, she downed the rest of it and felt her muscles begin to twitch and pulse to the music.

Floorfilla, she remembered. It was the music she'd listened to when she was younger. She'd been in and out of foster care her whole life, but she remembered one family in particular, the only ones who really showed that they weren't just in it for the money. There was an older girl, in her teens. She used to drink cider in her bedroom with her friends and listen to an album that Arabella secretly liked. It helped her to escape her thoughts. The music made her want to dance and she would often be allowed to sit in with her foster sister and her friends while they got ready to go on a night out. The song playing now, 'Anthem 3', was from that album and it took her back so quickly that before she could stop herself, Arabella was turning the sound system up and dancing on the coffee table.

Amy began whistling and clapping her hands. 'On yersel', Arabella. That's what it's aw aboot hen, fucking let it go!'

Arabella smiled down at Amy and suddenly she was her friend. She was the best friend she'd ever had in her life. The whole room erupted then, everyone taking lines off the table at Arabella's feet, the beat of the music thumping in her chest. It felt euphoric. It wiped her memory of all the shit she'd been through, and it didn't matter that it wouldn't last forever. Any moment was better than nothing.

She felt a tap on her hip and when she looked down, Arabella saw Amy offering her another can. Taking it in her hand, she cracked it open and climbed down from the table before snorting up a second line. Then a third.

Her heart pumped in her chest and she finished her can. Arabella danced her way across the room, out of the hall and into the small kitchen of the flat she was in, remembering that she'd left some cans in the fridge. When she opened it, they were gone. She must have drunk them all.

Reaching into her pocket, Arabella felt for the small amount of cash that she had put there and headed for the door.

'Where you going?' Amy asked, suddenly by her side.

'Shop. Need more booze.' On some level, Arabella knew she should go home to Ed and sort things out, but she felt fuelled for the night, ready to dance away all the shit going on in her head.

'I'll come with you,' Amy said. 'I need more booze anyway.'

Shrugging, Arabella headed out the door and down the street. The shop was busy and suddenly the paranoia became too much. Amy was in her ear, telling her to take the cider to the counter, leave the money and go. But Arabella didn't want to go anywhere near the front. People would see her for what she was, a waster on drugs. No, she'd wait. But Amy egged her on, telling her that no one would care and that it would be quicker than waiting in the queue. Shona was outside waiting on them.

'Hurry up, Arabella. Just do it.'

Before Arabella knew what was happening, she was at the till, the shopkeeper telling her to calm down or she'd have to call the police. Arabella was shouting, saying that if she didn't accept the cash then she was going to take the cider anyway. Fists flew, her own fists. She beat down on the man trying to restrain her, telling her to calm down. She *was* fucking calm.

There were blue lights. Arabella was screaming for the police to let go of her as she was huckled into the back of a meat wagon. Arrested? For what?

As the van began to move, and the effects of the coke began to wear off and the hangover and comedown kicked in, Arabella knew she was in deep shit. Attempted robbery and GBH. The one thing that she couldn't get over was the officers telling her that she was carrying enough coke in her pocket to bring a charge of intent to supply.

She'd only had one line back at the party, or was it more than that? It wasn't something she often did. So, where the hell had the coke that the police had found in her pocket come from?

She'd been set up.

'Fuck!' Arabella said, before beginning to sob in uncontrollable waves. What the fuck had she done? Eddie had warned her against going out with that crowd and she hadn't listened. Now look at the state she was in.

An officer slammed the back door of the van and she let out a long, painful wail of a cry.

Chapter Ten

The door to the prison transport vehicle opened and natural light flooded inside. Arabella squinted and glanced up at the building. It didn't look much like a prison from where she was standing, but that didn't help the intense nausea she felt now as she stepped out of the van and onto the ground. However, she quickly realised that actually, she didn't know what the inside of a prison was supposed to look like, given that she'd never served time in one. Arabella wondered if the television representations of prisons were what she could expect. For her, real life had always been worse than television dramas.

After her initial arrest, she'd been out on bail for just eight weeks before her case was up in court. She'd pleaded guilty to assault and robbery, as advised by her lawyer. He'd said that in doing so she'd get a lesser sentence. How naive she'd been. She'd expected community service, but when the judge threw ten months at her, Arabella had almost collapsed in the dock. The metal cuffs around her wrists forced her to think of the stretch ahead of her and how her freedom was waiting for her back in Glasgow.

'Right hen, come on. I'll show you inside and we'll get you processed, eh?' The male guard said, offering a soft smile.

Hearing the echo of keys on chains and the slamming of security doors, a feeling of displacement hit her hard as she stood at the entrance desk to be processed. 'Processed' like she was just a number. A barcode. How could she have been so stupid to have let this happen? Her life had been going fine until she'd bumped into her old group of friends from high school.

'Right, Arabella MacQueen?' The female behind the desk asked. Looking up from her cuffs, Arabella nodded in response.

If she'd just said no to their invitation to catch up, she could be sitting at home with Eddie right now, having a normal day. If she'd just listened to him instead of putting her guard up, she wouldn't be here right now. Shaking her head at her own failings, she closed her eyes.

'And do you have any concerns that we could assist you with? Any kids at home? Pets? Left your door unlocked?' The woman asked, interrupting Arabella's thoughts again.

'No, my boyfriend's at home. We don't have any kids,' she replied. Thank god she didn't have any of that to worry about. Although the guilt of what she was putting Eddie through was hitting her hard now. Eddie was a tough guy, not someone to show his feelings, but she knew deep down that her absence would affect him.

Thinking about her past and what had led her to prison, Arabella knew that she'd lived her life via the self-destruct button, doing whatever she could to block out the pain of being abandoned by her mother. Her downward spiral had started early – drinking cider with her mates. A group of them had gathered in the local woodland which connected the village she lived in with the next town, a place notorious for local teenagers' parties. Even the police avoided it at times, unless it became too rowdy. One of the lads in the group had managed to get his older cousin to buy everyone a cheap bottle of cider each and a couple of packs of cigarettes to share between them. Arabella had only been fifteen at the time and knew it was wrong. Her foster parents would have killed her if they'd caught her. But for her, that was the thrill of it. Knowing that at any moment, she could be found out and likely grounded. The foster family said they cared about her, which was why they gave her a curfew of eleven pm. The rest were allowed to roam the streets for as long as they wanted. She'd found it unfair, but thinking back, that was the kind of thing her own mother should have been doing. Caring for her instead of choosing the bottle.

'Any alcohol or drug dependencies that we can offer you support with, Arabella?'

'No. I used to. But not anymore,' she said, keeping her head down.

'And you're here on possession of?' The woman prompted.

Clearing her throat a little louder than she'd anticipated, Arabella said, 'Cocaine.'

'Okay,' the woman scribbled something down with her pen. 'And is that still a problem?'

Was it still a problem? Arabella asked herself. Well, yes, she supposed it was. The fact that she couldn't say no to it after being clean for eight years – then the minute she was back with those people had fallen under their influence again – spoke volumes. 'If you're asking me if I'm *addicted* to coke then the answer is no. I'm more addicted to pleasing people, that's a less expensive habit. Well, in monetary terms at least.'

The woman's expression didn't change as Arabella told her the truth. That was how she'd got into trouble in the first place, trying to please her mates into thinking she was a hard nut. And she was, to an extent. But to end up in jail because of it was beyond what she'd ever expected to happen.

That first night in the woods with her mates all those years ago, the cider and the cigarettes had just been the start. What came afterwards was worse. The need for the buzz of being drunk at the weekends had led to an addiction to getting high from harder substances than alcohol. That was when she'd started smoking weed. The rest of her friends were doing it, so why shouldn't she? But weed wasn't the kind of buzz she'd been looking for.

That was when she'd found cocaine. One of the lads had stolen a small amount from his older brother and Arabella had been one of the first to try it. She'd volunteer to try anything first to make herself look good. And she had no fear of what she was putting into her body because there was nothing worth living for. Not that she was suicidal; she didn't want to die, she just wasn't particularly fond of living either. The rush had been incredible and she knew from then on that it would be her downfall. It was lucky for her that she didn't have enough money for the coke to become a habit, unlike addicts who did have the cash to fund it. All Arabella could get was a line or two off someone else's stash, or the chance to chip in for a couple of grams with someone at a party. It didn't matter how long it had been since the last time she'd taken it, she always ended up saying yes to it.

Now, Arabella was being led to a cell, away from the world she'd built with Eddie. A nice flat, nice clothes and a boyfriend who cared for her. He was patient with her about how she dealt with her past. But she'd fucked up, royally fucked up and because of that, she'd lost her job and would be spending the next ten months in a cell with a stranger. Although Eddie had been angry, he'd said he'd wait for her. But would he? If she lost Eddie, what would happen to her? Not knowing the answer to that scared her more than being in prison.

'Okay, Arabella,' the male guard said. 'This is you.'

Peering in, she saw another female sitting on the edge of the bottom bunk bed. She was reading a book, and glanced up from the pages when Arabella stepped inside.

The guard disappeared, leaving Arabella on her own with this stranger, who was still looking up at her from the bunk.

'A'right hen?' she said. 'First time inside, is it?'

Arabella moved further inside the cold room and sat on the chair. 'How did you know?'

'Your face says it all. You don't have to look so terrified, I'm not a murderer,' the woman said.

Arabella managed a smile and felt herself relax when the smile was returned.

'I'm just in for attempt.' She winked and then laughed. 'I'm Roxanne.'

Arabella laughed with her, but wasn't sure if Roxanne was kidding or not. 'Arabella.'

'How long you in for?'

'Ten months. You?'

'That's fuck all, love. I've been in here for nine years. The last year is dragging. Just think, you'll be out of here just before me.'

Arabella felt her stomach roll. Ten years was a long time to be in a place like this. Maybe she wasn't kidding about the attempted murder. She'd have to get on this person's good side if she wanted to survive her own sentence.

'Fuck's sake,' Arabella says.

'Och, my choice, hen. Battered fuck out of someone because they owed me money. Was worth it though. I did get my cash in the end. Well, my man got it for me.' Roxanne closed the book. 'So, what did you do to land yourself a sentence in this shite hole?'

Arabella thought about that night. Her memories were still hazy. If it hadn't been for the CCTV and several witnesses, she may not have remembered much at all.

'Attempted robbery, GBH and possession of cocaine,' she replied in a quiet and guilt-ridden tone.

Roxanne pursed her lips. 'You don't seem like the type.'

I'm not, Arabella thought.

'Just goes to show the saying is spot on. It's the quiet-looking ones you've got to watch out for, eh?'

Arabella regarded Roxanne and her observation. They'd only met just moments before and there were already assumptions in Roxanne's head about the kind of person Arabella was. It caused an unsettling feeling within her, because she'd been clean for eight years, trying to stay on the right side of the law, until that one stupid night she'd gone against everything she'd worked so hard to achieve.

Roxanne turned her attention back to her book and leaned back against the wall. As Arabella took in the surroundings, her new home for the best part of the next year, she swallowed back the lump in her throat. She couldn't cry in front of this woman. She couldn't cry in a place like Kirktonhill Women's Prison.

She placed her belongings on the bed and didn't really know what to do next. If she'd never known the meaning of lost before, she did now.

'So, what did you attempt to steal, then?' Roxanne asked, slamming her book closed so loudly that Arabella jumped.

'Booze,' she sighed. 'And cigarettes.'

Roxanne laughed. 'Wisnae really worth a ten-month stretch, was it?'

Arabella shook her head. Was anything worth a stint in prison?

'Don't look so down in the dumps. Least you've got a decent cellmate. I heard this one lassie in here say that she was sharing with a woman who had night terrors. Apparently, she woke up many a night, fighting with the fresh air. That would do my nut in. Imagine waking in the middle of the night to see some rocket trying to knock seven shades of shit out of someone who isn't there.'

Arabella couldn't help but laugh at the picture Roxanne painted. The woman smiled at her and Arabella felt her shoulders loosen. 'I hope you're not a sufferer of night terrors.'

'No chance of that, love. But I can't promise I won't snore.'

'Ha, I can't promise that either,' Arabella joked.

They fell silent again for a while and Arabella watched as Roxanne pulled a pack of cigarettes from her trouser pocket and lit one. A wave of confusion washed over Arabella then.

'You want one?' Roxanne said, as if seeing the look on Arabella's face and mistaking it for something else.

'No thanks. Won't the officers be able to smell that?'

'Don't worry about it. It's not a problem.'

Arabella watched as Roxanne got up and moved to the window. Already Arabella was beginning to sense that this woman had some kind of presence at Kirtonhill. Perhaps becoming friendly with her would be a good thing, she thought.

The smell of the cigarette ignited in Arabella the need for some nicotine. 'Changed my mind if the offer's still going?'

Roxanne removed the packet from her trouser pocket and flicked it open before holding it out. Arabella slid one out and took the lighter from inside too.

Feeling the nicotine as it gushed into her system relaxed Arabella further and soon she sat down on the chair and the women smoked their cigarettes in silence. As much as Roxanne had been nice to her up until this point, Arabella didn't want to make a nuisance of herself. For all she knew, this woman wanted to be on her own, but being in prison meant she didn't have much of a choice in the matter.

She thought about Eddie now, and what he might be doing. He'd be at the van centre no doubt, sorting out the diary for MOTs and services, arranging hires and sorting wages. She remembered the process of his job, having worked there for a short time before going into hairdressing. As the owner, he'd be busy and the ten months would go by in the blink of an eye for him. Arabella was beginning to miss him already. Instead of being at home with him, she was stuck in this place with a woman she didn't know.

Pulling deeply on her cigarette, Arabella held it in her lungs and stared out of the window. She hadn't expected much of a view when she pictured herself in her prison cell but the room she was in with Roxanne faced out onto a housing estate around half a mile away on the other side of the fence which surrounded the prison. It wasn't just any old council estate either. The houses were brand new, by the look of it. Arabella could see that there was still a sign up stating that the show home was still open for viewing. She was thankful for the view, for still being able to see some sort of civilisation on the other side. It helped her to keep a connection with the outside world.

'Why would you want to buy a house that sits opposite a prison?' Roxanne remarked. 'And those houses aren't cheap either. I've looked them up on Rightmove. Some of them start off at one hundred and eighty grand. I mean, why pay that for something that has a prison overlooking your garden?'

Arabella laughed. 'They're not that close.'

'Hen, that guy?' Roxanne pointed. Arabella glanced in the direction in which Roxanne was pointing and saw a very small outline of a man in a garden. 'He's hanging his boxers on the line. You can practically see the stain where his skid marks used to be.' Roxanne giggled.

Arabella snorted and the women started to laugh uncontrollably together. This wasn't how she'd expected her first moments in Kirktonhill to go. She'd imagined sitting, long day after long day, wondering how she'd managed to get it so wrong, even with someone like Eddie by her side.

She'd have plenty of time to work out where she went wrong. Ten months was a long time to think things over.

2021

Chapter Eleven

The wheels hit the tarmac and the passengers did that weird thing of applauding the pilot for not killing them all on the flight. Why? Cole thought. It was stupid. You wouldn't applaud a bus or taxi driver, would you? Of course, these thoughts were just distractions for what he was about to do. Getting to Glasgow was stressful enough without thinking about retrieving his case and getting through the customs barrier. He had practised his poker face many times, the innocent look that he needed to perfect for when he came face to face with the customs officers behind that desk in the airport.

As soon as the plane pulled into the stand, everyone started to unclick their seatbelts and get to their feet to retrieve their hand luggage. Cole sat perfectly still, as the flight attendants had advised, remaining in his seat. Maybe that in itself made him look suspicious but he couldn't make his legs work at that moment. Even if he could stand up, he'd probably shit himself through nerves.

Moments later, he was moving slowly along the aisle of the plane towards the exit at the front. The low thrum of voices around him echoed loudly in his ears and he chose to focus on that to get him through these next few minutes.

'Thank you for flying with EasyJet,' the woman said as he reached the exit. He nodded, gave a smile but kept moving along the airbridge, towards the terminal. The rain battered off the outside of it and the wind rocked it slightly. His stomach lurched with the movement. Soon, he was through passport control and on his way to the next part of the journey.

Baggage reclaim. He saw the sign and followed the rest of the crowd towards the carousel. It had already started; he could hear the alarm sounding that warned passengers to stand back. There was no way out of this now. He had to get his case and hope that he'd get out of the airport a free man.

The carousel was already moving when he reached it. Men stood next to it with trolleys, women and young children stood back while they waited for husbands, boyfriends and parents to collect their bags. Cole stood at a spot on his own at the end of the winding carousel and waited. And waited. The thing went around roughly five times with nothing on it before slowly, one by one, bags began appearing. His appeared after around ten minutes of waiting and he pulled it off and began wheeling it along the floor towards the last of the security doors. That was the one he was most fearful of. Customs; Nothing to Declare. He was behind a family of six. Two adults, four kids. The kids were all roughly the same age and causing an absolute riot, shouting, singing and having a carry-on. Each child had a small pull-along case. One of the zips was burst, Cole noticed. As one kid shoved another, the case fell and the contents spilt onto the floor. Four cartons of cigarettes, each containing two hundred. Right in front of a customs officer.

The dad turned, glared at them and the kid started to cry. The customs officer stepped out in front of the family and Cole stopped, before manoeuvring around them. He listened as the dad began to stumble over his words and the family were pulled aside.

Cole's heart thrummed in his chest as he made his way under the green sign that read 'Nothing to Declare' and out towards the main terminal building, silently thanking the dad and his kids for distracting the officer. He saw the exit. Could smell the fresh, Glasgow air and hear the taxi engines outside.

He had to refrain from bursting through the doors and into a taxi. Slow and steady wins the race, he told himself.

'You want that in the boot, mate?' The driver asked as he approached the vehicle.

'Nah, mate. I'll take it in here with me.'

'Nae bother pal. Where to?'

Climbing into one of the taxis, Cole sat the case at his feet. He took a breath. He'd already organised his accommodation before arriving in Scotland. He gave the guy the address and sat back as the taxi pulled out of the airport and onto the motorway.

Cole exhaled loudly and had to stop himself from smiling. He'd done it. He'd managed to get the case out of Majorca and through the airport at the other side unscathed. His enemies were long behind him. They'd have discovered his betrayal by now. He was proud of himself, wishing he could see them now and their reactions to what he'd done.

This called for a beer and a night at the casino. Those were the two things that helped to numb the pain of his loss. His heart had been shattered; a black hole punched through his chest. The beer and the money would make him forget that for a while.

Chapter Twelve

Standing at the edge of the sun-drenched balcony overlooking the pool, Jez Kennedy bared his teeth as he held the phone to his ear. He may well be living in Majorca, but right now he felt like he was smack bang in the middle of hell.

'You're absolutely fucking sure of it?' Jez hissed down the phone. 'The money's gone?'

'Aye boss. It's gone. He's cleared out the safe instead of depositing it,' the voice said, sounding equally as furious as Jez. 'Word has it he's long gone, caught a flight back to the UK about six hours ago. But that's not all he's taken.'

'What do you mean?' Jez felt his breath catch in his throat, and then he remembered. He'd taken his mother's diamond wedding ring to the jeweller's to be cleaned that week. He'd picked it up and put it in the safe so that he could take it home. But he'd forgotten about it because he'd been so busy getting ready to launch the club. It should have been completely out of harm's way in that safe.

'The ring, mate. It's gone. I have hunted everywhere for it, hoping that it would have fallen on the floor during his bid to clear the cash out, but it's not here. I'm so sorry mate, I know how much that ring meant to you.'

Jez gripped the phone, feeling like he could crush it with his bare hands. The sun shone down on the complex Jez owned and had worked so hard to build. Blood, sweat and tears had gone into making a life for himself in Majorca. Not all his own of course, he'd had to bump a few off along the way. But that was business, wasn't it? You had to look after number one in order to get to the top of your game. And he was reaping the benefits of all that now. Well, he was until six hours ago. One hundred grand was nothing to someone like Jez. It was replaceable. But his dead mother's diamond wedding ring. It was the only prized possession she'd ever owned, her mother's before that. A family heirloom.

Jez Kennedy sat down at the patio table. The housekeeper set a bottle of beer in front of him. She always did that when he was stressed. Not that she ever asked him about his phone calls. Not even his wife, Charlene, did that. Jez always made sure that the lines were never blurred between business and family.

'*Esta bien señor?*' Maria asked. 'Can I get you something else?'

Jez always felt bad for not learning to speak better Spanish, but Maria assured him that he coped just fine, and that she liked speaking English.

'Fine. Thank you, Maria.' Jez said quietly, while offering a tight-lipped smile.

Maria sensed that Jez needed to be alone and left him to finish his call. 'Housekeeper' seemed an unfair title. She was more than that. She had also been the boys' nanny, someone who cared for the children and kept their home in order while Jez was out earning money and Charlene was out spending it. She'd been more of a mother figure than Charlene had been in the beginning.

'What do you want to do, Jez?' The voice at the other end of the line asked.

Jez knew exactly what he wanted to do. He didn't take too kindly to being screwed over by one of his own, especially not when they had stolen the only thing that had any kind of sentimental value from him.

'We find the bastard, even if that means bringing him back to this fucking island in a box. I want my money and that ring and I'll be damned if I let him get away with this. So, get a team together and find him. Preferably sooner than later. You got that?'

'Aye boss. Loud and clear. I'll let you know how things pan out.'

Slamming the phone down on the table, Jez exhaled loudly and ran a hand over his face. The season had started off well, with Jez launching a new nightclub, Martini Beach Club. It had only been open for a month and the place had already made him enough to see him through to retirement. But now the safe had been cleared of takings for the previous week and he was being laughed at all the way to the UK.

Getting to his feet and lifting his phone, he called his ex-colleague's number. It went straight to voicemail. Of course it did. There was very little chance that he had even taken his phone with him on that plane and if he knew what was good for him, he'd go into hiding when he got back to the UK. Because Jez was going to make sure he found him.

And when he did, bones wouldn't just be broken, they'd be shattered.

Chapter Thirteen

Martini Beach Club was buzzing with party-goers and Jez Kennedy sat back on the white leather sofa and smiled. This place was making him a fortune, setting his kids up for life. The place had only been open for one month but he knew there was many a successful season to come. It had quickly become one of the most popular places to visit on the island for stag, hen and birthday parties. Open eighteen hours a day, six days a week, the place was keeping Jez and his employees afloat all on its own. Yet he still didn't feel contented, not fully.

He'd been screwed over by someone he'd thought he could trust. But worst of all, a friend. And that was something that Jez wasn't able to swallow.

'How's things going with you and Charlene?' Danny asked, sitting across from Jez on the other side of the room.

Jez felt himself tense. 'Fine,' he lied.

'She's still acting off?'

Jez took a large mouthful of Jack Daniel's so he didn't have to answer. His relationship with his wife had been strained practically from day one but he'd stuck it out for the sake of the boys. In the last couple of weeks, she'd been off with him more so than usual. He suspected something was up, that she'd done something she shouldn't have, but when he'd questioned her she'd done the usual and told him to fuck off. He didn't want to think about his relationship and the state it was in right now. What he needed was to find out if there had been any development on bringing that bastard Cole back to Majorca. He'd already been gone a week.

'You found him yet?' Jez said, after swallowing the amber-coloured liquid and savouring the burn in his throat.

'Not exactly, but we think he might be in Scotland. Rumour has it he's working on a big deal that could see him earn fucking thousands,' Danny replied, shifting in his seat. 'But that's as far as I know and I don't want to dig too much too soon in case word gets back to him and he flees again.'

'He's got big fucking balls, I'll give him that.' Jez exhaled loudly. The bastard had stolen from him and then fucked off to Jez's homeland. Like he'd said, big fucking balls. 'Any idea who he's working with?'

'Not yet. But it won't be long before he's sitting here in front of you Jez. Then you'll be able to do whatever the hell you want with him,' Danny said with menace to his tone.

Jez nodded in agreement. He wanted that day, that very moment, right now. He thought about going to the UK himself. Nothing would give him more satisfaction than coming face to face with the guy who stole his money. Seeing the look on his face would be like all his birthdays and Christmases coming at once. However, Jez had commitments in Majorca, the club needed him present.

'I just don't get why he'd choose to go to Scotland when he had it all here? The sun, girls, money. It truly baffles me,' Danny said.

'Some folk always think the grass is greener, Danny. Thing is, you need to water your own grass, not shit all over it,' Jez replied.

'Couldn't agree more, Jez. We'll get him back, you won't have to wait long,' Danny said.

'Good things come to those who wait,' Jez replied. 'I can take it from here. I know someone who might be able to help. If I need you, I'll call on you.'

Jez thought about his connection back home in Glasgow. His old best mate, Billy Drysdale was at the very top of his own game by all accounts. Their lives had taken very different paths since that first time they'd visited Majorca together back in 2001. Jez just hoped that their friendship was strong enough now that he could call on Billy and ask a favour.

He pulled Billy's number and hit call. It rang only twice.

'DS Billy Drysdale...' The line went quiet for a moment.

'Billy boy, how's it going?' Jez said.

'Jez,' Billy replied. 'Good to hear from you. Long time no speak. I didn't even know you still had this number. You still over in Spain?'

'Aye,' Jez replied before he sucked air through his teeth. 'It's been a long time since we last spoke. Twenty odd years?'

Bloody hell, Jez thought. Two decades. Had it really been that long?

'Aye, sounds about right? How's things going with you?'

'Ah, you know, wife, two boys. Running a successful business. You?' Jez said.

'Successful career. No wife, no kids. Couldn't be bothered with all that on top of the job. You know me, I always liked to fly solo in that respect,' Billy replied.

'Look, I'll not hang about. I've something to ask you, a favour.'

'I thought as much. A gangster doesn't contact a DS for anything else,' Billy replied.

'Why would you presume I'm a gangster, Billy?'

'I'm a copper, Jez. I know these things. And it's not as though you weren't heading in that direction before we even went on that holiday, is it? So, what's this about?' Billy replied, his voice low.

'I wondered if you had someone on your radar back in the UK. I've been done over here in Spain and the bastard has fucked off with a lot of money that belongs to me. Apparently, he's in Scotland and planning a big deal. I trust you won't have to ask what kind, given how long we've known each other.'

Billy was quiet for a few moments and Jez wondered if the line had disconnected. Then he said, 'Why would I help you?'

'Do you really need me to answer that? Come on, Billy. Do you need me to remind you of that night? Of what happened?'

'How did I know you were going to throw that in my face?' Billy asked. 'That was almost twenty years ago.'

Jez exhaled noisily. He didn't want to have to use it against Billy, but he had to. It hadn't been easy to build a new life for himself in Spain, and for it to have started off by having to get rid of a body that had nothing to do with him had been a massive risk. He'd needed insurance, something that he could use if he had to, although he'd always hoped that it wouldn't come to that.

'And if it wasn't for me, Billy, you wouldn't be sitting at your cushty wee desk at Police Scotland. You'd be in prison yourself for a murder you committed while off your face on drink and a shit ton of drugs. You know I have the evidence, don't you? Your memory isn't so bad that I have to remind you of that.'

He listened to the silence on the other end of the line, the breathy sounds of Billy contemplating his position on the matter. Jez knew Billy as well as he knew himself. He wasn't going to let anything fuck up his life, not after he'd worked so hard to get to where he was.

'You're a bastard, Kennedy,' Billy said.

'Aye, I know. You know me better than anyone. Or at least you used to. Not much has changed. So, are you going to help me or not?'

Chapter Fourteen

Roxanne pulled Arabella in and held her close, so close that Arabella worried her friend might crush her. The emotion she felt caught her by surprise. Arabella hadn't expected to make a friend inside, and she certainly hadn't expected to feel sad about leaving. Naturally she couldn't wait to get out of prison, but it was hard to leave Roxanne behind. She'd been Arabella's rock on the inside, the person who had kept her on a positive path when she was feeling low about being in prison and leaving Eddie to wait for her, worried that she might come out and return to her old ways. Roxanne had been honest, often blunt. 'Get a grip, hen. You're in here for ten months, no' ten years like me. Thank yersel' lucky.'

'Feels like you've only been in here five minutes and you're off already,' Roxanne said now, loosening her grip on Arabella and leaning back to look at her face.

'Doesn't feel like five minutes to me,' she replied before she could stop the words. At least she was getting out, unlike Roxanne who still had a few more weeks to go. 'You'll be out with me soon enough.'

'Aye, and the first thing we're doing is going out and getting hammered. Understood? And I want to meet this man of yours, Eddie. He and my Jake sound like they would get on like a house on fire.'

Arabella laughed at the sly grin on her friend's face. 'Definitely.'

During their stretch together, Arabella had felt their friendship clicking into place. Their discussions led to her realising that they weren't all that different. They'd both grown up with alcoholic parents – although Arabella thought that Mandy, Roxanne's mum, sounded worse. But that was probably because Roxanne had had to put up with her a lot longer. Arabella had been removed from her own mother's care before she was old enough to truly understand what was going on, whereas Roxanne had had to wait until she was old enough to get away from her toxic parent. They'd made light of the fact that they both had boozed-up mums and had both ended up in prison. Was it any wonder? Would that happen to their own kids, if they ever had them?

Roxanne was like the big sister that Arabella had never had. Even though there was only a ten-year age gap between them, with Roxanne being thirty-eight, Arabella would go as far as to think that Roxanne was like a friend, sister and mother figure all in one, although she'd never say the latter out loud.

'Thank you, Rox,' she said in a whisper, fighting back tears.

'See you on the other side, wee yin.'

Letting go, Arabella turned and headed out of the room she'd shared with the woman she now classed as a best friend and followed the female officer along the corridor to the office at the end. She didn't turn around, not wanting Rox to see her crying like a stupid little girl.

Arabella entered the office and sat down at the table. The female officer on the opposite side smiled across at her and Arabella felt like the weight on her shoulders was already beginning to lift.

'Right, Arabella MacQueen. I've got a few things here for you to sign, just to say we've handed you back your possessions,' the officer said, sliding a pen and paper across the table. Arabella didn't bother to read it all, she simply signed her name at the bottom.

'Do you have somewhere to go when you get out?' The woman asked.

Arabella nodded. 'Yes, my boyfriend is picking me up.' Following the officer out of the room and down a series of corridors, she was led to a desk where she was handed a bag of her belongings – her mobile phone, a pack of cigarettes, a half-eaten pack of mints and a set of house keys along with a pair of jeans, a T-shirt and leather jacket. As she took the bag in her hand, the woman directed her towards a cubicle and she went inside to get changed out of her prison attire. Once inside on her own, she slipped out of the trousers and jumper and stepped into her own clothes. It made her smile how much she already felt like she was at home, feeling the familiar material against her skin.

Before Arabella could process what was happening, she was stepping through the security gate and into the open air, sucking muggy air into her lungs and smiling as she exhaled. Her ten-month stint in HMP Kirktonhill was over. She'd done it, served her time. Now she was free to do whatever the hell she wanted. And she would.

Arabella stepped off the kerb and crossed the road towards the parked car. She recognised it a mile off. Her beloved Audi TT.

'A'right babe?' Eddie said as he leaned against the bonnet of the car. 'I had her valeted especially for you coming out.'

Arabella grinned ecstatically at her man as he picked her up and spun her round. Wrapping her legs around him, she pushed her lips against his and squealed with excitement. 'God, have I missed you.'

'A'right babe, Jesus, at least let me drive us home first,' he laughed, putting her down on the ground.

'Keys,' she said, holding out her hand and wiggling her fingers.

'Really? You're just out the jail and the first thing you want to do is drive?' Eddie said with a raised brow.

'Eddie, I haven't driven this girl in almost a year,' Arabella replied. 'Keys. Now.'

Rolling his eyes, he tossed the keys in Arabella's direction and made his way around to the passenger door.

As she felt the weight of the keys in the palm of her hand, she glanced back at the prison she'd spent the last ten months of her life in. It hadn't been too bad. She'd made friends. Acquaintances, at least. The women and the girls had respected her in there. Some more than she'd expected. And she'd made a friend for life in Roxanne.

'What you hanging about for? You want to go back in or something?' Eddie called out from the passenger seat.

'Fuck that,' Arabella said, sinking into the driver seat of her beloved car. As much as she was going to miss her buddy, she was more than relieved to be out of that place. Running her fingers over the steering wheel, she gave a pleasurable sigh. 'Ugh, I've missed her.'

'Who?' Eddie said, pulling on his seatbelt.

'The car, you idiot,' she giggled, leaning over and kissing him again. He cupped one of her breasts for just a second and Arabella shivered with his touch. 'Oi, I don't want to have to go back in there on indecent exposure.'

'Ha,' Eddie laughed. 'You'd better get a move on then and get us back to the flat.'

Turning the key in the ignition, Arabella felt the engine vibrate in her bones. It felt incredible to be free. To know that she was driving home, that she would sleep in her own bed in the arms of her man. There was nothing like a man's arms around her.

Pulling away from the prison and out of the main gate, she turned the car onto the road before realising she didn't know how to get home. She'd arrived at HMP Kirktonhill in a van, cuffed inside a small compartment with only a tiny square window she'd barely been able to see out of, so she didn't know the way home. Before her sentence, she didn't even know where Kirktonhill was, let alone the prison.

'You'll need to direct me to the motorway from here, Eddie. I dunno where I'm going,' she said. Not that it mattered, she thought. She'd happily drive in any direction as long as it was far away from Kirktonhill.

Following Eddie's directions onto the M8, Arabella headed westbound towards the west end of the city. As the car came to the brow of the hill, the city came into full view on the horizon and for a moment, Arabella was stunned. She'd forgotten how amazing Glasgow looked from a distance. She'd missed it more than she'd first realised.

'So, how does it feel to be free?' Eddie asked, taking a cigarette from his packet and putting the window down. Lighting it, he handed it over to Arabella, who gladly held it between her lips.

'Fucking outstanding, Eddie. Honestly, that place was a shit hole,' Arabella said, pulling on the tip.

'Well I wasn't thinking it was the Hilton.'

'Far from it. At least with the Hilton you get a decent amount of men coming and going,' she winked.

'Oi, I hope you didn't swing the other way in there because you were missing me.'

Rolling her eyes, Arabella shook her head. Not that Eddie noticed. He was too busy laughing at his own joke.

'So what have I missed then?' Arabella asked, putting the window down slightly and blowing smoke through the gap.

'Nothing much.' He shrugged, but Arabella could see a mischievous grin creeping across his face.

'Liar. Tell me.'

'Okay fine, there is something. It's pretty huge but I need you to promise me you'll stay calm when I tell you.' His face was serious now and Arabella felt the panic beginning to build in the pit of her stomach.

'Oh shit. What is it?'

'I bought a hair salon,' Eddie said, connecting his phone to the stereo as if he'd just told her he'd picked up a loaf of bread for her arrival home. Oasis began to blare from the speaker as he sat back in the comfort of the leather seat.

Arabella eyed her man, wondering if she'd heard him right.

'What the hell would you want with a hair salon?' she asked, turning her attention back to the road.

77

'It's for you, Arabella.'

Her stomach flipped excitedly and she shot him a look. 'You *bought* me a salon?'

'Well, aye. Let's face it Arabella, you're not exactly going to be people's first choice at an interview when they see you've got a criminal record now, are you? I got a good mortgage rate on the place because the owner wanted a quick sale. So, if you want it, it's yours. I was going to keep it a surprise until I took you to see it tomorrow. But you know me, cannae hold things in if they're too good.'

'You've *bought* me a salon?' Arabella repeated, feeling dumb-founded. 'So what? I'm the manager?' she suggested. 'Like head stylist? Ed, I need to think about this. I've not touched a hair on anyone's head in almost a year. I'd barely got started at all and any skills I did have will be rusty.'

'Look, the place is already fully staffed with a full client list so you can take your time with it without having to worry about losing money. You really won't have anything to worry about.'

Arabella was stunned. She and Eddie had only been together three years, including the time she was inside. But in that short time, their relationship had moved quickly. Arabella had been physically drawn to Eddie and vice versa. Once the passion and fire between them had settled down, they'd decided that they still wanted to be around one another and Arabella had moved in with him.

'Eddie, is this all legit?' She pushed. 'I mean, I know the business is doing well. But enough to be able to buy a salon for me?'

'Right,' Eddie sighed. 'Look, I'm a business owner, Arabella. And because of that, the bank is very happy to lend me the money to start up a new business. That's all you have to know.'

Eddie sucked on the end of his own cigarette and Arabella kept her eyes on the road. The sun was high that May morning. The month that Scotland has its summer and she was out. Smiling at the thought, her mind was still on how Eddie could afford to do what he'd done for her.

'Are you sure?'

'It's not dirty money, alright? I told you, it's all legit.'

Silence hung between them for a moment before Arabella accepted the situation for what it was. A fresh start, offered to her by the guy who'd stood by her while she served her time. Who'd stood by her from the very beginning. She struggled to believe that anyone could love her that much.

Arabella couldn't wipe the smile off her face even if she'd wanted to. She finally had everything she'd wanted. But she still had to inspect the new place before she agreed to go ahead. If he had the savvy to buy the salon without her knowing, then he would have the savvy to sell it if she wasn't happy. But Arabella knew herself; she would love it even if it wasn't perfect. The salon was going to be her fresh start, her happy ever after. Did those still exist? After being sentenced, meeting Roxanne and now coming out to find that she was going to have her own business, things were almost too good to be true. Whilst in prison, she'd tried to stop herself from thinking negatively about things. But she always lost what she loved, in the end. Why should now be any different?

'I wouldn't do that to you, Arabella. I wouldn't buy you a salon with dirty money. You've been through far too much shit in your life. I know you struggle to believe that people can love you. But they can and I do. I want you to have a good life, Arabella. And this is where it's going to start. I promise I won't leave you like your mum did. I won't let you down like those so-called bastard friends did. Okay?'

Arabella fought against the tears. For once, they were happy tears. She nodded and smiled.

For the first time, she really believed that someone loved her.

Chapter Fifteen

Jake Cairney sat back on the seat in the kitchen of his flat and pressed send on the untraceable mobile phone that he used purely to contact the boys when they were out on a job.

> USUAL DROP OFF POINT BOYS. LET ME
> KNOW WHEN YOU'RE ON YOUR WAY.

Eastblane Designer Outlet, that's where the boys were headed. In fact, they would be there by now. Jake was nervous. Thousands of pounds were at stake here. There was no room for error.

This particular designer outlet on the outskirts of Glasgow hadn't been targeted before but that wasn't to say that Jake's team didn't know the place like the back of their hands. They'd made sure that they knew the layout, where each shop was in relation to exits, how long it would take for them to get from the exit of each designer store to the car park. One man, one store each. Jake had no concerns about his team. They were experts who knew exactly how much time they had, how much merchandise they needed and which brands to get. Specific orders would be honoured. Jake didn't get his hands dirty, not anymore. Back in the day, he and Roxanne had loved the thrill of a robbery. Leaving large gaps of time between them and making each one far different from the last kept them from getting caught. Being young, they loved being able to do the jobs themselves; it was exciting and kept their passion for each other alive because they were in it together. When Roxanne went to prison, Jake decided to screw the nut and keep his hands off the job. He needed to keep himself out of prison not just for Roxanne but for himself, too. He was getting older now, not as young and spritely as he used to be. If he was the one orchestrating the robberies and the hits, then his face was out of the picture and that kept him out of prison. They weren't exactly going to be making money if they were both behind bars. Jake did miss the feeling of exhilaration that came with it but after ten years off the job, he'd become used to being in the background.

Robbery wasn't their only source of income. Their main business was drugs. Mainly recreational, as that made the most money. Coke was their biggest earner. At between thirty and forty quid for a gram, it certainly set them up nicely. Jake had never touched the stuff himself, he didn't feel the need to. However, he saw what people liked about it. The cocaine high was what people wanted. And they never thought twice about paying large sums of cash for such a small amount. If people paid, Jake and Roxanne provided. Not just coke. Cannabis and speed too, but on the same scale. Coke was what had landed Rox in jail in the first place. The guy had been an idiot to think he'd get away without paying for his stash. It was just that Rox had gone a bit far in her punishment.

He thought about seeing Roxanne when she got out of prison, without the need to have prison guards at every corner of the room, watching them. Without having to be across the other side of the visitor table and not being allowed to touch her. Although he had paid off most of the guards to turn a blind eye, not all of them were as forthcoming as others. He had to take what he could get over the ten-year stint his missus had had to endure. And all because that prick Munro hadn't paid off his debt. It wasn't so much the debt; it was the attitude. He'd thought that because he was dealing with a woman, it didn't matter. Well, he'd found out the hard way, hadn't he? She'd near on bloody killed him. If it hadn't been for the two officers arriving on the scene due to a neighbour complaining about a disturbance, Munro would have died that night. Thankfully for Roxanne, he hadn't. The police had searched their home due to the nature of her crime, beating him up because he owed her money for drugs. Jake and Roxanne's flat was clean as a whistle. Not so much as a speck of dust, no loose bank notes. Nothing. Jake's storage unit company had been a good front for the income. He wasn't stupid. Another reason he hadn't yet bought them the house of their dreams. He didn't want the police to see that they were giving it the big guns by buying a large property. Not until the storage unit caught up in terms of income. However, Jake was happy to continue living in the flat. He didn't need the big flash house to know how successful they were. Maybe one day, when they were too old to carry on in the game they were in, they could buy a house out of the city and finally live a quiet life together.

Almost two hours had passed when he received a reply from his team.

DONE. ON OUR WAY.

Jake got up and headed out to his storage units on the industrial estate five miles from his flat in Glasgow. All twenty units were full. All of them were genuine punters storing their worldly possessions. Unit twenty was his gold mine. It was the only one with a hatch door on the back corner of the floor space. No one knew it was there apart from his team and Roxanne. Beneath was where it all happened. Drug production and storage. And a safe where all of their criminal income lay.

–

Arriving at the storage units, Jake got out of his car and walked towards unit twenty. A small van was sitting outside, the engine off. The boys were inside and waiting. Jake's stomach flipped with anticipation to see how much merch they'd managed to pull from the order. He wondered what Roxanne would make of it all if she were here. Would she praise the team, or simply tell them to get onto the next job?

Roxanne McPhail was a force to be reckoned with, as a criminal and a woman. Jake would do anything for her, be anything for her if it meant she was happy. Not only that, but Jake knew that having Roxanne in his life was the nearest thing he would ever have to being normal. He was prepared to do anything to protect that. He thought back to when he met Roxanne through a crime ring years ago. He knew as soon as he set eyes on her that she was the one he couldn't let get away. She was feisty, full of ambition to be successful and live a luxurious lifestyle but she would never shy away from hard graft. He saw a little of himself in her, knew that she was intent on going places and he wanted to be part of that with her.

That first job they'd done together had been brutal but such a thrill. Robbing the post office before they'd had a chance to bank their takings had been incredible. No other job had matched the feeling he'd had when he saw her with the gun in her hand and the mask over her face. He loved a powerful woman and Roxanne was the walking definition of that. They'd got away with a five-figure cash sum that day and never got caught. When Roxanne was involved, no one was ever found out. She knew how to work the system, avoid the cameras. But most of all, she wasn't afraid to pull that trigger if she had to. She was the smartest of all of them.

Jake smiled inwardly as he remembered. She would be coming home soon and he couldn't think of anything else. But for now, he had to focus on the job in hand.

Opening the door, he stepped inside the unit. Four boys stood at the back, all of them with boxes and holdalls at their feet. One of them was smoking a cigarette, another glugging back a can of Red Bull. All of them chatted amongst themselves.

'Nice one, lads, Rox will be delighted,' Jake said as he stood next to them.

'Nae bother, boss.'

'You managed to cover the entire order?' By the look of what was at their feet, it seemed that way.

'Aye boss. Couple grands' worth each,' one of the lads replied.

Jake nodded and kept his eyes on the merch. He pictured the look on Rox's face when he told her about it. And this was just the beginning. There would be plenty more where that kind of cash came from. Plenty more. On top of the drug deals, things were going to be fine. Jake had worked so hard to build the business, to grow their income.

When Rox got out, things would only get better. And Jake was planning on asking Roxanne to marry him. That was the only thing missing from their lives. Being married to Roxanne would hopefully help to conceal his secret even more.

Chapter Sixteen

Arabella allowed Eddie to guide her inside the flat. He'd insisted he blindfold her and that there was a surprise waiting.

'Is this really necessary, Eddie?' Arabella asked, stumbling over her own feet and feeling Eddie correct her stance.

'Yes it's necessary. This is the first time we've been together on our own in almost a year. I want it to be special.'

Arabella rolled her eyes behind the blindfold. Eddie was always trying to be a romantic but failing miserably. The last time he'd surprised her was after she'd mentioned seeing the new Shark vacuum cleaner advertised on the television and thinking it looked amazing. He'd gone out and bought it for her. But not just because she liked it. He'd wrapped it up for her birthday. The look on her face must have given her away because he'd insisted he return it, but he still hadn't understood. He hadn't realised she was disappointed about getting the Shark for her birthday – he'd just thought it was the wrong model. That in itself had made her laugh, and his failed attempt to be romantic made her love him even more.

'Right, stand there,' Eddie said before letting go. She felt him move away and listened as he busied around her. 'Okay, take it off.'

Arabella did as requested and removed the blindfold. As her eyes adjusted to the light, she took in her surroundings, amazed at what she was seeing.

'Welcome home, Ms MacQueen,' Eddie said, standing by the coffee table in the centre of the living room. A huge grin spread across Eddie's face as he drank in her reaction. An ice bucket with champagne sat in the centre of the table, two flutes either side. There was a vase of flowers on the window ledge to her left and a 'welcome home' banner hung on the centre of the back wall.

'Eddie…' Arabella started. Then she stopped, the sudden lump in her throat almost suffocating her.

'You like?'

She manoeuvred around the coffee table towards him and slung her arms around his neck before kissing him gently. 'I love it. But I have to admit…'

'Oh god, what? Did I get the wrong champagne?'

'No it's not that. It's just… well, I was expecting the latest vacuum cleaner.' Arabella gave a devilish grin and Eddie laughed.

'It's good to have you home wee yin,' he said. 'Just do me a favour, eh? Don't get involved with that crowd again. They're bad news, Arabella. I swear if I ever see any of them again I'll knock fuck out of them.'

Arabella winced at how quickly Eddie's mood changed when he talked about her old friends. She'd been stupid to go along with them. But it wasn't just their fault. It was her. She was the destructive one, the one who couldn't say no to a couple of little lines of coke, along with the booze.

'Let's not waste our breath on those idiots. I'm back now and I won't be making the same mistakes again. From now on it's just you and me.'

Eddie's expression softened and he bent down to kiss her. 'Hey, why don't we take the bottle to the bedroom?'

Arabella smiled and lifted the bucket. She wanted to forget prison, forget being locked away from Eddie and her life for the past year. Getting drunk and having sex with Eddie was a start.

–

Arabella rolled onto her back and lifted the cigarettes from the bedside table. Opening the box, she pulled one out with her teeth and lit it.

'How's that for a welcome home present?' Eddie laughed, adjusting his position on the bed and leaning over Arabella. Taking the pack from her, he lit up too and the room was filled with a double haze of blue smoke.

'You really do rate yourself highly,' Arabella smiled.

As much as she was joking around, Arabella was more than glad to be home and back in Eddie's bed. Her stupidity had landed her in a place she never could have imagined she would have ended up.

Arabella's thoughts of her friend were interrupted by Eddie leaning in for a kiss. 'So tell me, was your head turned in there?'

Pulling away, Arabella frowned. 'Eddie, don't be so disgusting.'

'Ah come on, I'm only kidding.'

'Actually, if you must know, there was one good thing to come from being in that hellhole,' Arabella said, flicking the ash into the ashtray on the side of the bed.

'Oh aye?'

'Her name is Roxanne. She's just about at the end of her sentence of ten years. If it wasn't for her I don't know if I'd have gotten through my own time.'

Eddie raised a brow and Arabella knew he would be thinking the typical guy thing. Had there been more than just friendship? She chose not to dignify the thought with a response.

'You were in there for almost a year, Arabella. How come you never mentioned her before?'

Thinking about the question, she had to be honest. She didn't really know why she hadn't told him. Rox was part of Arabella's life on the inside. When Eddie had come to visit her at prison, she'd kept inside life and outside life separate. Not that she had anything to hide.

'There was nothing to tell. Anyway, she's getting out soon and she wants to meet up.'

Eddie paused, giving Arabella a hesitant look. 'What is she in prison for, Arabella?'

'Attempted murder,' she said without hanging back. 'And before you say anything, no, I don't have to worry about her.'

'Attempted *murder*?' Eddie's frown grew deeper and Arabella could feel herself getting annoyed.

'It's not like it sounds.'

'Oh, so she accidentally tried to kill someone? Or was she falsely accused?'

Arabella sighed. 'No, but all I'm saying is, don't judge. She's my friend and I really want us to stay that way once she gets out.'

Eddie held his hands up and pursed his lips. 'Hey, I'm not judging. If you're happy then that's all that matters.'

Arabella smiled in her victory. Eddie was protective but he could also be a softie if she wanted him to be. She was glad their relationship was still intact after her prison stint and that she still had someone like him to protect her from herself.

'Good. Because I want you to meet her. She has a partner too, so maybe we could all get together at some point.'

Eddie smiled and nodded in agreement, but Arabella knew deep down that he wasn't convinced that her friendship with Roxanne was going to last, or that it was a good thing at all.

She'd just have to prove him wrong.

Chapter Seventeen

Eddie shook his head as he sat back on his seat in the office at the van centre. Was this really his life? Would the only excitement he was ever going to get come from hiring out vans? Yes okay, he owned his own business and yes, it brought in good money and his credit score was good enough that he was able to buy a business for his girlfriend. But there was something so dissatisfying about it all.

His thoughts were pulled from him when there was a knock at the door. 'Mr Corrigan, here are the time sheets from the staff for this week,' Sandra, his secretary, said.

Eddie smiled as she sat them on the desk. 'Thanks.'

He swung on his chair and watched as Sandra left the office. He stared down at the staff time sheets and sighed. He remembered the days when he was just a young teen, riding around on his dirt bike down by the fields at his old primary school, often not sober. The buzz of knowing that he could come off at any moment was what had kept him going. Or when he wouldn't think twice about taking ecstasy, just so he could have the night of his life with the boys. The number of life-threatening activities he'd pursued told him he should have died a long time ago, but he didn't. He was still very much present, yet he didn't feel alive.

Those days were long behind him. But he missed them greatly, so much so that when Arabella had been arrested on suspicion of attempted robbery, possession and GBH, he couldn't help but feel a little jealous. How could her life be so much more exciting than his? Before they'd met, she'd been a tearaway teen. Always getting into trouble with the people she called friends, taking drugs, drinking and partying. Now she was friends with a proper criminal, and Eddie's life was plain and boring.

He was glad she was home, of course he was. When she'd been in prison, he'd found the need to feel close to someone overwhelming and he'd had numerous one-night stands with other women. He was a man and he had needs. Arabella didn't need to know about that and she would never find out. He'd been careful not to allow them into his life, except for one. The last one had turned into somewhat of a relationship. That hadn't been his plan. He regretted the conscious decision he'd made to invite that girl back to the flat, back to the bed which he shared with Arabella. As good a shag as she was – as they all were – it still made him feel like shit to think of his inability to be faithful when things got tough. But he just couldn't seem to stop himself. If she hadn't gone to prison, he'd never have done it. He'd never have dreamed of cheating on her.

Shaking off the memories and the guilt gripping his stomach, he pulled his mobile out of his pocket and stared at the screen. No messages from Arabella. He wondered how she would get on, as the new owner of Hair Envy. As much as Arabella had no clue how to run a business, he was sure she'd get the hang of it. Even if she didn't, she had Scarlett to do all the leg-work. Scarlett. He closed his eyes as her name floated around inside his head, before shaking it out again. Hair Envy was a thriving business in the heart of the city and he couldn't let either himself or Arabella mess that up. Eddie had come too far in his life to ruin things.

He hadn't been in trouble since he was a teenager, when his dad would bail him out of the mess he'd got himself into. The car thefts, house break-ins, the class C drug dealing. But he wasn't a teenager anymore. He didn't have a dad or his money to rely on to get him out of sticky situations. In fact, his dad was the only reason that Eddie had a business at all. The van hire company had been left to Eddie in his dad's will, on the strictest instructions that he hunker down and run it properly. With his dad dead, Eddie was responsible for himself and if he threw away the business for the sake of an adrenaline rush then he'd be left with nothing. His mum had left before he could remember who she was, and he had no siblings. That was one thing he had in common with Arabella, that their mothers had abandoned them.

His phone rang then, jolting him from his thoughts. He answered it, listened to how excited Arabella was about going to see the salon for the first time. Eddie couldn't help but wonder how Scarlett would cope with Arabella as her new boss. He was only half listening when she said, 'I'll see you later on tonight? Maybe we could go out for dinner or something? I wanted to talk to you about meeting Rox. She's getting out soon and I really want to introduce you to her. She was my rock in there.'

'Sure, I'll see you back at home.' Eddie hid the annoyance from his tone. He didn't like the sound of Roxanne. Not because she was a criminal. But because Arabella seemed so besotted with her. He'd seen this kind of thing happen with her before. Growing up in care, not knowing how to create bonds and relationships with people, Arabella tended to jump into a new friendship with two feet, without truly seeing a person for who they really were. Those bitches, Amy and Shona, were a perfect example of that.

Opening Google, Eddie typed in Roxanne's name. If she'd been in prison for ten years then maybe there would be something online that he could find out about her. And he wasn't wrong. What he read surprised him. Arabella either didn't know what this woman had done, or had been desensitized by her crimes due to spending so much time with her on the inside.

March 2010 – Glasgow

Female Glasgow Gangster Found Guilty

Twenty-eight-year-old Roxanne McPhail was found guilty today at the High Court in Glasgow of possession with intent to supply Class A drugs. She was also found guilty of attempted murder. Roxanne, who has quickly become one of Glasgow's most feared female criminals, was sentenced to ten years in HMP Kirktonhill after the verdict was revealed.

Ms McPhail is said to have hospitalised Johnnie Munro after it is alleged that he owed her the sum of just twenty pounds. Ms McPhail was arrested at the scene of the beating, where she was later found to be in possession of cocaine and ecstasy.

The victim was not present in court for the sentencing, but it is believed that he is recovering from the attack and his drug addiction at home with his family. Johnnie Munro suffered a broken wrist, punctured lung and head injuries on the night of the attack, which left him in hospital for a month. No one from the Munro family was available for comment.

Roxanne McPhail's partner, Jake Cairney, was seen leaving the court alone.

Eddie read over the ten-year-old article and raised a brow. Now this woman was 'besties' with his girlfriend. Roxanne sounded out of Arabella's league, but highly interesting to Eddie. And by the sounds of it, it wouldn't be long until Eddie got to meet her or her boyfriend.

Maybe these people were just the thing Eddie needed to fill the void. Maybe hanging out with them would give him his spark back. He missed the dangers of living life on the edge of a knife, and it had to be better than cheating on Arabella.

Chapter Eighteen

The boys on his team had done their jobs. Retrieve and sell.
The merchandise was gone, sold on for plenty of cash. Jake had
given them their cut and the rest went in his pocket. He smiled.
It was a good side earner, something that Roxanne could take
over perhaps once she got out. But only if she wanted to. She
would be on probation, so she might want to lay low for a while.
She wouldn't want to risk going back inside. Ten years was long
enough, he thought.

The phone in his pocket began to vibrate and Jake pulled
it out. He glared down at the screen as the name flashed up at
him and Jake did a double take. The sight of the name made
him feel sick. Of all the people to get in touch, why him? Why
now? It had been a good few years since they'd last spoken.

His stomach rolled as he hit the accept call button.

'Jake Cairney. Long time no fucking speak,' Cole said, his
thick London accent snaking through the receiver.

'Cole, what you been up to?' Jake asked, feeling a genuine
fear.

'Funny you should ask, Jakey boy. Just so happens I'm in
your neck of the woods. Looking into some business. Fancy a
beer?'

Jake took a deep and steadying breath before he agreed to
meet Cole. Meeting this man face to face was certainly going
to bring back some memories that Jake would rather forget.

'You're in Glasgow?' Jake swallowed hard and silent, but his
throat was dry.

'Yeah, I've got a proposition.' Cole's words hung between them and Jake knew he had to agree.

'Aye, mate. Would be good to see you. Where you thinking?'

'How about that strippers' place up at Charing Cross? Around ten?' Cole suggested and Jake heard the smile in his tone.

'See you there,' Jake said before they hung up.

The sensation of wanting to throw up became a reality as Jake hunched over, allowing the contents of his stomach to exit his body.

–

Standing outside the strip club, Jake knew that there was no going back when it came to Cole Woods. If he showed an interest in becoming involved with him in his line of work even just by answering a phone call, then there was no backing out. However, Jake checked himself as he waited for Cole to arrive. Jake wasn't some measly wee ned off the street. He was a well-known criminal. Both he and Rox were known in the city and people knew not to mess. Cole was on *Jake's* patch, and he wanted to make it known that he wasn't going to be made to feel threatened, regardless of the past. And Jake had killed before; he could do it again if he had to. Even Cole knew that.

With his mind in overdrive, thinking of scenarios that hadn't even happened yet, Jake looked up to see Cole strolling towards him with a huge grin on his face.

'Jake fucking Cairney. How are you?' Cole said, sounding particularly cheerful.

Taking a deep breath to calm himself, Jake returned the smile. 'Cole, my man.'

The men shook hands and Jake noted the determined grip Cole had. It was a reminder that Cole thought of himself as the harder man, without having to say the words.

'Let's see what these Glasgow strippers are all about, eh mate?' Cole raised a brow and released Jake's hand.

He followed Cole inside and they headed for the bar before taking a seat in one of the booths at the back of the room. Sipping on his pint of Peroni, Jake began to relax.

'How long's it been since we last saw each other?' Cole asked, although Jake suspected that he was just testing the water to see how Jake would react to being reminded of what happened. It had been three years since that job.

'Three years,' was all Jake said in response.

'Yeah, that sounds about right. That job you did with me and the lads down in London was fucking epic, mate. We made a shit ton of money.'

Jake nodded. 'Aye,' he said, hoping that Cole wasn't about to mention the one thing from that job that made him sick to his stomach. 'It was a good one.'

Jake unwillingly thought about that night, about what had happened. An unfortunate mistake. It hadn't been part of the job, a drug run from London to Glasgow, which otherwise went smoothly. Somehow Cole found out about it and while that helped Jake deal with it at the time, he always knew Cole would call in the favour one day. He was clearly here to collect.

'So, anyone up here tickle your fancy then? You know, aside from the missus?' Cole laughed. 'I tell ya, Jakey boy, I didn't take you for a kinky fucker. Sex games aren't my thing, but each to their own and all that. Shame it ended so tragically.'

Jake shot Cole a warning look, shaking his head. 'Oi, it was a one-off, alright? Not something I'll be making a habit of. It was three years ago, and out of my head. And I intend for it to stay out. So I'd prefer you didn't mention it again.'

Cole smirked. He wasn't going to allow Jake to get away with that.

'How can you keep something like that out of your head? Get real, Jake. If I killed someone in the way you did, I'd never get over it,' Cole said quietly, a sly smile still set on his face. 'And to know the family could take you down if they found out... I mean, they're wealthy fuckers, aren't they? They'd have paid good money to show the world what you did to one of their own. It's lucky I was on hand to help dispose of the evidence; you know?'

Cole watched Jake as he took a breath, composed himself.

'Like I said, I don't want to talk about it. So I'm assuming this isn't just old buddies catching up?' Jake started.

'Ah, you know me so well, mate,' Cole replied, taking a large mouthful from his own pint. His eyes narrowed and Jake felt them burn into his skin. 'I've got a business proposition for you.'

'Oh?' Jake asked, pretending that he didn't know what was coming. He noticed how Cole's eyes drew away from his as he watched one of the girls walk past them in her black lingerie. Cole licked his lips, sucking air in through his teeth.

'And how does it involve me?' Jake pressed, bringing Cole's attention back to the table.

'You've got a good work ethic. You know how to get shit done and I *know* you're loyal. I'm expanding my business; the market is growing because demand is higher. You've good connections and I want you to run my shit up here. Organise runs, set up teams who will move my drugs around, up and down the country and that. I'm in with some of the high-end suppliers up here in Glasgow and they asked if I could get someone to manage the hubs up here and I thought of you.' Cole took a sip from his pint, regarding Jake through narrow eyes. Of course he'd put Jake forward. He always knew that his involvement with Cole would come back to haunt him one day.

'When you say "up and down the country"?' Jake asked.

'Like the job you did for me back in London. You get a team together – although try to hang fire on shagging any of them. I wouldn't wanna have to be in a situation where I have to sort things out for you again.' Cole laughed loudly.

Jake held his tongue. If Cole was going to be around for a while, he'd have to bite his tongue at every little dig.

'Right, I get it.' He gritted his teeth, hating that Cole had dirt on him and so had a lifelong way to blackmail him.

'So, who're the connections then?' Jake asked, wondering what kind of potential trouble this could lead to. At the same time, he was thinking about the money that could be made from this. Cole wasn't lying when he said he'd paid Jake well. Tens of thousands for the runs and an extra bonus for ensuring the police were none the wiser.

'Nah mate, no can do.' Cole shook his head.

'Cole, if I'm going to do this, I need to know who the bigwigs are. You've got to remember that I run my own production line, so if I'm going to be in this with you, using someone else's product, then I need to know who I'm getting involved with.'

Cole hesitated. 'You're stuff is recreational, eh?'

Jake nodded.

'Well, these guys are of the hard stuff. You know, crack, heroin. That sort of thing. It involves big money, a good pay out for both of us. All you have to do is get a team of lads, girls, whoever together and I give you the jobs. They do the runs and we all get paid. Simple as fucking that. You arranged the job for me last time and it worked a fucking treat, Jake. I need you on my team.'

Jake considered his options. He had none. If he refused to work with Cole, he could make his life a living nightmare. Jake wouldn't put it past him. He and Roxanne didn't need the money from the job Cole was proposing, but Jake needed to protect Roxanne from the awful truth and Cole would expose it. Not only that, but he would tell Roxanne every little detail.

'How's that fine lady of yours doing? Still in the nick?' Cole asked, as if reading Jake's mind.

'She gets out tomorrow.'

Cole's eyes lit up upon hearing that. 'Good. That was another thing I was going to tell you. I want her at the front of the operation. From what I've heard, that Roxanne is a bit of a fox, knows her shit and how to get the job done. Just a shame she got put away, but I'm not going to let that part worry me.'

Jake didn't like the way Cole was referring to Roxanne. 'Nah, she's not even out yet and when she does get out, she'll be on probation.'

'Jakey boy, don't get yourself all twisted about something that can be so simple,' Cole said, disregarding what Jake had just said. 'I want to put this to both of you. So, I think you should introduce me to her before we go any further with this. Think of the money involved. It'll be life-changing for you both.'

Life-changing? Did he think Jake and Roxanne were on the poverty line or something? Jake wanted to knock him out just for his sheer cockiness. But at the same time, he knew that Cole spoke the truth. And he knew that Roxanne would be on board. She'd be craving getting back into things once she was out. In fact, Jake strongly suspected that Roxanne would be more into this than he was, probation or not.

Chapter Nineteen

Twenty-four hours. That was all she had left to serve in Kirktonhill. Needless to say, it was the slowest day of her life, but all she kept thinking about was getting out, seeing Jake. She'd missed him a lot, more than she'd thought she would. She'd learned to live with his absence but that didn't mean she could do it again. Roxanne vowed never to allow herself to get into a situation that would land her back in a place like Kirktonhill. Well, not one that would leave her open to getting caught.

It had been a godsend that Jake was able to pay off the prison officers. It was thanks to his cash and their discretion that Roxanne basically got to do what she wanted, when she wanted, even inside. Having her own mobile phone in her cell so that she could contact Jake regularly had proved most helpful. She still had a hand in things, and Jake still consulted her on business decisions. Not that she didn't trust him. He'd never given her cause to think badly of him. Ever since she'd been put away, Jake had continued to bring in the business, generate their income and he'd done a good job. Now that her release was just hours away, Roxanne couldn't help but feel a ball of anxiety settle in the depths of her stomach. What was life as a free woman going to be like? She'd been locked up for ten years. To most people that wasn't very long but to someone who'd become institutionalised, it may as well have equated to a hundred years. The only reason she knew half the stuff that went on was because she'd had her mobile; her only link to the outside world, a tiny phone. Her daily routine was going to change, but Roxanne was sure that her body clock would remain the same. Lights out at ten, lights on at six. She'd have to try to reprogramme herself, so that she could fit back into life as Roxanne McPhail, gangster, not prisoner.

Her new friendship with Arabella was partly what had kept her going for the last stretch of her sentence, and it had been painful to watch her come and go so quickly. They'd been in touch via text message since she'd been released and it made Roxanne smile to think that their friendship could last on the outside. Arabella was a good girl. A little messed up to say the least, but reliable, trustworthy. She'd done time for something that wasn't really her fault; Roxanne could see that in her the minute she'd walked through the door. There really wasn't a bad bone in her body.

The phone in her hand began to vibrate and Roxanne glanced down at it. It was Jake. He'd be calling to arrange to collect her tomorrow. Relishing the thought of having her freedom again, Roxanne smiled.

'Oi, McPhail. Make it a quick one, eh? I'm due on my break,' the male prison officer said. He was standing at the door to her cell with his back to her. Normally that kind of attitude would stir up an anger in her belly. She wanted to comment that he must be feeling annoyed that as of tomorrow, his 'bonus' would stop. But she chose to keep quiet. She would not start any shit. Not today.

Pressing the accept call button, Roxanne raised the phone to her ear. 'Jake?'

'How you doing, babe? Your last day dragging?' Jake asked.

Roxanne shook her head. 'It's not bad. So, you picking me up tomorrow?'

There was a pause and Roxanne instantly felt uneasy. Jake was never quiet, never left a question unanswered.

'Jake?'

'Aye, of course I'm picking you up.'

'What's wrong?'

Jake sighed on the other end of the line and Roxanne felt the unease begin to rise in her stomach.

'Nothing's wrong, so to speak. We just didn't seem to make as much cash on the operation as we thought.'

Roxanne sat down on the chair next to her bed. 'Why not, Jake?'

'Some of the security tags burst.'

She nodded, knowing full well what that meant. 'How much merch was lost?'

'About eighty percent.' She listened as Jake sucked air in through his teeth. 'But don't worry, it was a one-off and things are fine, business-wise. You have nothing to be concerned about. There's been a development, an old business associate of mine down south has been in touch and he's offered us a business opportunity.'

'What kind of opportunity?'

'He wants to speak to you face to face. So when I pick you up tomorrow, we'll be going to meet him.'

'Who is this guy?' Roxanne asked. She didn't like these kinds of things being thrown at her out of the blue.

'His name is Cole Woods,' Jake said, sounding hesitant. It was as if he knew she wasn't going to like this.

'Cole Woods, as in *thee* Cole Woods? The biggest supplier of drugs from London?' Roxanne closed her eyes momentarily. 'Are you fucking insane, Jake? That guy is a nut job. Have you heard the stories circulating about him?'

'*Was* the biggest. He left to go to Spain, and has only just come back.'

Roxanne raised a brow. 'Even so, he's still a nutter.'

'Oh come on, Rox, people probably called you the same thing when you went away. Every gangster from here to the moon has a story or two floating around about them. And the reason those stories began is because he was dividing his time between living and working in London and abroad. Folk were saying that he was laying low overseas. It's all just bullshit,' Jake said.

'You hope,' Roxanne replied.

'Look, he's no more a saint than us and the rest of our connections here in the city, Rox. We're just meeting him to discuss things. It's not like I've signed anything.'

Roxanne sighed heavily. If Jake was in front of her, face to face right now, she was sure she'd knock him out. Cole Woods wasn't someone she wanted to get mixed up with, not unless she knew the exact scope of the business arrangement. And *definitely* not until she was the one in charge. It was a good thing that she was getting out the next day. As much as she loved and trusted Jake, she wasn't sure he'd be able to handle this quite as efficiently as she would. Jake was the man you wanted in charge of the shoplifting operations. This new business opportunity could be anything from selling weed to being hired to shoot someone where Woods was concerned.

'Jake, why would you contact him of all people?'

'I didn't. He phoned me. If he didn't think he could put good business our way then he wouldn't have bothered to contact me at all.'

'Oh so he's our guardian fucking angel now?' Roxanne hissed, although she heard a slight hesitation in his tone.

'Rox, just chill out, eh? I'm just focusing on seeing you tomorrow. Anything after that can get dealt with at the time.'

Hanging up, Roxanne stuffed the phone back into her pocket and wished she could turn the clocks forward by one day so she could get out of here and see what Woods had to offer them. She wasn't scared of Cole by any means; she knew she would be able to handle him, especially on her patch. However, Cole was good at manipulating a situation to suit his own needs. Roxanne wasn't in the mood to be manipulated. She'd spent the last ten years stuck in Kirktonhill, allowing Jake to run things in her absence. She didn't want Cole Woods to step on her toes the second she got out.

'Enjoy your last day of luxury living, Rox,' the officer standing by the door said with a sarcastic grin.

Smiling in return, Roxanne thought about what she might be faced with when she got out. The thought turned her stomach. Was she truly ready to get back into that life of crime, the life that she'd fallen into after she'd come back from the disaster that was Spain? She didn't know how else to live her life, how else to be. She couldn't exactly go legit, not now after all this time. Not now she and Jake had money behind them. There was no such thing as wealth when you worked a minimum wage job. Who in their right mind would give someone like her a job after her time at Kirktonhill? No one, that's who and she would need something to keep money rolling in. What they had already wouldn't last forever if they kept spending but not replacing.

It didn't matter what reservations Roxanne had, she had no choice. The only thing she was sure of was that this time around, she would get people to do the dirty work for her. No more stamping on bodies to get them to pay up. If she was to be certain never to end up behind bars again, then she would have to keep her name out of the mud. They'd have to take on more people to do the deals. All Roxanne wanted was to stay out of prison and get on with her life. As tough as she was, she couldn't go back to prison. She may be free again tomorrow, but she only knew this life. It was like an addiction; once you started you couldn't stop. But Roxanne knew how to stay out of prison now. Don't get caught.

Chapter Twenty

Arabella looked up at the sign above the large window of the salon and couldn't help but smile. She couldn't believe that Eddie had actually bought her a fully functioning salon. Just a few weeks ago, she had been in prison and now she was her own boss.

'You like?' Eddie asked, stroking the back of her hand with his thumb.

'I love it,' she replied.

Getting out of the car, Arabella allowed Eddie to lead her across the road and into the salon. A woman in what Arabella guessed to be her mid-thirties greeted them at the front desk with a smile. She was the manager, according to the embroidered tag on her pink tunic.

'Arabella MacQueen?' the woman asked and Arabella nodded. 'I'm Scarlett, the manager here. It's nice to meet you.'

Arabella didn't know what to say. She was staring into the eyes of the manager of the salon and realised that she and Eddie were now this woman's employers, along with the rest of the staff here. Was she ready to become an employer? Someone who would be relied on every month to pay the wages, order the supplies, keep the place and staff in professional order?

'It's nice to meet you, Scarlett.'

'Scarlett,' Eddie interjected. 'I want you to go over everything with Arabella. How the salon operates, introduce her to the staff. She should know the ins and outs of it all. No detail left out.'

Scarlett was nodding, her eyes fixed on Eddie. 'Of course, Mr Corrigan.' There was a hint of sarcasm to Scarlett's tone and Arabella was beginning to wonder if the girl already felt like her toes were being trodden on. The tone, along with the narrowed eyes, dispersed as quickly as it had come. At that, Eddie disappeared through to the back of the salon and Arabella watched him go.

A rush of excitement caused a flutter in Arabella's stomach. Finally, she was going to have something in her life that belonged to her, something that she could be in control of and that would better her life.

'Come on, I'll show you around so you can see how I run things,' Scarlett said, moving through to the back in the same direction in which Eddie had gone. Arabella stood still and looked around, taking in her new surroundings. As much as she was qualified to do the job, she didn't exactly possess the experience to do it well. The apprehension of getting to grips with everything so quickly was overwhelming.

'Arabella?' Scarlett pressed.

'Sorry,' Arabella replied, smiling at the manager and following her.

Passing a few female stylists and two male, Arabella watched as they chatted at ease with their clients as they coloured, trimmed and blow-dried their hair.

'You're a qualified stylist?' Scarlett asked. 'Is that why you bought the place from Rory?'

Arabella didn't want to look stupid. Eddie hadn't told her a thing about the sale, or where the idea had even come from. So instead, she nodded. 'Yes.'

Arabella had gained a level three in hairdressing back in college a long time ago. She hadn't used her skills in years, other than trimming Roxanne's hair while they were inside. And just because she had the basics didn't mean that she was capable of running a salon.

'But I don't do it anymore. I like the business side of things,' she lied.

Moving to the back of the salon, Arabella eyed four porcelain sinks in a row, with black leather lounge chairs in front of them. Mirrors lined the right side of the wall, with more of the same chairs in front of each one. Each chair had its own styling station and Arabella felt the familiar ache of standing on her feet for hours on end as she remembered her first job as a salon junior. Endless hours of sweeping floors and making cups of tea. Nowadays, she felt that was all she would be good at in a place like this. The salon was clearly high end, based on its décor and the fact that the place was serving champagne in ice buckets next to the clients' chairs.

'So,' Arabella started, trying to distract herself from the self-doubting and self-loathing thoughts circulating inside her head. 'Tell me what it is that you do here on a daily basis, Scarlett.'

Scarlett smiled and Arabella watched as she drew back her shoulders a little, as if she was getting ready to deliver the biggest and most important speech of her life. A slight feeling of envy prodded Arabella in the chest as she listened to Scarlett proudly explaining the job she did. She didn't own the place but it was clear to see that Scarlett could have become the owner if she'd wanted to. She carried herself with such assurance and not in a cocky way.

'I take care of the day-to-day running of the place,' she said. 'I take bookings, order in the supplies, do wages and pretty much hire in new stylists when we need them.'

It didn't sound like much, perhaps not as difficult as she had thought? But Arabella was in no position to judge anyone on the job they did. She had just come out of prison, and had a business bought for her. Most people struggled to get a job after being released. This had fallen into Arabella's lap.

'Sounds like you're a great manager. Can I ask, Scarlett, why you didn't buy this place over yourself?'

Scarlett let out a laugh but Arabella knew it wasn't in humour. 'Being a salon manager, single mum and paying nursery fees doesn't leave a lot of spare time or cash to get a business loan.'

'Oh, you have a child?'

'Two. A three-year-old and a sixteen-month-old. Both boys and both drive me nuts.'

Arabella gave Scarlett's figure a sneaky glance. Two kids under the age of four and she had a body like that? How had she become single so soon after having the second baby? She chose not to ask.

'What's your secret?' Arabella smiled and Scarlett laughed.

'Not having enough time to eat because I'm so busy. I'd highly recommend the "soup and sandwich whenever you get a spare second" diet.'

Arabella was beginning to like Scarlett. She wanted to build a friendship, make Scarlett see that she wasn't going to be one of those bosses who clicked their fingers and barked orders while she sat back and did nothing. For this to work, Arabella wanted to roll up her sleeves and show Scarlett that she could be useful.

'You look after the boys all on your own while you run this place?' Arabella asked.

'Well, my mum helps. And so do my ex-partner's parents. But he's not around at all. And I was seeing someone for a while there, but he broke it off with me.'

Arabella frowned. 'I'm sorry.'

'Don't be. The guy is a total dickhead.' They laughed together and Arabella relaxed more. 'I want to give my boys the best life I possibly can. I don't want them to be fucked up because their parents couldn't get it right. If I can get things right for them then I'll be happy.'

Arabella liked hearing that. It was far more than her own mother ever did for her.

'So, you pretty much do everything around here?' Arabella steered the conversation back to business.

'Yeah. This place is like my home. I've worked here since I was a junior. When Rory decided to sell up and move abroad, he did give me first refusal. Like I said, I couldn't afford it.'

A feeling of guilt and sympathy washed over Arabella then. As much as she had no intention to, she felt like she was pushing Scarlett out.

'Look, I don't want you to think that I'm here to push you out of your job. Truth is, I've had a shitty couple of years and Eddie and I just want something good to focus on. I'm not here to take over.'

Scarlett nodded. 'That's reassuring. Thank you. However, this is your business so anything you want to change, I can get on board with and help out. I've got almost fifteen years of service with this place.'

'And that will continue, Scarlett. I can tell just by looking around that you run a tight ship. I'd probably run this place into the ground. Fancy a cuppa?'

Scarlett nodded and Arabella followed her into the small kitchen at the back of the salon. Eddie was standing by the counter, already boiling the kettle as if he'd heard their conversation. Knowing Eddie, he'd probably been listening in. Arabella wouldn't blame him. He'd be worried that she would quickly end up back on that path of self-destruction. Well, not this time.

'You making some for us then?' Arabella smiled and raised a brow at Eddie.

'I was. And I'm just about to go back to the office. Got loads on this afternoon,' Eddie replied as he made up two mugs of tea without bothering to ask how Scarlett liked it.

'I'll stay here for the day then, see how things work around the salon. You can come back to pick me up later,' Arabella said.

Scarlett stood in silence as Eddie kissed Arabella and headed out of the kitchen and through the salon. 'Glad you two got to meet. Think you'll make an excellent team.'

As much as she knew he hadn't meant it to, his words made him sound like a cocky bastard. Like he was in control of how things were going to go.

'Ignore him,' Arabella said. 'He likes to think he's in charge.'

Scarlett cleared her throat. 'I think he's right, though. I think we'll make a good team. Us girls need to stick together, eh?' She smiled, before turning her attention to the door and moving towards the chairs.

Arabella and Scarlett sat down and chatted about the salon and how it ran. Scarlett had only been sixteen when she started working there. That was impressive. When Arabella was sixteen she was getting into all kinds of trouble at school. Mixing with the wrong crowds and falling into an alcohol and drug-fuelled spiral. Even though this woman had two young children, she was still able to get her shit together enough to provide a life for herself.

Arabella cringed inside at the thought of how easily manipulated she could be without even noticing. That particular trait had always been her downfall.

'Scarlett, I want you to know that nothing will change here. I want you to keep running this place as you are. I want you to make this salon the best in the city and for people to come from all over the place to get their hair and beauty treatments done here. I want us both to gain from this. Does that sound all right to you?'

'Sounds perfect.'

'I'll be here to oversee things, so that when you need time off I can step in to cover your side of things. Except doing hair, obviously. I'm qualified but I'm no stylist.'

Scarlett seemed happy at the prospect and Arabella was equally happy to have something to focus on. It would keep her mind from wandering to other things. Reflecting on darker times was something that would have a negative impact on Arabella if she allowed it to, so being here with Scarlett at the salon would hopefully stop that from happening.

'You don't have to look so nervous, Arabella. You're my boss, not the other way around,' Scarlett laughed.

Arabella glanced at Scarlett and felt her face flush. 'Shit, sorry. I just feel a bit in the way, you know. But maybe if I just shadow you today, you can go about doing your job and I'll observe. Show me everything you can.'

Scarlett smiled and her brow furrowed. 'Yes, but we can have a laugh, get to know each other. I want to know who I'm working for and the best way to do that is to start by just chatting.'

Arabella felt herself relax. She really couldn't have asked for a better person to be running the place.

Being in prison had altered Arabella's views on life. It was about living, doing the best for herself so that she could continue to be free and happy. The one good thing to come from being locked up at Kirktonhill was finding Rox. And she was excited to be able to meet up with her soon so they could build on their friendship in freedom. It had been three weeks since Arabella had been released, which meant Rox would be getting out today. Glancing at her watch, she saw it was ten thirty in the morning, and wondered if back at Kirktonhill, Rox would be going through the process of being released.

Arabella wanted to show Rox the salon, introduce her to Eddie and meet Jake.

'So,' Arabella said as they sat down together at the front desk; the gushing sounds of the hairdryers and the clients chattering away eased her even more. 'Tell me more about yourself.'

Scarlett sipped at her tea and nodded. 'Well, like I said, I'm a mum of two young children. No dad. He left. Safe to say he couldn't cope with family life or sleepless nights. So, I'm doing it on my own. My mum helps out with the boys. They're pretty hands on. But it's a good distraction for her.'

Arabella frowned. 'A distraction?'

Scarlett's eyes seemed sad then and Arabella instantly regretted pushing. 'My brother Johnnie died, just last year. Drug overdose.'

Arabella felt her stomach drop at that point. 'Oh shit. I'm sorry to hear that, Scarlett.'

'I mean, I can't say I was surprised that it happened. He'd been on drugs for years. Started off on the softer stuff, if you can even call it that. Cannabis, pills. That sort of thing. But as time went on, he ended up becoming a heroin addict. We tried everything to get him off the stuff but when I had the boys, I had to distance myself from him. I only went to see if he was okay because my mum said she hadn't heard from him in a few days. He only ever contacted her for money so he could buy his fix. When I went to his drug den of a flat, I found him lying on the floor in his living room. Dead. He'd overdosed.'

Scarlett's face hardened then, as if the memory was too much to process and she had somehow managed to shut it out even when she was reliving it.

Arabella didn't know what to say. What could she say? Nothing that would make the situation better or less awkward.

'That must have been horrific, Scarlett. I'm so sorry for your mum, and for you.'

'I'm more angry than sad about the situation. Johnnie was a good lad growing up. A good brother. But then he fell into the wrong crowd and things just spiralled.'

Arabella nodded. She knew exactly how that went.

'So, tell me about you. Eddie hasn't said much about you.'

Arabella thought about whether or not to tell Scarlett the truth and decided that she had nothing to hide and that she shouldn't be ashamed of her past. Those decisions had brought her to where she was standing right now.

'Well, there's not much to tell, really. I'm just an average girl, trying to get through life without any dramas. At least that's how I try to live now. The biggest thing in my life is that I've just come out of prison.'

Scarlett's eyes widened in surprise and Arabella waited for it to pass. 'You were in prison?'

'Yes, unfortunately I was one of those people who was swayed by the crowd and I got myself into a bit of trouble with the police. I did ten months. But I'm a good person, Scarlett. I'm not one of these people who is going to use this place as a front for criminal activity.'

Scarlett laughed. 'I know that, Arabella. That's not where I was going. Eddie, your man. He seems… like a good guy. Like he wants to look after you.'

Arabella smiled. 'Yeah. He really is.'

Scarlett sipped her tea again, her eyes fixed on the computer screen in front of them. Arabella felt bad for her. Here she was, just out of prison and her life was in a better state than Scarlett's.

The phone rang, and Arabella glared at it before turning her attention to Scarlett. She was smiling.

'Go on then, answer your first call.'

'Oh god, no, I wouldn't know what to say.'

'Just answer with the name of the salon, your name and then when they start talking, pass them on to me. Honestly, it's a doddle.'

Arabella bit her lip and reached for the phone. Lifting the receiver, her heart pumped hard in her chest.

'Good morning, Hair Envy. Arabella speaking.' She waited, not even listening to the caller properly before asking them to hold so she could pass them on to the manager. Suddenly, her stomach began to churn. But she was proud of herself, as stupid as it was to be proud of answering a simple phone call. She was here, in her own salon answering the phone.

Maybe the salon was the distraction Arabella needed. It was more than a distraction. It was a way to show the foster kid still inside that she really could make a life for herself, and actually be proud of the person she could become.

Chapter Twenty-One

Roxanne had been released just two hours ago and already she was on her way into the city for a business meeting with a man she'd never met but had heard a lot about. Cole Woods was a dangerous man but a man in the know when it came to the underworld, not just in Glasgow but up and down the country and, she was led to believe, abroad too. She wasn't sure she believed that the rumours about him were all lies. Drugs, robbery, murder. Roxanne had dealt in drugs before, of course she had. There was real money to be made there, but it had always been a territorial game with her and Jake. Work within the area, make your money there. But murder? She'd gone as far as to beat someone to a bloody mess and it hadn't bothered her, but she wasn't sure she was willing to work with a man who would shoot you as quick as look at you. Cole was a bit of a loose cannon, everyone in this game knew that, but she had to admit to herself that she was a little intrigued by him. Maybe Cole's proposal was going to be much bigger than either of them expected. Was this Roxanne's chance to make a real go of her life?

'You're quiet,' Jake said, pulling the car into a space on the side of the road.

'I don't have much to say.' She paused. That wasn't a lie. This wasn't exactly what she'd had in mind for her first day of freedom. She'd thought Jake would have sat her down and shown her everything he'd done for the business since she'd been away. Now, she was walking into the prospect of a new deal, with a new gangster. Walking straight into danger almost immediately. The thought was scary, but there was no way she was going to voice her thoughts to Jake. Instead, she said, 'Not a lot has happened for me in the last ten years. I've been in prison, remember.'

Jake smiled. 'You don't have anything to worry about, Rox. Cole's an alright guy, once you get to know him.'

'I'm not worried about Cole.' Rox raised a brow. 'But you've heard the rumours, Jake. People are saying he's linked to some unsolved murders down in London. Just because I was in the jail doesn't mean I don't know what's going on. Is he stable enough for us to go into business with him?'

'And we're angels, are we?' Jake said, ignoring her question.

Roxanne sighed. Jake was right but it didn't shift the feeling of unease that weighed heavy on her chest right now. But she had to remind herself of who she was before she went inside. She was Roxanne McPhail and she had her own reputation. She might not operate as far and wide as Cole Woods, but in her patch, she was someone to be reckoned with. Jake had kept things going. The shoplifting operations had been working fine up until recently, a nice little side earner on top of the drug operations. However, Roxanne wanted to build her empire and maybe Cole had turned up at the right time, to offer something far bigger than she and Jake had done before.

'I *know* we're not angels. But I know us, how we operate. I don't know much about him or how he runs things. The only thing I've heard about him is that he's brutal. And how do you know we can even trust him?'

'Okay, firstly I don't understand why you're so concerned about brutality. Secondly, I don't know for sure that we can trust him, Rox, but that's what this meeting is all about. To see what he will bring to the table and what the margins will look like. If things don't look good, then we walk. And I've already told you, those rumours are exactly that.'

Roxanne could tell that last sentence was half-hearted, but she chose to keep her mouth shut about that for now. Jake opened the door and stepped out of the car and Roxanne followed. They crossed Duke Street and entered the Old Duke Bar on the corner. As soon as they were inside, the smell of stale beer hit Roxanne in the face. The place was packed with older men, all sat around the edge of the bar sipping pints and reading papers. Some watched the dog racing on the television on the wall in the corner of the room. As Jake approached the bar, Roxanne turned to find somewhere for them to sit. As she moved towards a table just by the door, she was stopped by a man slightly taller than her. His dark hair and transparent skin made her stare into his eyes. He smiled widely at her and she knew who he was.

'Roxanne McPhail. It's a pleasure,' he said in his loud, thick cockney accent while holding out his hand. 'Where's the main man, then? Getting us all a beer, I hope?' His eyes moved away, searching the room for Jake before quickly resting on hers again. He smiled again, more gently this time. 'Cole.'

Roxanne regarded him with a smile that slightly raised the corners of her mouth. In her thirty-eight years, she'd only met two men with that same grin and charm. He reminded her a little of someone from long ago. Jez, her first love and heartbreak. That charm never lasted in any man; it always fizzled out into something else. Deceit, lies.

'Good to meet you, Cole. Jake's just getting us a drink,' she replied, noting how he hadn't yet let go of her hand or broken his gaze. Roxanne quickly rectified that and pulled her hand away before sitting down at the table. Cole sat across from her and she tried to study his face without staring. His features were dark, mysterious. She wasn't sure if it was because of the rumours of his links to the unsolved murders of various gang members down in London, or because he reminded her of Jez, but Rox had to remind herself that Jake was present and that ultimately, Cole's stare wasn't something she wanted to linger on for too long. She had to admit that he was handsome, but he had a snake-like stare that was almost predatory as he took in every inch of her.

'Cole,' Jake said as he placed the beers on the table and brought Roxanne out of her thoughts. 'Glad you could make it, mate.'

Cole stood up and the men shook, each placing the opposing hand on the other's shoulder. Roxanne glanced up at them and raised a brow. The embrace and enthusiasm was forced on Jake's part. She knew him well enough to know when he was playing someone for his own gain. That was what worried Roxanne about this whole situation. Cole Woods was not someone to be played, she could tell that just by his presence alone.

They sat down and Roxanne could feel the tension, along with Cole's eyes on her. Shrugging it off, she turned to Cole and smiled. 'So, what's this proposition you've got for us then?'

'Ha, I do like a woman who gets straight to the point.'

Roxanne smiled and glanced at Jake. His expression was hard and she could sense that he was feeling put out. She'd bet most men would feel put out by Cole, in business and otherwise. He was charismatic, she'd give him that.

'Right guys,' Cole started. He sat forward and lowered his tone. 'I'm looking to expand. The demand for my supply is higher than it ever has been and I need team leaders. People who can run a team of distributors, keep them in line, you know how it goes. You've both done this for a long time. Glasgow is a city we can make real money in but then, every major city is full of junkies crying out for supply,' Cole said, eyeing Jake. 'Jakey boy here worked on a couple of runs for me a few years ago when you were inside. Made himself a pretty penny so I know he's trustworthy.'

Roxanne frowned and turned to Jake, a fury building inside her she'd never felt for him before. 'Is he now?'

'Ah,' Cole interrupted, sitting forward and focusing all his attention on Roxanne. She took a breath and wondered what he was going to say next. 'You served a fucker of a sentence. What was it? Ten years?'

Roxanne drew her eyes from Jake, angry that he'd failed to mention his previous dealings with Woods. Cole didn't seem to notice. 'Yes, ten years. Got out this morning.'

'This morning, and you came straight here to meet me?' He held both his hands against his chest, eyes and smile wider than Roxanne would have thought possible. 'I'm fucking honoured, mate.'

Sarcastic bastard, Roxanne thought.

Dropping his hands to his lap, he reached for his pint and took a large gulp. Roxanne didn't know what to make of Cole. He seemed on edge; he was calm one minute then high on life the next. It made her feel uneasy, yet intrigued.

'Thanks,' was all she could think to say.

'I've heard all about you and Jake here and what you're both capable of. And word on the street is that you both have fierce reputations and can be relied on to get the job done. That's the kind of characters I'm looking for. And Rox – can I call you Rox? You've just done a ten-year stint and by the looks of it you've coped well. Looking beautiful for having been locked up, if you don't mind me saying. Anyway, my point is that you're both hard as fuck and I need you. You run a good business. You're experienced in organising and distributing. I did my research. You don't suffer fools gladly, Rox, do you?'

Roxanne felt in a trance-like state listening to Cole. The speed of his words meant her brain took a little time to catch up but she was getting there. He knew everything about them. He knew everything about her.

'Meaning?' Roxanne pressed.

'I heard what you did to that lad. Nearly fucking killed him, by all accounts. You're one rough girl and I like that. That's what this industry is missing. Too many women in this world on the edges, and not enough leading things. You could be the one who changes all that.'

Roxanne felt her eyebrows knit together. Cole had a way with words, knew how to use them to pull her in. It was working.

'You read about my trial?'

'Call it an interview, one of those police check things that people get when they're starting a job with the public. You see, I had to know who I was taking on. I already knew all about Jake but I didn't know much about you.'

Jake shifted in his seat. 'Give us all the details, Cole. We can't agree to anything until we have all the facts.'

'Right. Fair enough,' Cole swallowed loudly, baring his teeth and licking his lips. 'Seems as though there was a bit of a bust-up between the rivals on the west end and south side. One of 'em's dead and the other's in jail waiting to be tried for murder. Rest of 'em have gone into hiding by all accounts, left their shit wide open for the taking. Fucking mental, and I thought London was bad for territorial shit.'

Roxanne frowned and looked in Jake's direction. Why hadn't he told her about this? Unless he didn't know?

'Yeah, I heard that rumour too. Although we're east end so it doesn't affect us, not really,' Jake replied, not meeting Roxanne's eye.

'It affects us all, mate. That's why I'm here. We could be the ones to take it over. I'm talking thousands upon thousands of pounds here, mate. With those pussies leaving their shit open for anyone, we'll be the next ones to step in. No one else has the balls like us, Jake.'

Roxanne couldn't hide the smile on her face. She knew this was going to happen. Cole was already speaking as though they'd shaken on a deal. There was no going back now.

'So, remind me. What drugs you deal in then? The small time stuff? Cannabis, coke?'

'Aye,' Jake replied.

'Right, well, now you're in with me, you're dealing with the big time gear where there's real money to be made. And not just here in Glasgow, or across the other side of the country, Edinburgh and the likes. I'm talking county lines material, mate. But you'll need to assemble a team for distribution. People you know you can trust but who won't take the fucking piss out of you. Because if they take the piss out of you, they're taking the piss out of me and we don't need that kind of negative shit.'

Roxanne listened as Cole and Jake discussed details. They'd need to pull together a team. They'd need a hub. They'd be organising drug runs, but they would have to know how they were going to do this discreetly. Cole mentioned the cities the drugs would travel to. Manchester, Liverpool, Cardiff, London. The list went on and on. The details ran deep. And the more she listened, the more she could see on Jake's face just how serious this was, and how nervous he was about the operation. All the while, Roxanne's excitement grew. It was the way Cole talked about it. With passion and excitement. He knew what he was doing and how things would work. He'd been doing this for years in London.

'So, Cole. I hear you were living abroad for a while?' Roxanne asked. He shot her a look, as though he hadn't expected her to ask about it. 'Can I ask where?'

He hesitated, clearly not wanting to go into detail. 'You know how it is in this business. I was here and there. Doing deals for the big clubs all over the islands, you know?'

'The Canaries and Balearics?' She pressed. 'That must have been a laugh.'

Roxanne thought about her time in Majorca. The memories were still raw, not just because she'd had her heart broken by losing the man in her life and her best friend, but because she'd lost a life opportunity. How different things would be for her now if Jez hadn't been such a tosser.

'It was business. Making money,' Cole said, raising his drink to his mouth and keeping his eyes on her.

'I lived in Majorca for a while, back in the day,' she said, but she could tell that Cole was done with this conversation. He'd already moved on in his head. He didn't want to discuss his life abroad for reasons she might never know.

'You'll want to get hammered now that you're out of that shit hole, Roxanne,' Cole said and his words snapped her out of her thoughts.

'Aye,' she replied. 'Not had a proper drink in a decade.'

'Jake, grab your woman a proper drink. What ya like? Tequila? Whisky?' Cole said. Roxanne was surprised by how quickly Jake seemed to do what Cole said, as he was already getting to his feet.

'She likes vodka,' Jake replied, bending down and kissing her. She knew the kiss was a warning to Cole without the exchange of words. He'd noticed the attention Cole had been giving Roxanne.

'Right then, shots of vodka all round. Make mine a double. I think this is a cause for celebration, don't you?'

Jake left the table and Roxanne straightened her back and pushed back her shoulders. Why did she feel excited when she knew that she should be feeling the exact opposite? Jake had his reservations; that was obvious to her. What was also obvious was how blatantly Cole was flirting with her and she liked it.

'So, you got anyone in mind for the team you'll need to get the goods moving?' Cole asked. He'd moved around the table and was now sitting next to her where Jake had been.

'Aye,' she replied. 'I can think of a few people.'

Roxanne didn't have many friends, mostly acquaintances. But she'd think of someone.

Roxanne looked up to see Jake return to where they were sitting. He looked at Cole through narrowed eyes as he laid three glasses on the table. 'Here.'

Cole got up from his seat and moved back around the other side of the table. It was as if he knew not to overstep the mark with Jake. Sighing inwardly at the idea of being an object which both men fought for possession of, Roxanne lifted her glass and held it at her mouth.

'Here's to making a shit ton of cash,' Cole said, raising his glass.

Roxanne nodded and knocked hers back, allowing the burn to take over. She rose from her chair and excused herself from the table, leaving the men to compare cocks and went outside for some fresh air. Feeling their eyes on her as she exited the pub, she felt like telling them both to fuck off. That she would happily go about this all on her own, that she didn't need one man to help her earn some cash, let alone two. But in truth she couldn't do this alone. And she did love Jake, but not as much as she used to. Being away for ten years had created a space between them that even Jake couldn't deny. Roxanne was angry at him for not being truthful about his previous dealings with Cole. Perhaps Cole had seen it too and that was why he was behaving the way he was.

Pulling her phone out of her pocket, she punched in Arabella's number and waited for the ring.

'Well, hello there, Ms McPhail. You're out then?' Arabella answered.

'And it feels fucking glorious,' Roxanne replied with a smile. It was good to hear her friend's voice. 'Listen, why don't we meet up?'

'Oh, well I can't right now. I'm kind of at work.'

'You're at work?' Roxanne couldn't hide her surprise. 'What are you doing?'

'I'm a business owner now. A salon in the west end.'

'Oh. My. God! I have to come and see this place. And you of course. I could come now?' Roxanne felt excited to see the salon. 'I've just finished up at a meeting.'

Arabella was silent on the other end of the line and Roxanne knew fine well why. She wouldn't want a convicted criminal just out of prison that very day, swanning into her business and driving away customers.

'You still there?' Roxanne pushed.

'Yeah, I'm here. It's just, well, I don't know if you coming here today is such a good idea. I've literally only just started myself, getting to know the place and the girls who work here.

I don't want them to think that I'm taking the piss by having all sorts of people dropping in unannounced to see me just because I own the place.'

Roxanne felt her expression change, her brow furrowed. 'All sorts of people? Thanks for that, Arabella.' She forced a laugh.

'Oh god, no that's not what I meant. Fuck, sorry. I'm shit at this.' Arabella paused and Roxanne wondered what exactly it was that she was mulling over in her head. Maybe she didn't want people to know she was friends with a convicted criminal. But then, wasn't that what Arabella was? Except Arabella was a bit of class. Well, compared to Roxanne she was. She was young, beautiful, and surely intelligent if she just put her mind to it, rather than allowing people to carry her away and put her at the heart of their shitty games.

'Okay,' Arabella said. 'I'm sure it won't do any harm for you to come by for a while. I suppose I am the boss. But we can't stay for long. I don't want people thinking that I'm just using the place as some kind of entertainment venue. I know what you're like, Roxanne. You're going to want to crack open the voddy as soon as you get here.'

Roxanne laughed. 'Just text me the address, I'll be there soon.'

Roxanne hung up and flagged down a taxi and told the driver where to take her. She had cash in her pocket and Jake could pick her up later if he wasn't wasted.

She travelled through the east end and across the city to where Arabella was, thinking about the morning's events. So much had happened in the last few hours. She'd been released after ten years, met up with one of London's top gangsters and learned that parts of Glasgow were now for the taking. Jesus, she thought. A lot to take in on her first day as a free woman. Now she was going back into the drug business with Cole and Jake. Things were moving so fast that Roxanne's head was swirling. As the taxi pulled up outside the salon, she paid the driver and got out.

Staring up at Hair Envy, she smiled. Nice one, Arabella, she thought. She'd certainly landed on her feet with this place. Pushing through the door, Roxanne moved inside and saw Arabella standing at the back of the salon, chatting with a woman who was around the same age as Roxanne.

'Do you have an appointment?' one of the stylists asked Roxanne.

'No, I'm here to see the owner,' Roxanne replied. At that, Arabella looked across the room and smiled widely at her.

'Oh my god!' she almost squealed. 'I can't believe we're both here.'

Roxanne smiled as she hugged Arabella. She looked entirely different to when she'd last seen her, with a face full of make-up and her blonde hair styled in loose curls. Roxanne expected nothing less.

'Ah, freedom suits you,' Roxanne said. She noted the look on the other woman's face but ignored it. 'We have some catching up to do. Coffee?'

Arabella nodded. 'Yes, we can go to the kitchen. You don't mind, Scarlett?'

Roxanne regarded Scarlett. Clear skin, the type who could get away without having to wear make-up to look decent. Shoulder-length dark hair. She was the type to look down her nose at the likes of Roxanne.

Scarlett smiled at Arabella, but when she looked at Roxanne, there was something in her eyes that told Roxanne she was right. She was looking down her nose at her. Maybe Arabella had mentioned how they'd met, that they'd become friends while sharing a prison cell. Scarlett might be the type of woman who would prefer not to mix with the likes of Roxanne, but she certainly wasn't going to be made to feel like scum by a woman she'd just met.

'Not at all,' Scarlett said hesitantly. 'You own the place, after all.'

Drawing her eyes away from Roxanne, Scarlett moved away, her heels clicking on the tiled floor. Sarcastic little bitch, Roxanne thought.

'Right, first things first. Where the fuck did you get the money to buy a place like this? Three weeks ago, you were in the jail.'

'Let me get the kettle on first and then I'll tell you everything.'

Roxanne followed Arabella through to the kitchen at the back of the salon. She took in her surroundings and imagined just for a moment what it would be like to own a legitimate business. That kind of thing was so far removed from a life like Roxanne's that she allowed the thought to disperse. This place could be perfect for a not-so-legit venture, she thought to herself.

This could be the hub Cole was talking about.

Chapter Twenty-Two

'This feels so weird, doesn't it?' Arabella said, sitting down in the kitchen at the back of the salon. She watched as Roxanne smiled and sat down on the chair across from her. 'I mean, the last time we did this was back in that hellhole of a place.'

'Aye,' Roxanne said, glancing out at the salon floor with a look of wonderment. 'So, how's that lassie? What's her name, Scarlett? She seems a bit up her own arse if you ask me.'

Arabella frowned. 'Why would you say that? You don't know her. I don't even know her.' She chose not to share the conversation she'd had with Scarlett earlier. That wasn't her story to tell.

'Just the way she looked at me when I got here. Like she thought she was better than me or something.'

'She's actually lovely, really nice. I only just met her today but so far, she's been so lovely and showed me everything she could in such a short space of time. I've kind of been shadowing her. She knows her stuff, has the place running like clockwork. She's going to go over the books with me later but if I'm honest, she'd be as well showing me in Japanese because I don't have the first clue how to run this place. But I know that I can trust her; she's worked here for years and I couldn't step on her toes even if I wanted to. She's a mum too, so I know she's working hard to give her kids a good life. She's unlike my own mother, that's for sure.'

Roxanne shook her head. 'You'll pick it up quickly. If you can get through almost a year of living with me in the jail, you'll be running this place single-handed within the week. And look how far you've come now, without that woman in your life. We don't all need a mum; we can survive without them. I mean, look at me. I turned out just fine without mine.' Roxanne gave a sarcastic grin.

Arabella laughed at Roxanne's attempt to ease her. She had been able to do that ever since they met in Kirktonhill, somehow instilling in her a confidence that she'd never really felt before. It was different with Eddie, although their relationship was loving, romantic. Roxanne was the first friend that Arabella had ever had. A *true* friend.

'So, you like her then?' Roxanne asked.

Arabella noted that this was the second time Roxanne had asked about Scarlett's character. She watched as Roxanne's eyes trailed towards Scarlett and saw her expression change. Was there more to it than Roxanne was letting on? She didn't strike Arabella as the type to care what people thought of her.

'Is there something you're not telling me? Do you know her or something?'

Roxanne didn't answer. Scarlett and Roxanne had locked eyes with one another, but Arabella watched as Scarlett looked away first. What the hell was going on?

'I just don't like how she's looking down her nose at us, Arabella. Because we've been in prison.'

'No, she's not. Rox, she doesn't even know anything about you. I haven't told her about you other than that you're my friend. She only knows that I was in prison, not you.'

Roxanne's expression softened then and Arabella felt relief wash away the tension she hadn't realised was there. 'Ah, I've got an idea. Why don't you get your hair done?'

'Here?' Roxanne failed to hide her surprise. 'Now?'

'Why not take advantage of the fact that your bestie owns the place? I'll get mine done too. We can get a bottle of fizz and really celebrate being out. Oh come on, it'll be a laugh.'

Roxanne's surprise switched to delight as a smile raced across her face. 'Go on then, you twisted my arm.'

Arabella smiled widely and got up from her chair. The feeling inside was like waking up as a child on Christmas morning. The excitement and butterflies almost caused her to start giggling. She half-walked, half-skipped towards Scarlett who was wiping down the surfaces of the front desk.

'Scarlett, a few questions. The first is, would you mind if I spent some time catching up with Rox here? We've not seen each other in a while and have a lot of catching up to do. And do you happen to have champagne or prosecco on the premises? And lastly, could you arrange for me and Rox to have our hair done today? I know it's short notice but I'd really appreciate it.'

Scarlett hesitated, stole a glance at Roxanne then smiled. 'Yes to all,' she said glancing down at the diary. 'I can do Roxanne's hair and I can fit you in with Leanne over there. She's had a cancellation today so it won't be a problem. Means you'll get to see the kind of treatments we offer here at Hair Envy. And the prosecco is in the fridge in the kitchen. Help yourself to however many bottles you want.'

'Great,' Arabella replied, turning her back to head for the fridge. Before she got far, she turned and thanked Scarlett for her hospitality. 'You could join us if you wanted?'

Scarlett shook her head. 'I couldn't possibly. A few glasses of fizz and your friend would look like she'd had a perm from the eighties. Let me get your chairs sorted and I'll grab some prosecco glasses too. Oh and I think we've got some nibbles.'

Scarlett excused herself from the conversation and Arabella smiled. This day was turning out to be a decent first day.

Chapter Twenty-Three

Roxanne stared at Scarlett in the mirror as she worked through a hair treatment. As much as the mix of lavender and coconut was relaxing, Roxanne still felt on edge about the way Scarlett had been acting around her. The woman had barely made eye contact or spoken a word. Roxanne didn't know why, but there was something familiar about Scarlett that didn't sit well with her and she wasn't the type of woman to sit back on a salon chair and keep her mouth shut.

'So how long have you worked here at Hair Envy, then? My mate here says you're part of the furniture,' Roxanne said, keeping her eye on the woman in the mirror.

'Since I was sixteen. Left school, started as a junior and worked my way up. The place has had three owners since then, Arabella being our third,' Scarlett replied, nodding and smiling at Arabella who was in the chair next to Roxanne.

'Third time lucky, eh?' Arabella giggled before drinking back prosecco from the flute in her hand while the young stylist, Leanne, curled her hair.

'You'll be the *best*,' Roxanne replied with encouragement. 'This place needed someone like you and you deserve it after a shitty year at Her Majesty's pleasure.'

'You were in the jail?' Leanne asked. 'Jeezo. So what for?'

Arabella didn't answer, she seemed embarrassed and Scarlett didn't push. But Roxanne wanted to see Scarlett's reaction.

'Och come on, just tell them, minor drug offence and attempted robbery. You're lucky you didn't get a couple year up your arse,' Roxanne laughed, drinking back the last of the prosecco from her flute and holding it out to Scarlett for her to refill.

'Oh my god, Arabella!' Leanne exclaimed, her eyes wide. There was a hint of a smile teasing the corners of her mouth but she didn't let it out.

'That's where we met, in the jail,' Roxanne said.

'Okay so if we're sharing offences, then why don't you tell Scarlett and Leanne here why you were inside… for ten years, may I add,' Arabella hiccupped and giggled.

Roxanne sighed. 'It sounds worse than it actually is. But basically, I got sent away for drug dealing. And… now, I'm not proud of it,' she mocked, 'but I done someone in because they owed me money. I mean *properly* done them in.'

That was it, the look on Scarlett's face that Roxanne had been waiting for. Disgust, hatred. She pretended not to notice for the time being. But that was when it clicked in Roxanne's head, where she knew Scarlett from. It wasn't just the way she had been looking down her nose at Roxanne. There was something else there that Roxanne could see in her eyes. A hatred.

'Okay, it *is* as bad as it sounds. But I'm a changed woman now. Honestly.'

Scarlett hesitated, her hands hovering in Roxanne's hair before she dropped them to her side and excused herself. Roxanne eyed her as she walked away. Arabella seemed not to have noticed, like the bubbles had gone straight to her head.

Roxanne watched Scarlett leave and knew that this was the only opportunity that she was going to get to have it out with her, while it was still fresh in her head.

'Just going to the toilet. Too much fizz,' she said as she got up from her seat. Again, Arabella didn't pay much attention as she chatted to Leanne about hair styles and make-up.

Crossing the floor of the salon, she headed straight for the bathrooms. Pushing through the door, she came face to face with Scarlett, whose face matched her name, eyes glistening against the light.

Roxanne closed the door behind her and slid the lock across. She turned to face the woman who so clearly had a problem with her.

'Right, are you going to keep pretending that you don't know who I am? Or are we going to get this sorted right now?'

Scarlett kept her stance steady. She didn't falter or take a step back. Instead, she raised her chin and looked Roxanne in the eye. 'I didn't think I'd ever come face to face with you, not after your trial. And I certainly didn't expect to find you here. Hearing you talk about it the way you do just brings it all back. But you're the reason things went so wrong for my family. I always vowed if I came across you, I'd fucking kill you myself. I never actually thought it would happen.'

Surprised and frankly a little taken aback by Scarlett's nerve, Roxanne raised a brow and nodded. 'Go on then, you seem like a big brave lassie. Say it out loud.'

'Johnnie was my brother, the guy you battered, almost killed for the sake of a measly twenty quid.'

Roxanne searched her memory for the face of the guy who was the reason she'd ended up in prison. Scarlett was right; he had owed her twenty quid which in itself sounded ridiculous. However, it hadn't been the first time he'd taken the piss out of her. He'd attempted to run a side business of his own off the shoplifting ring Roxanne and Jake had had on the go at the time. He'd tried to sell some of the goods and keep a larger percentage than she'd agreed with him. That had got her back up. Of course it had; it would get anyone's back up if they thought they were getting screwed over. But Scarlett had used the past tense when talking about her brother. That wasn't right.

'And thanks to you, he's dead.'

'What do you mean, thanks to me? I didn't fucking kill him,' Roxanne said. 'Whatever the hell happened to him had nothing to do with me. I'd have been in the jail before he died.'

'You didn't kill him with your own hands, but he died of a drug overdose last year. An overdose that was caused by an addiction that you fed before you went to prison.' Scarlett's eyes were wide, her voice growing in anger.

'Look love, if he died last year, it's fuck all to do with me. Your brother was a druggie long before he met me and long after I went to jail.'

Scarlett's eyes narrowed as she stared at her. Roxanne took Scarlett in. Her face, her voice. Then she remembered the moment she was sentenced ten years ago. A member of the public from the gallery had called out to her, saying it was what she deserved. That she was scum.

'If I remember rightly, you gave me abuse from the gallery that day at court. You were brave that day as I was led away in cuffs. But now we're standing here, I wonder if you'd have the balls to take me on? If you don't want to end up with your face caved in then I'm telling you right now, back off or I'll do something that could land me back in the jail. Don't push it.'

Roxanne stood face to face with Scarlett. Was Scarlett stupid enough to push Roxanne on this subject? Dealing in drugs, whether you were the runner or the addict was a business in which there was no room for empathy. Both parties knew the risks.

Scarlett didn't say a word, but instead stared through Roxanne. Maybe she had more balls than Roxanne had given her credit for.

'I'm here to spend time with my mate. She's your employer. Don't do something that will not only put your job at risk but will make your life a living nightmare.'

Turning her back on Scarlett to leave, satisfied that she'd taken the hint, she felt a force push hard against her back, slamming her against the door face first. Fingers snaked around the back of her neck but they weren't quick enough. Roxanne used all of her weight and pushed back against Scarlett, spinning so quickly it caught her off guard and caused her to fall back.

'I fucking *warned* you,' Roxanne hissed, rushing forward and shoving Scarlett so hard that she fell through the doorway of one of the toilet cubicles. Grabbing her by the throat so she was half suspended over the toilet seat, Roxanne punched her in the ribs with her free hand, revelling in the sound of the air leaving her lungs. 'Your brother was nothing but a coke junkie and if it wasn't me it would have been someone else supplying him.'

Scarlett fought against Roxanne's grip but it was apparent that she was too strong for her. She gave up quickly when Roxanne struck into her ribs another once, twice, three times.

'Don't ever challenge me like this again, or next time you might not be so lucky. Oh and while we're on the subject, no one ever gets to call me scum and gets away with it.'

Scarlett kept her head down, coughing and spluttering against the blows Roxanne kept on giving. She was careful to stay away from anywhere above the neckline. She didn't want Arabella seeing evidence of a beating. Stepping over Scarlett, who had dropped down onto the floor now, Roxanne pulled on the handle for the flush and listened as the room was filled with the sound of water gushing through the pipes.

Fixing her clothes back to a presentable fashion, Roxanne washed her hands and dried them in the fancy Dyson hand-dryer, creating more noise which masked Scarlett's splutters. Then she calmly unlocked the door and stepped back into the salon. Her fist throbbed from the blows but she hid the fact from Arabella.

'What do you think?' Arabella said, spinning in her chair to show off her new hairstyle. 'You like?'

Sitting back down in her own chair, Roxanne smiled and lifted the flute that Scarlett had refilled before having the shit beaten out of her. 'You look like a proper entrepreneur. Here's to freedom, new business ventures and happiness. Cheers.'

'Cheers,' Arabella lifted her own flute and raised it in the air.

Roxanne smiled. This day had been unexpected. After just a couple of hours of freedom, she had met Cole Woods who had thrust a business venture in her direction, and had her own past thrust in her face. But there was one thing she knew for sure. She was back, she was free and no one was going to put her back inside. She would make sure of that.

'So, when am I getting to meet the lovely Jake then?' Arabella smiled.

'Why not later on tonight?'

Arabella was giddy, like a kid on Christmas morning. Roxanne almost felt sorry for her. But business was business.

Chapter Twenty-Four

Jake stared across the table at Cole Woods, feeling an overwhelming urge to knock the mobile out of his hand and punch him in the face. Cole had him by the balls with this one. He knew about Jake's affair in London, knew about how Jake had put a stop to it. Cole had all the cards to play with the new venture and his insistence on involving Roxanne. Jake couldn't exactly put a stop to it or Cole would reveal his secret to everyone and he'd lose everything. He'd warned as much at the time. A direct threat.

'We'll be seeing each other again, Jakey boy. And when I come looking for you, you'd better make yourself available for me or I'll make sure that every police station from London to the fucking Shetlands receives a copy of what you did. Do you get me?'

'That woman of yours sure is something, ain't she?' Cole said, pulling out a pack of cigarettes and lighting one inside the pub. Jake kept his mouth shut. He wasn't going to challenge Cole on anything.

'Aye, she is that,' he replied blandly.

'So, you two been together long?'

Jake blinked, holding his eyes closed for a second longer than normal. Cole was playing with him, trying to back him into a corner to intimidate him. It was working.

'Since long before she went to prison. We met not long after she came back from living in Spain. Two thousand and one, something like that.'

'And she's been away ten years? So you've been with her twenty odd years? Fucking hell, Jakey boy. That's like a life sentence mate,' Cole laughed, taking a long drag on the cigarette and eyeing the barman, who did his best to ignore the fact that the law was being broken, as did everyone else in the bar. It appeared that they either knew who Cole was, or they simply didn't want to challenge him.

'Why do people always say that? *If I'd killed her, I'd be out by now?* Bollocks. If you kill someone in this country, you'd get at least twenty-five years up your arse.' A menacing smile crept across Cole's face as his eyes fell on Jake again. 'If you get found out, that is.'

Jake swallowed the angry lump in his throat. It was like being held to ransom being in Cole's company. In truth, that was exactly what was happening here. He was being forced into a situation with a guy he wanted nothing to do with, even though it would make him some serious cash. But the risk of Rox finding out what happened when she was inside was too great. He ran the risk either way. If he refused Cole's proposal then he would tell Roxanne what Jake had done. And if Cole was feeling like a bigger prick than usual then he would tell her anyway.

'So then,' Cole said, blowing smoke into the air above them. 'You think this woman of yours will find us a hub for our operations?'

Jake nodded. 'She will. And she'll do it quickly. Once she has an idea in her head she will go with it until it runs out of steam.'

'Ah, I like the sound of that, Jake,' Cole said, sucking air through his teeth. 'Good business is the result of someone who goes after what they want. She sounds like the type to get what she wants.'

Jake gritted his teeth. He didn't like the sound of that. It wasn't the words themselves, it was the *way* Cole put it. As if he was insinuating that Rox wanted some*one*, rather than some*thing*.

Chapter Twenty-Five

It had been a long day and DS Billy Drysdale's back was killing him. A day at the desk filling out paperwork did that to him. He wasn't in the job for the paperwork, he was in it for the action. To be able to slap a pair of cuffs on a criminal and stick them behind bars gave him nothing but pleasure. The last thing he'd wanted to do when he got home from the station was to get in touch with Jez Kennedy and inform him of what he knew. He didn't want to be involved in this situation, but Jez was an old friend from back in the day. In his youth, before Billy knew he wanted to be a police officer, he would spend his time hanging around with the boys, getting smashed on cheap cider and spending his money on boys' holidays. He and Jez were like brothers back then; neither of them had thought that one day, their lives would take very different paths.

He thought back to those days, when Jez moved in with Billy after his mum died. They were together all of the time, getting into and out of trouble constantly. Dealing and taking recreational drugs, getting into scraps with the young team from the next town, even down to things like bike theft, stripping the bikes for parts, or respraying and selling them on. They had each other's backs. Jez never lost a fight because Billy was always there to back him up. Always. Their loyalty to one another unquestionable.

Billy had seen the fire in Jez from the early days, how criminal activity gave him a thrill. Billy had always suspected that Jez wanted more than anything Dunmuir or Glasgow could offer and knew that one day, he'd leave for bigger horizons.

However, back then Billy would never for one second have thought that all these years later, they'd be on opposite sides of the law.

At the moment he was about to call Jez, the phone rang by his side. Glancing down at the screen, Billy wasn't surprised to see Jez's name flash up.

As close as they'd once been, Billy wondered if all that would go out the window because all Jez truly cared about now was finding the guy who had stolen from him. He wouldn't let anything or anyone stand in the way of that, even Billy. He'd dump him in the shit if he had to, no questions or hesitations. That scared Billy more than anything else. It would end not just his career, but his entire life and everything he'd tried to build since going into the police. An honest life, an honest career. Everything that Jez didn't have. Lifting the phone, he hit the green receiver icon and placed the phone to his ear. He took a steadying breath, ready to speak to the man who used to be like a brother to him. Now, he could become one of the worst enemies he'd ever face because Billy worked for the right side of the law, had done for years. He couldn't turn his back on that for anyone.

Chapter Twenty-Six

'You found anything yet?' Jez asked as he paced the floor in the kitchen.

It was seven in the evening and Jez was getting ready to head to Martini Beach Club. His management team had organised a celebrity appearance for the evening and the place was expected to be packed out.

'You know I can't talk to you about that, Jez.' Billy replied.

Jez took a steadying breath. 'Billy, I know you value your job and all that, but I need a name. This bastard has fucked me over and you are the one connection I have. Is it who I told you it was?'

'Look, Jez, this is a massive operation. The police in the UK have been looking to take down this guy for years and I'm not going to be the officer who fucks it up. So, I'm sorry, but I can't give you a name. If you want to know for sure it's the guy you're looking for you're going to have to come to Glasgow yourself. Or give it up and accept the loss.'

Jez dropped his hand down by his side and stared out of the window which looked out at the pool from the lower level of the house. Charlene was sat on the terrace, sipping a cocktail. As per usual. The boys were out with their mates. Being twenty and eighteen and living in Majorca, Jez barely saw them nowadays. He'd always had the idea of his sons working for him in the family business, but they just weren't interested. Too busy living it up in Spain with their mates. Maria had gone home for the evening. The silence around him was deafening. He hadn't spoken to Charlene properly in weeks. Actually, if he was being honest with himself, he and his wife hadn't had a proper, honest to god conversation since the birth of their second son.

Raising the phone to his ear again, Jez closed his eyes and tried to keep his voice steady. 'I don't accept losses unless it's my own fault. So, if you're telling me that you can't help me, I suppose I'm just going to have to do what you suggest and come to Glasgow. It'll be nice to see the place again, take a look around the scheme, meet up with the boys again.'

He listened as Billy was quiet. He didn't like his old friend's response and the fact that he refused to give up the name of the guy he was looking for. He respected it, though.

'Then I guess we'll run into each other very soon.'

Jez didn't say goodbye, he simply hung up and slammed the phone down on the counter. He had hoped that someone would bring his money and Cole Woods back to him. Going to Glasgow wasn't going to be easy for him. There were issues from the past in Glasgow. He'd spent two decades keeping those issues in the dark while he'd built a better life for himself in Spain. Going back there could potentially uncover things he'd rather stayed hidden.

Chapter Twenty-Seven

Cole wrapped his fingers around the cold pint glass and raised it in the air. Jake Cairney did the same. Cole liked Jake, he was a good guy. Reliable, trustworthy and never did he fuck up on a job. He did everything he was supposed to, so going into business with him now seemed like a good idea. It was better than that, because Cole wasn't giving Jake a choice. He had dirt on Jake. Black, murky dirt that would stick if Cole ever needed to throw it at him. And that was the reason that Jake was allowing Cole to call the shots. And likely the reason he'd remained quiet when Cole had flirted with Roxanne. And she'd flirted back. He'd noticed the way she looked at him, or at least how she tried to avoid his gaze so she wouldn't give away that she found him attractive.

'Cheers mate,' Cole said. They eyed each other as they drank.

'I'm heading after this one,' Jake replied. 'Rox wants me to go and meet her and her friend. Wants me to check out the place we might be able to use as a hub. I just need to make sure it's secure, you know. I don't want there to be any fuck-ups if we decide to go ahead with it.'

'Good lad.' Cole smacked his lips together and swallowed hard. 'She gets things done quick, that woman of yours. You should hang on to her.'

Cole felt Jake's eyes on him, burning into him like hot embers. Pushing Jake's buttons was fun. It was something he was proud of, being able to do and say whatever he wanted knowing that the recipient couldn't rise to it. That was how he'd made his name. Building friendships and gaining trust, making people feel important, until he had them over a barrel and they were his to play with. Manipulation was his game and he loved it. Yes, he was younger than most in his position at this game. But he wasn't scared to get his hands dirty, get the job done right. That was why he'd made a name for himself, a reputation as someone not to be fucked with.

'I fully intend to,' Jake replied. 'So don't go getting any ideas.'

'Ach come on, I'm only messing with you.'

Jake offered a smile but Cole could see a warning in his eyes that gave him a thrill. Jake's girl was fair game if he thought she was worth it. He hadn't decided yet, but he knew that if he wanted her, he could have her. Women responded quickly to Cole, especially if what they were interested in was power. Roxanne struck Cole as the power-hungry type. If he did go for her, there would be nothing Jake could do about it because Cole could expose him for what he really was. A killer. Not just that. A killer with a secret that could seriously destroy his reputation if it ever got out.

'How's about I join you lot? Would be good to check the place out myself. I mean, I trust you, Jakey boy, but you know how it is, always good for the boss to have his say in a place.'

Jake's eyes widened. He began to shake his head and parted his lips to speak but before he could say a word, Cole jumped in. 'It's not a suggestion, Jake. My job, my rules. It's like when you've got a good little paper round going, you wouldn't have anything to post if the company didn't print them, would you? And if that were the case, you wouldn't make your pocket money. So, let's just say that you're the paper boy and I'm the printing headquarters. Got it?'

Cole was already getting to his feet and it was clear to him that Jake understood. It was Cole's way, no argument.

Jake walked through the exit to the street and Cole followed. He'd been in Glasgow many times before, knew most of the city well. He'd acquired colleagues and business partners up here.

Some a lot like Jake, others a lot more dangerous. Cole was top man in London, no one messed. But up here, the gangsters were different. In Glasgow, the drug lords and the high-up men took zero shit when it came to business and he'd learned a thing or two from them. They had a tendency to use violence at any opportunity they saw fit. They were far more dangerous than other people he'd come across in his time. There was a glint in their eye he'd never seen in any other.

'So, where is this place then?' Cole asked, patting Jake on the shoulder with a little more force than his friendly tone would indicate.

'It's not far from here,' Jake replied, his voice low. The sound of his words fought against gritted teeth and this made Cole smile.

-

Standing outside in the pissing rain in Glasgow, Cole glared at the building and nodded in satisfaction. So far, the premises were perfect. Glamour and beauty were the right ingredients for an operation like this. Cole was running drugs from all over the country, from small warehouses, taxi firms, leisure centres. But this would be the first salon.

'And you say that Rox's mate owns this place?' Cole said, rubbing his hands together.

'Aye, apparently her man bought it for her when she got out the jail just a few weeks before Rox.'

Nodding again, Cole raises a brow. 'And she's a criminal? Small time?'

'I don't know much about her. But there is one way to find out, eh? They're inside.'

Cole was already making his way to the entrance when he spied Roxanne through the glass. She was approaching the door and reached out for the handle to open it. She offered Cole a smile but quickly turned her attention to Jake.

'I didn't realise he was coming,' she said, giving a sidelong glance at Cole.

'He's the boss, wants to see the place before he makes any decisions,' Jake replied.

Roxanne stood in a way which blocked Cole from gaining access to the salon. She was sassy, fiery. He liked it. But he didn't appreciate this move.

'Out the way, love.'

'Look, Cole. I know you think you own this city already, you think you own us. But let me assure you, you don't. And I don't want us getting off on the wrong foot here. As much as I want this place to be in our common interest, I don't want us to get screwed over. So, I want to discuss things properly.'

Cole eyed Roxanne and something stirred inside him he hadn't felt in a long time. Excitement and intrigue about a woman didn't come by very often but for some reason, Roxanne's attitude did something to him that he hadn't expected.

Turning to Jake, he raised a brow. 'She's fucking cocky, mate, I'll give her that.'

'Oi, don't talk to him like I'm not here. You want to go into business with us then we all need to be equal. I'm not having you treating me differently because I'm female. I don't want you in there right now. Leave Arabella to me, let me suss things out with Jake and we'll report back as soon as we can. Watch from a distance if you have to but if you go wading in there waving your cock about then this isn't going to work. She'll shut down, even with me. I need to earn her trust about using the place. Just, go home or something. We'll be in touch.'

Cole was nodding. As much as he didn't care to admit it, she was speaking a lot of sense.

'Fine,' Cole replied. 'But earn it quick. I've got merch to move and you'll earn fuck all if you take your time about it.'

He noticed her inhale slowly, as if relieved that he'd agreed to her terms. She was wary of him. And she should be. He needed this deal in Glasgow. He needed the venture for his own good, for his own safety. If they fucked this up, he'd blow Jake's secret wide apart.

Chapter Twenty-Eight

Cole Woods closed the front door of his flat behind him and turned to face the lounge. His mobile phone rested in his hand. He'd hated having to leave Jake and Roxanne to finalise things at the salon, but he hadn't had much choice. He knew Jake would come through for him because there was no way he would do anything to risk Roxanne finding out about what went down in London. In fact, Jake wouldn't want anyone finding out about it. It was too risky for his reputation. And of course, Cole didn't want to have to reveal Jake's biggest secret because that would mean the deal not being finalised, leaving Cole in the shit. All that was just another headache on top of the one he already had. Stealing the one hundred grand from Jez Kennedy had been a stupid yet necessary move. Every time he thought about what he'd done and why he'd done it, that bloody Kenny Rogers song popped into his head. 'The Gambler'. That's what Cole was, a gambler and a bad one at that. He seemed to be on a losing streak recently. That was why he'd had to take the money from Jez. It wasn't as though he'd miss it. He was practically a fucking millionaire and Cole was as close to the gutter as he'd ever been. Cole needed to turn money into more money and quickly. If he hadn't had to deal with such a loss in his life, one that had almost finished him off, he might never have gone into this life in the first place.

As Cole paced the floor of his rented Glasgow apartment, the phone rang in his shaking hand. It was the fifth call in two hours. He'd ignored it each time, but the more he did, the more it rang. Jez Kennedy wasn't going to give up. Seeing the unknown caller come up on the screen had made him feel physically sick, but he wouldn't even admit that to himself. Before the gambling became a problem, Cole and Jez were tight. Cole was a man to be feared, and for those who knew nothing of the predicament that he was in, he still was feared. Jez and Cole had worked well together as business partners. Jez owned the clubs; Cole supplied them with the constant demand for recreational drugs. But the money was disappearing as quickly as it arrived in his pocket. He was practically keeping the casinos going single-handedly over there. He couldn't afford to lose more, and taking from Jez was his best option to get away from his debt to the Albanian gang he'd been working for in order to supply the clubs all over the islands. The Albanian gang he'd stolen five hundred grand from.

Five hundred from the Albanians, one hundred from Jez plus that diamond ring he'd found in the safe at Jez's club which he still didn't have the balls to have valued in case it was traced back to him. He wasn't scared of Jez. He was scared of the Albanians. If they got hold of him, he'd be dead before he realised they were on to him. Cole couldn't have that. He hadn't completed his quest to find out what had happened to his brother. That was partly the reason he'd stolen the money in the first place. Hiring a private investigator wasn't going to be cheap, but he needed to find out the truth. He had stolen more than enough when he was in Spain to cover the expenses.

That ring was real, he knew that just by looking at it. It was also his insurance policy: if the Glasgow deal went bust he could get it valued, sell it and use the cash to go into hiding. It was all such a mess.

'Fuck!' he screamed, squeezing the phone between his fingers. 'Fuck the lot of them!' Six hundred grand was nothing to these people. That was partly why he took it all in the first place. In truth, he knew he was in deep shit.

If he could just get Jake and Rox to pull this off, then things would be fine. He'd be able to pay off his debt to the Albanians, go back down to London, and hopefully get back to some sort of normality. Cole was ruthless; he wouldn't have stolen from a deadly group of gangsters if he wasn't. He couldn't tell Jake anything about that though, he had a reputation to uphold and if Jake found out about his dealings with the Albanians then he'd back out, regardless of the risk of the truth coming out about him.

The phone pinged again and vibrated in his hand. Buzzing twice, he glared down at it and his stomach rolled again.

> Cole Woods. You stupid piece of shit. You will be found, and when you are you will be buried for what you've done.

'*Fuck!*' The phone flew across the room, bounced off the wall and landed on the sofa.

This wasn't the way things were supposed to turn out. He was supposed to be top dog and now everything was fucked. He'd been stupid, greedy and weak and if he was found before Jake and Rox got things moving, got cash flowing, then Cole Woods would be a dead man. Jez Kennedy wasn't going to stop until he found him. He was a resourceful man, had people in his circle who would already be looking for Cole. And if Jez did find him, so would the others.

Chapter Twenty-Nine

Standing outside the salon and peering through the window, Eddie watched as Arabella danced around the salon floor, with a prosecco glass in one hand and the bottle in the other. The rest of the stylists had left for the evening except for Scarlett and another girl who was in the process of getting ready to leave. Arabella belted out the words to 'Starships' by Nicki Minaj in between gulps of fizz and Eddie felt his frustration building. Did she think the place was her own personal nightclub?

Pushing the door open, Eddie stepped inside and Arabella met his eye. She was pretty hammered by the looks of it. Having fun without him, it would seem, after he'd waited on her while she was in prison. After he'd bought her this place. Eddie swallowed down the bitterness on his tongue and tried to remind himself that all he ever wanted was for Arabella to be happy.

'You're here.' Arabella smiled widely and moved across the floor before placing the bottle on the counter at the front desk. As she hugged him tightly, Eddie wrapped an arm around her and took in her scent. 'I want to introduce you to someone.'

Pulling away, Arabella took hold of Eddie's hand and led him across the salon towards the kitchen. A woman appeared from the doorway. Tall with auburn hair and fiery eyes to match, Eddie knew exactly who she was, even though she looked a little different from the news report he'd found on Google.

'This is Roxanne, my friend from Kirktonhill. Roxanne, this is my Eddie.' Arabella kept hold of Eddie's hand, and squeezed it a little.

Eddie nodded at Roxanne and noted her expression. A sarcastic smile parted her lips as she raised a brow.

'Ah, the *famous* Eddie. It's good to finally meet you. I wish I had a man who'd buy *me* a salon.' Roxanne held out her hand and Eddie shook it.

'Always good to have a plan when you get back to the real world,' Eddie replied firmly. 'It's nice to finally meet you too. I hear you kept my girl in check while she was inside?'

'Erm, I'm standing right here, you know,' Arabella giggled, taking another sip from her glass. 'Oh by the way, Jake's just in the bathroom. You'll get to meet him in a minute. He's Roxanne's man.'

Eddie nodded, but he said nothing, unsure how to react.

'In all honesty, I don't know how I'd have got through the last ten months of my sentence without this girl. I'm glad you broke the law, Arabella.' Roxanne laughed.

Arabella leaned into Eddie's shoulder and smiled. 'Every crime has a silver lining, eh?'

Movement to his left caught Eddie's eye and he glanced in the direction of the salon manager getting ready to leave. Scarlett was putting on her coat.

'Mr Corrigan,' she said. 'Arabella, I'm heading now. You've got keys, haven't you?'

'Yes, yes,' Arabella replied chirpily. 'You get off. I'll make sure things are fine here. Well, Eddie will since I'm half scooped.'

Scarlett laughed and made her way across the salon towards the door. Arabella followed her, grabbed the bottle from the reception desk and turned the music up. He watched as she danced her way back to Roxanne. The pair were laughing and drinking and Eddie admitted to himself that he was proud of what he'd done for Arabella. No one else had seemed to care about her when she went to prison last year. No one had seemed to care about her at any part of her life, from what he knew of her before they'd met. He wanted to be the person who changed that, the person she could depend on.

'Scarlett?' Eddie called out. With one hand on the door, Scarlett turned.

'Yes?'

'Everything okay here, at the salon? Arabella is doing good?'

Scarlett parted her lips slightly but paused for a moment before replying. 'Yes, *Mr Corrigan*, she's doing fine. But what does it matter what I think? She's the boss. You're both my employers.'

Eddie took a short breath. 'And you're both getting on okay?'

'Yes, we're getting on fine. You have nothing to worry about. Honestly.' Her voice was low.

Relief flooded his veins. 'Thank you, Scarlett. I appreciate it must be hard having a new boss. But this means a lot to her and I need things to work.'

'Goodnight, Mr Corrigan.' Scarlett opened the door and went out to the street. He watched her go, disappearing around the corner. The slow-closing door clicked shut but Eddie didn't move. He simply continued to stare out to the street.

He heard the door to the bathroom open at the end of the salon and when he turned, he saw a man step onto the salon floor. Jake.

'Eddie?' The guy said.

'Aye, that's right. You must be Jake? Arabella was telling me about you.'

He knew who Jake was; the news report back from when Roxanne was sentenced had captured an image of him too.

'Seems they had a right laugh with each other while they were banged up together.' Jake smiled and held out his hand. Eddie shook it, applying enough strength to show that he was the alpha here. It was a bit pathetic, Eddie knew that, but he couldn't help it.

'Aye, so it seems.'

There was an awkward silence, as though everyone clocked on to the fact that Eddie was acting a little off.

'I think you two will get on.' Roxanne peered at Eddie as he sat down on one of the salon chairs. 'Aye, he likes those... oh what are they called again?' She raised her eyes and glanced up at Jake. 'Nissan GT-Rs. Got one in the garage back at the house. It's an old rust bucket but he likes it.'

Eddie laughed loudly as did Jake. 'An old rust bucket? You're clearly not into your classic cars then. What year is it?' He directed the question at Jake.

Arabella rolled her eyes. 'Car chat? Really? How *boring*.'

'Two thousand and one, mate. Love a GT-R,' Jake said. He pulled two beers from a bag on the counter to his left and handed one to Eddie. 'Bud?'

'Thanks,' Eddie said, taking the bottle in his hand and twisting off the cap.

Roxanne and Arabella looked as though they were pretending to listen but Eddie knew that Arabella would want to go out to a club later and that was fine. He didn't mind going out and getting smashed with her. And even though he didn't know Roxanne and Jake, it might be a laugh to go out with another couple. He couldn't deny too that part of him was attracted by their criminal links, wondering if this might bring him the buzz he'd been missing.

The four sat chatting for a few hours. Roxanne and Arabella spoke a little of their time together at Kirktonhill and Roxanne explained why she had ended up there for ten years. Eddie was surprised at how open she was being, and how brutal her crime had been. She had a classy look about her and certainly didn't appear as though she would be so violent. He supposed that was the kind of trait a gangster needed in order to operate: charm and class. Being female would also work in her favour.

'So, what's changed?' Eddie asked her, taking a drink from his bottle.

'Not much. I'd do it again if I had to. I don't let folk get away with something like that, Eddie. He owed me money, took the piss out of me for long enough. It's a shame I got caught, but then I wouldn't have met Arabella here if I hadn't.'

Arabella's eyes fell onto Eddie and he saw her shift in her seat.

'That's true,' Arabella replied. 'And our friendship has nothing to do with either of our pasts. Right?'

'Definitely,' Roxanne smiled and raised her glass.

The evening continued and the girls danced and chatted while Jake showed Eddie some classic cars on the internet that he was interested in. Eddie spoke about his van business and how he'd love nothing more than to be able to get his hands on a GT-R and do some work on one.

'You're a mechanic by trade?' Jake asked.

'Aye, although I mainly just sit behind a desk now. It's boring as hell running your own business, but I wouldn't have the bank balance I do if I was still just a mechanic.'

Jake laughed and Eddie smiled.

'Why don't I bring you my GT-R? It needs a new exhaust system fitted. I've got it sitting in the garage ready to go but I've not got around to booking it in yet,' Jake said.

'That would be brilliant. I'd love to see how she handles. But to be honest, I wouldn't want to touch her. You'd be better taking her to a specialist, Jake.'

'Fair enough. We'll give her a run once I get her fixed up?'

'Aye,' Eddie said. 'Sounds like a plan.'

Just as Eddie was about to crack open another beer, Arabella and Roxanne announced that they wanted to go to the new club that was opening in the Merchant City. Just as Eddie had suspected.

'Oh come on, it'll be a laugh. I've not been to a club in years,' Roxanne said.

'Actually, I know the owner,' Jake said. 'He told me he expects the place to be bursting at the seams on opening weekend. Why don't I give him a bell and see if he can get us on the VIP list?'

Eddie smiled as Arabella did a little happy dance.

'Jake, that would be amazing. I can't believe you know the guy who owns that club. Who is he?'

Eddie swallowed hard at that one. What was the difference between owning a club and owning a van hire company? A business was a business. He couldn't let it bother him that Arabella was impressed.

'Just an old business associate. Give me two minutes and I'll phone him now.'

–

A little over two hours later, Eddie and Jake were sitting in a VIP booth in Club Silver, while Arabella and Roxanne were up dancing. They'd been up on the dance floor for the best part of an hour, since they'd arrived. Eddie knew he wasn't going to get Arabella's dancing shoes off anytime soon, so he left her to it while he chatted some more with Jake about cars. This guy seemed all right and by the sounds of it had a bit of wealth behind him.

The music blared around them, the light sequences flashing in time with the beat. Jake had been right, the place was packed. People kept waving hello at Jake and Roxanne as they passed.

'So, you got a GT-R yourself?' Jake asked Eddie, calling over the music.

'I wish. Never quite found the right one though. Either the price or the timing wasn't right,' Eddie replied, keeping one eye on Arabella.

'Or maybe buying a salon for your girlfriend got in the way,' Jake remarked with a smile on his face.

'Had to mate, I didn't want her coming out of that shit hole to nothing. It was bad enough she had to serve time in the first place. I had to make sure that she had something to keep her focus.'

Jake seemed surprised. Not that Eddie blamed him. Buying a business for a convicted partner didn't seem like the everyday scenario.

'What I mean is, I wanted her to be able to support herself so that she didn't fall back into her old ways.'

'And what were those?'

Eddie sighed. Did he really want to talk about that with this guy? He was a stranger, someone he'd only known for a couple of hours. And anyway, if he wanted to know, then surely Roxanne would fill him in. She would be in the know if she'd spent ten months with Arabella.

'It doesn't matter now. It's in the past, hopefully,' Eddie said, hoping that Jake would sense his tone and end this line of conversation.

'Jakey Boy!'

Eddie looked up in response to the loud, London accent. A man stood by the booth, holding an ice bucket with a bottle of Grey Goose inside. Eddie could tell this guy thought a lot of himself. His stance, the way he loomed over the top of them told Eddie all he needed to know. He was the type who thought he was better than everyone, from how he dressed to how much money he had in the bank. The guy seemed like an arsehole.

'Cole. What are you doing here?' Jake replied, getting to his feet. Eddie saw how Jake gritted his teeth but tried to disguise it as a smile.

'Fancied a night on the town. Can't come to Glasgow and not try out the newest club on launch night, can I? I know the owner.'

Jake nodded and Eddie got up from his seat. 'Aw'right mate.'

'Cole,' Jake said. 'This is Eddie. Eddie, Cole.'

Cole put the ice bucket on the table and held out his hand. 'Good to meet you, Eddie. Mind if I join you? All my mates are back in London, you know how it is. My only mucker up here is Jakey Boy, ain't that right?'

Jake nodded and moved aside. Cole slid into the booth and the men all sat down. Eddie glanced over at Arabella again, but she wasn't paying attention. Roxanne, however, was staring over at the booth. Eddie detected a hint of concern in her expression and just as he did, she stopped dancing and headed towards them. Whatever the reason, it was clear both Roxanne and Jake were wary of this Cole character.

'Your missus don't look too happy, bud,' Cole said, taking the Grey Goose out of the bucket and placing it on the table.

Roxanne reached the table and smiled at Eddie before her eyes rested on Cole. 'Didn't expect to see you here, Cole.'

'Nah, I was just telling Jakey Boy and Eddie that I fancied a night out in Glasgow. Plus, I know the owner of Club Silver, so how could I miss launch night?'

Was this guy trying to impress, Eddie thought but he was distracted by Arabella as she danced her way over to the table and sat down on his lap.

'Let's get another drink,' she said. 'Oh, I've not met you before, have I?'

Cole's eyes fell upon Arabella and his smile lit up his face. 'Cole. And you must be Arabella. Roxanne has said a lot of good things about you.'

Roxanne's expression was soft, but her eyes gave away the lie. It seemed she wasn't happy about Cole's presence.

'Girls, why don't you get stuck into that vodka and I'll get us another from the bar,' Cole said.

Getting up, he squeezed out from the booth and disappeared into the crowd that was lining the bar. Roxanne glared at Jake, who said nothing.

'How'd you two meet then?' Eddie asked Jake.

'I worked with him for a bit down in London when Rox was inside.'

'Yeah,' Roxanne said as she sat down next to Jake. Taking a sip from Jake's beer bottle, she said, 'he's got some business coming his way up here and he's asked us if we want in on it.'

'Oh, that's exciting,' Arabella squealed, wriggling on Eddie's knee before leaning across the table and reaching for the vodka. 'Babe, pass me that bottle would you?'

Eddie handed the bottle to Arabella and watched as she held it close to her. 'What are you doing?'

'Why don't we take this back to our place? We could all go, grab some food on the way home and carry the party on there? I can't really chat to Rox in here with the noise and to be honest, I'm pissed and my feet are killing me. Not used to wearing heels.'

Roxanne nodded. 'Yeah, let's go.'

'Aye, clubbing's not really my thing these days. Rox will tell you, I can't dance to save myself,' Jake said.

Soon, they were all standing on the street outside and Arabella had put the vodka inside her jacket. They stood waiting for a taxi and Eddie was beginning to feel pissed himself. He'd not had a lot but then he hadn't eaten anything, with the garage being so busy today.

'Oi!' Cole shouted. 'Where you lot off to then?'

They turned and Roxanne muttered something Eddie didn't quite catch.

'Calling it a night, mate. We're all a bit old for this now,' Eddie said, sensing that whatever it was that Roxanne had said, she didn't want Cole with them.

'Right then, where we off to?'

'We haven't decided yet.' Roxanne said. 'But you'd be a spare part, tagging along with us couples.' Her sarcasm was hard to miss.

'Tagging along? Nice. Seems as though the only thing tagging along here is that bottle of vodka I paid for that your mate here seems to have nicked.' Cole nodded in Arabella's direction and raised a brow. 'So, like I asked, where we off to?'

Eddie stood still next to Arabella, straightened his back and glared at Cole. Who did this guy think he was, speaking about his girlfriend as if he wasn't there?

'Oi, she didn't nick it. You left it on the table and said you were going to get another. It was fair game,' Eddie replied.

'Right,' Jake interjected and Eddie could tell he didn't want things to kick off. 'Why don't we head to the casino?'

Cole's eyes lit up and the suggestion seemed to tear him from the brewing fight Eddie was ready for.

'Yes. Excellent idea, Jake, just excellent. Although, is the casino a place for the ladies here?'

'Well, prison is no place for a lady and we both managed to get through that fine. So I think we'll manage,' Arabella sneered, holding the bottle of vodka at arm's length and staring Cole dead in the eye.

Roxanne laughed loudly and linked arms with Arabella. 'Since we're just little women who can't do anything without you men, why don't you get us a taxi and we'll wait to be told what to do next.'

Eddie couldn't help but smile. He felt proud that Arabella had stuck up for herself. Yet he knew just by the look of him that Cole was bad news, a dodgy character. And the only way to keep an eye on those types was to stay close.

Chapter Thirty

Charlene needed a break from the sun and had gone inside to get herself a drink. When she did, she'd heard Jez on the phone, and from what she'd listened in on, it seemed that he was planning on leaving Spain on business. She wanted to quiz him, ask him where he was going. Who with? When? Of course, in reality it was likely that Charlene would keep her mouth shut and say nothing. It was easier to remain silent than to start an argument with a husband who was only just hanging on by a thread. She knew the only reason he was still there was because of the boys and they were getting to the age now where they didn't really need their parents to be together. It was only a matter of time before Jez left her. Or maybe he'd tell her to leave. The house was his. The businesses belonged to him. Yes, they were married and in normal circumstances a divorce meant everything split down the middle, but most women weren't married to millionaire gangsters who could make their life a living hell if they felt it necessary.

Being pregnant with his first son was the only reason they'd stayed together. She hadn't wanted to raise her child as a single mum, but choosing to stay with Jez purely for that reason was one of the worst decisions she'd ever made. She should have left him long ago. The boys were adults now, they didn't need their parents to stay together just for them.

Charlene replayed the scene in her head. Finding out about Jez and Roxanne that night had sent her into a rage she'd never felt before and that rage hadn't ever gone away. It simmered gently in the background most of the time, but it was always there. She just couldn't believe that it was Roxanne. Why did it have to be her? Her best friend? Charlene wasn't just humiliated by Jez, but betrayed by the one person she thought she'd be able to confide in. That in itself she could have got over in time. Old wounds fade. But he'd continued to cheat. Over and over. Of course she'd never actually caught him in the act, but she'd had every reason to suspect him of infidelity. He pulled every trick in the book, out 'working late'; and coming home smelling of other women's perfume. She'd confronted him, but his answer was always the same, *I work the club scene, Charlene. Of course I'm going to be home late smelling of stuff. Booze, perfume, smoke. You're being paranoid.*

'I have to go away on business,' he said, interrupting her thoughts.

Charlene began picking at the skin around her thumb nail and thought about how to respond. What did he expect her to say? *Okay darling, but do hurry back because I'll miss you?*

'I don't know how long I'll be gone,' Jez continued, seemingly unaware of the thoughts going on in her head.

A few moments of silence hovered between them and Charlene could feel his eyes on her. He was expecting an answer.

'And will I be honoured with the knowledge of the location of your business trip? Or shall I sit here and guess where you'll be until you get back?' The words trailed from her lips like the hiss of a snake and Jez rolled his eyes.

'What's with the fucking attitude, Charlene?'

'And what's with the years of pretending you want me around when you couldn't give two shits about me? You spend more time talking to the bloody housekeeper than me, your own wife.'

She despised the exaggerated sigh that was forced from his mouth. He always did that when she was making a valid point because he didn't have a comeback.

'I'm going to Scotland.'

Charlene's stomach lurched. Scotland? *Why?*

'Don't look at me like that, Charlene. It's a business trip.' Jez turned away and Charlene didn't know whether to feel relieved or offended that he couldn't look her in the eye while he lied straight to her face.

As much as it was a long time ago, Charlene couldn't help but think that if he was going back to Scotland, he might bump into Roxanne. What if their relationship started up again? She hated that she thought this way.

All she could say was, 'Look at you like what?'

'You know what. Like you're sizing up what I'm going to be doing when I'm there.'

'And you're trying to tell me you won't be catching up with your little bit on the side?' The words came before she'd even thought about it. He looked as surprised by them as she felt.

'Jesus, Charlene. It was twenty years ago. Give it a *fucking* rest, eh? I've not looked at another woman since.'

Sighing, Charlene raised a brow. 'So you say.'

Jez spun around and slammed his fist on the counter, making her jump. 'Is it any wonder our relationship is fucked when you continually accuse me of having an affair?'

Charlene let out a breathy laugh. 'That's because you did.'

'And you could have walked away,' he shouted. 'We had it out, a long-winded discussion about what was best for you and the baby. You said you wanted us to be together and I said I did too. But you've never let me live it down, have you? Always picking, always digging about it. I've had you in my ear almost every day, and when you're silent I can tell by that death stare of yours that what happened back then has turned you into a bitter and twisted...' He stopped, took a breath.

'Carry on,' Charlene said, eyeing him with suspicion. She knew that he was going to say she had become a bitter and twisted bitch. With all his infidelities, who could blame her? Staying with him had made her this way, she knew that. But for some reason, she'd never felt the strength to leave.

'If you really need to know why I'm going to Scotland, it's because I'm going after someone who has fucked us over.'

'Who?' Charlene asked, folding her arms and challenging him to lie to her.

'Cole Woods. He's stolen a hundred grand from the club and fucked off with it, as well as my mum's diamond wedding ring. I swear I'll fucking kill the bastard.'

Charlene frowned. She almost felt sorry for him. Jez was a hard bastard but when it came to his late mum, he always softened. This might just push him over the edge. 'But I thought he was one of your best suppliers. Why would he do that?'

'Because he's a greedy bastard, Charlene. But I'll fucking kill him before I let him get away with it. I'm going to pack. I've got a flight to catch.'

With that, Jez marched out of the kitchen and headed down the long hallway towards their bedroom. He slammed the door so hard Charlene thought that the wood might crack and the hinges come loose.

Then the house was deathly silent, aside from Charlene's thudding heart. The blood rushed inside her, a whooshing sound in her ears. She was angry. Livid. But she felt a sadness creep over her. A sort of loneliness that only came from being in a marriage that was dissolving. Two very different souls who'd once connected but no longer fit together like they used to.

She understood that he had to go and find Cole, not for the money but for the ring. It was the last thing he had that was connected to his past. Not that she knew a lot about his past.

She summoned up a strength she hadn't known existed; she wasn't going to just sit around and wait for her husband to return. She was going to get on the next flight to Scotland and follow Jez's movements. She knew that he was going for Cole, but there was every chance he could try to find *her*. The idea infuriated her so much that she worried what she would do if she saw them together. She didn't actually care about Jez, it was more that he had treated her like an idiot their entire marriage and she'd let him get away with it. And she'd lost her best friend because of him. The best friend she'd grown up with. The destruction of that relationship had left her broken.

Chapter Thirty-One

Jake watched as Eddie won yet another hand. That was five in a row. Anyone else would stop now; the fear would be creeping in that their winning streak was about to come to a halt. But not Eddie. He was a winner. He'd bet a hundred quid on the roulette table and was up five hundred. Jake had never seen anything like it.

'Bloody hell, Eddie. This is the best streak I've ever seen,' Jake said.

'I don't play often. I know when to stop. My uncle was an addict; I always had it drummed into me that money wasn't a game. But I do like the odd bet here and there.'

'I'd have stopped long before you,' Jake said, sucking air through his teeth like a tradesman giving the verdict on a heavily priced job.

'Fuck!'

Jake and Eddie turned in the direction of Cole's voice. He was standing by a slot machine, pulling on the handle like a madman.

'What the fuck's up with him?' Eddie asked.

Jake shook his head. 'Looks like he's losing.'

Eddie raised a brow. 'Aye, looks like it.'

Cole turned his back on the machine and slid his wallet into his back pocket before he walked towards Jake and Eddie, his expression twisted.

'You lost then?' Eddie asked.

'I'll win it back. I always win it back, one way or another. In fact, I'll *double* my money, just you watch.'

Cole ordered a beer from the bar next to the roulette table and when it arrived, he drank half of it in just two gulps. Jake looked on, wondering what was going on inside his head.

'Sounds to me like it's time to stop, mate.' Eddie said.

Cole slammed the bottle down on the counter. 'What did you just say? Who the fuck are you to tell me what I should or shouldn't do?'

Eddie blew out a mouthful of air before laughing. 'Calm it, I wasn't telling you what to do. I was only making an observation. I couldn't give a fuck what you do with your money. If you want to go ahead and try to make it all back twice over then on you go.'

Jake watched Cole, expecting him to blow up at Eddie as he'd seen happen before when they were working together down in London just three years previously. He didn't take too kindly to people speaking their mind about him. He remembered one night in the pub, the night before the job. Cole had skelped someone for bumping into the back of his chair. Jake had to break up a fight that the other guy would lose. It was then that Jake realised Cole was an off-the-scale nutter, but it hadn't occurred to him that he'd ever be on the receiving end of his wrath. To Jake's surprise, Cole didn't say a thing. Instead, he turned away and finished his beer before turning back and smiling widely.

'So, what do you do for a living?'

Eddie frowned and Jake wondered where the question was headed.

'I own a van hire company. What do you do?'

Jake saw the confusion on Eddie's face.

Cole licked his lips. 'Bit of everything, you know how it is. So, a van hire company. You must make a shit ton from that?'

Eddie frowned again. 'We do all right.'

Jake watched as Cole's eyes fell upon him. He knew then why Cole was asking. He wanted to know if Eddie was going to be of use to Cole's new venture. And judging by the answer that Eddie had given him, it would seem that Cole thought he would be.

'You don't sound so convinced?' Cole pressed.

'To be honest, before I took over the business from my dad, I lived a bit of a wild life. I was a dirt biker for a while. Took drugs, drank a lot. Went from girl to girl. But now, life's a bit... well, let's just say it's more boring than it used to be.'

Jake noted how Cole began to charm Eddie, and how Eddie seemed to relax a little more while being in his company. This was exactly what Cole had wanted. Someone just like Eddie, who was looking for a little bit more from life. Someone who was looking for a buzz. Eddie sounded like he was in need of that buzz, and Cole had managed to sniff him out very quickly. Like he always did with people like Eddie. People who were attracted to the darker side of life were his prey.

Cole put his arm around Eddie.

'Why don't we go somewhere a little quieter? Jake's place, perhaps? I want to put something to you, Eddie. Something I think you'll be *very* interested in.'

Eddie got up, collected his winnings and followed Cole out of the main casino room, down the stairs past the club below and out to the street. Jake followed behind and Eddie didn't look back to see if he was still there. Which possibly meant that Eddie was entirely interested in what Cole had to say.

Once outside, Cole turned to Jake and smiled. 'Your place?'

Jake gritted his teeth. He didn't want Cole at his house. Not when Roxanne would be there later in the night for Cole to leer over. But how could he say no? Having Eddie on their team could mean easier distribution possibilities.

Jake thought about how Eddie could get himself into real trouble working with Cole. But then, who was Jake to care? He didn't know Eddie, didn't owe him anything. Eddie was a grown man who could make his own choices. It had nothing to do with Jake either way.

Before he could answer, Cole said, 'Right then. Let's go.'

Chapter Thirty-Two

DS Billy Drysdale watched them climb into a taxi and followed it as it drove out of the Merchant City area of Glasgow towards Maryhill. As he drove two car lengths behind, he could see into the back of the taxi and noted that only one of them was acting rowdy. Drunk. Off his face. Or angry? Arms flapping all over the place, large gesticulations with his hands. The other men didn't seem to mirror his actions.

The taxi took a right turn off Great Western Road onto Queen Margaret Drive and headed past the Botanic Gardens. Wherever they were headed, it wasn't Cole Woods' rented flat. That was in the west end, nearer the Partick area. Billy had done his research, knew everything there was to know about Cole Woods. This man was dangerous, a massive drug dealer. He was known to many in the city of London as 'The Loner'. He'd made his business deals alone. No one wanted to have many dealings with him because rumour had it he was a tad unstable. A gambler, a guy who could fly off the handle at the slightest loss. People didn't want to be around him when that happened. Not only was he a gambler, he was a heartless shit. Rumoured to be linked to a few unsolved murders down south before pissing off to Spain for a couple of years. Of course, Cole was a resourceful man and left no evidence behind, so he had escaped prosecution. But DS Billy Drysdale had been tasked with the job of bringing this guy down because Cole was now doing his business in Glasgow. And he would bring him down. He wasn't going to allow this guy to deal drugs on his streets. A gambling addict and lone gangster didn't mix and it would only be a matter of time before Cole made a mistake. Billy just had to be there waiting when he did.

They reached the top of the road, just making the green light. The taxi turned onto Leyden Street and stopped outside the first sandstone building. Number two. Billy turned into the street and pulled in just ahead of the taxi. He pressed the button, releasing the window just an inch. He needed to be able to hear as much as possible.

The three got out of the taxi. Cole stumbled and Billy could just about make out what he was saying. His thick London accent was loud, yet his words slurred a little.

'You lads are going to fucking love it. I'm telling ya, just you wait. We'll be fucking—'

'Right, Cole,' one of the other lads said over the top of him. It was as if he knew that what Cole was about to say would cause them problems. 'You up for a game of poker?'

'Is the pope a *fucking* catholic?' Cole replied before roaring with laughter at his shit joke.

The taxi pulled out of the street and Billy killed the engine. He watched in his mirror as the two men Cole was with helped him up the external stairway before going inside. Billy needed to turn the car around and position it so that he could get a better view for when they finally came out again. That could be in the next few hours, or it might not be until the next morning. Either way, Billy was staying put.

He quickly turned his car around and parked it in the small private car park directly across from the flat. Killing the engine again, he took out his phone and noted the time. Almost midnight. Billy glanced back up at the building and to his surprise, he could see them. He was staring straight into the kitchen. One of the lads threw the window wide and another lit a cigarette before sitting by the window. They were loud. Well, Cole was loud. The others listened.

As did Billy.

Chapter Thirty-Three

Jesus Christ, Arabella thought. What the bloody hell was in those cocktails? Her head spun as she hung onto Roxanne, who was helping her out of the club and onto the main road. She was vaguely aware of people. People everywhere. Yet all she could see were their feet. High heels, sandals, painted toenails, trainers. She tried to put one foot in front of the other, yet her legs were like Bambi on ice.

'Watch where yer gawn hen!' someone shouted. Was that to Arabella? Had she bumped into someone?

'Sorry,' she tried, yet her words slurred and slithered out of her mouth, barely audible.

'Come on,' Roxanne said.

Her friend's voice was close to her ear but Arabella could hardly lift her head to smile in response. She didn't want to attempt to talk again, it was embarrassing trying to get her words out when she was so drunk she'd forgotten how to speak. And walk. And hold herself upright.

Roxanne, please get me home, Arabella thought to herself.

Barely aware of Roxanne flagging down the taxi, Arabella found herself being bundled into the back seat. Thank god her friend was there to help her.

'Let me strap her in first, mate,' Roxanne said, this time her voice sounding far away. 'She's had a bit much to drink.'

'Nae bother, hen. You know there's a soiling fee of fifty quid if she's sick.'

'Aye, she'll not be sick. She just needs to get to bed and she'll be all right,' Roxanne said, sitting down next to Arabella.

The movement of the taxi, the bumps in the road and the speed made Arabella feel woozy. You're wrong, Arabella thought. I might just throw up.

She tried to focus on something still. The folded-up seat in front of her. The advert for a funeral company. The words swam in front of her eyes and she closed them to stop the motion but that made her feel worse, so she opened them again and tried to focus on something else. The red light on the door. The red light that indicated the doors were locked. The sign said as much. She could just about read it.

'You still alive down there?' Roxanne's face came into focus as she dipped down and stared at Arabella.

Down there? Down *where*? Arabella realised that she had been focusing so hard on watching the stillness of the red light on the door that she was practically folded in half.

'Sit up, Arabella. That's going to make it worse.' She felt Roxanne's hands on her, forcing her back onto the seat.

'I'm so drunk,' Arabella said, her head lolling. She heard Roxanne laugh.

'Aye, I can see that. You'll be at home in your bed soon enough. Almost there.'

Time seemed to speed up then, yet Arabella couldn't comprehend how long it had been since she last saw Eddie. Where was he and why wasn't he the one looking after her? Did he even know where she was? Come to think of it, she didn't even know where she was.

'Cheers, mate,' Roxanne said.

A door slammed, and they were no longer in the taxi. Her skin felt chilled by the night air. Her feet throbbed in her shoes. She bent down to take them off before falling forward, her face crashing down against the concrete. She was consumed by darkness, a black shadow coming at her from all directions inside her head.

She was beyond drunk. She was unable to comprehend what was going on. Suddenly, she was being rushed along, dragged. Traffic noise in the distance. A voice echoed above her, like she was in a tunnel or under an archway. It was so dark that Arabella couldn't see where she was going. Suddenly she was a little more sober, but still fuzzy enough that she couldn't piece together how she'd come to be here. In this place.

'Roxanne? Rox?' She tried to call out, but a hand was thrown across her mouth.

'Sssh!' Roxanne hissed in her ear. 'Move quicker.'

'But what's…' Arabella's words trailed off as Roxanne dug her fingers into Arabella's arms, forcing her to stay as upright as possible while pushing her forward.

'Unless you want to end up back in jail, then move your fucking feet, Arabella.'

Why would she end up back in jail? What the fuck was going on?

It was beginning to rain, and the cool breeze on her cheeks made her realise how hot she felt. The wave that came before the alcohol-induced vomiting began.

'Stop,' Arabella said, tugging away from Roxanne. 'I'm going to be sick.'

'No. Not here. You'll get caught.'

Hunching over, hands on her knees, Arabella began to retch as the multitude of cocktails and fizz came back on her. It burned intensely in her throat, the acidic taste making her retch even more.

'Fuck's sake, Arabella.'

Before she could answer, even before she could stand up, Arabella threw up the last of the contents of her stomach. As she retched, she questioned why she was so ill. She hadn't drunk *that* much, had she? Not enough to make her so violently sick. In the past she'd been used to drinking and taking coke all through the night as she partied; she knew her body could handle much more than she'd drunk tonight.

'I'm sorry,' Arabella murmured as she wiped at her mouth with the back of her hand.

Jesus, she thought. Just out of prison, reunited with her best friend and look at the state of her. A drunken mess.

'I'm sorry,' she said again. But Roxanne didn't answer her as she tugged at her arm, pulling her along.

Chapter Thirty-Four

He'd drunk too much. Enough that it was beginning to distort his vision, his perspective on the situation he was now in. Cards lay scattered across the kitchen table, empty beer bottles sat on the side of the sink and a half litre of Jack Daniel's sat between Cole's knees. Memories from his past floated around in a drunken haze inside his head. His head ached with the confusion of it all. But he had to focus, get his head back in the here and now.

'Another game, Cole?' He heard a voice ask. It was coming from the other side of the kitchen. Taunting. He'd already lost a few hundred at the casino earlier, although he wasn't going to tell them that. He was surprised that was all he'd lost when he came to think of it. Or was it more? Possibly, that had happened before, losing more than he'd initially thought.

'Nah. I need a pick-me-up.'

Cole placed the bottle of Jack down on the floor and used his fists to push himself off the couch that sat under the window. Sliding his hand into his pocket, he pulled out a small bag of coke and poured the contents onto the table.

'Anyone for a line? Liven this so-called *fucking* party up a little?'

He eyed both Eddie and Jake, who were stood by the hob both clutching bottles of Peroni. The music had been turned down and Cole could feel the annoyance in his stomach beginning to build.

'Nah mate, I'm driving early doors tomorrow. Can't have booze and drugs in my system,' Eddie replied.

'You're the fucking boss, Ed,' Cole said as he began sectioning the coke with a business card, he'd picked up from one of the lap dancing clubs the night before. 'Just get someone else to drive.'

Pulling a tenner out of his pocket and rolling it into a thin tube, he bent down and blocked off his left nostril before snorting the white powder up the right. The sound was loud, piggish. Standing up straight, he stared Eddie in the eye. 'And anyway, our little business agreement will mean you'll never have to drive a fucking hire van ever again. We'll be the men in the high castle and all the little fuckers will be running around after us.' Cole pointed at Eddie and Jake, and then to himself, prodding himself in the chest.

'I'll have a line,' Jake said, placing the beer on the counter and stepping towards the table.

'That's it lad, get right in about it.' Cole slapped him on the back and Eddie laughed.

Jake glared at Cole and for a moment, Cole thought he was going to get punched in the mouth. Not that Cole would have blamed him. He had Jake by the balls, knew the one thing about him that no one else did. If it got out, it would ruin him. It would break him as a man, as a gangster.

'You taking that line or what?' Cole said, glaring back at him.

'Aye,' Jake said, bending down and snorting loudly.

'Ed? Come on, you know you want to. No women here to tell us what to do. In fact, I've got this card right here. And *apparently*, they do house calls; open twenty-four seven. Just like the doctor ordered.' Cole laughed loudly. He felt the coke taking the desired effect.

'No chance,' Jake said. 'Rox would kick seven shades of shit out of all three of us.'

Cole raised a brow at Eddie. He saw something in Ed that slightly resembled temptation. 'You're up for it, mate? Come on, call it a way to celebrate our new business venture.'

Eddie laughed. 'We couldn't have girls come here, though. I mean, Jake's right. If Roxanne and Arabella came back here to find lap-dancing hookers here, I think we'd all die in this very kitchen and the girls would end up back in jail.'

Cole's smile widened, his fingers tingled. 'But you're up for it?'

'We need to celebrate somehow. Come on Jake, it'll be a laugh,' Eddie said, seemingly deciding to take a line himself. He leant down and snorted up the third line.

'I don't cheat,' Jake said, eyeing Eddie. 'Roxanne deserves better.'

'Is that right?' Cole said. His voice had a menacing tone to it. 'So, you didn't cheat on her down in London when you were working with me, when she was in prison?'

Eddie's head span as he turned to look at Jake and he let out a laugh. 'You dirty bastard.'

'I *didn't* cheat.'

'You mean to tell me shagging someone else isn't cheating?' Cole shook his head sarcastically. 'Fuck me, then all my ex-girlfriends seriously overreacted.'

Jake shook his head and looked away from Cole and Eddie. His fingers began to twitch, Cole noticed. Maybe he was going to get a punch in the mouth. It was about time Jake lived up to his reputation. This Eddie guy seemed to have more balls than Jake and he was running a legit business.

'Go and fuck yourself, Cole.'

'Ah come on, you know I'm only having a laugh. It's not like we're going to tell Rox what you did down in London. Us lads need to stick together, innit?'

Jake's expression remained the same and Cole knew he was pushing his buttons. Good. It was about time Jake knew that Cole wasn't to be messed with.

'Right boys, come on. Let's have another drink and then we can go to the strip place. Get ourselves a few dances and relax. Come on Jake, you don't have to do anything. Like Cole says, it's just a laugh,' Eddie said. It was obvious to Cole that he was trying to defuse a potential outburst from Jake. Not that it would help. If Jake wanted to go off on one then he would. There was no one to stop him from doing that. Cole knew better than anyone; he'd witnessed it for himself.

'Call it a team-building exercise,' Cole laughed. Jake stared straight at him, a warning and pleading look. Cole was planning to keep his mouth shut – it was in his own interests to do so, but he liked playing with Jake. He enjoyed feeling like he had the balance of power, even though in reality, he needed the deal to work more than Jake did. He needed the money more too. And if he did have to use Jake's secret against him then there would be consequences for him as much as Jake. Concealing information was a criminal offence in itself, not to mention his involvement in the disposal of a body. If Cole went away for that, he wouldn't be able to finish the job he'd started for himself. No one knew the real reason why Cole was doing this, and he intended it to stay that way.

Jake expelled air from his mouth in protest before lifting his jacket from the sofa and walking out of the kitchen.

Cole and Eddie watched him before Eddie turned to Cole and asked, '*Did* he cheat on Roxanne when you were working together?'

Cole smiled. 'What the fuck you take me for? A gossip? Nah, that's not my style. I'll let the man himself tell you all about it.'

Eddie raised a brow before turning his back and heading for the front door. Cole's smile faded then. He wouldn't have to tell anyone about Jake's story from down south if he just did everything that Cole asked. Everything and everyone would be fine if things went exactly how Cole had planned them.

Chapter Thirty-Five

As they entered the club, Eddie realised that it wasn't your every day, run of the mill lap-dancing club. It was underground for a start, in the basement of some seedy hotel in the Parkgrove area of the city. In the day, this place was fine. Families out walking their dogs, kids playing in Kelvingrove Park. But at night, it became a very different place.

The neon sign outside already gave the place a seedy feel. But then, all lap-dancing clubs had those signs. This place felt different, he couldn't quite pinpoint why.

'Right lads, who do you fancy?' Cole said, rubbing his hands together as they stepped into the soundproof club. The sign on the door said 'members only' and only members could sign people in.

Eddie looked down to see Cole signing a book at the door. It didn't surprise him that Cole was a member of this kind of establishment. He came across as the type.

'You're a member?' Eddie asked, patting Cole on the back.

'One of the first things I did when I got here, mate. Aren't all you Glasgow lads members? You've got some banging birds here, I thought you would have been.' Cole smiled widely, and Eddie wondered if the rest of the men inside were just like him.

'I need a drink,' Jake said as he headed in the direction of the bar.

Eddie stood still, taking in his surroundings. There were girls everywhere, dancing on the bars, dancing on the tables. He wondered if any of them were there against their will. Most were foreign, some British. He watched as a small group of younger lads sat at one table in the corner, leering over the girl on their table. She wasn't dancing, but lying down on it. One of the lads snorted a line of powder off her stomach and the rest of them howled and cheered, like a pack of preying wolves. Eddie looked away. As he understood it, in most establishments like this one you weren't allowed to touch the dancers. Maybe this wasn't like the rest. It had a dangerous feel to it, like perhaps the girls weren't *just* dancers. He asked himself the question again, were they here against their will? It was likely, going by what he'd just witnessed. A mix of nerves and excitement stirred in his stomach. This was a side to Glasgow he'd never seen before. Perhaps he was out of his depth and he should get out while he still could. But did he want to get out?

'Ed, who you thinking? That blonde over there with her arse in that lad's face seems your type. You like blondes? Arabella's a blonde, is she not?'

Eddie shot Cole a warning look. 'I think I'll join Jake at the bar.' The words were hissed through gritted teeth as he pushed past Cole.

'Make mine a double vodka,' Cole called out after him.

So, Cole was like the rest of the men in here. Eddie didn't think it would take long before Cole was the one snorting a line off that girl's torso. But was Eddie any better for actually being present, even if he wasn't partaking in the activities around him? He reached the bar and stood next to Jake who was gulping back a whisky. 'You alright? You've been acting weird since we left the flat.'

'I'm fine.' Jake replied sharply, placing the glass down on the bar harder than Eddie expected.

'Look, I'm only asking because I could tell that Cole was pushing your buttons back there, talking about you cheating on Roxanne when you were down in London working with him.'

'He's a fucking prick. He might be able to sling a few quid our way with this deal, but don't for one minute think he's your mate. He'll stab you in the back as quick as shake your hand, Eddie. Let that be a warning.'

Eddie didn't reply, instead he ordered two whiskies from the barmaid. Turning to locate Cole, he wasn't at all surprised to see three girls dancing around him. One on his lap wearing nothing but lace knickers and the others on their knees next to him.

'He really is a bit of a prick,' Eddie said as he turned back to Jake. 'But then I can't say anything. I'm not much better than him.'

The barmaid placed two glasses in front of them and Jake knocked his back in one go before he said, 'Why's that?'

'I kind of cheated on Arabella when she was in prison too.'

'Kind of?' Jake said in a sarcastic tone.

'Well, I slept with a few girls. Aye, I know. Weak. But there was one girl I got involved with and it backfired.'

'What do you mean?' Jake seemed more interested now.

'It doesn't matter. But what I'm trying to say is that it doesn't make a difference so long as the missus doesn't find out. And before you go judging me, I've stopped now.'

Jake let out a laugh and shook his head. 'Aye, only because she's out and you can get it from her whenever you want.'

Eddie didn't know whether to laugh with him or knock him out. 'Alright then, Mister High and Mighty, I've told you my story, you tell me yours.'

The music boomed around the club, yet Eddie could still hear Cole whooping and whistling at the dancers. He really was quite the creep. Eddie may have shagged about but he wouldn't pay for sex and certainly not from girls who were forced into this line of work. It was bad enough he was present at all. Yet if he was thinking of working with Cole, earning big money, then he would have to swallow his pride and get on with it.

'I don't want to talk about it,' Jake replied.

'Aw come on; it can't be that bad. Oh, don't tell me you've married someone and got kids? You've got a fake identity and living two different lives?' Eddie laughed loudly, yet it still didn't drown out the sound of Cole on the other side of the bar. He certainly wasn't subtle.

'In some respects that would have been the easier option.'

Eddie saw Jake's expression fall then and he instantly knew there was much more to Jake's past than he was ever going to let on. Cole had something on him; it wasn't that hard to work out. Like Jake said, Cole would stab you in the back as quick as shake your hand.

'Look Eddie, I haven't told anyone about what I did in London. The only reason Cole knows about it is because he was there. He saw the whole thing. Used it against me. Continues to use it against me. Like I said, keep one eye on him while you're doing the job. Don't let your guard down with him. He's dangerous, one of the most dangerous men I know. He'll do whatever he can to get to the top and he doesn't care who's in the firing line. The worst thing is, he doesn't know you so he won't give a fuck about sorting you out if you let him down.'

Eddie turned and stared at Cole who caught his eye. Cole raised a hand, gave him a thumbs up while a sly smile took over his face. The three men had met just hours previously and now Eddie was thinking of going into business with them. He knew he shouldn't; there was no need to financially. But Eddie still had an itch that needed scratching. Something more exciting than filing the tax return and paying people's wages.

Jake was right; Cole didn't know Eddie. Knew absolutely nothing about him. Eddie was prepared to take risks for the tax-free cash that could come out of the deal he'd agreed to. But if Cole Woods thought that Eddie Corrigan was a pushover just because he wasn't a big-time gangster like him, then he was wide of the mark.

It would be stupid to risk everything he'd built up, to go against his dad's wishes of leading a simpler life. But deep down, that just wasn't Eddie. It was pathetic that he was jealous of Arabella being friends with Roxanne and the danger that could bring. If he was jealous, why shouldn't he do something to rectify that for himself?

Yes, Cole was a bit of a dick, but then so were he and Jake. None of them would know faithfulness if it smashed them in the face. So, working alongside them to earn a bit of cash and excitement surely wouldn't do much harm. He'd already convinced himself that working with Cole and Jake was going to be good for him. He loved Arabella; he didn't want to live his life without her and yes, he could go through life now that she was out, having date nights and relaxing with her like they'd both wanted. But going into business with Cole and Jake would bring back the excitement in his life that he'd been craving. And if it hadn't been for Arabella meeting Roxanne, then he wouldn't be sitting here with them now.

Chapter Thirty-Six

Feeling like she'd been smacked over the head with a hammer, Arabella failed to open her eyes even though she was awake. What the hell did she drink last night to feel so horrific? As she searched her memories from the night before, she drew a blank.

Groaning, she slowly turned on her side and realised she was not in her bed. Forcing one eye open, Arabella looked around the room. She was alone on the living room floor.

'Urgh,' she moaned, pulling herself into a sitting position. 'Eddie,' she called out.

The flat was silent. There was no sign of life anywhere.

'Eddie?' She called again more forcefully, pushing herself onto her feet. 'Where are you?'

Why the hell had she woken up on the floor in the living room? And why couldn't she remember anything from the night before? All she had in her head was when they were in the salon, there was nothing after that.

Head pounding, she moved through to the hallway and into the kitchen to get a glass of water. Opening the door, she almost jumped out of her skin when she saw Roxanne standing against the counter.

'Jesus *fucking* Christ, Rox,' Arabella gasped, clutching her chest. 'What the hell are you doing here?'

Roxanne looked at her, her face pale and eyes wide. 'Are you okay?'

'I feel like I drank every drop of alcohol in Glasgow. Can't remember a bloody thing.'

Passing by Rox, she pulled a glass from the drainer and filled it with water. Sipping it slowly, she fought the urge to gag.

Arabella turned to see Roxanne staring at her intently. 'Why are you looking at me like that? Oh god, did I do something embarrassing last night?'

'You don't remember *anything* at all?' Roxanne asked.

'I remember being in the salon and Eddie and Jake showing up. But after that, nothing. I don't remember anything. I made an arse of myself, didn't I?'

Roxanne exhaled, lowering her eyes down to the floor.

'What's wrong?' Arabella asked, a sudden icy chill trailing down her spine. 'What happened?'

Roxanne nodded. 'I think you should sit down for this.'

Arabella followed Roxanne back through to the living room and sat down on the couch. Terror and fear ripped through her, just like any normal hangover. But there was something else. A blank space like a black hole in the centre of her memory hung between them. Roxanne was about to tell her something that was going to shift the ground beneath her.

'Did I try it on with Jake or something?' She attempted light humour.

'So, we left the salon and went on to Club Silver. Do you remember that?'

Arabella shook her head. 'No.'

Roxanne raised a brow. 'Okay. Well, we weren't there for long. We chose to leave and then the boys decided they wanted to go on to a casino. They're still there, I think, although I haven't heard from them. Anyway, we started on the cocktails. You were pretty hammered – wasted, actually. I had to carry you outside and get us a taxi… Do you remember any of this?'

'No. I only remember being at the salon. Just get to the point, Rox. What happened?'

Narrowing her eyes, Roxanne shifted on the sofa. 'Okay, but please realise that it's going to be okay. I've sorted it. You won't get caught and things will carry on as normal. Do you trust me?'

Arabella felt her stomach flip. 'Of course I trust you. Just bloody tell me.'

'Good. Because in order to survive this, you have to trust me. You were sick in the taxi and the driver threw us out. He wouldn't have if you hadn't got so aggressive with him when he said he had to pull over.'

'Aggressive?' Arabella repeated. 'In what way?'

'You were basically calling him every name under the sun, telling him that he was just a scummy taxi driver taking hard-earned cash off the public for overpriced fairs. He asked you to calm down, I asked you to calm down but you were having none of it. You tried to punch him but were so pissed you lost your balance and fell over. When I went to pick you up, the guy drove away and left us in the street. The place was deserted because all the pubs and clubs had closed by that point.'

'What happened?' Arabella asked, trying as hard as she could to conjure up the slightest memory from Roxanne's story and coming up with nothing.

Roxanne took a breath. 'A guy approached us. A really dodgy guy. I think he was homeless, maybe. He became irate quite quickly, asking for money, asking for cigarettes. I told him a few times that we didn't have anything that he was looking for but he kept following us. You turned off the main road and took us onto a side path that leads to your flat and he kept on at us. Calling us names, taunting us. I tried to see him off but he wouldn't listen. I tried to tell him that I was just out of prison for GBH but he was having none of it. Arabella, I don't know what came over you, but you fucking lost it. You picked up a rock, turned and smashed it into the guy's face. Knocked him off his feet. But you jumped on top of him and just kept hitting and hitting. It was brutal, even for me. I had to pull you off but you were in a frenzy. I just grabbed your wrist and fucking ran.'

Arabella's eyes were wide and she got to her feet, gipping the hair at the top of her head. 'Oh my fucking god, Rox. Shit. Shit, shit, shit!'

'Ssh, it's okay. It's going to be okay,' Roxanne said, grabbing her by the shoulders.

'How is it going to be okay? What if he goes to the police? I can't go back to prison, Rox. I can't.'

Arabella was crying now. Huge waves of panic and terror made her gasp with each breath as she paced the floor.

'He won't go to the police,' Roxanne replied.

'How do you know that? He could be there right now. They could be on their way to arrest me right now.' Arabella's voice was high, she'd gone into panic overdrive.

'Hey, he isn't going to the police because he's dead.'

Silence filled the room and the air turned to ice. After a few moments, Arabella said, 'I thought you said you grabbed me and ran. How do you know he's dead?'

No, no, no. Arabella was shaking her head. No, this didn't happen. It couldn't have. She would have remembered. She tried so hard to see into her memories. Nothing came. Not an image, not a sound. Nothing.

Arabella looked down at her hands. Her fingernails were short, clean. Frowning, she looked up.

'I managed to get you back here, get you cleaned up. You were hysterical, crying and saying that you didn't want to go back to prison but you were still so drunk. I finally managed to get you to calm down and you passed out on the sofa. That's when I went back to check on him. He was dead, eyes open, staring blankly up at the sky. Blood *everywhere*.'

Arabella gasped, threw her hands over her eyes. 'Oh my *god*.'

Oh fuck. Fuckfuckfuck.

Fear and terror crept up from her stomach and clawed at her throat. 'Rox, how the actual fuck did I do this? I'm not a killer. Oh my god, oh my god.'

Roxanne gripped her shoulders tighter this time and held her steady. 'Hey, look at me. It's fine. I've sorted it. There were no cameras, no traffic. It was four in the morning and we were on a path off the road. No one knows anything except us. I promise, you're going to be fine.'

Tears trickled down her cheeks as she stared into the eyes of her friend. Her only friend. She had no choice but to trust her.

'How do you know I'm going to be fine? It's not fine. I'll get caught. Oh fuck, I killed someone, Roxanne. I took someone's life away from them.'

'Oi, he fucking deserved it. What kind of man follows two women down a dark path at four in the morning and gives them abuse? Fuck knows what would have happened if you hadn't stopped him in his tracks.'

Arabella shook uncontrollably, her eyes unblinking and wide with terror.

'I got rid of the rock and pushed his body down to the River Kelvin. When they find him, there won't be a murder weapon to link you to it. It'll look like he's been in a fight and lost. His injuries are pretty brutal, as if he was in a fight with a guy his own size. I *promise* you're going to be fine; this won't come back to you, Arabella. But you can't tell anyone about this. Not even Eddie. The less people who know, the better. Do you understand?'

Arabella nodded in rapid motion as Roxanne pulled her in and hugged her tight. She started to cry again, her body shaking in fear as Roxanne held her close. How could this have happened? How could she have got so off her face that she couldn't control herself? She'd blacked out and murdered someone.

'My clothes… they'll have his blood on them?' Her voice shook, the words came in a whisper.

'I've already dealt with it all. I made you change as soon as you got in last night. It's okay. I've got you, girl. Stick with me and you'll be fine.' Roxanne held her at arm's length and locked eyes with her.

'Thank you,' Arabella whispered. 'I don't know what I'd do without you.'

'You'll never have to find out. I'll be by your side forever now.'

Those words somehow made Arabella feel better. If she could trust anyone with this, it was Roxanne.

Chapter Thirty-Seven

Stepping off the plane at Glasgow airport, Jez felt his blood run cold at the shock of the temperature. If nothing else, this was a good reason to have fucked off out of Scotland. The weather was always a let down, no matter what time of year it was. He was never homesick for his country. When he and Charlene got married after she'd had their first son and their relationship was more manageable, they'd talked about how neither of them had wanted to return to Scotland to raise their family. There were many reasons on both their parts, but most specifically for Jez; he would be walking back into a crime scene he'd left behind. Only he and Billy knew about the things Jez had done in the past; he'd never disclosed them to Charlene, didn't feel the need to. All he'd said was that he'd left some bad omens behind and would prefer not to face them. Charlene had no reason to go back either.

She'd left Glasgow to get away from the scheme she'd been raised in. Her parents were alcoholics, drug abusers. Same as Roxanne's, she'd said. That had suited Jez; it meant he wouldn't have to argue with Charlene about returning home. He thought about their relationship in the beginning and how after their son was born, they'd both really tried to work at it. Of course, he knew that Charlene would hold Roxanne against him forever, but he wanted their family to work, so much so that she'd fallen pregnant with their second child just two years later. It hadn't worked out purely because Charlene just couldn't let things go. She threw Roxanne in his face at every given opportunity, especially when he was spending a lot of time at work. The accusations of cheating were relentless and, in the end, had led directly to him being unfaithful. He was damned anyway, so he ended up feeling he might as well do what he was being punished for.

The airport transfer bus was already full, but he managed to squeeze himself between the doors before it drove across the tarmac towards the main terminal. Nostalgia took over then as he thought about the last time he was in Glasgow airport. He was only nineteen, heading out to Majorca on a boys' holiday. He never went home. The opportunities were too good to pass up on. There was nothing for him in Glasgow. No job prospects after leaving school with next to no qualifications. That was his own fault, he'd admit. But he didn't want to spend the rest of his life working in a shitty, dead-end job on minimum wage.

He'd started off as a barman for one of the bars in the resort once he'd chosen to stay. He was eye candy, according to his boss. The offer of a free cocktail worked a treat almost every time and the girls always hung around a little longer. That and the fact that there was always at least one in the group who fancied their chances with him. He was happy to admit that too. After a few weeks, he became friendly with a couple of the lads who worked for some of the other bars on the strip. They were dealing on the side, another way to entice the punters in, especially the lads. They were always after a bit of coke or speed, anything they could get their hands on that would enhance their clubbing holiday experience. And enhancing their experience also enhanced Jez's cash flow. The more he sold, the more he made. He was a popular rep, had the right kind of banter with the lads and a charm with the girls. He'd get in amongst the party-goers, lead the booze challenges, dance with the girls… Jez was the life and soul. It was where he was supposed to be, what he was supposed to do.

Before he knew it, he was climbing the ladder, making more money than he'd thought possible as a rep. A year went by and soon Jez was managing the bar he'd started off in. The owner,

Rafa, had been impressed with Jez and his ability to get punters through the door. The bar's reputation climbed, word of mouth spread and it was packed out most nights.

Only a few months in, Jez was making serious money. Then Rafa hit him with the biggest news. He was dying from cancer and with no family to leave his business to, he signed it all over to Jez. It had all happened so fast that Jez didn't have time to think about it. It was happening and there was nothing Jez could do except roll with it. Years later, Jez had gone on to sell the place, and it had made him a shit ton of money, enough to enable him to buy more clubs, his latest being Martini Beach Club. Now, he was Majorca's wealthiest businessman, although it hadn't come easily. He'd had to adopt a business-like manner that hadn't come naturally. He'd been a young lad, fresh on the club scene. Not just managing, but running things. Associates hadn't taken him seriously at first, so Jez had had to adopt a firmer approach. It wasn't as though he didn't know violence, and it was useful in his new line of work. People really sat up and took notice when he was able to secure agreements with the drug traders. People really knew who was boss.

Jez stepped off the air bus and made his way through the terminal towards passport control. The place smelled exactly as he remembered it. Cold air stung his nostrils and he held his nose, attempting to pop his ears after the flight. He got to the front of the queue quicker than he'd expected and glanced down at the passport scanner before placing his passport on the glass. The barrier raised above him and he stepped through.

He waited by the conveyor belt for his case. It was yet to start moving, which meant the baggage handlers hadn't finished unloading the hold yet. Jez took his phone out of his pocket and switched it on. Pulling up the number on his phone, he called Billy. It was early in the morning, but surely he'd be up and ready by now, being a bigwig in the police and all that. Two rings later, Billy picked up.

'Mate, how's it going?' Jez asked, keeping his voice low.

'Good. I take it you're back in Scotland then?'

'Just waiting on my case now. Fancy a beer later?'

'Not a good idea, mate. Sorry, you know how it is. I can't get mixed up in your shit when I'm running an investigation.'

Jez gritted his teeth. He respected his old friend and the fact that he was doing the right thing for his career. But that didn't mean he liked it.

'Look Billy. Aside from the reason I'm here, we go way back. It would be nice to catch up, for old times' sake?'

Jez listened as Billy hesitated. The alarm above the conveyer belt rang and it started moving.

'Okay, fine. I've got a few hours free later. Meet you in the old place at two?'

'I'm surprised that place is still standing,' Jez laughed as he pictured his old local.

'I've heard the place looks the same. Still old Evans that owns it but his boy runs it now, apparently,' Billy replied.

Jez smiled. 'Great. I'll see you then.'

He hung up the phone just as his case appeared. Heading out of the airport, he climbed into a taxi and headed straight for his hometown of Clydebank. It had been a long time since he'd last seen the place. It would be interesting to see what, if anything, had changed.

As the taxi drove across the Erskine Bridge, Jez took in the scenes to his left and to his right. He could just about make out the path which led up Dunmuir Hill towards the Dunmuir Loch. A place he and his mates used to go as teenagers to drink their cider so they wouldn't get hassle off the police. To his right, he saw the old schemes. He couldn't help but smile at the memories of dodging the police by jumping the garden fences at the back of the golf course when he was fifteen. If someone had told him then that he would grow up to become one of the most successful club owners in Spain, he'd have laughed in their face.

As the taxi pulled onto the A82 and headed for Clydebank, he passed the cemetery on the left and bowed his head. Both his parents were buried in that place. His home life had been decent up until that point, before death tore it apart. He'd had normal, hardworking parents. It was why, he supposed, he went off the rails as a teenager, ending up in all sorts of trouble. He hadn't been back since his mum's funeral. If it hadn't been for Billy and his family, Jez would have ended up in the system. When Jez got to Spain, he didn't want to remember anything from his life in Glasgow. And up until this point he'd had no reason to come back.

The taxi continued on its journey, passing his old primary school on the left hand side just a mile or so up the road. It looked exactly the same as it had when he and Billy had attended in the late eighties, early nineties. As did the street running adjacent to it. The old car garage had changed though, that was now a funeral home.

Passing the village of Dunmuir, Jez quickly glanced across at the old grounds of the hotel and pub which he used to frequent when he was underage. It had been knocked down and replaced by flats and new houses. That was some pub back in the day, Jez remembered. But it was also always the place that rival schemes would meet to have their weekly brawls. Jez was often involved in those. Another reason he had to get away from the place. Too many bad omens.

After another ten minutes of travelling, the taxi pulled up outside the Beardmore Hotel and Jez paid the driver before stepping out onto the pavement. Pulling his case from the boot, he walked along the path towards the main entrance and into the lobby.

He checked in quickly and made his way up to the top floor where his luxury suite was waiting for him. He wanted to have a shower and a sleep before he started on his quest to find Cole Woods. That fucker had one hundred grand of his hard-earned cash, had treated him like an idiot. Cole Woods might have been a bigshot back in his day, but he was nothing compared to Jez. He wondered if Cole knew that and that was why he'd done a runner with the cash. He must have known that if Jez ever did catch up with him, he would end up dead. Did one hundred grand seem worth that to Cole? Perhaps it did.

Jez slid the key card into the lock on the outside of the door and let himself in to the suite. It was a decent size with a good view of Erskine across the water. Not that he gave a shit about the view. The only thing Jez wanted to see was Woods staring down the barrel of Jez's gun, pleading for his life. Apologizing for taking his cash. Not that it mattered. Not now. Jez had already made up his mind that once he found Cole, once the money and his mum's ring were safely back in his possession, he would kill him anyway. No one got away with taking the piss out of Jez Kennedy.

No one.

Chapter Thirty-Eight

Arabella closed the door behind Roxanne, locked it and headed straight for the bathroom. She needed to throw up, to get rid of the dread and fear inside her left over from the hangover and the knowledge that she'd murdered a man the previous night. A murder that she couldn't remember taking place. There was no evidence on her, no blood spatters, no scrapes or signs of a struggle. Nothing.

Arabella turned on the cold water tap and splashed her face. She needed to wake up from this nightmare. But it wasn't a nightmare. It was real.

As she glanced at her reflection in the bathroom cabinet, the sight of the dark circles under her eyes and pale complexion made the nausea feel even worse. She stepped back, pressed her shoulder blades against the wall behind her and felt her legs give way as she let out a cry that sounded like a wounded animal.

Just out of prison, just free. And now it looked like she would be going back there because of what she'd done. She'd read somewhere that thirty-seven per cent of offenders were likely to reoffend within the first three years of release from prison. Surely a few weeks out of prison was a record.

A memory came to her then, of that time in the school playground. She hadn't meant to hurt the girl so badly; it was just that a red mist had descended and she couldn't stop herself, like someone else had taken over her body. That was when she was just eight years old. The violence was in her then. It hadn't taken much to provoke her; a few stupid comments. At least she could remember that, even though it was twenty years ago.

Last night, however, was an entirely different situation. Now she was an adult, she should know better. She'd tried hard to get her life on track, to steer herself in the right direction. After going to prison, she'd promised herself that she wouldn't let anything get in the way of her freedom again. Already she'd compromised that.

Gathering herself together, Arabella got to her feet and took a breath, glaring at herself in the mirror again. No. She wasn't going back to prison. She trusted Roxanne with her life. She'd looked after her in prison, stayed by her side the entire ten months. They'd bonded in a way that Arabella had bonded with no other. She hadn't had friends like Roxanne when she was in school. She was always the outcast, always the one to take the flak when a window was smashed, or someone was caught with alcohol in the common room. Roxanne wouldn't throw her under the bus like that. Never. She'd proven that by getting rid of the evidence of Arabella's involvement in that man's death. She'd gone above and beyond to protect her. It was possible there would be no one else on the planet who would ever do something like that for Arabella other than Roxanne.

A key scratched on the front door of the flat and Arabella froze. Her fear quickly faded at the sound of Eddie's voice.

'Hi,' he called out. His voice was groggy and Arabella looked down at the time on her watch. It was ten in the morning. How had she not noticed he'd been gone for so long?

She opened the bathroom door and looked at him. He looked like shit. The dark circles under his eyes almost matched hers. Standing just a few feet away from him, she could smell the alcohol as it wafted in her direction.

'Where have you been?' she asked, trying to keep her voice steady.

'Casino and then back to Jake's flat,' he replied, rubbing his hand over his face and stumbling a little. He steadied his stance and turned his attention back to the front door to close it.

'You were at Roxanne's?' she asked. If they'd just gone back there instead of her own place, then that guy would still be alive and she'd have been with Eddie, blissfully happy and drunk. Instead, she was about to keep the biggest event of her life from the man she loved. The man who had waited for her, bought her a business and stood by her side while she served her time.

'Aye. What happened to you and Roxanne?' He slipped his jacket off and hung it up on the coat rack.

'We ended up back here. You just missed her. I can't remember much from last night actually. I was pretty wasted.'

'You and me both,' he replied, heading to the kitchen. He barely looked at her. He hadn't noticed how wound up she was.

'Good night?' Arabella called through, taking one last look at herself in the bathroom mirror to check that she didn't look as though she'd been crying before following him into the kitchen.

'Er... aye, it was alright.'

She hesitated. 'What's wrong?'

'Nothing. I'm just rough as a badger's arse and I need a sleep.'

He kept his back to her as he sipped some water. Did he know she was keeping something from him? Did he know she was lying?

'Fair enough,' she said. 'I'll catch up with you later then? I told Scarlett I'd pop into the salon today to check in, see if they needed anything. Although I don't think she really needs me around to run the place. She's got everything covered. I feel like an imposter over there, if I'm honest.'

Eddie turned, smiled and gulped down the last of the water from his glass. 'Sorry babe, I'm too rough. I'm heading to bed. I'll see you in a few hours, yeah?'

Feeling rejected, Arabella smiled and nodded as Eddie kissed her on the cheek as he passed by and headed for the bedroom.

She didn't know whether to be offended that he hadn't noticed how shaken she was as she tried to hold everything in, or relieved that he hadn't clocked on that something was wrong.

Within seconds, Arabella could hear Eddie snoring loudly, oblivious to the world. Oblivious to her.

The only thing that Arabella could do in order to keep her mind off what had happened was to go to the salon and carry on as normal. As normal as she could, anyway, considering she'd been released from prison just a few weeks previously and had inherited a business.

But first, she had to go back. In doing so, she might be able to remember what happened. By now, the police would be there. There would be forensics, possibly press. But she had to know.

Arabella quickly dressed, pulled her hair back from her face and tied it on top of her head before grabbing her phone and heading out of the flat. Roxanne had said she wasn't to tell Eddie about what happened. But she didn't say that she couldn't go back and check things out for herself. If her mind wouldn't show her the memory, then she had to create the image from the present.

Leaving the flat, she headed along the road and turned down onto the footpath. Stopping at the top, she listened. She'd expected sirens, voices, people, traffic. If there was a drama – a murder – then normally people rallied around to catch a glimpse of the action. But there was nothing.

Pulling her phone from her pocket, she opened the Google app and typed in 'body Kelvin River' and waited for the searches to load. Again, nothing.

Sliding the phone back into her pocket, Arabella started down the path, looking into the bushes and trees at either side. Her head thumped with each step she took, the alcohol clearly still in her system. Not surprising – she must have drunk her weight in the stuff, based on the hangover.

That was when she heard it. The cacophony of voices. A flashing blue light highlighted the end of the path and as she edged closer to the centre of the pathway, she saw a gathering of people. Police tape. Officers telling people to stand back to allow the police and forensics to do their job.

ShitShitShit. It was real. She'd killed that man.

Voices chattered excitedly and Arabella couldn't help but overhear.

'I heard he was walking along the path and someone pushed him down the embankment towards the river.'

'Nah, apparently the guy who found him said his face was caved in. It's definitely murder.'

'Poor guy. No one deserves that.'

'Apparently he was found a few yards from where it happened. Someone said he'd tried to crawl back to the main road for help and just died on the spot. What a way to go, eh?'

Arabella turned, clutching her throat. She couldn't breathe as she retched over and over before finally she fell to her knees. Bile left her mouth, her body trying desperately to expel the horrific secret she was trying to keep inside.

'Oh good god, are you alright, love?' a woman said, her voice by Arabella's left ear, a hand on her back.

'I'm okay,' Arabella shrugged her off and got to her feet before running back to the flat.

Once inside, she locked herself in the bathroom and bit hard on her bottom lip while texting Roxanne.

> I need to see you. NOW! Meet me at the salon later. A

Chapter Thirty-Nine

Staring at his mobile phone, DS Billy Dyrsdale shook his head. He thought it might be good to see his old mate again. They'd been so close, like brothers. His memories of their friendship were all good ones. But their lives had gone down very different paths. Billy had always wondered why that was. Possibly because Jez had lost his parents at a crucial time in his life. Billy remembered how his family had taken Jez in, like he was one of their own. He and Billy had been best friends growing up, Billy's mum was friendly with Jez's mum. She'd later told Billy that she felt it was her duty to take care of Jez. However, as much as Billy and Jez were friends, they'd always had different lives planned. Billy had always wanted to become a police officer, whereas Jez had always aimed to earn as much money as he could, no matter what the job entailed. It would seem that both men had achieved their goals.

Almost twenty years had passed by since they'd last been together in the same room. They'd spoken on the phone on the odd occasion, sometimes video called. They never fully lost touch. Their worlds were always so far apart, but now Jez needed information from Billy on a professional level. Usually, the police were the ones looking for the informant, but on this occasion, it was the criminal.

He picked up his coat and headed to the front door. It had been a long time since he'd been to their old local. It had been a long time since he'd lived in Dunmuir, having moved away before going to police college.

As he drove to the pub, he thought about how Jez would try to manipulate him into giving up information. Billy wasn't stupid; he knew that if Jez truly wanted to, he could turn on him. He did have dirt on him after all, from when they went on that boys' holiday. The one where Jez had decided he wouldn't use his return ticket.

Thinking back to that time in Majorca, Billy winced. It was a mistake, a drunken and stupid act where he'd allowed himself to lose control. He could just about remember what he'd done. If he could change things, go back and undo it then he would. Of course he would. Jez covered for him, got rid of the body and the CCTV from the club so there was no comeback. He'd gone with Billy to the airport and made sure to get him on the first flight back to Scotland the next day. If it wasn't for Jez, Billy wouldn't be where he was now.

Stopping at the red light at the end of the scheme where he used to live, Billy felt his stomach flip. Could he do this? Could he walk into that pub, the west end bar and sit in the company of his old mate, knowing that Jez could throw that night in his face if he didn't get his own way?

If what Billy did back in Majorca got back to his boss, he could lose his career. He could lose everything. Yet equally, if he didn't show up to meet Jez, things could go the same way. This was always going to come back and bite him one day. His former best friend held his biggest secret and that scared him, because even though twenty years had passed, there was still a friendship there that could be destroyed by the secret between them.

The light turned green and Billy drove along the street, pulling into the pub car park. As he got out of the car, the smell of cigarette smoke hit him almost immediately. Without seeing them, he knew that there would be a gathering of the regulars outside the front entrance, smoking and talking about the bets they'd put on at the bookies directly across the road from the pub.

He walked towards the pub, head held high. Some of these people used to be his friends. In a way they still were, they hadn't fallen out as such, just lost touch over the years and he'd gone on to live a very different lifestyle to them. They'd been born in the scheme and would die in the scheme.

'Jesus Christ!' One man said. 'Here, Stevo. Look who it is!'

Billy recognised him as Marty Crawford, one of the lads he used to hang around with in his teens. He was also one of the lads on that holiday. As was Stevo.

'Boys,' Billy replied. 'Long time no see.'

'You're not kidding,' Stevo replied, patting Billy on the back as he exhaled cigarette smoke into the air. 'What brings you round these parts?'

Perfect, Billy thought. That question itself meant that Jez hadn't arrived yet.

'Not much, just catching up with some family,' Billy lied. 'How's things?'

'Awe you know, same shite different day,' Stevo replied. 'So, how's the police game treating you? Put away any bad bastards recently?'

Marty Crawford laughed and took a long draw on his cigarette. 'Here, were you involved in that post office shooting up the town last year?'

Billy shook his head. 'Sorry boys, I can't talk about my job.'

'Och, that's shite,' Stevo said. 'Good to see you, big man. You coming in? Can I get you a pint?'

Before Billy could answer, all three men turned as a taxi pulled up next to them. As the door opened and Jez Kennedy stepped out, Stevo and Marty fell silent.

'Boys,' Jez said before closing the door. Reaching in, he paid the driver and Billy watched as Stevo and Marty looked on in shock. They weren't expecting their old mate to turn up at the same time as Billy.

'What the fuck year is it, Stevo?' Marty asked. Billy detected a hint of nervousness in his tone.

'Ha,' Stevo laughed. 'Last time we were all together was Majorca, two thousand and one. Not that I can mind much of that holiday, right enough. Was smashed for two weeks straight.'

Good, Billy thought. That's the way it should be.

As the taxi pulled away from the pub, Jez held out his hand to Billy as a smile crept across his face. Billy shook it and returned the smile.

'Good to see you Jez,' Billy replied.

'What the *hell* are you doing back?' Marty said, as Jez shook the hands of the other men.

'Bit of this, bit of that. You know how it is.'

'Naw, we don't. You never came back from Majorca and we've not heard a peep out of you since. We've got a lot of catching up to do, boys. I'd better phone the missus and tell her the sesh is on and I'll not be home till tomorrow,' Stevo replied.

Marty and Stevo laughed. Jez smiled but shook his head.

'As much as I'd love a sesh, boys, I'm not here for long and I've got a lot of things to do.'

Marty and Stevo shrugged.

'Aye, fair enough, big man. I've got to go to the job centre to sign on anyway. If I'm not there by two they'll not give me my money. If you're still here when I get back, surely we can have a pint? Old times' sake?' Marty asked. The nerves in his tone were gone now.

Jez smiled. 'Aye.'

Stevo and Marty shook hands with Billy and Jez before disappearing across the road and heading into the bookies. Billy wondered if Marty spent all his dole money at the bookies and the pub. He certainly had the glowing red nose to prove a lot of his cash went on booze.

'So, shall we?' Jez said, motioning towards the entrance of the pub.

Billy stepped inside his old local and even though he'd heard that the place hadn't changed, he hadn't expected to feel like he was walking back in time. The walls had the same yellowing tinge, the dark mahogany wooden beams still stretched across the ceiling. The same old village images hung in dusty frames that could be the same age as the pub itself. But when he turned towards the bar, he couldn't quite believe that the same person was stood there, cleaning glasses and pulling pints.

'Jeanie *still* works here?' Billy said in wonder.

'Bloody hell, she'll die with this place,' Jez whispered. Billy couldn't help but laugh.

'What you having?' Billy asked Jez.

'Pint. Peroni if they've got it on draught?'

'In here? If the décor and the bar staff are the same after twenty years, then I doubt you're getting that. At best I'd say you're getting Tennents on draught,' Billy replied as he pulled his wallet out of his pocket.

'Get me a bottle then. I'll grab us a table.'

Jez moved towards the seating area and found a quiet spot in the back corner. Billy stood at the bar, waiting for Jeanie to serve him and wondered if she would recognise him.

'What can I get you?' she asked.

'Two bottles of Peroni, Jeanie.'

Her eyes didn't flicker at the mention of her name. Instead, she fetched the beer and took Billy's cash. Carrying the beers to the table, Billy sat down across from Jez and passed him a bottle.

'Cheers,' Jez said, taking a large gulp. 'So, how's things?'

'Aye, good. And you?'

Jez nodded and it was clear they were both feeling the tension of having been separated for so long, with such a big secret hanging between them. Billy couldn't stand it.

'Just get to the point, Jez. What you after?'

Jez gave a wry smile. 'You know what I'm after. The bastard fooled me, fooled the lot of us over in Spain and I'll be fucked if he gets away with it. He has one hundred grand of my cash and I want it back. But worst of all, he took my ma's wedding ring, thieving little bastard. I want info on Woods. I need to know where he is.'

Billy took a breath and shook his head. Straight to the point then, Billy thought. 'You know I can't do that, Jez. If I find that information for you and he turns up dead, how's that going to look? Folk around here aren't stupid. They've seen us together now. They know who you are, what you do. They know what I do, for Christ's sake. The connection would be made before this Woods character even took his last breath. It's police corruption, pure and simple. Sorry but I just can't help you.'

'Funny that. You were quite happy for me to help you out back in the day when you killed that lad from London. You remember, don't you? How you stamped on his head? How I got rid of the body – sorry I meant how we, as in me, Marty and Stevo, got rid of the body. And I took care of the footage from the club, made sure you were covered? Don't you think you owe me a favour?'

And there it was. The very reason that Billy wouldn't be able to say no. But he had to. He couldn't put the investigation at risk. It would come back to him. He'd be done with perverting the course of justice.

Billy shook his head. 'Yes, I *do* remember. And yes, I'm always grateful. You think I don't regret what I did that night? You think I don't regret taking those drugs, getting off my face and killing someone? I didn't ask you to help me, Jez. You did it because we were like brothers. But you couldn't handle the fact that I got my shit together and chose the career I did. I know you never approved of my choice, that you'd have preferred I was into the life you live. It's not me, Jez. That night wasn't me. I was off my face on drugs and you've been planning on using it against me ever since. Tell me, are you going to throw Marty and Stevo under the bus too? Aren't their lives shit enough here without sending them to jail because of something we all did?'

Jez shook his head, ran his tongue across the front of his teeth. He was angry that Billy wasn't backing down. But he would use that anger to get what he wanted. Billy knew how Jez worked.

'Och, like Marty and Stevo will even remember. They were just as fucked up as you were that night. They'll have drunk so much over the years that their cells will be so fried they'll remember fuck all from that night. But you do.'

Billy said nothing, just sipped his beer quietly. How could Jez think that they wouldn't remember moving a body? That was probably one of the reasons they were in such a state these days. No jobs. Alcoholics. He only had to look at their noses and the state of their clothes to know they were in a bad way. And how had they felt about being part of it back then? Jez wouldn't have given a toss, so long and he and Billy were in the clear. Billy felt like shit as he thought about how he'd played his part in not only killing a man, but potentially wrecking the futures of two others. He sensed that Jez shared no part in his guilt.

'Fuck Marty and Stevo. They were just handymen back then. Come on, Billy. We were like brothers growing up. We lived together, remember? You needed me that night and I was there for you. I need you *now*, Billy. This isn't some little thing. Cole Woods has taken the piss right out of me. I can't let him get away with that. Now, I know he's here. I know you have information on his whereabouts. I don't need anything else. Just a location. That's all. Then we can go our separate ways again. You won't have to see me again.' Jez paused for a long moment and Billy knew there was something else coming that he wasn't going to like. '*Unless* you want that CCTV footage of what you did that night to fall into the lap of your boss. Or the press?'

He felt his jaw fall open, almost touching his chest.

'Tell me you're joking?'

'Do I look like I'm fucking joking? You don't think for one minute I didn't take out some kind of insurance on myself that night, Billy? Come on, what do you take me for? I made sure that I was covered if I ever needed to be.'

Billy's stomach felt like it had dropped out of his arse. How could Jez do this? Even back then he was thinking about himself.

'But you'd be implicating yourself, too?'

'No, I wouldn't. I've fixed a copy that leaves me out of it.'

'I can't fucking believe you. Why? We were best mates. Brothers. Why back then did you think that you would need to use it against me?'

'It wasn't about using it against you. It was about using it for myself. It's not personal. It's business.'

'Fuck off, Jez, *business*,' Billy spat. 'You wouldn't dare do this to me.' His words sounded powerless as he said them. Would Jez really destroy him just to get his hands on Cole Woods? Jez wasn't one to be messed with. Never had been. When they were teenagers, the majority of the lads at school were either scared of Jez or wanted to be in his gang just to stay on the right side of him. But Billy knew the real Jez, the one that only he got to see. The softer side of the young lad who'd lost his parents too young. Maybe that side of him had disappeared over the years.

'Try me,' Jez replied, resting back on the seat and taking another large gulp of beer. 'Just try me.'

He searched his mind quickly for ways that he could sort this. The first thing that came to mind was to destroy the evidence that Jez had. But he had no way of knowing where it was. He knew it would be in Spain, but where? His house? One of his businesses? And how many copies would there be? Surely Jez wouldn't be stupid enough not to have copied the original?

Billy felt sick. This could end his career, see him go to prison if Jez followed through on his threat. Being an ex-copper in prison would mean living out the rest of his days in hell. There had to be a way out of this.

Of course there was a way out of it. Bring Cole Woods in before Jez did. They were both looking for the same guy. Billy couldn't allow himself to become involved in the bad blood between the two. He was part of a police operation to bring

Cole Woods down. Yes, if Jez got to Cole first then the world would be rid of the scumbag, but in Billy's line of work, legal justice was the only way. And if he got to Cole first, had enough evidence to prosecute him, then Jez wouldn't have to grass him up. Would he?

Chapter Forty

Arabella stood by the door of the salon and stared out at the street. Still no sign of Roxanne. She was over an hour late. After what had happened last night, Arabella had thought Roxanne would have been by her side a lot quicker than this.

'Are you okay, Arabella?' Scarlett asked. 'You don't seem yourself.'

Arabella shot Scarlett a look. 'How would you know? You don't know anything about me.'

Scarlett's eyes widened, seemingly shocked by Arabella's outburst.

'Sorry,' she said, throwing her hands over her face. 'That was out of order. Yes, thank you. I'm fine.'

Her apology didn't seem to take the sting out of Arabella's words, because Scarlett moved away from the reception desk and headed for the kitchen at the back of the salon.

Sighing, Arabella pulled her phone out of the back pocket of her jeans and glared at the screen. Still no reply from Roxanne. No message to say she was running late. Nothing. Where the *hell* was she?

Glancing up, she looked down the street again. Still no sign. Then her phone rang. She answered it without registering the name on the screen.

'Roxanne?'

'Yes, it's me. I'm on my way. Got held up. Sorry, it's a business venture. I promise you I'll be there in the next fifteen minutes. But do you want to go somewhere more private to talk?'

Arabella bit on her bottom lip to stop herself from crying. How was this happening? What the hell was she supposed to do? Her nerves were shot and she wasn't sure how much longer she was going to be able to hold in the fact that she had murdered someone last night.

'Can we go to yours? Eddie is asleep at mine. He didn't come home until just a few hours ago. Is Jake rough?'

'Nope. Fresh as a daisy. I seriously don't know how he does it,' Roxanne replied. 'Look, if it's easier why don't you just come straight to me? It's probably best we don't talk about this around other people.'

Roxanne went quiet and Arabella felt like she was going to explode. 'Then why didn't you just tell me that when I messaged you this morning?'

'Calm down,' Roxanne replied. 'There's no need to get so stressed. I said I'd sorted it. I'll text you my address and you can come straight here. Okay?'

'Fine,' Arabella said, sighing loudly before she hung up. She grabbed her coat from behind the reception desk. Calling out to the stylists, she said, 'Tell Scarlett I'm away. I've got something to do and I'll be back later.'

They smiled and waved her off over the sound of blow dryers and the radio playing in the background, blissfully unaware that their new employer was a cold-blooded killer.

–

The buzzer sounded and Arabella stepped into the building. The place wasn't as glamourous as she'd thought it would be. She'd expected something a little less dingy. As she climbed the stairs, she decided to breathe through her mouth to block out the stench. Someone was either smoking, or growing grass somewhere in the building. The sweet smell was so strong, she could taste it on her tongue.

Rounding the corner onto the first floor, Arabella noted that Roxanne had left the front door open for her. Music played from somewhere inside the flat.

'Rox?' She called out.

'In the kitchen. Just come in,' her friend replied. She sounded as though she didn't have a care in the world. How could she be so calm after what had happened in the early hours?

A thought struck her then. Arabella really didn't know Roxanne very well. They'd spent ten months together. Not even a full year. Roxanne had been inside for ten years for GBH among other things. Was this the kind of person she really wanted to be associating herself with on the outside? Roxanne was the kind of person that Arabella had been around when she got herself into trouble. Although it was too late to back out of this friendship now. Roxanne had sorted out her problem last night. She'd have that hanging over her for the rest of her life. She couldn't very well turn around and tell Roxanne that she'd changed her mind about being friends with her. Arabella felt suddenly trapped.

Stepping into the flat, Arabella located the kitchen at the end of the long hallway. The music got louder the closer she edged to the door and when she opened it, Roxanne was dancing on the spot as she poured water from the kettle into a mug.

'You want one?' She spun to face Arabella, a smile plastered across her face.

'No. I don't want tea. Why are you so *fucking* calm? It's not normal. Do you have any idea how I'm feeling right now? I went out to check that path after you left. The police were there, forensics. They'd cordoned off the walkway. There were crowds of people, talking about what could have happened. Roxanne, the press will be all over this. And you're dancing around in your *fucking* pyjamas, making tea. Seriously Roxanne, what the fuck?'

Roxanne stopped, her smiled faded. She placed the mug back on the counter and moved towards Arabella.

'Why did you go down there? You didn't have to do that. I told you I took care of it.'

'Yes, you did. But it seems as though you didn't, Rox because there were police *everywhere*.'

'You think I can just make a body magically disappear? Ha,' she laughed. 'I might have my ways but I'm not a magician. I put him in the river, Arabella. Shoved rocks in his jacket pocket so he'd sink. I didn't say that I was able to make him disintegrate. The water will have washed away your DNA and I've already told you that there will be no evidence to lead the police to your door. Just trust me on this.'

'You know that for a fact? That my DNA will have washed away?' Arabella asked, once again silently questioning herself as to who Roxanne really was.

'Well, no. But you have to trust me. I've got your back, Arabella. I wouldn't let anything happen to you. You're a good girl at heart. You've had a shitty upbringing and that wasn't your fault. You're like a wee sister to me. You'll be fine, the polis won't come back to you on this.'

Arabella eyed her friend. She'd never heard anyone refer to her as a good girl, or a wee sister. It softened her suspicion. 'You promise?'

'Come here,' Rox said, opening her arms. Arabella went to her and allowed herself to relax. '*Of course* I promise.'

'Thank you,' Arabella said, her voice cracking.

The pair sat down at the table and Arabella felt the tension on her shoulders begin to loosen. But she couldn't get the images of the crowds out of her head. The police would be all over this; the press would be all over it. People out there would be looking for justice for a family member. She'd taken someone's life. How could she have done it?

'You'll get through this, Arabella. I know what I'm doing.'

Arabella frowned. 'What do you mean, you know what you're doing?'

'Arabella?' Roxanne smirked. 'I didn't go to prison for ten years because I stole a packet of crisps. I'm a criminal. I know how to conceal things from the police, I know how to make problems go away. Jake and I both do. And I have done that for you. You just have to *trust* me, ask no questions and you will be fine. This will disappear if you just do as I say. Okay?'

Arabella glared at Roxanne. 'But what if—'

'Ah,' Roxanne interrupted, wagging her finger. 'I said no questions. Just do what I say and all this will disappear. Now, how about that tea? Or coffee?'

Arabella nodded and Roxanne got to her feet, moving towards the counter.

Ask no questions? But she had a ton of questions that she needed answered. Did Jake know about what happened? What exactly had she done to keep Arabella from conviction? Got rid of the rock that had killed him, yes. But what about CCTV? Eye witnesses? Surely Roxanne couldn't stop all of those things from getting in the way of Arabella being convicted?

'Sugar?' Roxanne asked, suddenly pulling Arabella from her thoughts.

'Actually, can you make mine an Irish coffee? I need something stronger than sugar.'

Roxanne laughed. 'Even after last night's cocktails, shots and fuck knows how much prosecco? You're hardcore, lady. One Irish coffee coming up. Whisky okay?'

'Whatever you've got. I don't care,' Arabella said, turning to look out the window.

She noted the car that was parked across the road. There was a man sitting in the driver seat, staring up at the kitchen window. When she made eye contact with him, he pulled the sun visor down. She kept an eye on him, watched how he busied himself. He put the phone to his ear. The visor went back up and the man stared straight at her, before pulling the car out of the space and heading up the road behind the flat.

'Here you go,' Roxanne said, placing a mug on the table in front of her. 'Get that down you. You'll feel much better.'

'Did you see that car?'

'What car?' Roxanne looked out of the window.

'There was a man inside, staring up here. He was looking straight at me,' Arabella said.

Roxanne raised a brow. 'The flat above us is up for sale. It's probably the estate agent or a buyer. Seriously Arabella, you need to get a grip and stop being so paranoid.'

Arabella lifted the mug. 'Erm, I have every right. I killed someone and can't remember a single thing about it.'

'Yeah,' Roxanne said. 'And if you don't stop going on about it and acting suspicious, people are going to start to notice that something's wrong. So, do yourself a favour and shut up. I don't mean to sound harsh but you do need to keep your mouth shut, Arabella. It's not just you involved. I'm an accomplice. Never mind you not wanting to go back to prison, I'd prefer I didn't, either.'

Roxanne was right. Arabella had to pull herself together. But the question was, could she? Could what she'd done be pushed to the back of her mind? Could she pretend nothing had happened? The feeling of an impending panic attack was her answer. Tears of terror sprung to her eyes as she thought about the possible consequences of her actions. Prison. But not for a miniscule ten months this time. They'd throw away the key for what she'd done to that man.

Chapter Forty-One

'Fuck me,' Eddie said. He stared wide-eyed at the small room and whistled loudly. He'd never seen anything like it in his life.

Drugs packages, piled on top of one another, halfway up the wall.

'This is what is going to make us fucking rich, Ed,' Cole said. 'All we need is your vans and we'll be raking it in before the end of the month. I'm telling you, this stuff is like gold dust.'

Eddie turned to look at Jake. He raised a brow but stayed quiet.

'So what we talking here?' Eddie asked, noting how wired Cole seemed to be. 'How much is all this worth?'

'Close to a few hundred grand,' Cole said, lowering his tone. He winked, as though he'd just given Eddie a top tip on the horses. 'And we could earn so much more, Eddie. So much more just by selling this lot.'

'Fuck,' was all Eddie managed. 'How the hell have you managed this without the police sniffing around?'

'I'm resourceful. Discreet. Know a man who had a super-market van and he delivered them in parts.' Cole smiled. Eddie was impressed. 'But he's moved away now, away up to Aberdeen. Shame really. It would have been a good way to move all this.'

He watched as Cole moved towards the bags sitting along the back wall. Eddie was shocked by how much was there and a little apprehensive about the risks involved. Getting caught with just one of those bags could lead to a lengthy prison sentence. Did he really need to do this? He had a successful business. A good life. But there was a little voice in the back of his head, a whisper that no one else could hear, telling him that his life was boring, predictable. His missus had more balls than he did, which was why she'd ended up in prison in the first place. If it hadn't been for her going to jail, then he would never have met Jake. Never have met Cole. A case of serendipity. A chance meeting that could lead to huge benefits.

Cole picked up one of the bags and just by looking at it, Eddie could tell it was heavy. He was surprised to see that the bag itself was an Aldi bag. Most of them were.

'We've got the best of gear, Ed. I'm talking opiates, stimulants, the lot,' Cole said.

Eddie nodded. 'What kind?'

'Usual street stuff: heroin, cocaine, speed, cannabis.' Cole placed the bag back on the floor and rubbed his hands together, laughing to himself. 'The streets of this city are fucking crawling with people looking to get their hands on this stuff. Not just in Glasgow. I've seen it down south too. People will spend all night on the phone at a party trying to get a hold of someone to get them something to help keep them going into the small hours. It's all about demand and we have the means to supply it.'

'How the hell did you get hold of all that?' Eddie asked.

Cole shot him a look. 'That, my friend, is none of your concern. But if you must know, I know someone who knows someone. All I need from you is to take care of the distribution. If you can do that, you get your cut.'

Eddie was up for this. He had the vans. Could literally deliver the goods. There was decent money involved here, a good few hundred grand. He'd be stupid not to take up the opportunity. If it meant an even better way of life for him and Arabella then he would do it. He'd been stupid when she was in prison. Being unfaithful was fun but not worth the hassle. It was partly why he'd bought the salon, a way of paying off his guilt. The only thing concerning Eddie now was who else was involved. Cole had said that the drugs came from someone else, somewhere else. Another source.

'I made a deal with you, Cole. You and Jake. If I'm working for someone else, then I need to know who. I can't go into this blind, especially when I'm putting my legit business on the line.'

Cole smiled. 'You don't work for anyone else, just me and Jakey boy here. We're the top dogs in this.'

Eddie wasn't sure he believed Cole. He was a right dodgy bastard and if Eddie was honest with himself, he knew nothing about him or Jake. He'd shaken on a deal while he was off his face and he had a feeling that he wouldn't have the option to change his mind now. Not that he was planning to do so. The money aspect outweighed any doubt he had in his mind about going ahead with the job. Maybe he'd only do one, make a small fortune and never have to do it again. Yes, that's what he'd do.

'Arabella can't know anything about this, boys.' Eddie said.

'We won't say nothing, will we, Jakey boy? Good at keeping a secret, aint ya?'

Eddie noticed how Jake drew his eyes off Cole.

'Aye, lips sealed,' Jake said, his tone sparking in the air. Cole chose to pretend he hadn't noticed.

'No worries, mate. I've got potential for another base. So I could double our profits. But for now, Ed, I'll tell you to keep your head low. Do your thing and I'll be in touch. Got it?'

Eddie nodded and Cole smiled.

'Got to get a shift on. I've got more business to attend to,' Cole smiled.

Eddie and Jake followed him out of his flat and watched as he walked along the street and headed into the bookies. Eddie shook his head.

'Why do you let him talk to you like that, Jake?'

'I don't let him talk to me like anything,' Jake replied sharply.

'Alright mate,' Eddie said, holding his hands up in mock defeat. Eddie knew when to keep his mouth shut. He hardly knew these men, didn't want to make something out of nothing if there was serious cash involved. All he had to do was get on with the job and earn the cash and keep his nose out of whatever was going on between Jake and Cole. The only thing he had to worry about was keeping Arabella in the dark.

Chapter Forty-Two

'Oi,' Jake shouted, catching up to Cole as he walked along the main road in Maryhill. 'I want a word.'

'You can have two. Fuck off. I've got things to get on with,' Cole laughed, only half turning in response to Jake.

'Nah,' Jake replied, grabbing hold of Cole's sleeve and pulling him round to face him. 'I said I want a word and I want it now.'

Cole shrugged Jake off and stopped walking. He had a mischievous look on his face, a glint in his stare. 'Go on then.'

'Where do you get off, speaking to me like that in front of Eddie? You think I'm just going to put up with it?' Jake said, not allowing his nerves to get the better of him.

'I *know* you'll put up with it, Jake. Are you forgetting what I did for you? Are you forgetting that the reason you're still walking around, free as a fucking bird, is because of me? You could have been banged up just like your missus, for longer than you could have ever imagined because of what you did. I stopped that from happening. Do you really want me to start talking? Tell people that Jakey boy likes a bit of BDSM and during a wild sex game down in London when your missus was in the nick, you got a bit carried away and done someone in? Nah, I didn't think so. You owe me, you owe me big bollocks and if you think I'll ever forget that then there's something seriously wrong with that nut of yours.' Cole jabbed his finger into Jake's temple.

Jake stepped back, pulling away from Cole. 'You think I've forgotten that you helped me out? I *know* I owe you, that's why

I agreed to this fucking job. You think I'd be doing this if I didn't have to?'

Cole spat out a laugh. 'You think one job is going to pay off what I did for you? No chance. I own you now, Jakey boy, and I will own you for the rest of your sorry little fucking life. You think you're a gangster? You think you and Roxanne are the ones people will be scared to walk past in the street? You two haven't got a fucking patch on me, Jake. And I'll make sure everyone fucking well knows it. I'll be sure to tell that big stunner of yours about your little sex fetish gone wrong.'

Jake breathed through his nose, gritted his teeth. Woods really was so sure of himself, wasn't he? He may well be a dodgy guy, someone people would be wary of, but he was no Glasgow boy. He was a Londoner, and he had no idea what the streets of Glasgow would do to him if Jake or Roxanne gave the word. Jake still knew some lads from back in his scheme days. He could ask around, have Cole sorted without question. But it was still a risk. If Roxanne ever found out about his infidelity, it would kill her. It would kill both of them.

'Fuck up, Cole. I'm not scared of you.'

Cole stepped forward. 'Well, you fucking well should be.'

'You know what, Cole,' Jake started. 'You go ahead and tell her. Tell the whole world if you want to. She won't believe you. No one will. You think people will believe you? A gangster who's hooked on his own coke, a gambling addict? Someone who would sell their own fucking granny to get what they want?'

He tried to hide it, but Jake could see the shock written all over Cole's face. He wasn't expecting Jake to say that.

'I aint no addict. But I'll tell you what I am. I'm someone who never forgets to take out an insurance policy. I've already lost enough in my life because I didn't have all the facts to hand. I will never make that mistake again.'

Jake shook his head in confusion. Whatever that meant, it was something from before Jake's time. Cole took his phone out, tapped on the screen and turned it so that Jake had nowhere else to look but at it. He watched the video footage play out, just how he remembered it. It was consensual, they'd both wanted it. A game of asphyxiation gone wrong. He watched himself, heard his own laboured breaths as he fell to his knees, muttering that it was an accident. He hadn't meant it. Hadn't planned it. Jake had been pushed to his limit. It was only ever meant to be a bit of fun. Just sex. It had turned into something tragic that he could never change. The fact that Jake played the scene over and over in his head every day since it'd happened was bad enough, but to know that Cole had footage… The guy was sick in the head.

Grabbing for the phone, Jake almost fell forward as Cole pulled it from his reach. 'Ah, ah, ah,' he wagged his finger. 'You can't have what isn't yours, Jakey boy.'

'You're a fucking bastard, Woods. I'll have you for this.'

'Ha, I don't think so.' Cole laughed menacingly. 'I'm not as thick as you might think, Jake. Far from it. You see, I set up cameras for all the staff I have working for me on a job. None of them know about it, but it's necessary. It means that if someone fucks me over, or if something goes wrong with someone, I have leverage on them. But you're the first person that I've ever caught getting up to something he shouldn't have. I have this video footage backed up on as many devices as you can imagine. USB sticks, memory cards, hard drives. You name it, it's on there. This is my lifeline to make sure you stick to your end of the deal. You need to make sure that you secure that base for my drugs. You need to make sure your dealers will sell as much as physically possible, like you said they would. I don't want your excuses. If you step out of line, do or say anything that could jeopardise me or the job then I'm going to make sure your entire life comes crashing down around your ears and I will make sure I am there for episode two.' Cole waved the phone in front of Jake's face. 'Then I'll make sure that the police know exactly where to find your victim's remains. You've got to remember, Jake, I'm a hardened criminal. I'm clever and resourceful. I've never been caught, hence why I don't have a record. It's your DNA and prints all over that body. Your semen inside them. That, along with the video evidence... well, you're a prosecutor's dream, aren't you?'

Jake's heart thundered inside his chest and his breath shortened. Cole had him exactly where he wanted him. There really was no other way. He had to do what Cole said. If he didn't, he'd lose everything. Cole wasn't stupid, he'd have backed up the back up of the incriminating footage on Jake. Even if Jake did choose to take Cole out like he'd already thought about, he suspected Cole would have a way of getting the footage to the police even from the grave. Someone would be paid to do it, in the event of Cole's death.

Chapter Forty-Three

A week had passed since it had happened. A week since she'd brutally murdered someone. The media had reported him as a forty-six-year-old man who'd been living in and out of hostels for the best part of twenty years. No family. No friends. A loner. That made Arabella feel worse than ever. Now there was a character, a real person behind the crime she had committed.

The police hadn't shown up. The chat around the area had died down and the gossip had moved on to something else. She didn't know how to feel about that. Relieved that she might just get away with it? Or ashamed and disgusted with herself? She hadn't looked in the mirror since the morning after. Not properly. She couldn't look herself in the eye. If it wasn't for the salon, she was sure she'd have lost the plot by now. The place had kept her distracted as much as possible. She'd wanted to distance herself from Roxanne to keep her mind from what had happened, but hadn't managed to do so. Eddie had spent more and more time at the office. The business had picked up a lot in the last few days and Eddie had said he wanted to be there to oversee everything.

Arabella flicked through the appointment book as she sat at the front of the salon. The girls were all busy with clients, the sound of hairdryers blasting hot air around and music playing from the radio reminding her of how she'd felt the day she was getting ready for her end of year high school dance. A time Arabella would much rather forget.

'Come on Arabella, you know you want some,' Shona had said, waving the bottle of vodka under her nose.

Arabella had tried to laugh it off, she remembered. 'No thanks. That stuff is rank.'

'Och, are you fear't the teacher will suspend you or something? They're probably all be on it too. Come on, you'll be the only one not doing it. You want to feel left out?'

Arabella had shot Shona a look before grabbing the bottle from her hand. She didn't want to feel left out. That was the worst feeling, not being part of things. She'd do anything to make herself fit in because it helped to distance her from the memories of feeling rejected and let down by her alcoholic mother, the person who ultimately was the cause of Arabella struggling to create relationships with others throughout her entire life.

Unscrewing the lid, Arabella took a large mouthful and suppressed the urge to gag as the rancid liquid burned its way down to her stomach.

'Nice one,' Shona said, pulling out a small bag of coke from her bra. 'Now for a line.'

'No thanks,' Arabella had said. 'I'll stick with the voddy.'

Shona and some of the other girls started to laugh. 'Aw, little care home girl doesn't want to do drugs. Who you trying to kid, think you're a Goody Two-Shoes or something?' one of the girls said.

Arabella felt so belittled it made her angry but she didn't show it.

'Goody Two-Shoes kids don't end up in care,' Arabella said, reaching out her hand and taking the small bag of powder from Shona.

She smiled at Arabella then. 'Honestly, you're a laugh when you just join in, Arabella. You should just loosen yourself up all the time.'

That was how these friendships had formed, if she could even call them that. Arabella had friends so long as she went with the crowd. If she did the same as them, they didn't take the piss out of her. They'd been standing in the school toilets when one of the female teachers came in to check on the girls. Shona pulled more bags of coke out of her bra and shoved them into Arabella's bag.

'What are you doing?' Arabella hissed, trying to give them back to her.

'Unless you want a kicking, keep your mouth shut,' Shona had said.

Luckily the teacher hadn't searched any of them. Arabella knew at that point that she wasn't friends with any of these girls. They were using her. She just wasn't friendship material and people would only give her the time of day if she did what they told her to.

Fast-forward into her adult years and she'd realised that Shona was the same person now as she was back then. She'd used Arabella and Arabella had allowed her to. She'd made a right mess of her life. Before she'd gone to prison, she'd been working a few shifts for Eddie, answering phones and cleaning the offices. She'd got a job in a salon but lost it quickly when she'd failed to show up for a few shifts because she'd had a hangover after spending time with these people the night before; the 'friends' who'd ultimately been the cause of her prison sentence. Yes, she'd had Eddie at home, but he wasn't a friend. She'd needed friends, a group she could fit in with. In truth, she knew she'd never fit in with anyone. Eddie had commented on how often she'd be out with them and not him, but Arabella hadn't toned it down until it was too late. Now things were finally going in the right direction. Or at least they had been. Not so long ago, Arabella had thought she'd never get to live a life like this. Being in prison wasn't exactly good for the CV and she had worried that she'd struggle to get a job. Not in a million years could she have imagined that Eddie would have bought her a salon. Not in a million years did she think she'd have murdered a complete stranger.

The phone rang, pulling her from her thoughts.

'Hair Envy, Glasgow,' Arabella answered. She was getting better at this by the day. And so she should; she did own the place after all.

'Hey, it's me,' Eddie's voice came from the other end of the line. 'How's things going?'

'Oh hi,' she said, surprised to hear from him. 'Yeah, nothing much to report. I'm just manning the phones while the girls get on with their clients. I suppose I have to since Scarlett's done a bunk.'

'Scarlett isn't at work?' Eddie asked.

'No. She hasn't turned up. The girls say it's not like her. I've tried to call her but her mobile is switched off.'

Eddie started to speak but Arabella didn't hear what he was saying with the commotion going on at the front door of the salon. A woman had appeared. Barely a woman, a young girl in fact and she was pregnant. She couldn't be older than sixteen, Arabella thought. She looked ill. Her face was pale and beads of sweat trickled down between her brows. She seemed out of breath. She wasn't alone.

'Arabella, can you help?' Roxanne said, holding the young girl up. 'I found her on the street like this. I think she's in labour.'

'Bloody hell,' Arabella said a little too loudly. All of the stylists and clients turned to see what all the fuss was about. 'Eddie, I have to go. I'll call you back.'

Hanging up the phone, Arabella rushed around to the other side of the desk and stood in front of her friend and the young girl.

'I'll call an ambulance,' Arabella said.

'No, I'm not in labour. I just need a glass of water,' she said, tears pouring down her cheeks. She looked like she was in pain, Arabella thought.

Roxanne looked on at Arabella, panic-stricken. 'Can we go through to the kitchen, let her sit down for a bit?'

Without saying a word, Arabella led them through the salon to the kitchen. Allowing them to go ahead of her, she followed them inside and closed the door, creating a private space away from prying eyes. The young girl was helped down onto a chair by Roxanne while Arabella grabbed a glass from the cupboard and filled it with water. Turning, she held it out to the girl who was now sobbing.

'Right, calm down, hen,' Roxanne said, her expression hardening. Arabella frowned at how harsh her friend sounded.

'Are you okay?' Arabella asked as the girl took the glass and held it tightly. 'Do you want me to phone someone for you?'

The girl stopped sobbing as though someone had flicked a switch. Her actions were robotic. She looked up at Arabella, shook her head. Her expression was neutral, but Arabella saw the fear in her eyes.

'Right, shirt off,' Roxanne said to the girl. Arabella's eyes widened in horror at the request.

'What?' Arabella said, but Roxanne ignored her, keeping her eyes on the girl. 'Wait a minute, Roxanne. What the hell is going on here? Why does she need to take her shirt off?'

The girl got to her feet slowly and silently pulled the shirt over her head. As Arabella took in the scene, she was as confused as she was horrified. A moment ago, this girl had looked like she was in labour. She was crying, terrified. Roxanne was helping her. But now?

Roxanne spun the girl round and began to untie the straps at the back, allowing the fake pregnancy bump to fall to the floor. Bending down, she picked it up and studied it. 'Good work, Stephanie. Good work indeed. Did you think this was real?' Roxanne turned to Arabella.

Arabella's eyes darted between her friend and the girl who'd just revealed that her pregnancy was fake. 'Did I think she was really pregnant? Are you kidding, Roxanne? What the *actual* fuck is going on here?'

Roxanne didn't respond as she opened up the inside of the suit and began pulling envelopes out. They were stuffed full, by the looks of them.

'Is that what I think it is?' Arabella asked, staring as Roxanne's hands went to work pulling the envelopes out.

'Arabella, just give me a second. I need to count this and get Steph here paid.'

Arabella scoffed, 'Are you two having a fucking laugh here? This isn't serious, is it?'

Stephanie stood in awkward silence in her jeans and bra, arms folded over her chest as she watched Roxanne check the envelopes she'd pulled out of the suit. Five, to be precise.

'Good girl, Stephanie. Right,' Roxanne opened one of them, took out a handful of notes, counted out one hundred pounds and shoved it into the girl's bra.

'Payday has come for you,' Roxanne said, smiling at Stephanie. 'Now, remember what we talked about?'

Stephanie nodded quickly as Roxanne shoved the pregnancy suit at her. Sliding it on, she turned so that Roxanne could strap her back in securely. 'Yes, you said I've to wait for a call for the next job.'

'Good girl. Keep that phone I gave you on you at all times. Make sure it's on loud and vibrate so you don't miss it. You answer, take instructions and do as you're told. Got it?'

'Am I fucking invisible here, Rox?' Arabella said, the words hissing through her teeth.

Roxanne tightened the suit, tugging hard on the straps before securing them. Stephanie expelled air and almost lost her balance, gripping the counter to support her. Roxanne said nothing.

'Right,' Arabella said, standing with her back to the door and folding her arms across her chest. 'You're not going anywhere until you explain what the fuck you've just dragged me into.'

Roxanne stopped pulling on the ties for the suit and Stephanie gave a sidelong glance before turning her back and putting her shirt back on.

Roxanne frowned, as though she had no idea what Arabella was talking about.

'Is this a problem?'

'Are you joking? You pull this girl in off the street and pull fuck knows how much money out of her fake pregnant belly and you think I'll not bat an eyelid?'

'It's only money, Arabella. It's not like I'm forcing a needle into her arm.' Roxanne's tone was how Arabella had always known it. Friendly. Straight to the point.

Arabella felt her eyes narrow, her brow crease. Was she over-reacting a little?

'Well, what's the money for? Where did it come from?' Arabella pushed.

Roxanne turned to Stephanie and gestured for her to leave. 'Mind now, that phone should be practically glued to your hand for the foreseeable.'

'No bother, Roxanne.'

At that, Stephanie gave Arabella a tight-lipped smile and headed out of the kitchen via the back door. Roxanne saw her out and Arabella waited for the door to be closed and for an explanation.

'Look. I'm doing this job. It's not exactly legit, but it's a job. Something to bring the cash in, you know? We don't all have a boyfriend to buy us a salon when we get out.'

Arabella felt instant embarrassment, like a spoiled brat. 'Well,' she continued to press. 'Can I ask what sort of job?'

'Some of the same of what I was doing before going to the jail. Shoplifting, wee bit of dealing. That sort of thing.'

'So that girl,' Arabella eyed the door. 'What's her role in all this?'

Roxanne smiled thinly. 'She works for me. And for Jake. This is our thing. Together. Like this place is yours and Eddie's.'

Arabella sighed, shook her head. 'Ed might own this place but he has nothing to do with the day-to-day running. To be fair, that's not even down to me. Scarlett does all that. Or at least she did until she done the off.'

Roxanne raised a brow but didn't comment about Scarlett. 'Look, I'm sorry. I didn't mean to startle you by bringing her in here. Stephanie, she's a good girl. She gets the job done, some of her mates help her out. I send out the list of goods, she gets hold of them, sells them and brings the cash back to me. Jake has a team working for him too. I just, well I didn't know where else to bring her. When I met up with her, she said the polis had been watching her. Or at least she thought they were. I panicked, made her pretend she was going into labour and before I knew it, I saw this place and thought you'd be alright with it. I should have checked with you first that it was okay.'

Arabella noticed the softness in her friend's eyes then. A silent apology to go with the explanation.

'It was a one-off, yeah?'

'Absolutely. I'll make sure that my shoplifting business doesn't cross over the threshold of Hair Envy again.'

Nodding, Arabella smiled. 'Good. Look, I don't mean this to sound harsh, but things have been pretty shitty for me the last week what with… well, you know what with. I just don't think I'm cut out for all this illegal shit. Ed bought me this place so I could start over. I don't want him thinking I'm falling back into something that's going to send me back to prison. I am so grateful for what you did, I really am, Rox. You'll never know how much. But I can't get involved in your shoplifting game.'

Roxanne opened up her arms and stepped forward. 'Then you don't have to. I promise. And I know how grateful you are for what I did for you, Arabella. You're not a bad person, you don't deserve to go to prison for what happened. The guy was a sleaze, you dealt with him the best way you knew how. You did it to keep us safe. I won't hold that against you, if anything I thank you for it.'

Arabella accepted Roxanne's open arms and hugged her best friend. Not just her best friend but her only friend. She didn't want to do anything to jeopardize that.

Chapter Forty-Four

Eddie sat in one of his vans outside the block of flats and stared up at the window. His hangover was kicking in now, and he needed something to take the edge off. Glancing out of the window to make sure there was no one around, he took the little bag of coke out from inside his pocket and poured some onto the back of his hand before snorting it. He didn't bother to use a rolled-up note. Seeing some residue left over on his skin, he licked the back of his hand. Almost immediately he felt less foggy.

He'd rung the number stored in his phone three times and there had been no answer. He had no choice but to go to the door and sort it out in person.

Getting out of the van, Eddie pointed the fob at the door and hit the lock button before heading into the building. He climbed two flights of stairs before reaching the door. Standing outside, he balled his fist and rattled the wooden surface.

'Fuck off,' he heard a voice from inside.

'We need to talk. Let me in for a minute, please?' he said, trying to make his tone sound calmer than he felt.

A few seconds passed and as he raised his fist to pound on the door again, he heard a click and it opened. Eddie stepped inside and closed the door behind him before making his way through to the lounge.

'Boys not in?' Eddie asked.

'They're at their grandparents' today,' Scarlett said. 'Not that it's any of your business.'

'Why aren't you at the salon today?' he asked, looking at Scarlett as she sat back on the sofa, sipping on a glass of wine. He looked down at his watch. It wasn't even midday yet. What the hell was she playing at?

'What's it to you?' she slurred, not meeting his eyes.

'Erm, I'm you're *employer* and you didn't show up to work. You didn't even let Arabella know you were taking the day off.'

Scarlett pulled a face that told Eddie this wasn't going to get resolved the way he'd hoped. Her eyes focused on the television but when Eddie looked over, he saw it was switched off.

'Look, Scarlett, I'm just going to be blunt with you here. You knew I was in a relationship when we first met. I told you straight up I had a girlfriend who was in prison. You said that didn't bother you, and that you wanted the same as I did. It was only ever sex with us, you knew that. So, I don't get why you're being so fucking unreasonable about this?'

Scarlett snapped up at him, getting to her feet in an instant, albeit swaying a little. 'You don't seriously think I'd want to work for you and that girlfriend of yours, knowing the company you keep? I mean, gangsters, Eddie. You think you're one, don't you? Wee Eddie the gangster.' She sniggered. Eddie bit his tongue. He didn't want to say anything about Jake or Roxanne and fuel her fire. When he didn't respond, she continued.

'You think I'm being unreasonable? Eddie, you *bought* my place of work. You could have at least given me advanced warning. How do you think it made me feel when I found out? All of a sudden you rock up to the salon with your bit of fucking skirt and tell me she's my new *boss*! And you think *I'm* the unreasonable one? You just came into my life and fucked everything up. I told you about my brother, you gave me a fucking shoulder to cry on and then you shat on me from the greatest of fucking heights. You should have pulled out of the sale when you realised I worked there.'

'It was too late by then, Scarlett. We went over everything and you said you were fine about it.'

Scarlett swayed again, her wine sloshing out of her glass and dripping onto Eddie's shoes. Glancing down at them, she sniggered and then before Eddie could stop her, she threw the remaining wine in the glass over his face.

'Well, I'm not. You're a selfish, self-centred fucker, Eddie Corrigan. You deserve everything that's coming to you.' She jabbed her finger into his chest and Eddie caught her wrist, squeezing it tight and shoving her down onto the couch.

'Shut your mouth, Scarlett.'

'Ha,' she laughed. 'What you going to do about it? Tell Arabella? Sorry, I should really be calling her Miss MacQueen. That's what you want me to call her, isn't it? She is my boss. Well, I wonder what my boss would think if I told her I was fucking her man when she was in prison?'

'I said, shut your mouth, Scarlett.'

'What, you think she wouldn't believe me? Come on then,' Scarlett grabbed her phone from the arm of the sofa. 'Let's give her a call and see what she has to say about it?'

Eddie lurched forward and grabbed the phone from her hand before launching it across the room. It slammed against the back wall and fell to the floor, the screen shattered to the point where it was unreadable.

Leaning down, he saw that the action had given Scarlett a fright. Her eyes glistened behind pooling tears.

'Now you listen to me, Scarlett. If you think I'm going to let you ruin what I have with Arabella then you're sadly mistaken. I'm not putting up with this shit.'

Tears spilled over her face. Eddie had never noticed how pathetic she looked until now. What had he been thinking, getting involved with her? At the time he'd thought it would be a laugh. Buying the salon hadn't been intended to upset Scarlett, he'd just seen an opportunity. It just so happened that he'd been involved with Scarlett beforehand.

'You're a bad bastard, Eddie. You know that? She needs to know what kind of man you really are. And I'm going to make sure she knows about what you got up to when she was behind bars. You don't get to do this to me, not anymore.' The words were hissed through the gaps in her teeth as she threw the wine glass at him.

At that point his anger began to cripple him. He couldn't let her do this. If she contacted Arabella, if she told her that he'd been having it off with Scarlett then bought the salon she was in charge of, he'd lose her.

'Shut up, Scarlett,' he said. 'You're drunk and I'm late. Get a grip of yourself, eh?'

'What? You think I won't do it? Go on then, try me,' Scarlett said, getting to her feet and heading towards the door.

'Where are you going?' Eddie followed her out to the hallway.

'I'm going to work, I'm going to tell her everything.'

Eddie rushed ahead of her, blocking the door so she couldn't get out. She stopped in front of him, her eyes bloodshot with tears. She hesitated and for a moment he thought she was going to relent. Go back to the lounge and finish her sad little bottle of wine. Then out of nowhere, she slapped him so hard his ears began to ring. It did little to knock him off balance, but the anger he felt was like a volcanic eruption.

He lifted his own hand in retaliation. Knocking her to the ground with a dull thud, he kneeled down over the top of her and grabbed a fistful of hair. Her mouth was bleeding but he chose to block it out.

'You'll be sorry you done that. You'll be sorry you ever *fucking* met me.'

Chapter Forty-Five

The terror inside had kept her cowering in the corner. She hadn't expected him to lose it the way he did. She'd never seen that side of him before, didn't think he had it in him to do something so violent. Yet here she was, balled up in the corner of her own living room.

Opening her eyes, she looked around and saw that he'd turned the place upside down. It could have been worse; he could have broken every bone in her body rather than the furniture. She'd thought he might, by the way he'd looked at her. The threat had been enough to make her back off. The words he'd said before shoving her out the way and beginning to trash her home. She was glad that was all he'd done. Although the way she'd crashed into the console table in the hall when he'd thrown her to the side exacerbated the pain she still felt in her ribs from Roxanne's attack. She'd got up and followed him into the living room, tried to stop him. But he'd gone into some kind of frenzy and there was no stopping him. Upturned furniture, broken mirrors and glass everywhere. It was over quickly, but she'd genuinely believed he would turn on her next so she'd cowered in a corner, trying to stay out of the way.

'Jesus,' Scarlett said as she attempted to get to her feet, surveying the mess. If she'd known this was the kind of man he was, she'd never have got involved with him in the first place.

Standing up, she ran a hand over her ribcage and winced. She'd need to get that seen to. But first she'd have to call the police. There was no way she was going to let him get away with this. Arabella needed to know what Eddie had been up to. Come to think of it, she needed to know what her new friend, Roxanne was capable of, too.

Looking around for her phone, she headed out to the hall. She couldn't remember what she'd done with it before Eddie had turned up. Everything was such a blur. She glanced up at the door and noticed that it was slightly ajar. He hadn't closed it properly when he'd left.

Reaching for the handle she went to close it but before she could, it swung open. She looked at the person standing in the doorway and frowned.

'What are you doing here?'

They didn't reply, just stepped inside and closed the door behind them. Scarlett's eyes moved down, noted the black gloved hands and returned to meet her unwelcome visitor's gaze.

White noise filled her head before the pain hit her. She fell to the floor, clutching her head. Her sight blurred before she could get a look at the weapon in the hand of her attacker. Then the white noise stopped. Everything stilled.

Chapter Forty-Six

Eddie watched as Cole and Jake sat down at the desk opposite him at Eddie's van hire centre. They were suited and booted, looking like real businessmen. Cole was normally in his designer clothes, DKNY jeans and Jack & Jones T-shirts. Even wearing casual clothes, he looked smart. Jake looked smarter than normal too, his attire much the same as Cole's on any other day.

Seeing them like this felt odd but Eddie didn't question it.

'Right Ed, let's talk business. I laid all my cards on the table, now show me yours,' Cole said, sitting back on the seat and raising his left leg over his right, resting the ankle on the knee.

Eddie was shaken after his encounter with Scarlett. It had only been an hour since it had happened. He wasn't going to let a little bitch like her ruin his chances of earning more money. This part of life was what he'd been craving for a long time. The affairs, the one-night stands, the occasional blow out on recreational drugs, the booze… it was all a pathway in search of something more.

'So I've got three vans that can be used; it just depends on what you want to do with them. Your stock, your call,' Eddie said, matching Cole's body language. 'They're often hired out to companies for delivery purposes. Small businesses like florists, bakers, that sort of thing. But big companies sometimes use us. Like Amazon, online retailers. They're all road legal.'

'You have drivers for me?' Cole asked, his eyebrow raised as if he wasn't interested in anything Eddie had just said.

'That wasn't part of the deal. I don't hire out drivers with the vans.'

Cole turned and glared at Jake. 'This guy having a laugh?'

'Cole, he's right. That wasn't part of the deal. Look, I know plenty of guys who would be looking to earn a bit of cash. I'll get in touch with some of the shoplifting mob and see who's up for it.'

Cole swung his chair side to side and Eddie noticed how the suit crumpled with the movement. This guy didn't just look good in a suit. He looked like a rough and ready bank manager.

'Fine, but make it quick. I don't want my drugs sitting in that flat any longer than necessary. I've got a list of orders waiting.'

Jake started saying something about the job, but Eddie had stopped listening when he caught sight of a bloodstain on the cuff of his shirt. He glanced up and saw that neither Jake nor Cole had seemed to notice.

'Let me know who and when your guys are free, Jakey boy. But make sure it's in the next forty-eight hours. I don't want my clients going elsewhere because there's a hold-up with dispatch.'

Jake nodded and he and Cole got to their feet. Eddie rose with them. 'Just let me know what the plan of action is, who will be picking up the vans and when.'

'Sound, mate,' Cole said. He reached over and held out his hand. Eddie raised his own to shake but Cole's eyes fell immediately to the bloodstained cuff.

'Nose bleed,' Eddie said almost too quickly.

'They're a bastard, eh?' Cole smiled. He held Eddie's gaze for a second longer than Eddie felt comfortable with. Did he suspect something? Maybe he wouldn't have if Eddie hadn't jumped in so quickly to defend himself against suspicion.

'Aye, get them all the time.'

Jake stood by the door and Cole moved out of the office. Before Jake followed him out, he turned and nodded at Eddie. 'You alright? You seem off.'

Eddie stared at him for a moment, not quite sure how to respond.

'That really a nose bleed?' Jake eyed Eddie's cuff. 'I mean, if you've done someone in then you might want to use one of your vans for disposal.'

Eddie glared at Jake who was smiling widely. 'Joke, Eddie. Fucking hell, man, you should smoke a joint or something. Don't worry about all this, it'll go smoothly. So long as you stay on the right side of Cole, you'll be fine and minted.'

Eddie's legs almost buckled beneath him at Jake's shit joke but he forced out a laugh. 'Very funny, Jake.'

Jake left the office and Eddie watched him and Cole through the window as they got into Jake's car. It drove along South Street towards the bus terminus and out of sight before he allowed himself to glance down at his cuff again. The sight of Scarlett's blood reminded him of the damage he'd caused. He should feel guiltier than he did, but she'd left him no choice. She was going to try to take him down, and in doing so she'd take Arabella down too. He couldn't let that happen. Who did Scarlett think she was? How dare she? He had to get home and burn that shirt *immediately*.

Grabbing his phone from the desk, Eddie slid his arms into his jacket, ensuring the bloodstain was out of sight before heading outside. Unlocking his car, Eddie reached for the handle when he heard a voice calling over to him.

'Eddie?'

Eddie turned and squinted in the sunshine. A man was walking towards him, a tall man. His hair was greying at the temples and his eyes crinkled at the edges. A punter looking to hire a van no doubt. Then he saw his face and the anger began to build.

'Not here, in the middle of broad fucking daylight,' Eddie said, just as he was about to climb into his car.

'I need a word. Need an update,' the man said.

'Aye, well, you'll have to wait.'

'Since when did you start calling the shots, Eddie?'

Eddie stepped back a little from the car and closed the door. 'I don't. But I do value my fucking safety, so if you want to talk to me it'll need to be somewhere discreet. Got it?'

The man reached into his breast pocket and produced an ID card. Eddie narrowed his eyes but could barely read the words.

'Do I have to remind you who you're talking to?' DS Billy Drysdale said.

Chapter Forty-Seven

Jez had decided to stay behind at the pub after Billy had left. It had been such a long time since he'd drunk in the dreary local, but there was something nostalgic about it. A feeling that took him back to his teens. He'd ended his time in Scotland on a bad note. He'd owed money to a local drug dealer and he'd been careful not to tell any of his mates before they'd jetted off to Majorca on their boys' holiday. It was one of the reasons he'd decided not to return home. Out of sight, out of mind. It was Billy who'd told Jez about the body that had been found up at the Dunmuir reservoir a few months later. An unsettled feeling had set in Jez's stomach. What if the police knew who did it? What if there were witnesses? Of course, Jez knew there weren't. He'd arranged to meet his dealer at the bottom of the road which led up to the reservoir. The guy was scum, a bit of a druggie himself. Now when Jez thought about it, he actually felt sorry for him. He was only out to make a bit of money. But that didn't excuse the fact that the guy had pulled a knife on him. It had been midnight, a time they'd both agreed on. Less people around, less chance of the police catching them. The road gates had been left open and the guy's old Vauxhall Nova, which looked like it was ready for the scrappy, was sitting in the small car park at the edge of the track road. He probably didn't even have a licence, or own the car. That was what it was like around the scheme where Jez and Billy had grown up.

Jez had walked along the back road to meet him. Diggo, his name was. Jez didn't know him as anything else until the news had identified him as Allan Diggins. A local down-and-out who was known for dealing class A drugs as well as motor theft. No one would miss him, which was just as well for Jez.

Jez had approached him and he remembered the distinct smell of sweat and cigarette smoke coming from Diggo's over-sized hoodie.

'Got my money, Jez?' Diggo had said. His breath had a bitter, disgusting odour and Jez wasn't even standing that close to him.

'Aye,' Jez had said. 'Well, not all of it.'

'What the fuck do you mean, not all of it? You owe me a hundred quid, Jez. I gave you a fucking extension the last time and I warned you it would be the last.'

Jez had noticed how Diggo's words had slurred. He'd been drinking. A good thing for Jez. It would mean that if need be, he could outrun him.

'Aye, well, I'm short. So, you'll have to take this now or wait for the full amount and I won't have that until next week.'

That was when Jez had noticed the blade slide out from Diggo's right sleeve.

'Ah, come on, Diggo. There's no need for that,' he'd said, taking a step back.

'And there's no need for you to tell me that I can't have what you owe. So, pay me in full right now or I'll fucking plug you. Got it?'

Jez had a few seconds to think. It was a fight or flight situation. One he could never have imagined he'd have to face, especially not against someone like Diggo, the junkie dealer, as he was known. It was a wonder he wasn't dead already. Rumour had it that he'd got high on some of the stash he was dealing out for someone higher than him and that he owed a shit ton of money himself. That was likely the reason he was pulling a blade on Jez, to make sure he paid up so that he could pay off his own debts.

Jez picked the option to fight. He wasn't going to go down against someone like Diggo. No chance. Jez was used to viol-ence and aggression, having grown up in the scheme. Getting into fights was a way of surviving. Jez and the boys didn't class themselves as a gang, but society did. Getting into scraps for territory, drugs, booze and girls was just a way of life. From time to time, there was an all-out scheme war. He wasn't scared to get into this with Diggo. So, Jez had balled his fists and jerked his body towards Diggo so quickly that he dropped the blade in fright. Jez launched himself at him with a swift uppercut, knocking him to the ground. He kicked the knife and it skittered far enough away that Diggo would have to fight with his bare hands.

'Get up, you fucking prick. You think you can pull a blade on me and get away with it?'

Diggo looked up at Jez through watery eyes as blood poured from his mouth. He said nothing but got to his feet, his body in a defensive stance before taking a swing at Jez who stood back and watched as Diggo stumbled forward and fell at his feet.

Jez saw an opportunity to finish the debacle and lifted his foot and brought it crashing down on the back of Diggo's head. He raised it again, and again. He stopped, watching for signs of movement, signs of life from Diggo as he lay face down on the track road. The back of his head was a bloodied mess and when Jez looked at his shoes, they too were covered in Diggo's brain matter, crimson red in colour. The metallic stench of blood mixed with Diggo's own rancid body odour made Jez gag.

He stood for a moment, wondering what to do. He couldn't walk away and leave Diggo lying there to be found. That could lead the police straight to him. Jez knew how forensics worked; he could be traced by a single footprint. Especially if the boot that matched the print was covered in blood. He'd have to get rid of them. But first, he had to get rid of Diggo.

Eyeing Diggo's shitty Nova, he bent down and searched his pockets for the car key. Locating it, he opened the boot of the car and wondered if he'd have the strength to drag Diggo's dead weight the few feet down the track, let alone lift it into the car. Would his body even fit? It would just have to. Jez wasn't going to let Diggo ruin his life, dead or alive.

Jez turned Diggo over and slid his hands under his arms. He pulled the body towards the car, the sound of the gravel underfoot deafening. There were no cars in sight; not a sound could be heard. Jez was safe to do this but he had to be quick.

He managed to haul Diggo into the boot and closed it before climbing into the driver seat. Starting the engine, he kept the headlights off and drove up the track road towards the reservoir. It took around ten minutes in second gear but he finally got to the top. The view was outstanding and Jez got out to admire it. He'd never been up there at that time of night and he had to admit, even the scheme looked amazing from up there.

Jez lit a cigarette and smoked it down to the tip to calm the adrenaline rushing through him, as he replayed the sound of his boot smashing into Diggo's skull over and over. The sound had surprised him. He would have thought it would be harder, like rock hitting rock, where in fact what popped into his head was the memory of his granny tearing celery for her pan of soup on a Sunday.

Jez finished his cigarette and dropped it to the ground. He stomped on it and picked it up to check that it was fully extinguished before placing it in his back pocket. He wasn't going to leave that behind. Again, forensics. They could find the most miniscule thing and it could be their breakthrough. Climbing back into the driver seat, Jez drove the car to the edge of the grass bank and put the handbrake on before getting back out again and moving around to the back. He had to get rid of the car and the body.

Jez found that getting Diggo into the boot wasn't as difficult as getting him out and into the driving seat. His body was stiff, heavy. He held his breath as he leaned over and put the seatbelt on the corpse. The smell was beginning to intensify and Jez didn't want to leave a pile of his own vomit anywhere near Diggo or the car.

Swallowing hard, Jez stood back and sucked in clean, fresh night air. He turned away from the corpse, needing a moment to think, to process what he'd done. This was never the plan. This was never something Jez had thought himself capable of. It seemed he was. It seemed that instead of feeling fear of being caught, the thrill of what he was doing was overwhelming. It shocked him but he accepted it. Jez's life had never been plain sailing so why should this be any different? Now he knew he had the stomach and the balls to take on the criminal world as a player, as a hunter, rather than the prey. *His* body would never have to end up at the bottom of a reservoir.

Turning back, Jez leaned in and released the handbrake. He rolled down the driver window too. He didn't look at Diggo's face – or what was left of it – before closing the door. He moved around to the back of the car and laid his hands on the hatch, before taking a breath and using all his weight to push the car forward. It took less effort than Jez had thought it would, but the Nova shunted forward and rolled down the bank before plunging into the water.

Jez stood back and lit another cigarette. He counted, one, two, three... It took seventy-eight seconds for the car to become fully submerged in the reservoir. Less time than it took for Jez to smoke the cigarette down to the tip again.

He sat on the edge of the bank and washed his boots in the water, rinsing away the blood and brain matter from Diggo's head, before getting up and wiping his boots on the dry grass.

'That'll teach you to pull a blade on me,' he said, before turning and heading along the track towards the top of Dunmuir Hill.

He'd enjoyed the walk home that evening. Enjoyed looking up at the stars and down at the view. The Erskine Bridge, Old Kilpatrick. The scheme which he came from. He could even see all the way to the west end of Glasgow, a place he and the boys would often go for a few bevvies, before realising it was full of snooty arseholes and heading into Partick where the real boozers were.

That night made Jez realise that he was capable of much more than he had given himself credit for. He would go on the boys' holiday and when he was there he would think about what he wanted to do with his life. There were a million Diggos in the world. Jez didn't want to end up like him and staying in the scheme would push him closer to becoming one of them.

–

Jez finished his pint and sat back, looking around his old local, taking in the familiar faces and the memories that came to him. Stevo and Marty had been a laugh back then but it was clear to Jez that they'd gone nowhere and done nothing with their lives. It had taken Diggo's murder to make Jez realise that the scheme was a place that would hold him back. That kill was a turning point in his life, even if he hadn't realised it back then. He'd stopped himself from becoming one of those petty drug criminals at the bottom of the barrel. He'd moved on, climbed the ladder in a world where you didn't need qualifications to get to the top. Jez was proud of how far he'd come. He was successful and wealthy – and there was much more where that came from. He'd come far enough to have people do his killing for him if it was ever necessary.

Coming back here to find Cole was a pain in the arse, but it reminded him of how ruthless he could be. Billy was a mate, but business came first.

He'd make a Diggo out of *anyone* who stood in his way.

Chapter Forty-Eight

Charlene stepped out of the hotel lobby and onto the street. Glasgow smelled exactly as it had all those years ago. Car fumes, cold air and burger and onions. Those were the three main scents that assaulted her senses as she headed along the road towards Queen Street station. Jez had no idea she'd followed him and unless he saw her, he never would.

Being in the city made Charlene nervous about what she would do if she found Jez doing exactly what she suspected of him. The thought turned her stomach. She didn't love him. In the beginning, she'd almost fallen for him, before she found out what he was really like, before he'd had it off with her best friend. Why hadn't she been enough for him? Why did he have to abuse her trust, rip apart a friendship she'd had before even meeting him? People said there was a fine line between love and hate. Charlene wasn't sure how many times she'd crossed it and come back again. It was his fault she felt like this. His fault that she'd wasted her life trying to be a good wife, a good mum. She'd focused all her energy into loving him, yet she'd struggled to forget what he did. He was good-looking, charming and once upon a time had made her feel good about herself. After they'd had their first son, things had got better for a while. She'd managed to somehow live with his infidelity, not just with Roxanne but with others too. They'd worked hard at being affectionate towards each other, but the lie was always there in the back of her mind.

She knew Jez had continued to cheat on her as the boys grew up. The older they got, the more she and Jez grew apart. The idea of him with other women didn't infuriate her as much as it had when he'd been sleeping with her best friend. That rage had never burnt out.

Purchasing the ticket at the ticket desk, Charlene headed down to the platform to wait for the train. She knew exactly where Jez was. The tracker she'd set up on his phone was accurate. Of course, he was unaware of her constant need to know where he was every second of every day. She'd managed to hide that from him for a very long time. It had only been during the last two years or so that she'd let the mask slip and he'd seen her bitterness and what it had done to her. She'd often wondered why he hadn't just left her. Maybe he didn't feel the need. They were barely ever in the house at the same time and when they were, they were at opposite ends. They said absence made the heart grow fonder, but for Charlene, absence made the raging fire grow.

If he was in the location the phone said he was, then there was a very strong possibility that *she* was there too. The one woman who had destroyed Charlene's marriage to Jez before they'd even got married. Before he'd even proposed.

The train pulled into the station and Charlene climbed on, sat by the window and took a steadying breath. What would she do when she got to the location which was flashing up on her screen? Would she confront Jez, or watch from afar? Could she bear to look at them together? Why did she want to torture herself like this? Ignorance was bliss, but she wasn't ignorant like she had been back then.

There was one thing she knew for sure: if that *bitch* was there, Charlene would deal with her. She would deal with them both.

The image of both her lying, cheating husband and her so-called best friend lying dead at her feet brought a feeling of calm so quickly, it scared her. Maybe she was more like her husband than she thought. Ruthless, vengeful. He was one for getting rid of people who stood in his way. Perhaps she'd learned from the best?

The train pulled out of the station and headed west, out of the city. Charlene looked up at the grey sky and found she was beginning to forget what it felt like to have the sun on her skin. Funny how Scotland made you forget what it was like to feel warm. Even though she'd grown up there, she felt no connection to the place. No family, no friends. That was why she'd never gone back, even when things were at their worst with Jez.

The train continued on its journey and Charlene continued to monitor the screen. Jez could go anywhere and she would know his exact location. Unless he turned his phone off. But Jez was a businessman and he hadn't turned his phone off since she'd known him.

A voice in her head kept telling her to stop what she was doing; that it wasn't healthy. *Just go back to Spain, pack your things and leave.* But she couldn't bring herself to do it. She loved him but she hated him. She wanted to know for sure if Cole Woods was the only reason that Jez had come back to Scotland.

Chapter Forty-Nine

Jake stood up and slung the holdall over his left shoulder as Cole packed a second. One was filled with coke and one filled with heroin. Eddie was waiting outside with a van and a set of keys and Jake had brought in one of the guys from his shoplifting mob to be the driver. He barely spoke a word to Cole, barely looked him in the eye. He was worried that if he did, he might not be able to control himself. He hoped that once this deal was over, Cole would just crawl back to where he'd come from and leave Jake to get on with the rest of his life. Although deep down, he knew that was never going to be the case. He knew that if this job went well, Cole would want to keep things going, even if he wasn't present.

'Right,' Cole said, rubbing the palms of his hands together. 'First round of deliveries ready to go. Ed outside?'

Jake nodded and headed towards the door. 'I'll take these two bags to the salon like you said; Rox will be there, ready for the girls to get them onto the street. Once they're sold and the money's in, we'll go again.'

'Good lad,' Cole said. 'Oh, by the way. You know it's nothing personal, it's just business.'

Jake turned, his hand on the door handle. He glared at Cole and waited for him to continue.

'The footage, me having dirt on you. It's just insurance, that's all. I like you, Jakey boy, but you understand that I've got to do what I got to do. I know you won't fuck me over if I've got something that can ruin you. If it wasn't you it would have been someone else.'

Jake kept his expression neutral. 'And what makes you think I'd ever fuck you over in the first place? I've never given you the impression that I'm anything other than loyal.'

Cole laughed loudly. 'Jakey boy, in this game, loyalty only exists until a better offer comes along. This way I know that if an opportunity turned up for you to make more money and you wanted to sack this off, you wouldn't be able to because I'd be able to show your good woman what you did.'

Jake gritted his teeth so hard that he thought they might shatter.

'Look, it was an accident and I'd rather you'd stop bringing it up. You came to me with a job, I agreed to all your terms, Rox found a base and you're still threatening me. What is it with you, eh? Are you sick in the head or something?'

Cole dropped the holdall at his feet and squared up to Jake. 'Nah mate, the question is, are *you* sick in the head? Are you forgetting what you did? Are you forgetting the circumstances which led to what happened?'

'And are *you* forgetting that you're the one that set up a fucking camera in my hotel room and filmed the whole fucking thing?' Jake spat. Cole stood back and a menacing smile crept over his face.

'Like I said, I film all my associates working a job for me. I'm glad I did it. I'm not sick – you're the one that got a little too kinky when you were ball-deep in some guy. I wonder what Roxanne would think if she knew that you prefer men to women.'

Jake dropped his own holdall then and shoved Cole hard. He stumbled back but stayed upright. He was laughing, clearly satisfied that he'd got a rise from Jake.

'You need to calm down, Jakey boy. What's this really about? Can't handle the fact that you're gay? Was it really an accident, Jake? Or did you want to have your wicked way with him and then kill him off to keep your secret buried?'

Jake stepped forward and shoved Cole again, harder this time. Still, Cole kept his balance but this time he wasn't laughing.

'Shut you're fucking mouth, Cole. If that's really what you think, what's to stop me from killing you right now to keep *you* quiet? Eh?'

Cole narrowed his eyes. 'Don't fucking threaten me. You're not as hard as you make out, Jake. I was the one who picked you up off that hotel room floor when you were crying like a baby. I've got contacts, ways and means to get the message out there that one of Glasgow's biggest gangsters is a closet gay. I could get that message out from the grave and don't you dare doubt it.'

Jake stepped back, lifted the holdall and turned away from Cole. He had to remove himself from the situation, get away from Cole for a bit and calm down. Pulling the door open, he picked up the bag that Cole had packed and left the room, slamming the door behind him. As he walked through the flat, Jake checked through the peephole before stepping into the communal hallway. Taking the steps two at a time, he reached the street and found himself in front of the van. Eddie was standing, his back against it, with a cigarette in his hand.

'Didn't know you smoked,' Jake said, opening the back of the van and slinging the bags in. He slammed the doors shut and moved around to the side next to Eddie.

'Only occasionally,' he said. 'What's up with you? You look like you could kill someone.'

'Doesn't matter, it's nothing,' Jake replied. 'You can get off if you want.'

Eddie shook his head. 'It doesn't look like nothing.'

Jake was about to answer when Cole emerged from the front door of the building, his eyes fixed on Jake. No words were exchanged as Cole approached, his eyes falling from Jake and settling on Eddie.

'Eddie, mate,' he said with a wide grin. 'You boys can take it from here? I've got something else to do right now.'

Jake nodded and Eddie said, 'Aye, no bother.'

Cole made his way along the street and up the hill towards the city centre. Jake knew where he'd be headed. The casino, no doubt.

'You two had a lovers' tiff or something?' Eddie said, humour in his tone.

'He's a fucking prick, Eddie. Like I said before, you can't trust him. The sooner this job is done and dusted the better.' As soon as the words were out of his mouth, Jake realised that the job would never be over. Jake would have to live his life bowing down to Cole Woods if he wanted to keep Roxanne in the dark about his sexuality, and the rest of the Glasgow underworld. If it got out, it wouldn't just ruin his relationship and his reputation as a hard man, but it would see him go to prison for murder. The murder Roxanne would be able to live with, but the reason behind it would end her.

Chapter Fifty

Cole marched along the road, seething from his altercation with Jake. How dare he think he could get away with speaking to him like that? Who did he think he was? He was nothing but a closet fucking gay who needed to be brought down a peg or two. But Cole had to be careful; he couldn't jeopardise having him onside. Jake was one of his few connections up here in Glasgow, one of the few people who knew who he was. He needed to keep his head low, make sure he didn't get into any altercations. Jez would find him, of course he would. He was a resourceful guy, one of the best and a Glasgow man himself. If Cole could go back and change what he'd done then he would. Stealing Jez's money had been one of those off-the-cuff, split-second decisions. He'd already taken five hundred thousand from the Albanian gang, but he'd got greedy. Gambling had always been part of his life, as had drugs – dealing and partaking. But when he got out to Spain, started working for Jez, the casino clubs had appealed to him more than he'd thought. The girls, the booze, the drugs and the bets. He'd quickly become addicted to it all.

Jez had been too busy to notice Cole's money troubles. He was spending as quickly as he was earning. He'd planned the timing of the robbery carefully, had booked his flight to Scotland so that there would only be a few hours between the theft he'd pulled on the Albanians and take off. Once he'd taken from them, he had just enough time to swing by the club to check he hadn't left anything behind. To his surprise, the safe had been left open. It was pure luck and Cole saw an opportunity to take more than he'd originally planned. He didn't think twice about it, didn't hesitate at all. Jez didn't give two shits about Cole, so why should he care about leaving him financially lighter?

Going to Scotland had its benefits. London would be the first place that the Albanians would look for him, and none of his connections in Spain even knew Jake existed.

As he turned the corner, the backstreet casino came into view. A dingy little place that he'd found the day he'd landed. He'd been there every day since.

Pushing through the door, Cole stepped into the main entrance and the doorman nodded but said nothing as Cole moved through to the bar. He ordered a beer and a Jack Daniel's before taking his usual seat at the roulette table. Black thirty-three caught his eye. He was drawn to it, as his hand was drawn to his wallet. Pulling out a twenty-pound note, Cole slid it across the table to the croupier and nodded.

'Black thirty-three.'

The man nodded and placed Cole's bet. The wheel spun, as did Cole's stomach. There was seven hundred pounds riding on that one bet. He was either going to be up or down and that made him feel sick. But as he watched the wheel spin, he forgot about everything. Jez, Jake, the job in hand. All he wanted was for the ball to land on black thirty-three, for his winning streak to return and things would get better; he would no longer have the black cloud of doom hanging over him.

'Black thirty-three,' the croupier said. 'Congratulations, sir.'

Cole stood up and punched the air. 'Yas! Get in there.'

'Another bet, sir?'

Cole looked at the man standing behind the roulette table and smiled. He was seven hundred up, seven hundred better off than he he'd been before he'd walked through the door and that was just the roulette table. The drugs would be making him a lot more than that if Jake, Roxanne and Eddie did their jobs right. Maybe he wouldn't even pay them for their part in it. Maybe he would take everything for himself and fuck off, start a new life somewhere else. But not before he fucked Jake over by telling Roxanne what her precious gangster boyfriend had got up to when she was in prison.

'Aye,' he said, his smile growing wider at the prospect of it all. 'Make it one hundred this time. Black eighteen.'

If he got enough money behind him, he would never have to worry about Jez or the Albanians finding him. He could change his name and start over somewhere entirely new where no one knew him.

The croupier spun the wheel and tossed the pill in. Cole watched as it spun around the outside of the wheel itself. Black eighteen, he thought. Another thirty-five to one bet. Only this time, the pay-out would be much more substantial. Just over three and a half grand.

Worst case scenario, he could stay here and make Jake pay back his debt in other ways. If Jez did find Cole, then maybe Jake could take care of him, take him out. Jake was a Glasgow gangster after all. Maybe if Jez did return to Scotland, Jake wouldn't want him here. He might get a bit territorial. Cole could use that, if he had to, to protect himself.

Cole swallowed the Jack Daniel's in one mouthful and watched as the ball was released onto the roulette table. He hoped he'd win big with this bet. The more he won, the more powerful he felt.

Chapter Fifty-One

Roxanne made her way across the street towards the salon. It was grey, raining a little and she felt the cold nip at the skin on her face. She looked into the salon window and saw Arabella standing at the reception desk, the phone at her ear. Good, she thought. She was distracted.

The text had come through from Jake. The van would be arriving in the next thirty or so minutes and she had to be there to take the order in. To anyone else, it would look like salon supplies being delivered.

Just as she stepped onto the pavement, she felt a hand on her shoulder. Turning, she looked into the eyes of a face she'd never thought she'd see again.

'Hi, Roxanne.'

She gasped, wondering if she was imagining it all. But of course, she wasn't. She was standing face to face with the first guy she'd ever fallen in love with. The guy who had broken her heart into a million pieces.

'What the hell are you doing here?' she asked, her mouth suddenly dry.

'Nice to see you too,' he replied with a smile.

'Sorry,' she said. 'I just didn't expect it to be you. I mean, aren't you supposed to be living it up in Spain?'

Jez smiled again. 'I am. Well, I was until I had to come back here to attend to some business. I won't be here for long.'

Roxanne frowned. If he wasn't going to be in the country for long then why had he bothered finding her at all? What was the point?

'Do you fancy grabbing a drink?'

'I'm sure your wife would disapprove. Does she even know you're here?'

The thought of Charlene brought on a feeling that Roxanne hadn't felt in a long time. She and her best friend had gone to Spain to get away from their shitty life in the schemes. They'd grown up together, done everything with the other by their side. They'd promised each other that they'd make a life for themselves over there. It had been twenty years since she'd last seen her best friend, since they'd last spoken. If Jez hadn't been in the picture, they would likely still be together now. A pang of sadness hit her at the thought. Things could have been different. They *should* have been different. It hadn't quite turned out that way.

Although, now that Roxanne was out of prison and embarking on even bigger and better things since Cole was in the picture, she would be able to move out of the flat in Maryhill and into a lavish house with Jake. That was something that she'd never been able to dream of when she was younger and living in the scheme. Jake had changed all that, even if she'd lost ten years of her freedom.

'Well, she knows I'm in Scotland. I swear I didn't know you would be here today, Rox. I came looking for someone else and you were crossing the street and, well, here we are.'

Bullshit, Roxanne thought. 'Don't call me Rox.'

He opened his mouth to speak but kept quiet.

She took a steadying breath and glared at Jez. The last time she was in his company, he was dragging Charlene off her. Not that Roxanne blamed her for losing her shit. She had been having an affair with her boyfriend. She felt shit about the way things turned out but she couldn't get over the fact that she'd fallen in love with Jez. He'd said he felt the same, but he was quick to drop her as soon as Charlene had revealed that she was pregnant. The whole thing had been a disaster from the second they met.

'Look, I've got to go. I'm waiting on a delivery.' She nodded towards the salon.

'Oh, you own the place?'

Roxanne shook her head. 'No, I just work for the girl who does. I met her in prison.'

The words slipped out before she could stop them. Shit, she thought. She didn't want Jez to think that she was some lowlife. But then why did she care? She knew what he was doing over in Spain when she was living there. Dealing drugs at the club had been the start. When social media exploded into the world, Roxanne had tried to look Jez up. She hadn't found him, but she'd found Charlene and there were a few pictures of the couple, looking happy and carefree, but she knew people exaggerated their lives on social media. There would be a reason he wasn't on Facebook or Instagram. God only knew what he was up to nowadays.

He stood there in a pristine suit that screamed money. His and Roxanne's worlds couldn't be further apart and for the first time ever, she felt low about herself as she stood next to him.

'Prison? What landed you in prison?'

'That's none of your business. Like I said, I've got to go.' Roxanne turned to move towards the road which led to the back of the salon when Jez gripped her by the elbow.

'Wait,' he said. 'I want to talk to you.'

'I said I don't have time.' She shook him off. 'Look, Jez, you can't just rock up here after almost two decades and expect me to just hear you out. You were with my best friend and shagging me at the same time. Then she tells you she's pregnant and all of a sudden you want to be this stand-up guy, leaving me with nothing. I had to come back to this shit hole. I lost my best friend. I lost my *future* because of you. You're an arsehole. You were back then and you are now. So, do yourself a fucking favour and bugger off back to Spain.'

'Hang on a minute. You're blaming me for all of it?'

'Yes, Jez. If you'd just stayed away from both of us, I could still be there living a better life. I might never have come back here and ended up in prison.'

She turned her back on him then, just like he had turned his back on her twenty years ago, and marched towards the salon. Glancing through the window, she saw Arabella was still on the phone. Jez called out after her, but she ignored him. She didn't need this right now. Not with the salon, the job with Cole and the fact that she had to keep Arabella sweet. Dredging up the past wasn't something she could cope with on top of everything else.

Reaching the end of the road, she turned the corner and stood in the delivery bay area as she waited for the van to arrive. Jake wouldn't be there. He'd be back at the flat where Cole was holding the supplies. Anger sat heavy in the pit of her stomach, but there was something else. Guilt? She felt guilty for being so rude to him. Why?

Leaning her back against the wall, she bit her lip. The feelings she'd had for Jez back then were flooding back now. What the hell was she supposed to do with them?

Roxanne closed her eyes, exhaled loudly and tried to force the memories out of her head. But before she could, she heard footsteps approaching and when she opened her eyes, Jez was just a few feet away.

'Fuck off, Jez. I mean it.'

'Do you though? Mean it?'

'Yes, I fucking mean it. You can't just show up here and expect me to be sweet with you. You're nothing but a self-centred arsehole, Jez.'

He parted his lips to speak, when the back door of the salon opened. Arabella appeared, carrying a bin bag. Roxanne turned away from Jez swiftly and smiled at her friend.

'Oh Jesus,' Arabella jumped. 'What the hell are you doing standing out here?'

Roxanne heard Jez walk away, his footsteps becoming distant. Her chest ached but she would not allow the pain to show on her face.

'I was just waiting on you getting off for a break,' Roxanne lied.

'Who was that?' Arabella asked as she tipped the rubbish bag into the bin.

'Don't know. Fancy putting the kettle on?'

Arabella hesitated, her eyes falling from Roxanne's gaze and out to the direction in which Jez had headed. 'Yeah, okay.'

Arabella went inside and Roxanne exhaled, relieved that she was out of sight before the delivery van arrived, along with the girls she had hired to deal out the orders.

Seeing Jez had thrown her off her track. Was this the real reason he'd come back to Scotland?

'Roxanne?' A voice interrupted her thoughts. Turning, she saw young Stephanie standing just at the edge of the building.

'Come here,' she replied. 'Where's Selina? She better not have done a bunk.'

'She's just stopped at the shop for fags. She'll be here in a minute.'

Roxanne nodded. 'Right into your suit I see?'

'Aye, well there's no point in carrying it in a bag. That'll not look suspicious at all, will it?'

Roxanne laughed but her attention was drawn to the van as it rounded the corner and stopped beside her.

'Keep him talking,' she said to Stephanie. 'I'll be back in a minute. Oh, and make sure you text Selina and tell her to get here pronto. She's got a job to do.'

Roxanne pulled the back door of the salon open and stepped into the small kitchen. The last time she'd been in there was when Stephanie had done her first round.

Arabella was pouring water into two mugs when she looked up at Roxanne. 'Milk and two?'

'Actually, you've got a delivery out the back.'

Arabella frowned. 'Have I? Scarlett must have done an order before her disappearing act.'

'Scarlett has disappeared?'

'Didn't even call in to say she wouldn't be coming into work. She's left me to deal with everything, although I shouldn't really be complaining, I am the boss after all.'

Roxanne shrugged. She couldn't care less about Scarlett. All she needed was for the contents of the van to be emptied into the kitchen at the back of the salon and for Arabella to keep her mouth shut.

'I'll let him in, shall I?'

'Yes,' Arabella lifted her mug and took a sip. 'If you don't mind.'

Roxanne stuck her head out of the door and nodded at the driver. He got out and took two holdalls from the back of the van and carried them into the kitchen. He left quickly as Roxanne beckoned the girls inside.

'Roxanne, what the hell is this?' Arabella asked as the two girls entered the kitchen, their fake pregnant bellies ready to hold drugs packages.

'You know what this is, Arabella. You've seen it before. You know Stephanie here. Well, this is Selina. She's one of the girls I've hired to help lighten Stephanie's work load.'

Arabella shook her head. 'No. No way. I said it was a one-off. This is *my* business, you can't just come and go when you please, treating it like a fucking halfway house.'

Roxanne closed the back door and walked over to the door which led out to the salon. She put the snib on.

'Arabella, you really don't have a choice in the matter.'

'Erm, I think you'll find I do.'

Roxanne stared at Arabella, narrowed her eyes and took a breath. 'Do you really think I'm going to let you stop me from doing this? Have you forgotten what I went to prison for, Arabella? I mean, we met in Kirktonhill not so long ago. I got ten years for GBH. Do you know what I did to that guy?'

Arabella's expression hardened, but Roxanne could see in her eyes that she was beginning to worry. Good, she should worry.

'I battered that guy black and blue because he didn't do what he was supposed to.' She paused, let the information sink in. 'Do you know what you're supposed to do, Arabella?'

Arabella shook her head so gently that if Roxanne had blinked, she'd have missed it.

'You're supposed to make the tea, take the bookings and stay out the front while me and the girls here get on with our jobs. Stephanie and Selina are good girls, they'll do what I tell them for a small price. I wouldn't even have to get my hands dirty if you got in the way. But you know, I wouldn't even have to go that far, would I? Because I have dirt on you, love. Hostel guy ring any bells?'

Arabella's shoulders slumped. Now she got it.

'Good. Now go out the front, let me get on with my job and you get to keep your freedom and all your bones intact.'

She smiled her sweetest smile as she watched Arabella walk out to the main floor of the salon. Roxanne hadn't lost her touch after all.

Chapter Fifty-Two

Charlene watched as Jez hung around outside the hair salon before turning and walking in the direction of the city; her stomach churned as she blinked away tears of anger.

She'd followed him to the outskirts of the city, to a place called Dunmuir and then into the west end of Glasgow. The whole time, Charlene had been wondering if she'd got it wrong and that perhaps he really was only in Scotland on business. But seeing them together, seeing them in the street and how he pulled Roxanne back when she'd tried to walk away was like a kick to the gut. It brought it all back.

Who should she confront first? Or should she just cut her losses and leave him, take the boys and her rightful share of the money and start somewhere new? But where? There were no real connections to Majorca other than Jez. And she had no one here, no family or friends. She'd given up everything to be with him.

'I should have finished her off when I had the chance,' Charlene said through gritted teeth.

And I will, she thought. I'll finish them both.

Chapter Fifty-Three

Just as Arabella was about to 'do as she was told' she turned back and stood her ground. This was her business, her life. She wasn't going to let anyone ruin that.

'You're my friend, but I'm not going to let you do this. If you want to deal in drugs then that's fine, but you're not doing it on my property. It doesn't matter what you threaten me with, Rox. Because you are involved too, and I know you don't want to go back to Kirktonhill.'

'Ha,' Roxanne laughed. 'You'd never have survived your ten pathetic little months at Kirktonhill if I hadn't looked after you.'

Roxanne took a step closer, like she was squaring up to her. Arabella noticed how the two teenage girls who were wearing the pregnancy suits didn't know where to look. Although Roxanne had threatened her with them, she doubted that they would want to get involved in this row. And she definitely didn't want them to hear what she'd done.

'Roxanne, we're supposed to be friends. You're being vile right now.'

'Vile? Sweetheart, you don't know half of what I'm capable of and unless you want to find out, I'd suggest you do as I say and go out to the front of the salon. That way, you won't see a thing, can't pass comment on what we're doing and we can continue to be friends. Run your mouth and I'll have to shut it for you, understood?'

Arabella felt tears prick the corners of her eyes. This wasn't the Roxanne she knew, the woman she'd met in prison. But she knew Roxanne was right about two things. One, Arabella couldn't phone the police. If she did, Roxanne could tell them that she'd killed that man. She could go back to prison for a long time. And two, Arabella really didn't know what her friend was capable of. She knew nothing about her, only what she'd seen of her and learned in prison. Arabella had made the very mistake with Roxanne that had cost her her freedom. She'd trusted the wrong person, made friends with someone who was quick to stab her in the back. Because that was what Roxanne was doing right now, wasn't it?

'Och, come on, Arabella, put the crocodile tears away, will you? I've not got time for it.'

Arabella tried to swallow the lump in her throat. She didn't know if she was more upset at the way she was being spoken to, or at how far Roxanne was prepared to betray her. Maybe both. She'd never had a true friend before. Not until she met Roxanne in Kirktonhill. But that meant she had never had a true friend at all. So she really had nothing more to lose from this friendship. She'd been walked all over by people who called themselves friends her whole life. Well not now.

'Don't speak to me like that in front of people, Rox. In fact, don't fucking speak to me like that at all. If you want to deal drugs then you can go and fucking do it somewhere else. Now get the fuck out of here.'

Roxanne's eyes widened in shock and Arabella didn't know whether to feel exhilarated or terrified as her friend's face reddened with anger.

'Girls,' Roxanne exhaled loudly. 'Wait outside. I need a minute with Arabella.'

The young girls did what they were told and left the kitchen via the back door as quickly as they could. Arabella couldn't help but pity them. She knew what it was like to be them, to some degree. They probably just wanted to stay out of trouble, but this was the only way they could earn money. Being pulled into a situation you couldn't get out of was a familiar scenario to Arabella.

'Right, I'm sorry you're all uptight about this, Arabella. Really, I am. But you've been in prison, for fuck's sake. And you're one of the lucky ones to get out and walk into a place like this, a business handed to you on a fucking plate. I'm not so lucky. I need money to survive and this is how I'm making it. I don't have anywhere else to do this. You owe me fucking big time, Arabella. I covered up a fucking murder for you, so the least you can do is turn a blind eye.'

Arabella watched as Roxanne's eyes glistened. Was she about to cry? Jesus, she thought.

'I'm sorry I was horrible to you. I don't like to be that way but I felt backed into a corner. I don't want us to fall out over this.'

Shaking her head, Arabella sighed. Maybe her apology was genuine, but she'd still said some horrid things. 'I don't want us to fall out either, but you're not giving me much choice.'

'Let me make it clear for you,' Roxanne lowered her voice. She stepped forward and before Arabella could stop her, she gripped a chunk of her hair and dragged her towards the chair in the corner before throwing her down on it.

Stunned by fear, Arabella sat perfectly still as Roxanne pulled her mobile phone out and began playing a video. It was grainy, dark, but Arabella could see an image of a man lying face down on the ground. The sound of her own voice echoed out from the small speaker at the bottom of the phone, crying, wailing about him being dead.

Arabella closed her eyes tight, trying to shut out the scene in front of her.

'I will take this to the police, call it an anonymous tip-off. I have copies of this video in a pen drive and believe me, Arabella, I will use it if I have to. Don't make me. Oh, and don't bother telling your precious Eddie about this. He won't be able to help you. He's in on this too.'

Arabella opened her eyes and stared up at Roxanne. 'Eddie's involved?'

'He and Jake have come to an agreement.'

Gritting her teeth, Arabella forced herself to stay quiet. She got to her feet, fixed her hair and turned her back on the woman she'd been fooled into thinking was her friend, before walking back out into the salon.

Roxanne had her backed into a corner and a bloody tight one at that. This was a win–win for Roxanne and a lose–lose for Arabella. If the police got hold of that video, she'd go to prison. If they found out that her salon was being used to force teenagers to deal drugs, she'd go to prison.

Arabella would keep quiet about it all. How could Eddie get involved in something like this? Why would he buy her a salon and then allow it to be used as a site for drug dealing? The thought angered her. She'd already killed one man. Arabella was sure that when she got home, she would kill her second.

Reaching the reception desk, Arabella pulled her mobile out of her bag and sent Eddie a message. She typed out the text, jabbing at the screen angrily.

> You've got some fucking explaining to do. How could you do this to me?

Glaring out of the window, Arabella saw the two teenage girls waddle across the road, their fake swollen bellies on show under their clothes. Their fake bellies stuffed full of drugs. Roxanne had got them all into deep shit and there was really nothing Arabella could do about it.

She wanted to cry, to go after them and tell them to dump the drugs and run. But that would only achieve trouble, for them and for her. Roxanne had her over a barrel. Eddie had betrayed her.

Her phone beeped and as she looked down, expecting a reply from Eddie, she saw the Google alert light up the screen.

Woman found beaten to death in Glasgow flat.

There were no real details, other than the fact that the police had cordoned off the scene. She recognised the street name. Leanne appeared by Arabella's side.

'Have you seen the news? Do you think that's why Scarlett isn't here? You think it could be her?'

Arabella's stomach flipped and she felt hot tears spring to her eyes. How could this be happening? It was like hell had broken through from below and was coming for her. Swallowing hard, she tried to remain calm.

'No, it won't be. But she's not answering her phone. I'll head over, she's probably just got the flu, or a hangover and didn't want to tell anyone. You know what it's like when you've got the fear.' She attempted a smile but failed miserably.

Arabella took a steadying breath. So much had happened already in the last week. She'd killed someone, her friend was dealing drugs from her business and her boyfriend was in on it. Now there was a possibility that the manager of her salon had been beaten to death. All she could think right now was, what the actual fuck is going on?

–

Wrapping her jacket around her, Arabella took the fifteen-minute walk towards Scarlett's flat and while she did, her mind began to wander. What if the body of the woman mentioned in the news report was Scarlett? What then? And who would want to do something like that to her? She was a good woman, kept herself to herself and had run the salon for years before Arabella came along. But then, Arabella didn't know a lot about her, so perhaps there was an abusive husband or partner?

She reached the area of the west end of the city where Scarlett lived and headed up the hill towards her flat. She could already see the police presence, the crime scene tape.

'Jesus,' she said out loud, remembering the scene just a week previously when she'd gone to see what she'd done to the man she'd killed. She still couldn't remember it. But Roxanne had footage, her voice, her wailing cry as she stood over the body.

Arabella pushed herself to keep moving towards the scene. She had to know for certain if Scarlett was all right.

Standing at the edge of the tape, she saw an officer stood at the bottom of the stairs which led into the sandstone building. He looked straight ahead, his expression steady, his eyes unblinking. Crowds of people had gathered to watch what was happening and Arabella felt sick.

'Excuse me?' Arabella said. 'Has there been a murder?'

'This is a crime scene, you'll have to step back,' the officer said.

'My manager didn't show up for work today, I haven't been able to contact her and she lives in this building. Her name is Scarlett.' Arabella felt the muscles in her jaw tighten when she saw the man's eyes flicker. He'd reacted to the name. 'I just need to know if she's okay.'

A sound came from behind her then. A sound that chilled her to the core. A woman, crying hysterically and calling the name that Arabella hadn't wanted to hear.

Turning, she watched as a woman collapsed to the ground. Someone attempted to cradle her. She was screaming Scarlett's name and the lump in Arabella's throat cracked. Tears pooled in her eyes as she realised that the woman she was watching was likely to be Scarlett's mother.

Turning her back on the building, Arabella hesitated. What was she supposed to do? Stand here and wait? Wait for what? The inconsolable woman wouldn't know who Arabella was, and it would be inappropriate for her to approach a grieving mother right now.

Go home, she thought. Just go home, curl up in a ball and block it all out. Scarlett, Roxanne, Eddie. All of it. She would text one of the girls at the salon and ask them to lock up. She just couldn't face them now.

Arabella began walking away from the scene, failing to stop herself from shaking. Tears poured down from her eyes and she bit her lip to stop herself from crying out. She didn't feel safe around anyone, couldn't trust anyone.

Arabella's life was careering down a dangerous road at high speed, and she couldn't find the brake.

Chapter Fifty-Four

Roxanne took the cash from Stephanie and Selina and smiled as she counted it. They'd managed to get their stash sold in no time at all and she shared the triumphant smile spread across their faces. Although they were young, they were resourceful. Stephanie and Selina had said that their scheme was crawling with druggies looking for their next fix and that they had older siblings who would be able to sell to the people that Stephanie and Selina wouldn't be able to handle if they got a bit rough. Roxanne had warned them that if they fucked her over on this, it would be the last thing they ever did. In truth, Roxanne had faith in them. They were a lot like her when she was their age. The job she'd tasked them with was the same as the job she'd done before she'd left for Spain. It was one of the reasons she and Charlene had left Glasgow. Of course, Charlene had got to live the life they'd planned for themselves. Roxanne hadn't and had returned to Glasgow. But when she did, she'd sworn to herself that she wouldn't go back to those jobs, she would rise to the top. Meeting Jake had only accelerated that.

'My sister Kelly sold most of mine,' Stephanie said. 'She said she'd be up for doing it again but she'd want to meet you first.'

Roxanne looked at Stephanie, her interest piqued. 'Well, give her a call and bring her here then.'

Stephanie smiled widely. 'That's the thing, you see. She's outside waiting on me. She's quite impulsive. When she gets an idea in her head, she kind of runs with it and—'

Roxanne held up her hand and Stephanie stopped speaking. Roxanne opened the back door to reveal a girl standing outside.

She was smoking a cigarette and Roxanne noted the lines at the corners of her eyes, how shifty she seemed.

'Kelly?' Roxanne asked.

'Aye,' Kelly replied, taking a step forward.

Roxanne stood in the doorway and regarded the girl for a moment before moving to the side and allowing her to step into the small salon kitchen.

'Kelly, this is my boss, Roxanne,' Stephanie said, as though they were all about to sit down in an official interview. Roxanne stifled a laugh. She liked Stephanie. There was something about Kelly that didn't sit well with Roxanne though, but she couldn't quite put her finger on it.

'Your sister said that you helped her out with some sales?'

'Aye,' Kelly replied. 'Some of the folks in my scheme are older than her. I didn't want her getting in trouble with some of the chancers, you know?'

'And you can handle yourself better than Stephanie can?'

Kelly knitted her brow, in an 'of course I can, you idiot' kind of expression. 'Well, she is twelve years younger than me. And I know the tricks of the trade to dodge the polis. Had to do it a million times before and not once have I been caught.'

Nodding, Roxanne pulled her mouth into a thin line. 'You're very sure of yourself, Kelly. I like that.'

'Have to be in this line of work, don't you? You have to pick off the weak ones to keep yourself out the jail.'

Roxanne couldn't disagree. She would have to think about what to do with Kelly. Perhaps give her a bigger run than her younger sister. Maybe Stephanie could punt Jake's own cannabis grow, rather than the class A drugs.

Terminating the interview so abruptly that she could see Kelly was shocked, Roxanne bent down and pulled a pay-as-you-go mobile out of the holdall on the floor and handed it to Kelly.

'What's this?'

'It's what I'll use to contact you on. Don't use it for anything other than taking calls from me. Don't give the number out, don't switch it off and do not put it on silent. I need to be able to get hold of you at any time and if I can't…' Roxanne left the words to hang between them.

Kelly nodded and turned to her sister Stephanie who said, 'Just do what she says and we get paid. We get to feed ourselves, keep the flat. It's better than what Maw's doing for us now, what she's ever done.'

Something clicked in Roxanne's head then, as to why Stephanie seemed older than her sixteen years. She'd had to fend for herself for a long time, the same way that Roxanne had when she was that age and younger. Her own mum – 'the village bike' as she'd later found out she'd been nicknamed – was only interested in earning enough money to buy herself booze and drugs for the weekends when Roxanne was a kid. It seemed that growing up on the scheme was a way of life for Kelly and Stephanie, as much as it had been for Roxanne back in the day. Kelly was tough and she saw a little bit of herself in there.

These were the type of people that Roxanne could pull in to do the job. These were the kind of people who would want to do it. It was fast, easy money so long as they kept their heads low.

Kelly turned to Roxanne, a controlled expression on her face. 'You call, I'll answer. We need the money, so you don't have to worry about any fuck-ups on our end.'

Roxanne nodded. She was glad to hear that kind of attitude. She needed girls like this for the job and if Kelly did well, then Roxanne would ask her if she knew of any others who would be up for the challenge. As much as Roxanne didn't like Cole, there was every possibility that this arrangement could see her and Jake become very wealthy.

Chapter Fifty-Five

Sinking back on the sofa, Jake stared down at the screen of his phone. Cole could end his life as he knew it at any second, regardless of the job. Cole knew enough people to replace him in the deal and Jake would bet his life savings on Cole going ahead with the threat just because he could.

The way Jake saw it, he had one of two choices. Tell Roxanne everything, cut his losses and leave Glasgow. Or end Cole before he got the chance to ruin him. Jake was a private person and Cole had exploited him. It had been easy for Cole to do what he did. Finding out Jake was gay was one thing, but to be as sick in the head as to film him with his lover, that was something else entirely. Jake knew that Cole was always looking forward, making sure he had insurance – dirt on people so they could never say no to him.

Jake thought about Mark and the familiar feeling of dread gripped him. It was always lurking in the background. Mark had been working for Cole too; that was how they'd met. The attraction between them was instantaneous. What had happened that night was an accident. People do stupid things when something bad happens, like allowing Cole to take control. And what happened after the accident was a bad judgement, on his part.

The memories of those days in London flooded his vision and even when Jake closed his eyes, there was no way of stopping them as they played out. Jake had met Cole three years ago, in Glasgow, during a night at the pub with some of the lads from the shoplifting operation. They'd been successful in their latest haul and Jake had taken them out for a few beers. Cole had been in the pub that night and had approached Jake on the way to the toilets.

'You're Jake Cairney?' The voice had come from behind him, at the top of the stairs, as Jake had made his way down to the ground floor where the toilets were – in the dingiest pub in the city. He'd chosen it because it was the only place that sold Buckfast on draught and most of his boys were Buckie drinkers.

'Depends who's asking,' Jake had replied as he turned and caught the eye of the man with the thick London accent.

They stood on the stairs, Cole at the top and Jake almost at the bottom. Staring. Sizing each other up. Then Cole started to make his way down, slowly but with a strong presence. Jake tensed for a moment but then remembered that his boys were just at the bar. If there was a commotion just a few feet away, then they'd hear it. They'd know their boss was in trouble.

Just as Jake was about to ball his fist, Cole held out his hand. 'Cole Woods.'

Jake hesitated, glared down at Cole's hand and then back to his face. He took Cole's hand and shook firmly, as did Cole. He'd heard of Cole through the underworld grapevine. Drugs, violence, that sort of thing. And it had seemed that Cole knew who he was too.

'I wanted to talk to you about something business-related,' Cole said, letting go of Jake's hand. 'I've heard a lot about you, Jake, and how successful your drug business is up here in Glasgow, not to mention your little side business of designer gear robbery. I'm looking to open up my business from London to Glasgow and I think you'd be a perfect fit.'

Jake turned his back and went into the toilets. Cole followed. Jake stood at the urinal, very aware of Cole behind him. The bathroom echoed the sounds of the lads laughing up at the bar. They wouldn't hear Jake down here.

'And what makes you think I'd work with a complete stranger?' Jake asked as he tucked himself back in and headed towards the sinks.

'Well, I'm not a complete stranger to you, am I? I'm in the same business as you. Drugs, shoplifting operations. But I need someone who can run things for me down south, get some runs on the go from there to here. I've been watching your crew for a while now and I'm impressed with their ability to be discreet.'

Cole hadn't moved in the time they'd gone into the toilets, kept his hands by his side. It was clear to Jake that he wasn't a threat.

Jake pulled a handful of paper towels from the dispenser and dried his hands. 'You've been watching my crew?'

'Yeah, your lot know what they're doing. But they follow your lead, yeah?'

Jake nodded as he chucked the wet paper towels in the bin and headed for the door. How had this guy come to know about Jake and the lads?

'What are you doing in Glasgow anyway? Who you working for?' Jake asked.

'I work for myself,' Cole said, before Jake could get a chance to question him further. 'I was in that centre in town, what's it called? Buchanan Galleries? I watched one of your lads doing his thing and I followed him out to the car park. He had a fucking grand's worth of gear on him, all designer. Not one security guard stopped him. Not one member of the public even looked in his direction. Then he got to his car, and that's when I followed him. I was going to ask him about it, how he managed to do it so subtly. But when he got to his destination at that plot of units within the industrial park, that's when I saw that it was more than him. There were at least ten and I knew it was a team effort. Then I saw you. Listened as you talked, gave them instructions as they packed the gear into boxes. I was impressed that you were able to keep a group of lads like that in check and get them to do exactly what you said.'

Jake raised a brow, surprised by Cole's words. He'd been watching them and Jake hadn't even known. That wasn't something he was happy about. He'd taken his eye off the ball when it came to making sure they were discreet. The security guards at the centre may not have noticed the crew doing their job, but this Cole character had.

'Aye, well, they're a good team I've got,' Jake said, before shaking his head. 'So, what exactly is it you want again?'

'Just think, if you and your boys can get away with lifting so much designer gear, think about how many kilos of drugs you could move around the country. Think of the money involved. Let's talk about this over a drink?'

Cole had taken Jake up to the bar and bought him and his boys a round of drinks before asking Jake to join him at a table where they could talk. Jake wished now he'd never agreed to that conversation, wished he'd never agreed to the deal. If he hadn't gone anywhere near Cole, he'd never have met Mark. He remembered his first encounter with him, in a pub down in London. They'd sat together at a table, talked about the job. But they'd talked about other things too, and Jake felt like he could be normal around him because no one knew him in London. They'd clicked almost instantly and if it hadn't ended so tragically, the memory would have made him smile.

Jake opened his eyes and exhaled loudly, trying to breathe out the Images from his past. His mind was plagued with guilt.

Getting rid of Cole Woods was the only way Jake could get on with his life. The idea of ending Cole terrified and exhilarated him in equal measure. But could he really do it?

Jake Cairney wasn't a coward and there was no way that he was going to leave behind a reputation that said he was.

Chapter Fifty-Six

Eddie sank back into his seat at the opposite side of the table, in some little back street boozer away from the city and wondered what he'd managed to get himself into. Just before Arabella got out of prison, the worst thing he'd done was cheat on his girlfriend. Now he was in deep shit.

DS Billy Drysdale leaned back in his seat too and looked ever so comfortable as he made Eddie squirm. All Eddie had been looking for was some excitement in his life. How the hell was he supposed to know that it would lead to this?

'We've had Mr Woods under surveillance since he came back into the UK just some weeks ago. Police forces in London and here in Glasgow have been working together to bring him to justice. He's a dangerous man, Mr Corrigan. And I have been watching your involvement with him. I've seen you offer up your vans to allow him to move his drugs freely around the city. I've watched you handle drugs packages from Mr Woods flat. I've even seen you out on a boozing session with Mr Woods and Mr Cairney. So, I will put it to you again, Mr Corrigan...'

Eddie shook his head and looked down at his clammy hands.

'I can either arrest you right now for your involvement with Woods and Cairney, or you can co-operate with our invest-igation into Woods and help us to bring him down. We have enough to bring him in, but we're waiting for him to give us the bigger fish in this pond. He's not producing himself, he's buying in and we don't know who from yet. If you help, in return, you will be offered anonymity and immunity from prosecution of any offences in relation to Woods.'

Jesus *fucking* Christ, Eddie thought. How was he going to get around this? He was screwed either way.

When he'd first met Jake and Cole and they'd gone that night to the casino, Eddie had been taken in by the money and the glamour. That was just the face of it all though; it ran a lot deeper than that. As deep as the shit running through the sewers. If Jake and Cole ever found out that he was in cahoots with the police, they wouldn't hesitate to kill him; there would be nothing the police could do to protect him. And what about Arabella? They'd get to her too, surely.

Grass, or go to jail. Just as Arabella was getting on her feet.

Shit, shit, *fucking shit*!

DS Drysdale kept his eye on Eddie the entire time, his arms folded as he sat back comfortably. 'Come on, Mr Corrigan. I've not got all day.'

Eddie shook his head but sat up straight. He'd made his decision.

Chapter Fifty-Seven

Opening the door, Cole saw Eddie standing there with a bottle of whisky in one hand and a pack of cans in the other.

'Come in, mate,' he said, standing aside to let Eddie inside. 'What's this all about then?'

'Well,' Eddie replied as he walked through the flat and into the small living room at the back; he avoided the back room where the drugs were being produced, 'I thought since we're business partners now, we should get to know each other a bit better.'

Cole closed the door behind him and shrugged. 'Fine by me, so long as you crack open that whisky and pour me some first.'

Eddie smiled and placed the bottle on the coffee table. Cole went to the kitchen to get some glasses and took a deep breath. Everything was riding on this business deal with Eddie and Jake. It would earn him enough to hire that private investigator he'd looked into. The only problem he would have to face was keeping away from the casino, the online betting websites and the bookies. Surely he could do that in order to find out what happened to his brother.

'Right then,' Cole said, moving through to the living room and setting the glasses down on the table. 'Let's have some of that then.'

Eddie nodded and poured two large measures of whisky. He raised his glass and Cole clinked his off Eddie's.

'Here's to business,' Eddie said.

Cole smiled and downed his measure, before reaching over and cracking open a can.

'So, I'm just going to be blunt here,' Eddie said. 'Is it true about you being a gambling addict?'

Cole shot him a look, but was in awe of how openly and bluntly Eddie had said it. Cole needed someone like him on his team, not someone like Jake. A wet blanket who couldn't face up to what he'd done. Jake used to be hard, fearless. Now all he cared about was his girlfriend finding out he'd been living as a closet gay who'd murdered his lover.

'Ha,' Cole laughed. 'Blunt is your middle name, then? Yeah, I like a bet now and again.'

Eddie took a mouthful of whisky. 'I don't mind the races myself. But I wouldn't say it's something that I'd obsess over. That's what addiction is, isn't it? Obsession about when you can do it next. Whether it's drugs, booze, hookers, even gambling.'

Cole narrowed his eyes. 'You a therapist or something?'

'Nah,' Eddie replied. 'I suppose I just know a fucked-up soul when I see one.'

Those words hit Cole right between the eyes. Fucked up was definitely the correct terminology. His life had been one big fuck-up since he was just a young teenager. It had all started after his brother went missing. His mum had died of a broken heart after he'd disappeared, his dad was never around to begin with and his brother was the only one he'd ever been able to rely on.

'Well,' Cole said, reaching for the bottle of whisky, deciding that the beer just wasn't going to cut it. 'You'd be right. Jesus, maybe you *should* become a therapist. You've been in the flat five minutes and already you've worked it out.'

Eddie didn't reply, just sat back on the sofa and took another sip. Cole watched as Eddie looked around the flat. It was empty, aside from some furniture that came with the place and a TV in the corner. Cole wasn't one for having sentimental things around him. No photographs. Those only reminded him of what was missing in his life. Gambling had become his escape and now, it had a grip on him. It had all turned him into someone he'd never planned to be. But it was the only things that kept him breathing. He couldn't let go of life until he found out what happened to his brother.

'That's twice you've said "therapist". Sounds as though you've got some stuff to get off your chest, mate,' Eddie said.

Cole glanced at his new partner. 'And you think you'd be a good listener, do you? Kiss the bad dreams away?' He laughed loudly then.

'You got any mates up here in Glasgow, other than Jake, I mean?'

'Ha, Jake's not my mate. He's a business partner, and even then he's only in with me because he owed me a favour.' Cole took a swig from his drink. 'I've been back and forth to Glasgow a lot over the last few years. Have associates up here, but no mates. I tend not to get close to people, they end up leaving in the end.'

Cole thought about his relationship with Jez Kennedy, before he'd stolen from him. There had almost been a friendship there. Cole had been closer to Jez than anyone since his brother. But the drive to find out what happened to him was stronger than his need to be friends with anyone. It was the one thing that drove Cole to keep living, but it was also the one reason why his head was so messed up.

'Yeah, I sensed a bit of bad blood between you both.'

'None of your business, mate.'

'Hey,' Eddie put his hands up. 'I never said it was. Simply voicing an observation. So, you think the deal is going well then?'

Cole nodded. 'Of course it's going well. That's the other good thing about having Jake in on the deal; his sexy missus is in on it too.'

'Roxanne?' Eddie said. 'You fancy her?'

'She's fiery. I like fiery. I think she could go a lot further in this business than her gay boyfriend,' Cole said. He saw the flicker on Eddie's face and an excitement stirred in him.

'Gay?'

'Yeah, as in *full blown gay*. He's not come out of his closet yet. He'll get to stay in there as long as he does exactly what he's supposed to do.' Cole took another glug of whisky and exhaled loudly.

'How the hell do you know he's gay?' Eddie asked, his face contorted as though he didn't believe Cole.

'Because he murdered his gay lover when we were working together in London.' Cole didn't care who knew. What was Eddie going to do? Run and tell the police? Very doubtful.

'Get to fuck! He murdered his gay lover?' Eddie laughed.

'I'm fucking serious, mate. I've got fucking video evidence to prove it.'

Eddie's eyes widened and his complexion paled. Now he believed Cole. Now he knew who he was working with. Then Cole stopped, glared at Eddie for a moment. He'd just revealed Jake's dirty little secret. Not that it would do Cole any harm, but he wished he hadn't said anything now. It was more fun when it was just Cole who knew. Maybe Eddie wouldn't believe him.

'Jesus, I didn't think Jake was that kind of guy.'

'What? A poof or a murderer?' Cole slapped his knee and laughed loudly. 'Look, each to their own and all that but he made his bed when he asked me to help him out of a sticky situation. I don't allow folk to walk away from their debt, you know?'

Cole looked at Eddie with a smile, a silent reminder that Eddie wouldn't be able to walk away from Cole either.

Chapter Fifty-Eight

Eddie's mind was buzzing from the information Cole had just revealed. He felt for the phone in his pocket. He'd put it on silent and had hit record before he'd got to the front door of Cole's flat. He hoped it was still recording now.

Pulling his hand away from his pocket, paranoid that Cole might notice and become suspicious, Eddie thought about Jake as a killer. Eddie struggled to see it in him, but if Cole said he had proof and that the reason Jake was in on the deal was because Cole had helped out with getting rid of the body then who was Eddie to argue?

'Going to grab some crisps from the kitchen, you want any?' Cole asked as he got to his feet. Eddie glanced up at him and nodded.

'Aye, cheers.'

Cole left the room and as he headed through to the kitchen, Eddie noticed that he'd left his phone on the coffee table. It lit up with a text message and he couldn't help but notice the image of the man that was Cole's screensaver. Frowning, he cocked his head to one side to get a better look. It wasn't Cole, obviously. Who would have a screensaver of themselves?

The screen died and Eddie sat back in his original position when he heard Cole coming back from the kitchen. Looking up, he saw a bag of crisps flying through the air towards him. He caught it in his hands and pulled the bag open.

'Your phone lit up by the way,' Eddie said, crunching on a mouthful of crisps.

Cole looked down and pressed the home button on the phone, shrugged and sank back on the sofa. He didn't say anything about the text or the picture on the screen. Why would he? He barely knew Eddie; he wasn't going to give anything up.

'Was probably Jakey boy, checking things are all on track,' Cole said. He sucked air in through his teeth before sinking back another half.

'Why do you say that?' Eddie asked. He narrowed his eyes and kept them on Cole. There was something on the tip of Cole's tongue and Eddie wasn't sure what was coming next.

'He won't want you to know he's gay, or a killer. He doesn't believe any of those things himself. He's in denial. Has been since it happened. Poor bastard's probably been gay his whole life but because of who he is, what he does for a living... well,' Cole paused. 'It doesn't exactly go, does it? Gay gangster. He's a dangerous bastard, Eddie. Don't get too close to him. He might seem soft on the outside, but there's a switch in there somewhere. That Mark, the lover, he flicked that switch. If I didn't have footage of what happened that night, no one would even know Mark was dead.'

Eddie swallowed hard as he watched Cole drink more and more whisky and set up a few lines before snorting them quickly. It was loosening his tongue and Eddie had so many questions he wanted to ask but couldn't risk raising Cole's suspicions. He was easing into a comfort zone with Cole, who was beginning to trust that he could talk around Eddie.

As Cole sat back, Eddie filled up their glasses, but decided to stick to the one beer he had been nursing since his arrival. He needed as clear a head as possible to deal with this.

'You know, Ed...' Cole slurred slightly, cleared his throat and shifted position on the sofa. 'I've been in this business a long time. You know, drugs, stolen goods. That kind of thing. It never gets boring. You'll come to learn that with each job, there's a new excitement. My brother always used to say...' He paused, took another gulp from his glass, '… that if you want to live a luxurious life, then you have to take risks. Do things that take you right out of your comfort zone.'

Eddie watched as Cole moved his hand in a swift motion through the air as he spoke and noted how his expression, albeit pissed, was sad. It was the first time he'd seen any real emotion from the man.

'Your brother?' Eddie pressed.

'Aye. Had a brother. He was five years older than me. Fucked off on a working holiday and I never saw him again. He told me he'd come back and get me when I was older, take me away to sunnier climates. But he never did.' Cole clicked his fingers. 'Just disappeared like that, not a word from him. Said bye to him at the front door when he left for the airport and I never saw or heard from him again.'

The sadness in Cole's eyes hardened then and Eddie wasn't surprised that the emotion didn't last long.

'What happened to him? Did he just go off and start a new life?'

Cole shrugged. 'Nah mate, he's dead for sure. He'd never have abandoned me like that. Someone took him from me. And it won't have been an accident either. You die in accidental circumstances or with natural causes and your body shows up sooner or later. My brother's been missing for two fucking decades. You don't just disappear into the black hole unless someone puts you there.'

Eddie nodded, he agreed with that. Accidental deaths were just that, accidental. Hit by a bus, fall off a ladder, heart attack, someone finds you.

'So, you think someone killed your brother? Where? Why?'

'I don't fucking know, Ed. But I'll tell you this, I am on the verge of finding out. The money from this job, I'll be putting it to a private investigator. I've already spoken to him and he thinks there might be something to work with.'

Eddie nodded again, wondering how he would feel if someone in his family went missing without a trace, with no answers after all this time. When Arabella was in prison, he'd felt like he was going insane, so much so that he'd ended up having an affair with Scarlett which was one of the biggest mistakes he'd ever made. He didn't want to think about it, or what he'd done to her.

He turned his attention back to Cole, who had sat forward and already poured another whisky. His eyes were bloodshot, his skin flushed.

'You think this guy will find out what happened to him?'

'Should bloody think so, I'll be paying him enough. I've got plenty pictures of him and I've dug out the information of where he was going. I don't even know if he made it to his destination. He could be lying dead somewhere back home for all I know.'

Cole reached for his phone and tapped on the screen, turned it around and offered it across the table to Eddie. He took it in his hand and stared down at the screen.

'That's him. It's the most recent picture I have of him, taken just a week before he left.'

Eddie was shocked to see how much Cole looked like his brother and realised that it was the same image on the screen saver.

'What's his name?' Eddie said, careful not to refer to him in the past tense in case it upset Cole. Or angered him.

'Brian. He was in the building trade, just done his apprenticeship. Was going to take me out on site when he got back, get me off the streets and away from the gangs. Mum told him to do it but to be honest, I idolised my brother, so I'd have gone with him anyway.'

Eddie wondered if Cole would be the way he was today if his brother hadn't gone missing. The hardened exterior, the fact that he was blackmailing Jake, was it all just Cole's way of coping with not knowing what had happened to the only person he'd had to look up to when he was a teenager?

'Anyway,' Cole got up. 'That whisky's gone straight through me.'

He headed out of the room and Eddie heard the bathroom door close. He quickly pulled his own phone out, took a picture of the screen and set Cole's phone back down on the table.

It didn't matter that the story of Brian Woods meant nothing to Eddie, or the case he was informing on. It was a starting point of trust and in order to get his own job done, Eddie absolutely needed Cole's trust. And he'd been told that any information he had was to go straight to Billy. Anything at all.

Turning to face the hall, Eddie wondered what would happen when Billy and his team came knocking. Would Cole know who had grassed him up to the police? It could be anyone really, punters, an ex-girlfriend, maybe even Jake. There was bad blood between them, so maybe Cole would think it was a possibility.

Getting to his feet, he peered out of the window and down to the main road and that was when he saw the CCTV camera sitting in the corner, pointed out towards the street. His stomach flipped. If Cole had CCTV, then he would be able to anticipate an incoming raid.

'Looking for someone?' Cole said, his sudden presence in the room startling Eddie.

'Nah,' Eddie replied, playing it cool. 'But if I was, I'm sure your CCTV would tell me they were here before they knocked on the door.'

'Ha,' Cole said, sitting down on the sofa and lighting a cigarette. 'It's a good kit, that is. Cost me enough. It's to keep an eye out for punters, some of my dealers and that. Also good if the cops come knocking, you know?'

Eddie nodded. Yes, he thought, he did know. If the cops did come knocking, Eddie would have to put his acting skills to the test.

'We'll need to get the CCTV in the salon linked up to this kit, right enough. Need to be able to warn Roxanne of any trouble coming her way.'

Eddie stopped, turned and stared at Cole. 'What are you on about?'

'The salon. Roxanne's using it as a second hub for the girls she's got operating out of it. You know, the pregnancy suits?'

Cole looked on expectantly at Eddie, as if he should know what he was on about. Again, Eddie had to put on an act.

'Oh aye,' he said. 'Good idea. You don't want anyone getting caught out, might lead them back to this place, you know?'

Cole nodded and picked up his phone again, stared down at the screen and seemed to gaze off into a far-off memory, leaving Eddie to wonder what in the fuck Arabella had agreed to.

Eddie finished off the beer and placed the bottle down on the table. 'Look mate, sorry about this but I've had a text from Arabella, she's not feeling well. I'll need to get back and see how she's doing.'

'Ah, women. They're always dragging us back to the nest.'

Eddie smiled. 'Yeah.'

Whatever the fuck Arabella was doing, Eddie was going to get to the bottom of it.

Chapter Fifty-Nine

'What are you doing here?' Arabella said as she opened the door to Roxanne.

She'd arrived home just a few hours ago, having discovered that Scarlett was dead and was still none the wiser as to how it had happened. It looked suspicious, based on the news report and the police presence. Surely the police would want to talk to Arabella, being her boss. Roxanne turning up now was something she didn't want to deal with.

'Charming,' Roxanne replied, pushing past her and entering the flat without being welcomed. 'I just thought I'd check in, see how you're doing after today?'

Arabella closed the door behind her former friend and sighed. All she wanted was for Eddie to come home. She needed him around and he seemed to be here less and less.

'I've had a really shitty day, on top of what you've brought into the salon. So, if you don't mind—'

'No, I don't mind at all. Actually, the salon seems to be the best place for my little money-maker. No one suspects and no one will because you're going to be a good little friend and keep your mouth shut.' She jabbed a finger at Arabella, poking her in the chest.

Arabella hesitated but kept her eyes on the bitch standing in front of her. 'Right now, I couldn't give a fuck what you say to me, Roxanne. You're just out of prison after a ten-year stretch. One sniff of trouble from you and the polis would have you back inside before they could slap the cuffs on you.'

Roxanne laughed loudly and towered over Arabella. It was obvious she was trying to intimidate her, yet somehow Arabella didn't feel like backing down, even though deep down she knew that Roxanne could knock her out with one punch. Arabella knew that the right thing to do would be to turn herself in, because no matter what, she'd killed someone. But she wasn't going to say that to Roxanne.

'Is that right? Well just you remember hen, I've got dirt on you. You just remember that one word from me and it'll be you straight back at Kirktonhill. You'd get a lot more than ten months for what you did, and this time you won't have me to walk you through it.'

Arabella shook her head. 'Just do one, Rox. I'm not in the mood for your shit.'

Roxanne stood firm, unmoving. Arabella could tell that she wanted confirmation that she wouldn't talk about her little drug venture.

Arabella eyed the open front door and moved towards it, holding the handle firmly in her grasp. 'Just get out, Roxanne.'

Roxanne turned, her brow furrowed and Arabella sighed, ready to tell her again to get the hell out. But then Roxanne said something that made Arabella's stomach lurch, her skin chill.

'Your Eddie's in a bit of shit. Saw him leaving that Scarlett's flat earlier. He was raging from what I could see. Then the police are crawling her street. Did you know she was found dead in her flat today?'

The nausea clawed at her throat as Arabella's body tried to reject the words that Roxanne was saying. Why would she say this? Why would she link Eddie to Scarlett like that?

'Yeah, he's her boss and she hadn't turned up for work. He was probably just trying to get hold of her and when he couldn't, he left.' Arabella failed to sound confident.

'Aye, you tell yourself that, love. But why don't you ask dear old Eddie how he met Scarlett in the first place? Why don't you ask him how well he really knows her? Do you really want to be with someone when you don't know who they really are?'

Arabella swallowed back the nausea as she watched Roxanne smirk and head for the door. She wanted to slam her head between the door and the frame, and in days gone by she would have. Arabella was a rough girl back in the early days. But she'd seen what life could be like on the other side now, seen a future ahead of her with Eddie and some money in the bank. There was no way she was going to let Roxanne be the reason she lost all that.

'I don't want to be around someone when I don't know who they really are. That's why I'm telling you to get the fuck out of my flat. I'm not scared of you and I'm definitely not going to let you stand there and try to intimidate me or lie about Eddie.'

Roxanne smiled, and a sadistic glint shone out from her eyes. 'Just ask him. I bet you he'll crumble at the mere idea that you have your suspicions.'

At that she left and Arabella slammed the door so hard that it shook in the frame.

And then the tiny cogs at the back of her head began to turn. Roxanne barely knew Eddie. So why would she say what she had about him, if there wasn't some weight behind it?

–

Pacing the floor of the flat, phone in hand, Arabella's head was now swimming with all sorts of thoughts. What was going to happen to the salon now that Roxanne had made clear her plans for it? What would happen to Arabella regarding the murder, of which she still had no memory? What had happened to Scarlett? What if Eddie *was* involved, as Roxanne had suggested?

She'd sent Eddie a message not long after Roxanne had left and he hadn't replied. She'd contacted the office but he wasn't there either. So where the hell was he? There were so many questions about how her life was quickly spiralling out of control. She couldn't even trust Eddie now.

A sound from the hallway halted Arabella on the spot in the living room. A key in the door. He was back. She marched out to the hall, ready to blurt it all out and ask him what was going on. But then she saw the look on his face.

'Hi,' she said, her tone soft.

Eddie closed the door behind him and his eyes narrowed. 'You got some stuff you want to tell me? About a certain Roxanne pulling you into a situation you shouldn't be in?'

Arabella felt her chest tighten. How did he know about that?

'Well?' he said, taking his jacket off. 'Go on then. Tell me what happened.'

His tone was firm, angry. Her eyes burned as she stared back at Eddie and her stomach flipped. She had to tell him the truth. But she had her own questions too.

'It was an accident. I didn't mean for it to happen. I can't even fucking remember because I was so blind drunk. That night, when we all went out from the salon, I drank so much and we got split up. When I woke up the next morning Roxanne told me what I'd done. I didn't believe her. I thought I'd changed; thought I'd got all the anger out of me after the last stint in jail. But then I went down to the pathway and the police were there, had cordoned off the place. How did you find out? How did you know I'd killed him?'

Eddie's eyes were wide, unblinking. His face paled and he stepped forward. 'You what?'

Arabella frowned. 'How did you know I killed him? I barely know how it happened. But Roxanne was there, she… dealt with it.'

Eddie moved closer, gripped Arabella by the shoulders. 'Arabella, what did you and Roxanne do?'

She realised then that when Eddie had come in and asked her about the situation Roxanne had pulled her into, he hadn't meant what she'd thought. Because Roxanne hadn't pulled her into that situation. She'd just sorted it for her, and then used it as blackmail against her.

'That's not what you meant?'

Eddie shook his head. 'You need to start from the beginning and tell me what kind of shit you've got yourself into with Roxanne.'

Arabella felt her legs buckle from beneath her, but she managed to stay upright and move through to the living room. Eddie followed, but instead of sitting down together like they normally would, they stood facing each other. Staring at one another.

'Start talking.' Eddie said.

So she did.

Chapter Sixty

The door was slightly ajar when she reached it. She went to step over the threshold when it was pulled open from the other side.

'What the fuck are you doing here?' *Scarlett said.*

'I'm here to warn you to keep your mouth shut,' *Roxanne said, closing the door behind her.*

'Who the hell do you think you are, coming into my home and telling me to keep my mouth shut? You,' *Scarlett pointed in Roxanne's face.* 'You are a murderer. A dealer and witch of a woman.'

Roxanne nodded, rolled her eyes. Then she pushed past Scarlett and moved through to the lounge.

'You've been shagging your boss?'

'What business is it of yours if I have?' *Scarlett said.*

'It's not,' *Roxanne said.* 'But it's good for me that you have been, because it means I've got leverage to get you sacked. I'm here to tell you that you'll be leaving the salon for good, whether you hand in your notice or whether I tell Arabella that you've been at it with Eddie behind her back.'

Scarlett laughed loudly. 'Oh do fuck off, Roxanne. I don't take orders from scum like you.'

Roxanne felt the words burn on her skin.

'You've already wrecked my life. My brother is dead because of you. My kids have lost their uncle, my mum has lost her son and you're just walking around here free as a fucking bird. I don't think so, scumbag.' *Scarlett moved to open the door, as though she were going to throw Roxanne out but before she could, Roxanne punched her in the side of the ribs and Scarlett fell to the floor.*

'What's up with you?' Roxanne asked Jake as he padded into the kitchen, wearing just his boxer shorts.

They'd both got home late last night and had barely spoken to one another. Roxanne had had a busy day, with Arabella's reaction to Stephanie and Selina, then dealing with Scarlett. That bitch had had to go. It was one thing to be accused of something she was guilty of, that Roxanne had mastered. But to be accused of something she hadn't done had pushed her over the edge. For Scarlett to say that Roxanne was the reason that her brother had died was below the belt. It wasn't her fault that he'd overdosed. She'd been in prison at the time, so how was she expected to take responsibility? If you were a junkie, you needed to know your limits and it was clear that Johnny hadn't. But after some time to think about what Scarlett had said, Roxanne had seen it as an opportunity to get rid of her so she couldn't bad-mouth her anymore. It had been so easy to make it look like someone else had murdered her. Eddie had walked right into that trap. He was such an idiot, whose brain was clearly in his crotch. Roxanne had known there was something going on between Eddie and Scarlett from that first night she'd met him. She'd decided to keep an eye on them, not just for Arabella's sake, but so she could use the situation to her own advantage if need be.

'Nothing,' Jake replied, switching on the coffee machine. He looked tense and Roxanne knew just how to sort him out. She got to her feet and began massaging his shoulders but he shrugged her off. 'Not now, eh? My head's bursting.'

Roxanne let her hands drop and tutted. They hadn't touched each other since the night she'd got out of prison. Any normal man would be all over his girlfriend when she'd been away for ten years. But not Jake.

'You know what? I don't even know why we're together, Jake. Sometimes I just wish…' Roxanne stopped, realising what she was about to say.

Jake didn't respond as he poured himself a coffee and stared out of the kitchen window. She thought about Jez. Was it a coincidence that he had turned up when things were going wrong between her and Jake? Now that she thought about her relationship, had things ever been right? She'd been in prison for half the time they'd been together and now all she could think about was Jez. He'd come to see her for a reason. She'd told him to fuck off because of what had happened between them. She'd lost her best friend. But that didn't change the way she felt about him, even after all these years.

'Are you depressed or something?' Roxanne pushed Jake for a reaction.

'No,' he said. 'Can't a man just have his coffee in peace?'

Roxanne shook her head. There was more to this than he was letting on.

'You've been acting weird ever since I got out. Is there another woman or something?' The suggestion made her laugh but maybe that was the case.

'Ha,' he said. 'If only it was that simple, Roxanne.' He turned. 'Look, there's no one else. It's just this job with Cole. It's hard going and he's a pain in the pisser to work with. A bit of a loose cannon and I need to stay focused. It's nothing to do with you.'

Roxanne watched him, taking in his expression. He could be lying, but she wasn't able to tell. But he was right about Cole. He seemed a bit riotous at times; there was a glint in his eye. The way he'd looked at Roxanne when she'd first met him told her that he could be an evil bastard if he really wanted to be. So maybe that was what was up with Jake, maybe he didn't like the fact that Roxanne was involved?

'It's so hard to read you at times, Jake.'

'Then don't try to. Alright?'

With that he turned and walked out of the kitchen. He'd left his mobile phone on the worktop the night before. She eyed it, wondering if there would be anything in there that would tell her what was really going on inside his head.

The sound of Jake switching on the shower made Roxanne reach for the phone and she slid her thumb across the screen. It was locked and she didn't know the passcode. Just as she was about to place the phone back down, she saw two messages ping onto the screen at the same time. One from Cole. One from Eddie.

The one from Eddie piqued her interest. Yes, he was involved in the job with Cole and Jake, but he hardly knew Jake enough to send a friendly text – if that's what it was. She couldn't open the full thing to check.

It started off:

> Mate, we need to talk. It's about…

The message trailed off then and no matter how many code combinations she tried, Roxanne couldn't open Jake's phone. What was it that Eddie wanted to tell Jake?

The one from Cole was two words.

> Packages ready.

That meant that Roxanne would have to go back to the salon and arrange for Stephanie and Selina to pick them up. Hopefully, Arabella had learned her lesson this time and would either stay away or not make trouble.

Roxanne had already killed one bitch this week, she didn't want to have to do another.

Chapter Sixty-One

The mug of hot tea warmed Arabella's hands as she sat in bed, her head resting against the pillow. She glanced out of the window and as the sun came up, she wondered what was going to happen with her and Eddie. In the time they'd been together, he'd stood by her in her darkest moments. Last night when she'd spilled her guts about the salon, about what Roxanne was doing there and what had happened on the river path, his reaction had surprised her. He'd been calm, focused.

'Hey,' he said now, his voice croaky from sleep. 'You okay?'

Arabella smiled. 'Everything is such a mess, Eddie. I was so caught up in what was going on with me, I never even told you about Scarlett.'

Eddie glanced up at her and frowned. 'What about her?'

'She's dead.'

He sat up so quickly that Arabella almost spilled her tea. 'What do you mean she's dead?'

She felt her eyes burn as the tears came. 'I don't know. I still don't have any details. But she didn't show up for work yesterday and I heard on the news that police had cordoned off her street due to a disturbance. I decided to go and check on her and when I got there, there was police everywhere and they were guarding the entrance to her flat. I saw a woman, hysterical crying. She was shouting for Scarlett. It was her mum. Jesus, it's awful. What about her boys, Eddie?'

Arabella was sobbing as she described the scene and Eddie put an arm around her.

'Do they know what happened?' he whispered.

'I don't know. But I expect the police will want to speak to us since we're her employers?'

Eddie paused for a moment and Arabella sank into him. 'Yes, they probably will.'

She felt his heart beat against the side of her face and it comforted her. Things were such a mess but she knew that Eddie would be there for her.

Arabella had to go into work today; she couldn't abandon the girls when their manager had just been found dead in suspicious circumstances. She had to pull herself together.

'Eddie, are we okay? I mean, after everything I told you last night I'm surprised you didn't up and leave in the middle of the night.'

Eddie pulled away and smiled down at her. 'Arabella, there's nothing you could say or do that would make me do that. Trust me, I have your back on this. You're not going back to prison. I promise.'

The words flooded her with relief, but the look of confusion and dismay on his face made her stomach flip quickly.

Chapter Sixty-Two

Jake sat at the corner of his favourite breakfast café just off Maryhill Road and waited for Eddie. His message had sounded urgent and if Jake was honest with himself, he needed to get out of the flat. Being around Roxanne was making him feel like shit. He'd been living a lie as far back as he could remember, and now with Cole on his back he felt like he was drowning in it all.

The waitress placed his second mug of coffee of the morning on the table in front of him just as the bell above the door rang. He looked up and saw Eddie striding in. His expression was sullen and Jake frowned.

'Morning,' Eddie said, sitting down opposite Jake and lifting the menu, before quickly letting it drop to the surface of the table.

'You okay? You look raging.'

Eddie shook his head and Jake regarded him through narrow eyes. 'What's the problem?'

'Your missus is my problem. You and Cole never told me that the salon was part of the deal.'

Jake glanced around the café and leaned forward. 'Keep your voice down, Ed. And you never asked.'

Sitting back on the hard plastic chair, Eddie sniggered. 'Oh, is that how it goes, is it? You make deals about one of my businesses behind my fucking back and because I don't ask, you just don't tell me? My missus is being taken for a fucking mug, Jake and I'm not having it. The salon is off limits and if you

299

don't pull it out of the deal then I'm off. You and Cole can find your own fucking transport.'

Eddie's voiced hissed across the table and Jake raised a brow. This was the first time Jake had ever seen Eddie lose his cool. So far, all Jake had witnessed was Eddie, cool and respectable businessman. Now, his brow was speckled with tiny beads of sweat and the vein in his neck looked like it was about to pop.

'I can't do that, Eddie. A deal's a deal.'

'Fine,' Eddie said. 'Then I suppose you won't mind when Roxanne finds out about your little London escapade. What was his name again? Mark?'

Jake's stomach began to roll. How did Eddie know about Mark? 'Eddie, if I were you, I'd keep that mouth of yours shut.'

'Touched a nerve, have I?'

Jake said nothing and watched as an unblinking Eddie smiled over at the waitress and ordered himself a coffee as though everything was normal.

'I mean, if both Cole and I were to tell her about it then she'd have no choice but to believe it, would she? Two against one? Doesn't feel nice, does it, Jakey boy?'

The mere sound of that name, the one that Cole used to wind Jake up chilled his skin. He ran through the options in his head. He couldn't allow Roxanne to find out about Mark. She wouldn't care that Jake had killed the guy, but she would care very much about why.

'Right,' Jake said as he lifted his coffee mug and took a sip. 'Let's talk. I'm sure we can come to some kind of arrangement.'

Eddie glared at him across the table. Maybe Jake could make this situation work in his favour?

'Yes, I'm sure we can. But we have to be able to trust each other, Jake. So, I think we should lay all our cards on the table and see where we end up.'

Jake nodded. This was going to be a long conversation.

Chapter Sixty-Three

The text message Billy had received from Eddie had been a short one. It told him an email would be coming through to him from the email address that Billy and his undercover team had supplied. Not that Eddie had ever met the others in the team. The less he got to meet, the better for him.

Billy refreshed his emails several times before Eddie's message came through. There was one attachment, a photograph. He read the email first and as he took in the words, his stomach leaped. It all sounded so familiar. It unsettled him. His thumb hovered over the attachment when the doorbell went, alerting him that someone was at his door. Not now, he thought.

Choosing to ignore his unwanted visitor, Billy opened the attachment and it began to download. It was grainy at first and he couldn't make out the face. But as it came into focus, Billy's leaping stomach almost shot up and out of his throat.

'Jesus fucking Christ,' he said as he stared down at it.

Never in a million years had he wanted to see that face again. It was the one that had almost changed his life forever back before he'd gone into the force. Back when he was just a young lad.

He shut the picture off and called Eddie.

'Tell me again where you got the image from that you just sent me.'

Billy listened carefully as Eddie told him that he'd taken a screenshot of the image from Cole Woods's phone.

'He said that the guy's his brother and he went missing twenty years ago. I know it's not relevant but you told me to

301

leave no detail out so that's why I sent it. Why, do you know who the guy is?'

Billy's heart pounded in his chest as he processed the question. But what could he say?

'Cheers for this, Eddie. I'll be in touch.'

He hung up the phone and began pacing the floor, back and forth and around the kitchen table. He tapped the phone against his chin, wondering what the hell was going to happen when all this came out. Because there was no way he was going to be able to get away with this. Murder always caught up with the killer one way or another.

He sank down onto a seat at the kitchen table before calling the only person he could think of who would be able to sort this out.

'Jez, it's Billy. Look, something's come up and I need to see you right now.'

'It's a good thing I'm at your door then. Did you not hear me ring the bell?'

'Sorry. I was distracted,' Billy said. Understatement of the fucking century.

Billy headed to the front door and let Jez in. Jez regarded him for a moment and smirked.

'You look like you've seen a fucking ghost.'

'I have,' Billy said, holding the phone up to Jez. He watched as his former best friend glared at the screen before turning his eyes to Billy.

'Why are you showing me this?'

Billy exhaled loudly. 'Because the guy I'm investigating, the guy you're looking for, is looking for him. This is Cole Wood's brother.'

Jez raised a brow. 'Are you sure?'

'Aye. My informant is getting closer to him and he showed him this picture. Said he went missing twenty years ago. It's the same guy, isn't it? This is the guy I killed in Majorca and the same guy you got rid of.'

Jez shook his head. 'Jesus fucking Christ, Billy. Just when you think the universe isn't listening, then bam!' He slapped his hand off the kitchen table and Billy glared at him. 'I got my fucking revenge on him before I even needed to.'

Billy shook his head. 'What the fuck are you on about, Jez? This isn't a game. This is our past catching up with us. Cole Woods has told my informant that he's going to hire a private investigator to find out what happened to his brother.'

Jez let out a cackle and grinned widely. 'No, Billy. This is exactly what we needed to happen. The guy who steals a hundred grand from me is the brother of the lad you killed all those years ago. It's like killing two birds with one stone. I get my money and we get rid of the guy who could blow our cover. It's a no-brainer.'

Billy's eyes were wide at the sheer stupidity of the idea. 'You're damn fucking right it's a no-brainer. You'd have to be brain dead to think that would work.'

'It will work, Billy. Have I ever let you down before? And be honest now. Remember the money we owed to that drug dealer back in the day? Diggo? Did I sort that? Yes I did. Did I get rid of the body in Majorca with no comeback? Yes I did. So what makes you think I'd fuck this up or that you'd get caught?'

Billy felt sick but on some level he knew Jez was right. Jez had been like a brother growing up and never once had he ever let him down. They'd been there for each other from day one. It had only been in the last couple of decades that their friendship had fallen away because of the distance between them and their very different life paths. But they'd never had any bad blood and if this situation had taught Billy anything, it was never to burn bridges.

'You contacted me about this, Billy. Not the other way around. I could walk away from this now. Find Cole myself, get my money and leave you to pick up the pieces. Do you want to go to prison? I mean, you work with a team of highly skilled investigators. Not to mention the private investigator that Cole is seemingly going to hire – with my fucking money, no doubt.'

Billy shook his head.

'You know, I knew this police officer once,' Jez smiled. 'He was sent to the jail for gross misconduct or some shit like that. Anyway, he ended up with a spinal injury while he was inside, for grassing up the guy involved. In a wheelchair now, paralysed from the neck down. Shame, that. He's still all there in the head, but he can't move.'

The former friends locked eyes, and Billy didn't care if the story was false or not. It was a warning.

Chapter Sixty-Four

Roxanne McPhail crossed the road and kept her eye on the salon. Peering through the window, she saw Arabella standing at the reception desk, looking glamourous as if she didn't have a care in the world. It annoyed Roxanne a little that Arabella had it all. Coming out of prison was a doddle for the likes of her when she had her dear old boyfriend to throw money at her. Money that came from guilt, of course.

Arabella looked up from the booking diary at the reception desk and locked eyes with her, before giving her a sarcastic smile and waving her in. She'd sent Roxanne a text first thing that morning, asking her to come to the salon to speak to her.

Roxanne reached the door and pushed it open before stepping inside. She glared at Arabella but put on a smile for the sake of everyone else.

'Hi,' Arabella said. 'I've got a little unexpected surprise for you.'

Roxanne regarded the tone and in an instant, it got her back up. There was a hint of sarcasm in there and from the look on Arabella's face, she could tell Roxanne was suspicious.

'Look, I don't want us to fall out,' Arabella said, stepping out from behind the desk and standing next to her. She placed a hand on Roxanne's arm and gestured for her to follow as she headed towards the back of the salon. 'But there's someone here that really wants to see you and they insisted they wait until you got here.'

Roxanne watched as Arabella walked away and had no choice but to follow her so as not to make a scene in front of the customers and the other stylists. The anger building inside was overwhelming. She didn't like that Arabella had some of the power now.

She reached the kitchen door and Arabella was already holding it open. Roxanne stepped inside and her heart almost jumped into her throat. Turning, she frowned at Arabella.

'What the fuck is this?'

'Look, there's obviously some air to be cleared. So, I'm happy for you to use *my* salon to do that. Have fun catching up with your old friend. I've heard all about what you got up to back in the day.'

Roxanne watched as Arabella closed the door with the most sinister smile she'd ever seen on her face. She turned to face her visitor.

'Charlene, long time no see,' Roxanne said.

'Not long enough, if you ask me.'

'Then why come here?'

Charlene was leaning against the counter next to the kettle, but pushed herself off and stood with her back straight and shoulders pushed back.

'Is he here to see you?' Charlene asked and Roxanne thought she detected a hint of emotion in her voice.

'Who?' Roxanne said, playing dumb. Of course, she knew Charlene was talking about Jez.

'Don't give me that shit. It just so happens that he comes to Scotland "on business",' she said, using her fingers to do air quotes. 'And suddenly you show up.'

'I can't show up if I'm the one who lives here, can I? Charlene, I really couldn't give a shit if you think Jez came here to see me. And I don't care if he wants to see me. I've got things going on here that don't concern my past at all. So, if you don't mind, I've got to get on.' Roxanne pulled out her phone and handed it to Charlene. 'Here, check it if you don't believe me.'

Charlene's eyes narrowed as she took the phone from her. 'Yeah, your little friend out there told me all about your drug-peddling here. Was ten years in the jail not enough for you? You want back in?'

Roxanne shook her head. 'Are you still jealous that I was shagging Jez back then? Do you know what, Charlene? I *did* know you and Jez were together, but I'd just arrived in Spain and I thought, fuck it.' Roxanne spun the lie so well, she almost believed it herself. There was nothing that she would be able to say to Charlene that would make her believe anything else. She truly believed that Roxanne had screwed her over willingly, so why not use it and wind her up about it? Roxanne would only hit the same brick wall she had twenty years ago if she tried to convince her that she'd had no idea that Charlene was seeing Jez.

'I wanted to live, I wanted to have fun,' she continued. 'Did you come all the way from Majorca to find out if your husband was *still* sleeping with me? Woah, that's intense, and a little psycho if you ask me.'

Roxanne laughed and watched as Charlene's shoulders tensed. It was crazy to think that they'd been best friends once.

'No, I didn't come here for that. Well, not *only* that. I came to do this.'

Charlene swung her arm up and back-handed Roxanne across the face. Her cheek exploded as Charlene's diamond ring connected with her skin and she fell to the floor. A foot flew at her face and Roxanne buried her head in her hands and tried to angle away from the blow. Charlene clearly anticipated the defence and changed her tactic and Roxanne felt a boot to the stomach. One, two, three more before she relented.

'That's for fucking up my marriage before it even got started. You can fucking have him, you two deserve each other. And you can tell him that the next time you see him.'

The sound Charlene made as she hawked back as much saliva as she could made Roxanne rage, but she couldn't get to her feet from the pain of the blows.

Saliva rained down on her before the sound of heeled boots left the room via the back door. Roxanne stayed down for a few moments, trying to regain some of her composure. She'd never been treated that way, not even in the early days at Kirktonhill. She felt humiliated even though she was on her own. Had Arabella known this was going to happen? Roxanne hadn't told Arabella about her time in Majorca, or about Charlene, so how could she have known? Unless Charlene had told her everything. But they were strangers, so why would Charlene spill all to Arabella?

Roxanne attempted to get to her feet but the pain in her stomach kept her down. She managed to pull herself to a sitting position and leaned her back against the cupboard. The door opened just a few inches. When she looked up, she saw Arabella's face peering through the gap.

'What happened?' she asked, slipping into the room and closing the door behind her. 'Did that girl do this to you?'

'Oh, don't give me that shit, Arabella. You knew fine well what was going to happen in here and you let it happen because you can't handle the fact that I have control over this place.' Roxanne winced as she moved onto her knees and stood up. Glancing in the small mirror on the opposite side of the wall, she saw the blood trickling down her face from where Charlene had hit her. Bitch, she thought. But the attack was not unlike the way Roxanne would have handled the situation herself. She had to give it to Charlene, she had some back hand on her.

'I didn't know she was going to physically attack you, Roxanne. I don't condone violence. Not anymore.'

'You mean after you murdered that guy on the river path?' Roxanne sneered. 'You're so full of shit, Arabella.'

Arabella didn't respond, instead she moved past Roxanne and opened a drawer, pulled out an envelope and handed it to her.

'What's this?'

'It's the papers for this place. Here, take them. You want full control then you can have it. I want nothing to do with any of it.'

Roxanne looked down at the envelope and took the papers out, glanced over them and smiled. 'What's the catch?'

'No catch. I had Eddie contact his solicitor first thing. He fast-tracked it. The place is yours. Run it into the ground, turn it into a brothel for all I care. I'm done. All you have to do is sign and the place is yours.'

Arabella turned and headed for the back door, but before she left, she said, 'Just make sure you read it. I don't want you coming to me and telling me that I've screwed you over when things go wrong here.'

'You're trying to tell me that you're signing this business over to me?' Roxanne winced again.

'Yes. I've told Eddie everything and I don't want anything to do with this place if you've got your claws into it. I'm not having you drag me down. I got out of prison and I want it to stay that way.'

Roxanne narrowed her eyes, tried to play things coolly even though her face was pulsing with pain and her ribs and stomach felt as though they were about to fall out of her arse. 'You do know what Eddie's been up to, don't you?'

Arabella nodded and smiled. 'Yes, I know *everything*. Have a nice life, Rox.'

With that, Arabella exited the salon via the back door and as it closed behind her, Roxanne stared down at the papers in her hands and smiled. As easy as that? It had taken a lot less time than she'd first anticipated, but Arabella had been very easy to manipulate. From the first time they met in prison, Roxanne knew that Arabella was someone that could be used to get what she wanted. But she'd never have betted she'd get a business out of her. Regardless of the pain from the beating Charlene had just given her, Roxanne couldn't help but smile.

Pulling the papers out, she read over the first page and it all looked legit. She'd run it past Jake. Or maybe she wouldn't.

He'd been so distant lately, maybe this was what she needed. A fresh start away from Jake. Maybe she'd go legit herself? She didn't know the first thing about business but she could learn.

Chapter Sixty-Five

'Hi,' Arabella called as she stepped into the flat. 'I'm back.'

Eddie appeared in the hall to greet her and smiled. 'Job done?'

Arabella nodded. 'Yep. She fell for it hook, line and sinker. Stupid bitch.'

'Good.' Eddie said.

'But there's something else. Something happened that I didn't expect. That girl that came to the salon to see Roxanne. She took her phone and when I left, she handed it to me outside. Told me that there was something on it that I should see and that I was stupid to ever have trusted Roxanne in the first place.'

Eddie smirked. 'I could have told you that from day one.'

Arabella didn't care that Eddie had a smart mouth on him. Right now, all she cared about was showing him the contents of Roxanne's phone. She grabbed his hand and led him into the lounge before sitting down on the couch. Eddie sat down beside her and watched as she opened up the phone.

'The stupid bitch didn't even have a passcode on it. That's what ten years in the jail will do to you. You miss the movement of technology.'

Eddie smiled and stared down at the screen as Arabella went into the video gallery and selected the first video.

'This is the one she showed me from that night. I still can't remember anything at all and you know what? I think she spiked my drink so that I would forget this. It makes perfect sense.'

Arabella hadn't had a long time to think about it, but Roxanne was a bad seed and Arabella had been drawn to the likes of her throughout her life, ever since she'd gone into the care system.

Glancing down at the screen, she talked Eddie through the short clip as they watched together. Arabella was standing over the body of the man on the river path, crying and wailing about what had happened. 'Looks cut and dried, doesn't it? I mean, with my record, this video isn't far short of a confession. But then there's this.'

Arabella shut off the clip, opened the next one and hit play. She was silent as Eddie took in what was happening on the screen.

'Jesus,' he said at the end. 'She filmed the entire fucking thing? What the hell did she do, prop the phone up against the wall? She's sick in the head.'

Arabella nodded. 'I didn't know her at all. I wouldn't be surprised if she'd got away with other murders if this is how she goes about her business.'

Eddie took the phone from Arabella's hand and slid it into his pocket before getting to his feet. 'We need to show this to the police. They need to get her off the street, Arabella.'

Arabella nodded. 'I know.'

Eddie took a breath and pulled out his own phone.

'Billy, it's Eddie. I've got something I think you'll be interested in.'

—

Eddie stood outside the building, Roxanne's phone in one hand as he smoked a cigarette. He glared down at the phone and felt the rage building inside him. Roxanne had made no effort to hide her crimes. They were all in her phone, like some kind of trophy that she could look at whenever she wanted. She was definitely sick in the head; that Eddie was sure of.

He stared down at the images on the screen of Scarlett lying there. Her lips blue and her face puffy, covered in blood and cuts, she hardly looked like herself. That was absolutely not the way Eddie had left her. Roxanne had gone in after he'd left and killed her. What kind of sick person took pictures of a dead person, especially one she'd just killed?

'Can you use this?' Eddie asked. 'Would this be enough to get her out of our hair for good?'

Billy took a draw of his own cigarette and nodded, keeping his eye out on the road. 'Aye. This should be fine. And your missus is sure she signed that confession?'

'Roxanne's reckless. Arabella is certain she'll sign it if she thinks it's business transfer papers. But we might not even have to use it now we have this.'

'Aye,' Billy said. 'Let's hope not because it's not exactly legal.'

Eddie frowned. He hadn't thought of DS Drysdale as a bent police officer. But with everything that had happened since Arabella's release, anything was possible.

Eddie couldn't help but think that Scarlett's death was his fault. If he hadn't bought the salon for Arabella, Scarlett would never have come into contact with Roxanne and she'd still be alive.

Chapter Sixty-Six

More drugs packages were set and ready to go. His supply had been flying out the door. Roxanne had been a dab hand at getting those girls to sell drugs and they were making a small fortune. That in itself was great, but on top of that Cole hadn't been near a casino or a betting shop in a week, since he'd told Eddie about Jake. It had been difficult, but he'd needed to do it so he could afford the fee for the private investigator to find out what had happened to his brother.

Opening the door to Roxanne, Eddie and Jake, he welcomed them in and closed the door. This little team they had going was working well and if Cole ever needed to return to Glasgow once he'd made his money, then he knew who he'd be coming to for work.

'Alright, mate?' Eddie nodded.

Cole sensed the tension in the air and regarded them all. 'What's going on?' Roxanne stood with her back to Eddie and Jake looked like a kid who'd woken up to fuck all presents on Christmas morning.

'Eddie here can't handle the fact that I screwed over his missus and he knew fuck all about it. Big businessman took his eye off the ball,' Roxanne sneered.

'Can I just get the gear so I can get the fuck away from her?' Eddie said. Jake shot him a look but said nothing.

'Are you going to let him speak to me like that?' Roxanne said, reaching out and giving Jake a shove.

'Wow, wow, wow. Seems the only person who took their eye off the ball is me. What the *fuck's* going on?' Cole said.

Before anyone could answer, the heavy footsteps outside the front door alerted Cole to the CCTV screen in the kitchen. He moved towards it and glared at it as it projected an image of the street. No police cars, no riot vans.

A gentle knock on the door caused a stir in Cole's belly that made him feel sick. Something wasn't right. He reached the hall and watched as Eddie pulled the door open. It all happened so quickly, Cole had to blink to check his eyes weren't deceiving him.

'Come in lads,' Eddie said, stepping back.

The two men stepped into the flat and Cole straightened his back. This was it. The moment he'd been dreading, yet expecting.

'I told you I'd find you in the end, Cole.'

Cole glared at Jez Kennedy and then at the other guy. Roxanne looked confused, but Cole noticed how the corner of Jake's mouth was raised in a very subtle smile.

'What the *hell* are you doing here?' Roxanne asked.

'Never you mind,' Jez replied. He glanced at her and said, 'Jesus, what happened to your face?'

'Your missus happened to my face. Did you know she was here?'

'No, I didn't.' He turned away from her and took a step forward, adjusting his coat. 'So, tell me Cole. Where's my money? And my mother's wedding ring?'

Cole narrowed his eyes and shook his head. 'I don't have them.'

'Please don't insult my intelligence by lying to me. You and I both know you took one hundred grand of my cash as well as my mother's wedding ring and I want them back. With interest, of course.'

Roxanne turned and glared at Cole. 'You stole money from Jez Kennedy? Jesus Christ, Cole. Are you on a death wish?'

'No, I didn't steal money from him. I don't know what he's talking about.'

'Shall I just contact the Albanians then? Have them come and deal with you?' Jez said.

Cole froze. The thought of the Albanians getting him was enough to cause him to drop dead with fear on the spot. Just as Cole was about to answer, there was a swift movement from Jez, his hand a blur as it reached in and grabbed the handgun from the inside pocket of his coat.

Before Cole could move, the side of the gun connected with his temple and he went down quickly.

'Jesus Christ, Jez. What are you doing?' Roxanne shouted.

Cole felt his eyes closing but before the light went out, he saw Jake kneeling down in front of him with that wry smile across his face.

'Good luck getting out of this one, Cole.' He stood up, and his face was replaced with Jez's.

'Shame I've not got the same carpet I used to wrap your brother in twenty years ago,' Jez whispered. 'Two brothers, one carpet. One bin lorry. Suppose I'll have to use my imagination with this one.' The words stung as the realisation kicked in, but he couldn't move. The blow to the side of the head had stunned him.

The last thing he remembered was Jez's foot coming towards his face. The pain as it connected with his mouth. A black shadow crept in from the sides of his eyes then.

Chapter Sixty-Seven

Billy Drysdale sat opposite Cole Woods and waited for him to come to. Jez had tied him up and sat him on a chair in the middle of the floor in the living room before heading into the bedroom to search the place for cash. He'd found plenty of it and had already bagged it up. There was more than he was owed and Billy had been promised a good amount of it if he went with Jez's plan. Go rogue. He'd had to, to keep his own crime out of the spotlight.

'He made any sounds yet?' Jez asked.

'Nah, nothing. He will, though,' Billy replied. 'Here, how did you know that girl, Roxanne?'

Jez shook his head. 'We were a thing once. After you went home from Majorca, I met her. I was shagging her and her mate at the same time. Trust me, don't ever do that. It's a bigger headache than it's worth.'

'Hang on,' Billy said. 'What about Charlene?'

'Aye, she and Charlene were mates. It all got a bit messy and Charlene found out, nearly killed Roxanne and I never heard the fucking end of it, mate.'

Billy couldn't help but laugh. 'So, you and Charlene made a go of it anyway?'

'Had to mate, she was pregnant at the time. It was shit from the beginning. We could have had our good times. It's just that she never got over it. She always said that the beginning of a relationship shouldn't be based on lies and cheating. I suppose in a way she's right. But the way she acted just drove a wedge between us, you know? If you're going to forgive someone, you can't throw their mistakes in their face at every opportunity you get.'

Billy nodded and wondered how Jez had survived in a marriage where his wife had zero trust for him. Billy had always felt a little jealous, that Jez was out in Spain living the high life while he was working hard to get to the top of his own game. But in truth, Jez had never been that happy at all. The thought exited his mind as Cole Woods began to shift in his seat.

'Here we go,' Jez breathed. He stepped closer to Cole and bent down. 'Oi, Woods. You awake?'

Billy looked away as Cole grunted in response. He knew that Jez would kill Cole, not just because they had to get rid of him to keep his brother's murder quiet, but because he'd crossed a line. Stealing that amount of cash was a stupid thing to do, but to take Jez's mum's ring was something else entirely. And to have thought he would get away with it was just baffling. Billy knew that Jez was a resourceful man. He'd make sure that the job was done with no comeback, hire a hit man if he had to. Billy couldn't be a part of that. He just couldn't.

'You're a fucking cunt, Kennedy,' Cole said through broken teeth and swollen lips.

'That I am, wee man. Now, DS Drysdale here is going to leave us to it. He has some police work to do,' Jez said sarcastically. 'It's just you and me, Woods.'

Billy looked at Jez as he nodded towards the door. 'Go. Do what you need to do with the rest of them. I couldn't care less. I got what I came for. I'll be in touch.'

Jez held out his hand and Billy took it in his, gave it a shake and turned. He headed for the door and didn't look back. Jez wouldn't tell Billy what he was going to do with Cole unless he asked. It was hard enough living with what he'd done to Cole's brother; he didn't want a second kill on his conscience. It didn't matter how many killers Billy caught and put behind bars, no amount would ease that guilt.

None.

Chapter Sixty-Eight

Jake opened the door and allowed Arabella and Eddie to walk through to where Roxanne was waiting. Arabella's mind swirled with what was about to happen, but she kept her composure.

'You signed those papers yet?' Arabella said, standing in the middle of the living room, staring down at Roxanne. Her stomach was churning with excitement but she didn't allow that to show on her face.

'Aye, I've signed them. Didn't hang about really, signed them when you gave them to me. So all that's left to do now is to hand over the keys,' Roxanne said, getting to her feet and reaching down the side of the sofa. She produced the envelope and passed it to Arabella.

Arabella took the papers and read the last page. Roxanne was telling the truth; she'd signed the papers. She'd signed a confession to murder, and it was clear that she had no idea she'd done so. Clearly, she hadn't read all of it.

'Keys? Now?' Roxanne said.

Arabella glared at her and burst into hysterical laughter. Roxanne frowned and glanced at Jake and Eddie before resting her eyes back on Arabella.

'What the fuck's funny?'

Arabella had to take a few deep breaths and compose herself. 'You're what's funny, Rox. You know, for a businesswoman of the criminal underworld, you're not that fucking smart. Did you really think I was just going to hand over my business to you? *Really?* It just goes to show that you didn't read all of this.'

Roxanne's expression was furious and Arabella was loving it.

'What the hell are you talking about?' Jake asked, stepping in between them.

'Mate, don't.' Eddie put his hand up.

Jake batted his hand away.

'Roxanne, even though you have signed this confession to murder, I won't have to use it. It wouldn't stand up in court anyway, but now that we have actual evidence, I can—'

Everyone stopped then, turning their attention to the front door. Someone was banging on it loudly. Arabella kept her eyes on Roxanne. She wanted to see her expression when this all kicked off.

Jake moved through to the hall and pulled the door open. Footsteps followed silence and Arabella nodded at DS Billy Drysdale as he entered the room. He had two uniformed officers with him.

'Roxanne McPhail?' DS Drysdale said.

Arabella watched as Roxanne glared at the officers through narrowed eyes.

'We're arresting you in connection with the deaths of Keiran Mitchell and Scarlett Kent. In terms of section fourteen of the Criminal Procedure Scotland Act nineteen ninety-five, I have reasonable cause to suspect you have committed the crime of murder. The reasons for my suspicions are that you have been identified via video footage from a mobile phone. You do not have to say anything, but it may harm your defence if—'

'Are you *fucking kidding*? I didn't kill anyone and I don't even know who you're talking about,' Roxanne said. Arabella noticed how she kept her arms by her side, her hands perfectly still as she spoke. She was trying to plead innocence through her body language.

Keiran Mitchell. Now that the man had a name, Arabella felt sick. He was a real person and Roxanne had killed him purely so she would have a hold over her. And Scarlett? Arabella felt the emotion catch in her throat.

DS Drysdale continued. 'You're not obliged to say anything, but anything you do say will be noted and may be given as evidence.'

Roxanne exploded into a rage that Arabella hadn't even seen when they'd shared a cell in prison. She lashed out, went straight for Drysdale but the two uniformed officers were too quick for her. They were on her, restraining her.

'Hang on a minute, you're a *cop*?' Jake said, staring at Drysdale. 'But you were at Cole's flat.'

Drysdale shot him a glance and turned to him. 'Jake Cairney, you are under arrest for the murder of Mark Robertson...'

Arabella stopped listening. She didn't care about Jake, or what he'd done. But she was shocked and hadn't expected this. Instead of mirroring Roxanne's actions, Jake simply stood still, listened to Drysdale and complied.

Roxanne continued to kick and judder under the restraint of the officers.

'You can't just come in here and arrest us for murder without any evidence.'

Eddie smirked. 'Did you not just listen to what he said? They got their evidence direct from your phone, Roxanne. Thanks to your ex's wife after she beat seven shades of shit out of you at the salon.'

Roxanne sneered at Eddie, then a sadistic smile formed on her face. 'I take it Arabella knows you were sleeping with Scarlett? Maybe it was *you* who killed her?'

Arabella frowned and shot a look at Eddie. 'What?'

Roxanne gave a sarcastic gasp. 'Oh, you didn't know? Yeah, he was sleeping with her. I can't be sure how long for, but don't you think it's weird that he bought you the salon she worked in? Maybe he wanted to have you both around, maybe he liked the danger of knowing you would find out.'

Arabella felt her jaw tense but she refused to look at Eddie. She wouldn't give Roxanne the satisfaction. She'd been through hell in her life because of other people. Roxanne was going to be the last one to make things hard for her.

The police dragged Roxanne out of the flat as she kicked and screamed about being innocent. Jake turned to face Eddie and shook his head.

'What are you, a fucking super grass or something? Or are you undercover?'

Drysdale slapped cuffs across Jake's wrists and began guiding him out. Eddie didn't reply and when Arabella glanced at him, she saw the real Eddie for the first time. A cheat and a liar. Yes, he'd got her out of a situation that could have seen her back in jail, but what Roxanne said had made sense. When she'd met Eddie, he'd had a girlfriend. Arabella had turned his head and she'd certainly been taken in by him. He'd made her feel things she didn't know existed. He was kind, caring, passionate with her. He took care of her, listened to her story of going into care at a young age. He'd bought her a business for Christ's sake. So what had happened? Why did he change? Maybe he hadn't changed: they say once a cheat, always a cheat. That was how they'd started off.

Drysdale turned and gave Eddie a nod before leading Jake out to the police van. Arabella followed Eddie down to the street and watched as the van took them away. All the time she could hear Roxanne banging on the sides, shouting and screaming.

She stood a few meters away from Eddie and felt tears threaten, but she held them back. There was no way she was going to break down in the middle of the street.

'Is it true?' she asked, tucking a stray hair behind her ear.

Eddie didn't answer. He couldn't even look at her. That was all the confirmation she needed. Pulling the salon and flat keys from her pocket, Arabella threw them at Eddie's face.

Chapter Sixty-Nine

The sounds of Cole's screams were muffled against the rag that Jez had forced inside his mouth. The tape that had been wrapped across his face and around the back of his head pulled at his hair. No amount of struggling could free his hands that were bound behind his back, because he was lying on top of them inside the wooden box.

Jez had been sick enough to tell Cole the details of how his brother had met his death out in Spain. He'd been a cheeky bastard with the wrong person and it had resulted in him taking a beating. Jez had said that he'd tried to stop the guy from doing it, but it was too late so he'd had to get rid of the body. It wasn't personal, it wasn't planned. It had just happened. But then twenty years later, Cole had come along and stolen a substantial amount of Jez's money.

'It's funny when you think about it, really. Such a small world. You come out to find your brother, start working for me and decide that you want to take my cash to hire a private investigator to find out what happened to him, when the whole time you were working for the guy who did it. Well, the guy who helped get rid of him. I told you I'd find you, Cole. I always achieve my goals,' Jez had said as he'd dug out the grave for Cole. 'You know the thing that gets me the most, Woods? It's not the money. It's the ring. Why did you take it? What possible need would you have with a dead woman's ring? To pawn it for money? I tell you, it's a good thing I got it back, otherwise your death wouldn't be so fucking kind.'

Tears streamed down the sides of Cole's face as he listened to the grit and soil thundering down on top of his coffin. There was no point in fighting, no point in hoping. This was it. He was going to die at the hands of the same man who killed his brother twenty years ago.

He'd been inside the box for what felt like an eternity. He was tired, sore and broken, barely able to breathe. The sound of soil packing him deep into the ground stopped after a while.

Maybe this was karma for all the things Cole had done over the years. The drugs he'd dealt, the deaths, the blackmail. Maybe this was his punishment for those crimes.

Cole closed his eyes and slowed his breathing. If he was going to die like this, then he wanted it to feel like he was falling asleep. But it didn't matter what he thought, how he tried to calm himself.

Cole Woods couldn't stop himself from screaming his way into death.

Chapter Seventy

Billy signed his resignation letter and put it inside the envelope. After everything that had happened, he couldn't continue to serve as a DS. His life as a cop had been a lie. How was he supposed to protect the public when he himself was a killer? He knew that Jez was going to kill Cole Woods and he stood back and did nothing because it would keep him out of prison.

He'd promised himself that if Roxanne and Jake pleaded not guilty, he'd see through the trial. But they'd pleaded guilty because the evidence was stacked against them. Thankfully, he didn't have to go through that.

He picked up his helmet and keys and headed outside to his bike. He needed to cycle to clear his head. It was how he'd always been. When he'd come back from Majorca, he'd cycled for miles. Not that it had helped.

Climbing onto his bike, he decided to head to one of the old haunts he and the boys used to hang around at when they were teenagers. It was a steep climb but worth it for the views. It wouldn't take long.

As he climbed Dunmuir Hill, his thigh and calf muscles burning, Billy thought about what he would do with his life once he resigned as a DS. Maybe he could retrain as something else? Maybe start his own business? If Jez could do it, so could he.

He hadn't heard from Jez since that day he left him with Cole. He'd managed to tell a convincing lie to his bosses that Cole had done a runner. That he must have caught wind that the police were on to him. They'd seized millions of pounds worth of drugs from his flat and Billy hadn't slept since, worried that he'd be caught and sent to prison himself.

He reached the top of Dunmuir Hill and just over the brow was the reservoir. The sunlight glinted off the water as he took in the view. He could see for miles, and out there in the vast space Billy wondered if Cole's brother's body would ever be found. The world was a big place, and twenty years had gone by and so far, there had been no news from Majorca about remains being found. Maybe they'd wasted away.

He thought about Jez and how he'd got away with so much in his criminal career. Before they'd gone off to Majorca, Jez had gone to pay off some of their recreational drug debt with Diggo, the local down-and-out drug dealer. He'd confided in Billy when they were abroad that he'd dealt with their debt without having to pay up. Billy hadn't been surprised when Jez had told him that Diggo and his shitty little Vauxhall Nova were at the bottom of a reservoir. When it was on the news all those years ago that they'd found Diggo and the car, Billy had known the truth of what happened and kept it to himself.

As Billy stood at the edge of the reservoir, staring down at the water, he knew that it was likely Cole Woods's remains would be up at the reservoir somewhere too.

He swallowed hard and realised that he was just like Jez. His friend had supported him in his desire to become a police officer, but he'd always said that he didn't think it would suit Billy. He'd been right. Billy used his police career to hide what he truly was. A boy from the schemes, a killer.

Chapter Seventy-One

Roxanne sat down on the bed of her new cell and took in her surroundings. Cold, clinical white walls. That was what she would look at every single day for the rest of her life. Or at least for the next thirty-seven years. She'd have put herself through a trial if she'd thought it would be worth it when she got out. But there was no point. After everything that had happened, she had nothing left to get out for.

Finding out about Jake, his secret sexuality and the fact that he'd murdered his lover so that he could keep it a secret had shocked her. Roxanne had expected to feel more hurt but instead, she was just angry for not having noticed the signs herself.

'You're back then?' one of the prison officers asked, popping her head around the door. 'I'd hoped you'd have sorted yourself out, made a life for yourself.'

Roxanne gritted her teeth. 'What can I say? I missed the food.'

The prison officer smiled wryly and went on her way.

She lay down and thought about what the judge had said when she'd handed Roxanne's sentence down. She'd described Roxanne as a dangerous, trophy killer. She'd said that it was clear Roxanne liked to film or capture her victims on camera and replay the incident as though she were watching it for entertainment purposes. The judge hadn't been wrong, Roxanne supposed.

'A'right, Rox. Good tae huv ye back, hen.' The voice came from the doorway. The prisoner's name was Helena. A woman in for murder. She'd arrived around the same time as Roxanne had the first time. 'If yer needing anythin' to help ye sleep, just give us a shout. Got a stash in ma cell.'

Roxanne smiled and nodded at Helena. 'Cheers.'

Sighing, Roxanne placed her hands behind her head and stared up at the ceiling. It was going to be a long sentence this time round. She'd get out, and when she did she'd find Arabella MacQueen. When she did, she'd fucking kill her.

Chapter Seventy-Two

Martini Beach Club Club was in full party mode, the sun shining down on the holiday-makers as they danced and drank their way through the day.

Getting his money and the ring back from Cole Woods had been á matter of principle for Jez. He'd had to end Cole's life, there was no other way. How would it have made Jez look, if he'd allowed him to walk away unpunished? Jez was the biggest, most powerful gangster on the island, he had to live up to that reputation. Well, he was on a par with the Albanians. He'd had no real contact with them until Cole disappeared. When they'd come to see him, they were angry. A lot angrier than Jez had been and for the first time in his life, he had feared for his safety. The Albanian drug gang had made him an offer. Find Cole Woods, retrieve the money he stole from them and he'd be rewarded. Having the barrel of a gun shoved into his mouth had swayed him to agree. Of course, killing Cole was always going to be Jez's choice, but the Albanians had made it clear. Make sure his body is never found.

'You did a good job, Jez. I didn't think you'd be able to pull it off,' Zamir, the top man, said. 'You proved me wrong. Cole Woods got what was fucking coming to him and I salute you for wiping him off the face of the earth.'

Jez nodded. 'One less thieving bastard walking around.'

'Yes,' Zamir replied. He unzipped a large holdall that he'd placed on Jez's desk and tipped it forward. Jez peered inside. 'It's all there. You followed through on your word, Jez and for that I reward you.'

Five hundred grand. That was how much they'd offered him to take Cole out. As if that wasn't incentive enough.

'Cheers, Zamir.'

Zamir nodded. 'I hope now that things are sorted here, we can come to a business arrangement to start supplying your clubs once again. And just for you,' he pulled a small bag from his inside pocket and placed it on the desk. 'See it as a "try before you buy" scheme.'

Jez knew by the look on Zamir's face that there was no option to say "thanks but no thanks". He would be going into business with Zamir and his brothers to supply the clubs and that was that.

Charlene entered the office and Zamir stepped back and excused himself and left. Charlene stood and glared at Jez for a few seconds and he glared back.

'Are you seriously not going to sign these papers?' Charlene asked, shoving the divorce papers under his nose.

Jez set up a line from the bag Zamir had handed him on the desk and snorted it loudly. He wasn't an addict, not by any means. But sometimes he needed a little pick up, especially being tied to Charlene. Zamir was right, it was good shit.

'No, I don't need a divorce. It's you who wants one. You really think I'm going to sign that and give you half of everything I fucking own? I'm not a fucking idiot.'

'That's debateable,' Charlene said, shaking her head and glaring at him with that judgemental look on her face. That was the expression she'd always looked upon him with and he was sick to the back teeth of it.

'Oh fuck off, Charlene.'

'Okay, fine,' she said. 'But you'll regret this. I promise.'

Jez watched as she stormed out of the office, barely able to walk in her designer heels. He laughed, the coke going straight to his head.

He was going to enjoy this season on the island, revel in the fact that all these holiday-makers' money would be sitting in his account, making him wealthier by the day.

The only regret he ever had was meeting Charlene. She was one miserable cow.

–

The next morning, Jez woke up to a pounding headache and a younger girl next to him. He couldn't even remember taking her home. Couldn't remember her name. Not that it mattered. There would be a new one next to him tomorrow morning.

Sitting up, Jez leaned across the bed and reached for the bottle of water. Just as his fingers gripped around the plastic, Maria knocked on the door and peered around it.

'I'm so sorry to interrupt, Mr Kennedy. But the police are here to see you. They're waiting in the hallway.'

Frowning, Jez got to his feet and pulled on a pair of shorts as Maria headed back to the main hallway. He followed her out.

'Mr Jez Kennedy?'

Jez ran a hand through his hair and nodded. 'Aye, that's me.'

'You're under arrest for perverting the course of justice and accessory to murder in the case of Brian Woods.'

'Who the fuck is Brian Woods?' Jez asked. And then he clicked. Woods. Cole Woods's brother. How the fuck did they know about that?

Jez considered his options. Turn and bolt or profess his inno-cence. But he *was* innocent: he hadn't killed Brian. That had been Billy.

'Who told you about Brian Woods?' Jez asked as the officer put him into a set of cuffs.

'That would be me.'

Jez looked up to see Charlene standing at the top of their marble staircase.

'You?'

Nodding, she remained on the middle step. 'I was packing, getting ready to leave you when I discovered a little USB stick. I'd never seen it before, so I popped it into the laptop and you know what I found? A little footage of you and Billy with this

Brian lad. I handed it in to the police and turns out they'd found his remains years ago just off the coast of the island. Badly decomposed because of the water. They've been looking for his killer ever since. Turns out I'd been living with him the whole time. Well, you as good as killed that lad when you got rid of his body.'

Jez launched himself at the staircase. He wanted to kill her there and then. But the police were heavy on him, dragging him outside.

'Just when you thought you'd got away with murder, eh? Told you you'd regret not giving me a divorce. I was going to leave the USB, forget I'd seen it. But then you told me no, that I couldn't have one. So, I decided to fuck you over. Have a nice life in prison, Jez.'

Chapter Seventy-Three

Sitting down with a beer, Billy reached for the remote control to switch on the television. There wasn't much else to do as a retired police officer. He'd thought about taking up a hobby. It seemed that hobby was drinking until he passed out and forgot all the shit he'd done to cause himself so much guilt and grief.

Just as the television came to life, there was a knock at the door. He got up to answer it and there were two of the officers from his station stood there, sullen expressions etched on their faces.

'Jenkins, Whitler?' he said. 'What you two doing here?'

'Billy, we need you to come down to the station.'

'Can't cope without me already? Christ, I've only been away a few weeks.' He laughed but they didn't share in his humour.

'Billy, we're sorry to have to do this,' Jenkins said.

'We're arresting you for the murder of Brian Woods.'

Billy didn't hear the rest of the spiel. The beer bottle slipped from his hand and smashed on the hardwood floor. His ex-colleagues cuffed him and led him out to the car.

In truth, he'd always known this day would come eventually. Jez had kept footage. It was bound to get out one day.

'Mind your head there, Billy,' Whitler said as he bent down to climb into the car.

He could plead innocence. But what was the point? Being arrested was almost like a release. He could finally stop living a lie, stop trying to cover his tracks. They'd get Jez eventually if they hadn't already. There was every possibility that Billy could be sent back to Spain to be tried there. It was only what he deserved.

He was a killer. He was an ex-cop. Billy recalled the story Jez had told him about the officer who'd gone to prison and ended up in a wheelchair. He tried to block it out, but it hung around in the back of his mind.

Chapter Seventy-Four

Eddie stood by the door of the flat, his suitcases at his feet and a solemn look on his face. Arabella hadn't allowed him to talk his way out of what he'd done. He'd been honest, and had said that he'd hoped that because he'd told her the truth, she would find it in her heart to forgive him. She'd laughed.

Eddie had told Arabella that when he bought the salon from a guy named Rory, he hadn't known that Scarlett was the manager of the place. If he had, he wouldn't have gone near it. That didn't change the fact that Eddie couldn't keep his dick in his trousers for the ten months that Arabella had been in prison. He'd bought her the salon out of nothing other than guilt. Good, she'd thought. He should feel guilty.

'Have you got everything? I don't want you turning up because you've forgotten stuff,' Arabella said, making sure her tone was flat.

'Yeah,' Eddie said. 'For what it's worth, I'm sorry, Arabella. If I could go back and change things I would.'

'But you can't.'

Eddie sighed. 'The salon's yours. I won't interfere.'

Arabella nodded and opened the door. That was the way she wanted it. She wouldn't stay at the salon forever. Eventually she'd move on. Maybe go abroad, start a new life away from Glasgow altogether. But for now, all she wanted was to be on her own. She had to learn to love herself for who she was, learn how to trust the people she surrounded herself with. Over her life she'd chosen to be around people who only cared about themselves; it was time for Arabella to be selfish for a change.

'Thank you,' she replied. 'Have a nice life, Eddie.' She didn't mean it in a nasty way, she genuinely wanted him to be happy. But she couldn't have him in her life.

'You too, Arabella.' He leaned in and kissed her on the cheek. It took her all her strength not to tell him to stay. Because that would be the easiest thing to do, wouldn't it? Just forgive and forget. But she couldn't do it.

Eddie turned and walked out of the flat and Arabella closed the door behind him, before sinking to her knees and sobbing silently into her hands.

—

When she opened up the salon the next day, Arabella decided that she wanted to change the name. 'Hair Envy' wouldn't have been her choice. There was only one name that would fit, and it was the least that Arabella could do after bringing Roxanne back into Scarlett's life.

'Morning,' Arabella said as the stylists started arriving.

She told them about her idea to change the name of the salon to 'Scarlett's' and they loved it. Arabella had a lot of work to do with the place: she wanted it refurbished and kitted out with the best of equipment. Eddie would be responsible for that. That would be the only contact she would have with him. It was the least *he* could do in memory of Scarlett.

If someone had told Arabella back when she was a kid in the care system that this was where she would be now, she'd have told them to fuck off. But standing at the reception desk, taking in her surroundings, Arabella was going to make sure that she turned her life around. No more crime, no more fake friends, no more prison.

—

Arabella stood outside the hospital room and stared through the glass at the woman in the bed. Her heart thrummed in her chest as a wave of nausea took over. She hadn't seen this woman in twenty years, but there were things that had to be said.

Pushing the door open, she stepped inside and the woman opened her eyes. Staring at her from the bed, it was clear that she didn't know who Arabella was.

'Mum?' Arabella said.

The woman's expression turned from fatigued to shock and she gasped, but said nothing. Arabella moved closer to her, and sat on the chair next to the bed.

The woman who she used to call Mum, was yellow in colour and looked a lot older than her fifty years. It was quite apparent that she was on her death bed. Arabella didn't know how to feel about that. She viewed her differently now to when she was just eight years old.

'I contacted the social work department to find out where you were. I just wanted to, well…' she paused. 'I don't know what I wanted to do. I suppose I just needed some sort of closure. I always wondered what happened to you after I was taken into care. I always wondered if you got sober, started a new life. Maybe had more kids? I don't think that's the case, is it?'

The woman shook her head gently.

Arabella stared down at her, and a mixture of peace and sadness came over her. Arabella had no other family. Her only surviving blood relative was this woman lying in a hospital bed, dying through liver failure and lung cancer from the smoking. If she'd done her job as a mother, maybe things would have turned out differently for Arabella. Maybe not. Parents couldn't always be blamed. Adults made their own choices. Just like Arabella had when she'd gone to prison. Just like when Eddie slept with Scarlett, or when Roxanne murdered Scarlett and Keiran.

'I—' the woman gasped. Arabella leaned forward to listen. 'I'm sorry.'

She hadn't expected that.

'Me too, Mum. I'm sorry I wasn't enough for you to get your act together and be there for me. It's been a shit couple of decades, but I've survived it.' Her throat throbbed against the emotion she fought hard to hold in. Seeing her mother lying there was harder than she'd expected. She couldn't watch this woman, her mother, die from alcoholism. She'd abandoned Arabella as a child. She didn't deserve Arabella's sympathy.

Arabella smiled, squeezed her mother's hand and got up from the chair before heading out of the room.

There were others who did deserve her thoughts and sympathies, like Scarlett and Keiran. They didn't have to die because of what she'd done in her life due to her abandonment issues. It wasn't their fault that Arabella had clung to the wrong people because she'd never had a real relationship with anyone.

The least that Arabella could do now was begin to build and live her life to the fullest, in memory of them.

The one thing she had learned from all of this was that not all people were bad, but then again, not all people were good. She would keep her guard up, always.

A letter from Alex

Firstly, I want to thank you for choosing to come back to me for the release of *The New Friend*, my sixth book with Hera Books. It's always so exciting and nerve racking when I know the book is out of my hands and into yours, but I really do love to see it out there in the world. I love when you get in contact via my social media pages, it really motivates me to get moving with the next one.

This is the first book I have written, having come back out of lockdown and gone back to work full-time. Having been used to writing 'full-time' between March and August 2020, I didn't know how I was going to manage it. But I have, and I have to say that this one has been my favourite.

I began writing *The New Friend* in July of 2020, so I did get a head start on it before going back into some sort of normality. I thoroughly enjoyed creating these characters, and taking them out of Scotland and down to Spain for part of the book and I feel like I pushed these characters to their limits. I particularly liked Roxanne, even though she was a horrid woman. I like creating a 'bad lassie' and she definitely fits that description.

I'd love to hear your thoughts on *The New Friend*, as I said, it really does make me so thankful that I do what I do, and motivates me with the next book.

You can contact me on my social media pages:

www.facebook.com/alexkanewriter
www.twitter.com/AlexKaneWriter
www.instagram.com/alexkanewriter

Or you can email me:

alexkaneauthor@gmail.com

Once again, thank you so much for coming back. I'm still blown away by how much my books have taken off with Hera Books, and I'll be forever grateful for the opportunity to write for them, and you.

Best Wishes

Alex Kane

Acknowledgments

I want to start by thanking all at Hera. Keshini Naidoo and Lindsey Mooney continue to work so bloody hard for their authors, and really put us first. I'm forever grateful to them.

Keshini, your structural edit notes always help me to see a bigger picture, and you're always there to answer my many, *many* questions. Thank you so much.

I want to thank my line editor, Jennie. You really went to work on this and helped me to pick out all the little details to make *The New Friend* the best version of itself. Thank you so much.

Thank you to my proof reader, Andrew Bridgmont. You did a fab job on the tiniest details.

Thank you to Jo Bell at Bell Lomax Moreton. I still can't believe I have you, Keshini and Lindsey supporting me. It's the best journey and I wouldn't want to do it with anyone else.

A special thank you goes out to a family member of mine, Graham Cordner. You answered my police procedural questions with great detail, and I feel very lucky to have an ex-DCI on hand to offer his expertise. Hope you're enjoying your retirement, you deserve it.

I want to thank my family. My mum and dad are always so encouraging and keen to know what the next project is, and my mum is always one of the first to read my books.

My final and biggest thanks of all goes to my husband, Chris. You sat down with me in the middle of the first draft when I had a mental breakdown, not knowing where to take the storyline.

You talked me through the characters, listened, helped me make a large story board and guided me towards solving a plot issue. You're incredible and I love you more than ever.